"TWO GUARD SHIPS JUST CAME OUT OF PLANET SHADOW!

They're accelerating toward us."

"Increase speed, Helm."

Janina blinked, startled. "But, sir, we have to offship—"

"Look again, Janina. Those aren't just guard ships," Captain Andreos said heavily. "They're orbital warcraft, the ships Tania's Ring used to put down that grain revolt a few years ago."

"Sir, the warships are gaining on us," Athena said in surprise. "They're angling to intercept, trying to cut us off."

"What?" Andreos said. "*Net* can outrun any planet-bound craft."

Athena shook her head. "My monitors say their engine emissions are star-drive frequency. They must have put jump engines on the warships. And, sir, I confirm launch of two torpedos . . . !"

THE CLOUDSHIPS OF ORION

Maia's Veil

▼

P. K. McAllister

A ROC BOOK

ROC
Published by the Penguin Group
Penguin Books USA Inc., 375 Hudson Street,
New York, New York 10014, U.S.A.
Penguin Books Ltd, 27 Wrights Lane,
London W8 5TZ, England
Penguin Books Australia Ltd, Ringwood,
Victoria, Australia
Penguin Books Canada Ltd, 10 Alcorn Avenue,
Toronto, Ontario, Canada M4V 3B2
Penguin Books (N.Z.) Ltd, 182-190 Wairau Road,
Auckland 10, New Zealand

Penguin Books Ltd, Registered Offices:
Harmondsworth, Middlesex, England

First published by Roc, an imprint of Dutton Signet,
a division of Penguin Books USA Inc.

First Printing, June, 1995
10 9 8 7 6 5 4 3 2 1

To Kevin, for all his help and support.

ACKNOWLEDGMENTS

I would like to acknowledge Jan Yoors for his inspired writing about the gypsies of Europe, especially his memoir of his boyhood travels with a gypsy family (*The Gypsies,* 1967). Through his eyes, I discovered a special people who inspired my creation of Pov Janusz and his beautiful cloudship.

My thanks to Tom for his patience and help; and to my editor, Amy Stout, for her enthusiasm and support in making my books better. *Sastimos!*

Chapter 1

The morning after *Siduri's Net* returned to Tania's Ring and docked at Omsk Station, Pov Janusz and Athena Mikelos, *Net*'s pilotmaster, stood in front of a viewing window high on *Net*'s prow, watching the repairs to *Siduri's Dance* in the docking bay nearby. During *Net*'s three-week absence at T Tauri, Omsk Station had replaced several of the senior cloudship's hull plates and had removed the damaged sail assembly, nothing more. Still crippled, *Dance* drifted idly at her mooring, with a single Omsk repair jitney hovering above her.

"Captain Rybak's first words," Pov said, "were, I quote, 'God, you took long enough, *Net*.' Then he berated Captain Andreos about this and that, sputtered himself into a total rage, and clicked off before Andreos even got a word in."

Athena grimaced and shook her dark curls. "Why am I not surprised? *We* took a long time, he says. Maybe next year, at this rate, *Dance* might be spaceworthy again." She turned away from the window and sighed.

"Yesterday I felt rich," Pov said gloomily, looking at *Dance*.

"We're still rich," Athena said. "Don't worry about it." She walked over to one of the lounge chairs and sat down slowly, then straightened one leg in front of her, then the other.

Pov turned and looked at her with concern. Athena looked deathly pale, a shadow of her usual energetic self. She saw his look and shook her head at him irritably, warning him off.

"How's the radiation treatment going?" Pov asked anyway, poking at her.

"Wonderfully, Medical says," she said, sounding cross. "On the green, sail."

"You shouldn't be on duty," he told her severely.

"Soar off," she told him. "I'm not on duty. I'm just sitting here."

"Oh, sure."

Athena looked stubborn. "I refuse to accept being sick. I will do what I please to do." She straightened and gave him a glare, then seemed to collapse slowly back on herself again. She sighed. "I do admit all those little radioactive atoms running around my body take their toll. It takes a while for that chelating goo to pick the atoms up, one cell at a time."

Pov looked her over. If the Medical Section's progress reports weren't as favorable as they'd been, he'd worry very much about Athena right now. She looked gray. "How much longer for the therapy?" he asked.

"Until the goo picks up every last atom, I guess." She grimaced. "Stop standing there worrying. Go do something useful."

"Ah, come on, Athena."

She tossed her head. "I'm sorry. I feel cross, and you're getting the brunt. I appreciate your concern, Pov, but you know skyriders and their image problems. Me, limited by anything? Radiation? What's that? Ho ho."

"That I do know. Kate'll probably tear apart half the ship by the time her baby gets born."

This time Athena's smile was more genuine, but still too wan. He looked at her with open concern, thought to say something more, then shut his mouth as Athena tossed another warning glare at him.

"At least go below and rest, Athena," he said patiently. "Let Gregori and your girls hover."

"Why do you think I'm up *here*?" she said, scowling grumpily. "They act like I'm made of spun glass—not that I'm minding, family is family and I love them too, and all that, but after a while I start to feel feeble just because they act that way. Mind over matter, the wrong way." She stood up and stretched her back, pacing a slow circle around her chair, and then sat down as if Environmental had suddenly boosted the ship's artificial gravity directly under her.

"Humph," he said, crossing his arms.

"Go grump at somebody else, Pov. I'll go rest in an hour or so when the watch is over. Okay?"

"Well, if you say so."

"I do."

Tully Haralpos walked out of the elevator and strolled over to join them, dressed formally in shipboard grays. All of *Net*'s captains had dressed in uniform this morning, expecting a call to an intership hearing with *Dance*, and Pov had asked Tully to join the formal horde. Tully took one look at Athena's face and added his own chiding look. As he crossed his arms to comment, he suddenly shifted uncomfortably, then pulled irritably at his uniform sleeve. The months since Tully had worn his uniform last showed in the tightness at inconvenient spots. Tully shrugged his shoulders, trying to settle the tight tunic, then squirmed. "I feel strangled in this thing," he complained.

"Wait long enough," Pov suggested lightly, "and you find you've grown like a crocodile. Another year, another inch."

"Nuts to that." Tully pulled at his collar. "Though I'm afraid it's more like 'another meal, another pound.' Christ." Athena snickered and crossed her trim ankles, then dangled an arm over the side of her chair. She opened her mouth. "Not a word, you," Tully warned, bunching his thick black eyebrows. Athena smiled broadly, then snickered behind her hand, making an act of it.

"That's a word," Tully told her severely.

"Is not. Check your dictionary."

Pov inspected Tully casually. "I've got a clean spare that's a little bigger. You want to try it on?"

"No, I'll suffer. Greeks are used to fatalism: read your myths. All that dire tragedy, capricious gods, those unrelenting Furies chasing folks everywhere, hither and yon, shrieking at the top of their lungs." Tully wiggled, then glared at Athena as she snickered again. Athena pretended to ward him off with her hand.

"Sorry, she said, her blue eyes dancing. Athena had the lithe curves to gloat safely.

"I doubt if I'll get called over to *Dance,* anyway," Tully said. "No reason to dress up."

"Don't count on it." Pov scowled. "If Rybak manages to dust me out of rank this time, you're it on Sail Deck as *Net*'s new sailmaster."

"I doubt that's an issue anymore, Pov. Not with three holds of tritium to buy *Dance* out of her problems."

"Yeah? Keep whistling." Tully frowned in concern, not liking Pov's mood.

Pov shrugged and turned back to the window to watch *Dance*'s repairs. Well, we've got the money, he thought tiredly, feeling a dull aching in his back and legs from accumulated fatigue and stress.

"This isn't going to be fun," Tully muttered as he joined Pov at the window. Tully's mouth set as he looked at *Dance,* sharing Pov's frustration and anger at their mothership.

Pov glanced at his friend. Even Tully showed the strain today, waiting like others on *Net* for new troubles, after so many troubles with *Dance* in recent weeks. Tully seemed more closed this morning, despite his raillery at Athena, his face drawn with a fatigue that matched Pov's own. The crew's celebration over *Net*'s fantastic success at T Tauri had muted into a sober elation, pricked now by new worries, and those worries showed most in her senior people today.

"Found out what's hatched?" Pov asked, prodding him.

"*Dance* is shut up tight," Tully said gloomily. "We'll find out soon enough."

"True." Behind him, Pov heard Athena sigh and shift position in her chair, as unhappy with waiting and doing nothing as he and Tully were. It felt far too much like target practice, with *Net* as the target, not the laserman.

Dance did not call, and Pov spent a quiet morning watch on Sail Deck, mostly sail drills and data analysis of the T Tauri runs, then stopped by his sister's apartment on his way to lunch. Now in her third month of pregnancy, Kate had been grounded from her skyrider duties for the duration, a restriction that made her fret. Athena had relented by allowing Kate to work with the skyrider checkdown crew, and even allowed an inspection flight in the relative safety of Omsk's placid orbit: it helped.

He found Kate cleaning the apartment, her head buried in one of the storage cabinets in the living room. Her ears muffled, she didn't hear the door chime, nor his footsteps, so when he nudged her foot he nearly brained his sister on the cabinet doorframe as she reacted to the touch.

"God, Kate," he said, helping her back out of the cabinet to sit down on the floor. She had hit her head hard enough to start tears, and he knelt down and hugged her close as she gasped, squinting with pain.

"I'm sorry, I'm sorry," he said. "I didn't mean to startle you."

"What an entrance," she muttered, then felt her skull gingerly. "Ouch, that hurt."

"Hell, Kate," he said in distress. She winced.

"Oh, I'll survive. Stop looking like the sky fell in on you." She fingered her head a few moments more, then narrowed her dark eyes, eyeing him. "I think it fell in on me, thanks to you." Pov backed away a step, wary that Kate might take some retribution, and heard her chuckle. "Ah, you're learning wisdom."

"Soar off. *Are* you okay?"

"The stars are out early, but yeah."

"What are you doing?"

"Cleaning. What does it look like?"

"That I can see. Are you *that* far down the list of things you could do?" Kate absently pushed her wiry black hair back behind her shoulders and smiled at him.

"I like the way you watch over me," she said. "I'm bored, true, but I'll survive it. Stop hovering. I told you not to do that, but you keep persisting."

Pov smiled as Kate bared her teeth warningly. He and Kate had always been close, even among a family as closely bound as their gypsy family. Just as she waged his wars for him, he involved himself in hers. "So I'm diligent."

"That you are, I agree."

He helped Kate to her feet and followed her into the

kitchen, where she clattered among her dishware in the cupboard, playing the hostess.

"You look nice dressed up," Kate said as she set out two glasses on the counter, tipping her head to admire him. She reached to adjust his uniform collar, then neatened his sleeve. "Adds dignity or something. I've been trying to figure out what."

"Dignity?" Pov smiled at her. "What's that?"

"Oh, nuts to that. Half my time on skydeck, it seems, I'm defending my stuffy older brother, so serious, so determined, such a *flat* orbit of a man. Lighten up, Pov. Listen to Avi."

"Avi likes me just as I am," Pov informed her.

"I'll talk to her," Kate retorted. "Love can blind."

Kate poured him a drink of something fruity and pink from the refrigerator. "Try that." She watched as he sipped at it.

"I don't recognize this," he said.

"This is from Patia's lab on *Dance*. Tawnie brought it back when she went over to visit the *Dance* Rom: some kind of clone of plums and Tania marshberry. It's certainly vividly pink. What do you think?"

"Sweet," he said judiciously.

"Too sweet, I think, but the children love it, Tawnie says." Kate capped the bottle and put it back in the refrigerator. "I keep expecting Patia to start making some weird kind of vat-meat or something, then expect us to eat it. Though, I'll admit, most of her experimenting hasn't been too bad. I'm not sure marshberry fits into the *marime* rules, though, and Bavol had a fit about this when Patia brought it home."

"He would." Their cousin Bavol, the middle son of Damek's three sons, had inherited most of his father's conservatism, a trial for the more modern-minded young woman he had married. He sipped at the glass again, rolling the liquid around in his mouth. "I like it."

"Tell Patia that. She wasn't expecting Bavol to get upset, and it always bothers her when she doesn't see it coming. I was thinking of going over to see her. Should I?"

"Why shouldn't you?"

"Because I'm the sailmaster's sister and Athena's probable spy, and it signals things maybe you don't want signaled. Why isn't *Dance* talking to us?"

"I don't know. I don't think it's going to end up to our good." He scowled.

Kate shook her head tiredly. "I get so tired of the divisions, Pov. I used to think all it took was reasoned talk, a few airy jabs to keep the other in place, but always there was some way to work it out. First came Mother's war against Sergei, and now *Dance* behaving like this. Will Captain Rybak really try to keep us here? Why can't he just let us buy free and go do what *Net* can really do?"

"Why can't Mother love Sergei like a son?" Pov smiled down at her ruefully. "I don't have many answers lately. It seems you answer one question and others pop up. It's called life, right?"

"Now, *that's* profound." Kate wrinkled her nose. "I feel truly enlightened."

"Airy jab—I can take it."

Kate grinned at him, then fisted his ribs. "Thanks for coming by. You don't have to come by so often: I'm okay. The baby's okay, Sergei's okay, the storage is okay, everything's simply okay."

"So I check up. When I'm a problem, let me know."

"That's on." She kissed him. "Stay awhile. Sergei'll be home soon—I hope. He and the physics lab have been going wild over the superheavy atoms you and Janina caught at T Tauri." She wrinkled her nose. "Sadly, the little beasties keep unpacking their little quantum shells or something, and Sergei can't figure out how to bottle them so they won't do that. Thinks I should give him a gypsy spell for quark stability. Is there one?"

"Not that I've heard." He smiled.

"I keep explaining to him that I don't *have* gypsy spells, him the scientific mind and all, and he just points to how I make him feel and says it has to be magic." She smiled softly. "Sweet man. Why can't Mother—?"

She turned away suddenly and clattered awhile with her dishes, her jaw muscles tightening. Pov sighed and put his hands in his pockets, wishing he did know some

spells, one in particular that could change a mother's
heart. If only it were that easy.

"I'm sorry, Kate," he said inadequately.

"It's not your fault, Pov."

"I'm trying to reason with her. All it gets me is more
fights. She just doesn't believe you would leave the tribe
for him, if she forces it."

"I would, believe me." Kate slammed down a pot hard.

"*I* know that, but she doesn't. She honestly doesn't.
I'm about out of ideas. It makes me worry for Avi. Avi
wants to get married, but I don't like the way the family
has been changing lately. Mother wars on you, Bavol
snipes at Patia, pushing and forcing and forgetting what's
supposed to count. Mother blames *Net* for it, calling it
gaje temptation, and she'll do something about it soon
and break up the family. I see it coming, and I can't do
anything about it, just watch it come at us." They looked
at each other bleakly.

"Why does it go this way, Pov?" Kate asked sadly.
"Why does family get all mixed up, doing the wrong
things? Why can't the Rom be part of *Net* and keep the
best of both? Why is it one way or the other and nothing
in between?"

"I don't know." He looked away unhappily. "I don't
have any answers for that."

"Maybe there *aren't* any answers," she said.

"Maybe not. God, I hope there are, but lately hoping
hasn't gotten me much of anywhere. So cheer me up,
chavali. Give me an airy jab. I could use another one."

"Oh, *sure* you could. Promise me, Pov, that you'll tell
me if I ever start turning wrong on you. Don't even let
me get started."

"I'll do that." He kissed her cheek.

Pov found Avi Selenko in the gym briskly wasting cal-
ories, thin and taut in an exercise suit and adamantly fo-
cused on staying that way. Raised in a Russki colony
devoted to physical fitness and other perfections of the
Great Rodina, Avi was better than he was about keeping
in shape, making a duty out of her workouts that she followed zealously. He perched on a convenient equipment

rack by the wall and watched appreciatively as Avi bent and swayed and jogged around the room, the several others in the gym making an odd but graceful dance around her.

Lev Marska, another of his Sail Deck crew, jogged by. Pov belatedly sucked in his middle, too late to be useful, and Lev hooted derisively as he bounded past, feet working smartly. Ah, well, Pov thought, eyeing Lev's hairy muscles with some envy. He wondered idly if Avi liked hairy muscles and whether he should get a few. As he watched Lev bob and weave around the gym, Pov decided the problem wasn't the initial investment but the upkeep. He went back to slouching loosely on the rack rail, watching Avi.

After a while, Avi sidestepped briskly over to him and jogged in place in front of him, her dark hair bouncing, damp wisps curling on her pale neck where the hair had escaped her hairpins. She considered him a moment, her feet bounding up and down.

"Lazy sot," she announced, deciding on the right label.

"That I am," he said cheerfully.

"Ten minutes after I'm done, I feel great."

"Good for you."

Avi chugged to a stop and put her hands on her slim hips, giving him a fearsome look. "And when you get fat, Pov," she told him severely, "remember why."

"God, why are fitness fanatics so fanatical?"

Avi wrinkled her nose and bent over a moment, breathing deeply, then walked around in a circle with her hands on her hips, strutting nicely as she worked her arms forward and backward. Avi had the length of leg and the smooth curves to make a strut worth watching. "*I'll* never be fat," she declared.

"I'm not fat," Pov groused.

"Oh ho. I saw you suck in your middle when Lev went by. Don't tell me that drift-gas."

"Come get naked with me and I'll show you who's fat."

"Hush, you." Avi glanced at the others in the gym, not that anyone on *Net* didn't know all about *Net*'s sailmaster and his pretty Russki Sixth Sail. "Brag on your own time, sailmaster, sir. *I'm* busy doing *important* things." She worked her elbows some more as she strutted another circle, showing off, trim and sexy and full of herself.

"Now when do I brag?" he asked. "I don't hear me bragging at all."

"Oh ho," she said mockingly. "Sure you don't."

He spread his hands, inviting. Avi stepped into the circle of his arms, then rested her forearms comfortably on his shoulders, dangling her hands behind his neck. He pushed back a damp tendril of hair from her face, then pulled out a hairpin to watch the dark curl fall down on her shoulder. She kissed him, then smiled happily.

"Want to go to lunch?" he asked.

"Sure. Russki's choice of the skyside lounge?"

He hesitated. "Okay."

She sighed. "It's still hard, isn't it, eating food outside your gypsy rules? You suggested this half-and-half compromise, you know. Half the time we're Russki, and half the time we're Rom. I don't mind eating by your purity rules. How you fix it doesn't change the taste."

"We've been over that. I'm trying to meet you halfway."

"To your discomfort, I'm afraid. I appreciate the effort, Pov, but you still squirm."

"And so do you, when we turn tables. Sorry." He smiled. "It's the way I was raised. Once a Rom—"

"—always a Rom," she finished for him. "All that's fine with me, but I still say you squirm, Pov Janusz." She suddenly slipped her fingers into his armpit and wiggled them, finding a ticklish place he unwisely allowed her to discover in bed. "See?" she said as he shied away from her poking. "I'd call that a squirm."

"Stop that," he complained. He grabbed her hand and then tussled with her as she laughed, pushing against his strength to tickle him again. "Stop it, Avi. That's an order."

"Order? What in the hell kind of order is that? Thank the stars *I'm* not ticklish anywhere." She sniffed and then gave it up. "Well, it's Russki choice today, so I've changed my mind—let's eat in at my place." He released her hand and she slouched her arms comfortably on his shoulders again, smiling at him. "I still don't understand why you backed off on asking me to do the whole *gaji romni* act, as Sergei does for Kate in keeping the rules. I'm willing to try—I think."

"It's the 'I think,' Avi." He pulled her closer, and she relaxed against him, the warmth of her body palpable through his clothes. "We're trading places: you were the one worried about pushing away someone who's special. Now look at you, secure and sassy and willing to try— and I'm the worrier."

She toyed with a lock of his hair, arranging it into a curve on his forehead, then smoothing it back onto his head in a caress. "I'm not going anywhere, Pov."

"That's good to hear."

She smiled sweetly, and he kissed her, tightening his arms around her as she responded to him. She opened her mouth and he pulled her even harder against his body, and the kiss got totally out of hand.

"Hey!" a voice said. "Save that for private."

"Soar off, Lev," Pov retorted.

Lev grinned and flexed the muscles on his bare chest, his blond hair slicked back wet from sweat, then flipped his towel briskly about his shoulders, making a breeze. Pov watched Lev's muscles flex and pursed his lips. "Disgusting," he said loudly.

"Just envy, sir." Lev's grin broadened as he snapped his towel again.

Avi half-turned and bared her teeth at the Slav computer tech. "Watch out, Lev. I'm not as nice as he is."

Lev rounded his mouth in mock dismay, goggling at her, then laughed and danced off, legs pumping high.

"It *is* disgusting," Pov said. "Come on, let's get out of this fanatic's den."

"Speaking as a fanatic, that's on."

Avi had the afternoon watch on Sail Deck, and Pov decided to catch up on some sleep he'd been missing since T Tauri, firmly bypassing more of the T Tauri scans that had kept him up too late, since he had a bad

habit of replaying endless data screens in his dreams. He
and Tully had almost finished the analysis of the magnetic flux that had made *Net*'s runs into the protostar's
gas-jet as much improvisation as planned intention,
though the theoretical physicists in Sergei's lab were still
arguing about the new theories that might fit reality. As
he walked through the residential corridor to his apartment, he felt the fatigue in his leg muscles, dragging at
his calves with little catches and twinges. The tiredness
seemed to seep upward, climbing his spine like sifting
ink the more he noticed it. He yawned, then yawned
again until his jaw joints cracked. Bed, he told himself.
What a wonderful idea.

As he snapped on the overhead lights in his apartment,
his eye caught a gleam of metal from the small triangular
table in the far corner by the window. He walked over to
the Rom shrine and picked up the gypsy token, then the
note that had lain beneath it. He looked at the slender
statue of St. Serena standing on the shrine table. Dissatis-
fied with the few hundred gaje saints handed to them by
the Catholic Church, the European gypsies had invented
St. Serena and a few other saints to be their special pa-
trons, untainted by gaje ideas of a proper saint. Serena
was the patroness of Rom families and of Rom tradition,
a gypsy queen beloved by all the Rom and welcomed
happily to every Rom wedding and baptism.

To Pov, St. Serena was also Siduri herself, the Babylonian goddess after whom *Net* had been named, as graceful
and lovely as *Siduri's Net* herself and somehow his
cloudship's essence. In Babylonian myth, Siduri had
loved the hero Gilgamesh for a short summer season on
her sea island, pleading with him to stay and give up his
heroic adventures. I am music and the dance, she had told
him: I could give you the security of a family, a wife, all
a man needs to be happy. Listen to me. But Gilgamesh
had not listened, and had left her behind on her sea isle,
bereft and longing.

Pov dropped incense on the small square plate in front
of the statue, then watched the thin curl of scented smoke
swirl upward. Grace to you, Siduri, he thought in Romany. Please look after Kate, I am asking.

The statue's face changed subtly as the wisp of smoke briefly shadowed the eyes, a flicker of expression he always noticed, as if, for a moment, Siduri had smiled at him. He smiled in response, as always, not at all minding that Rom ancestor worship was only superstition, that the illusion of movement was a simple combination of carbon particles and the angle of overhead lights. It suited him to think Siduri smiled at him.

He opened the note in his hand and saw Lasho's mark at the bottom. The token, a small pierced coin tied with a short length of colored yarn, showed Tawnie as the messenger. Half of the Siduri Rom lived on *Net,* half on *Dance,* with Damek's two younger sons and their wives staying behind on *Dance* when *Net* was built three years before. Until *Net*'s recent quarrel with *Dance,* the division had not interfered with his family's contact, with the two groups of Rom freely traveling back and forth between *Net* and *Dance* to share their Rom feast days or just to visit. Lasho was the third of his uncle Damek's sons, Karoly and Tawnie's youngest brother, about Pov's age. He read the brief note and scowled, wondering why Lasho wanted a private meeting—and why on Omsk Station.

He put the token back on the shrine by Siduri's sandaled foot for safekeeping until he could return it to Tawnie. Trust Tawnie to blaze ahead and visit the Rom on *Dance,* mere hours after *Net*'s arrival, indifferent to the opinions of any gaje who objected. He smiled, guessing just how Tawnie had carried it off, dressed gypsy-style to the hilt with flowing skirts and loud jewelry, her baby Cappi on her hip, flouncing onto *Dance* and tripping through the older ship's corridors, gaily greeting every gaje who passed, stiff-arming any security guard who dared to question her intention. On certain things, Tawnie Janusz, barely sixteen and just topping forty kilos, could not be outdone.

He put Lasho's note in his pocket for its Omsk location, some eatery on the space station, then walked into his bedroom to his computer and logged himself offship. He turned and looked at his bed for a long wistful moment, knowing how it would feel to stretch out and go boneless, drift away and do nothing but sleep and sleep and sleep. He shrugged fatalistically, then changed out of his ship's uniform into other clothes, repocketed the note, and left for Omsk.

Chapter 2

According to Omsk's wall map, Pov discovered, the small cafeteria lay halfway across Omsk Station, a good kilometer's walk through the connecting corridors. He checked the note again for the spelling, mentally converting the Cyrillic letters to the ship-Czech script he found more comfortable, then checked the map again. It was still on the other side of Omsk, immovably so. He frowned at the map irritably. Maybe Tully's Greek Furies were chasing him now, as if Rom deities weren't enough, shrilly insisting that a certain gypsy get some exercise, no excuses—and had snatched his nap away to boot, just to make their point.

He checked the clock above the map. Lasho had already been waiting a couple of hours. He sighed and set off, deciding to interest himself in the Russkis who passed him, each Russki brow furrowed with its owner's intent upon service to the Great Russki Rodina—or so Omsk techs learned to pretend.

With a new world discovered somewhere in Sol's vicinity every year, Earth's star colonies were given the latitude to tailor themselves to goals of their choice, free by charter to exclude anyone, free to control themselves with whatever laws were imposed by the majority, with certain exceptions regulated by Earth. A colony could not execute by torture or deny any colonist passage back to Earth upon request, but otherwise the colonies had free rein. And so the Russians of Tania's Ring pursued their Rodina, the mystical Russian motherland close to the Russki soul, created anew on a new world. On Ashkelon, the Arabs were busily building the perfect Islamic society, complete with medieval architecture, chadors for the women, and a science drawn from Muslim roots more Aristotelian than Einsteinian. On Perikles, where Pov had been born, the Greeks re-erected their Doric columns and built graceful cities by their many seashores, welcoming anyone who asked to immigrate but limiting governmental participation to ethnic Greeks.

The Rom had never bothered to vote anyway, even on Earth, and so found Perikles a comfortable new home with new roads to travel. Several hundred gypsies had joined the few million gaje on Perikles, fascinating the sophisticated Perikles Greeks with their colorful wagons, disdainful pride, and brazen fortune-telling. Most of Pov's nearer relatives still lived on Perikles, growing richer in children and gold each year. After Pov's father had died in a chance accident when Pov was a boy, forcing his mother into an unpleasant widowhood with her husband's family, she had persuaded her brother Damek to try another road on *Ishtar's Fan,* the aging cloudship that had just arrived insystem. Later, when *Fan's* daughter ship, *Siduri's Dance,* shifted star systems to Epsilon Tauri, Margareta's Rom family had gone with her, leaving Perikles and the planetbound Rom behind.

Unfortunately, the move had created a sizable tactical problem for Pov's mother. Uncle Damek had safely married off his children before *Dance* left Perikles, finding two sisters as brides for the younger sons, then adopting eight-year-old Del for Tawnie when the two grew up to marriageable age. During *Dance's* years at Perikles, Margareta had looked on and off for a bride for her teenaged son, not successfully. On the several occasions she had dragged Pov down to the planet surface to get looked over by a girl's family, Pov hadn't cooperated much, being far more interested in sail training at that age than in girls, let alone marriage. Then time had run out for Margareta when *Dance* left Perikles, leaving Pov a bachelor well into his late twenties, unusually late for a Rom to marry.

Last year Pov had involved himself with Dina Kozel, a Bulgar computer tech, and now would probably marry Avi Selenko, both gaje women. Even his mother had to admit Pov had no choices among the closely related

Siduri Rom, and Pov would not accept a planetbound girl from Perikles whom he'd never met and who had never lived on a cloudship. Whatever his mother's tentative wheedling a time or two, he saw only misery in that kind of marriage, with his wife longing for her family and the Perikles life she had always known and himself unwilling to give up *Net,* even for his wife. His mother would likely accept in time, if ungraciously, a gaje wife for Pov, if she had to. She refused to accept Sergei.

Maybe life is simpler somewhere else, Pov thought as he walked along the metal-floored corridor of Omsk Station. He looked at the faces of the people who passed him, wondering if they served aboard Omsk willingly and really believed in the Great Rodina that had oppressed Avi and had wrecked her earlier marriage. Sergei had not believed, especially after he was forced out of his university post and transferred to a minor nuclear-tech job on Omsk by an arbitrary bureaucratic decision. Most of *Net*'s Russki people had left Omsk Station for similar reasons, bringing their technical skills and fresh faces as a new mix to *Net*'s multinational crew.

Certainly the Omsk people scowled more than they smiled, Pov decided, even to each other in corridors—and when they did smile, especially when the smiler was a wily bureau chief named Nikolay Bukharin making deals with *Dance,* it wasn't real. But Avi's a Tania's Ring Russki, too, he thought, puzzling about it. Oddly, he felt his spirits lift a little as another frown walked by. Maybe it's the air mixture, turns the soul sour, he thought. Now that's a safely biased statement: call it science.

He passed a group of Omsk techs talking quietly among themselves, their coveralls more smartly tailored than Omsk's usual jumpsuit. And wearing pistols on their belts, Pov noticed belatedly. One of the men glanced at him coolly, his eye caught by Pov's darker complexion among the lighter-skinned Russkis. The man raked him with a single glance, classified the difference, then strode along after the others. Pov angled over to the wall to stand in front of another of Omsk's ubiquitous maps and pretended to study it while he watched the group walk away and turn neatly on booted heels into a side corridor.

Military, he thought, part of Tania's Ring Forcer troops. Out of uniform, but you can't hide the precision—or that raking glance. In the heavy ultraviolet outside the planet's atmosphere, some station personnel tanned as dark as Pov's natural Rom coloring, and apparently the man had labeled and dismissed him as an Omsk tech. Pov tried to remember how often he'd seen Forcer troops before on Omsk: not often. He heard more measured footsteps approaching from the right and watched another group of men pass behind him in the reflective glass of the map. More security forces—odd. The Forcers watched everything, knew everything, an omnipresent security police as useful politically to colonial bureaucrats as to Earth's old-time tsars and commissars. Why would Bukharin ask for extra contingents for Omsk?

He thought of a good reason, then another, both of them involving *Siduri's Net*, then he felt his gypsy instincts lift the hairs on his neck. The Rom had always lived by their wits in an often dangerous gaje society— Pov felt very Rom when other Forcers crossed the hallway ahead. He looked around cautiously, then walked onward, circling through Omsk from one corridor to another, hunting Lasho's eatery.

When he walked into the tiny lounge, a rather bare room with several tables and a wall of automated food dispensers, he looked around for his cousin. Two Omsk techs chattered briskly in Russian at a table on the far wall, their backs to the door; across the room, hunched over a half-empty glass, the only other occupant was Benek Zukor, *Net*'s former Fifth Sail.

In a secret still kept by *Net*, Benek had misread a dust reading during the cloudships' last comet run, delaying *Net*'s warning to *Dance* as the other ship followed in her wake. *Dance*'s bad luck that the comet had disintegrated in their faces; *Net*'s bad luck that Benek had sat at that station. When Dina Kozel meddled and erased the records of Benek's mistake, Andreos had booted them both off-ship and back to *Dance*. Pov hesitated in the doorway, wondering if Dina had told Rybak, if *Dance* knew everything now.

Benek looked up and saw him, and Pov walked over.

"Benek," he said quietly.

Benek's neck cartilage bobbed nervously. "You got your cousin's message? It was the only safe way I could think of to contact you without *Dance* knowing."

"To meet you instead of him?"

"That's right. I asked him to not put my name in the message. I'm glad he didn't, just in case." Benek sat up straighter, his thin face oddly determined. "Please sit down, sir."

Pov pulled out a chair with a scrape and did so.

"Would you like a drink?" Benek asked nervously. His face looked pasty white, as if he were ill, the accumulation of strain perhaps. Benek was not strong, never had been. Three paper shot glasses stood on the table in front of him, with the faint aroma of good Scotch obvious on Benek's breath.

"No, thank you," Pov said, waiting.

Benek swallowed hard. "I goofed up the sample reading," he blurted suddenly. "On the run that damaged *Dance*."

"I know, Benek."

"You do?" Benek stared. "Dina said you wouldn't . . ." Benek seemed to collapse in on himself, his expression changing from shock to sudden grief. "Then there's no hope."

"If you want to come back to *Net,* Benek, we can discuss it. But Andreos won't take Dina back, for reasons you know. You'd have to come back without her." Pov looked at Benek with sympathy. Benek was weak, but doggedly tried his best, such as it was. It wasn't wholly his fault that Dina Kozel had chosen him as a tool for her ambitions.

"Back?" Benek goggled this time. "You'll let me come back?"

Pov shrugged. "I objected to your transfer in the first place, but it was a message Captain Andreos wanted to send to *Dance.* But he also promised me we could make the offer when we got back. Don't you realize how Dina endangered *Net* by tampering with the Sail Deck record? How could she be so rash?"

"If I made a mistake like I did on the sample, I'd never

get my promotion to sailmaster," Benek said uncomfortably, then flushed to his hairline.

"I know all about that, Benek."

"You do?" Benek looked amazed again. "And you still ... She said that you'd ..." He swallowed. "She's told them, sir. She told them everything. *Dance* knows I goofed the reading."

"Damn," Pov muttered, his heart sinking. "Did Dina get any proof of it off the ship?"

"No. The security chief erased her tapes, I guess. She was so angry. They're planning to ..." Benek swallowed again and closed his eyes. "God, how I love her."

"So did I, Benek," Pov said quietly.

"Why does she do things like this? Why?" Benek's anguish was open on his face. "It's not needed. I could give her ..." He ran his hand over his face, then looked away, a muscle jerking in his jaw. "I don't understand it all, but *Dance* is planning to keep *Net* from buying out."

"They can hardly do that. We brought back three holds of tritium."

"*Three* holds? God, sir." He smiled, his face lighting for a moment, then clouded again into his misery. "But they know that, and it doesn't worry them." He frowned, then looked at Pov squarely. "It has something to do with 'production clauses.' Does that make sense to you?"

"Production clauses?"

"That's what Dina said. Then she laughed. It was an awful sound, the way she laughed." He bowed his head over his drink. "She blames you for her getting kicked off *Net*. Said it was your idea. She's really angry at you."

"Well, it wasn't my idea, though I thought it a good one later when I found out. Don't worry about it, Benek. I know how Dina sounds off: I had enough of that when she trashed me and took up with you."

"I'm not sure she loves me," Benek said in a low voice, his head sinking downward. "How can you be sure? Do you know?"

"Benek, come back to *Net* with me."

He flinched. "You don't want me," he said.

"Yes, I do." Pov wondered if he really did, but felt he should offer. Benek looked a pitiful wreck. Did I look like that when Dina got done with me? he wondered uncomfortably. Desperate and lost and torn?

"Maybe *you* want me," Benek said, "but the others won't."

"They'll come around. It won't be easy, I can't promise that, but you're still part of *Net*'s Sail Deck, if you want it."

"I do, more than you know. I just can't believe I misread the screen. All the times I've tried to get better at it, and I let *Net* down like that, then went along with what she did . . ."

Benek's voice rose in anguish, and Pov reached to grip his arm tightly. At his touch, Benek moaned and sank his face into his arms, his cup spilling across the table. As the thin shoulders started to shake, Pov glanced quickly at the Omsk techs, not wanting attention, not now. Both men still had their backs turned, occupied with their own conversation over their meal. Pov glanced around the ceiling corners for security cameras, but saw nothing. Apparently Bukharin hadn't rigged every room in Omsk, not yet.

"Come on, Benek," he said. "Get hold of yourself."

"No," Benek said with a muffled sob.

"That's an order, sail."

"You don't want me."

"I don't have time to convince you right now. Come on, pull yourself together. If you want to rehabilitate yourself with *Net*, I need you stronger than this. Can you do that?"

"No. No, I can't."

Pov looked at him with frustration, then waited impatiently as Benek struggled back to composure, though his face still looked ravaged. What was bothering him? More than what Pov already knew? But what? Benek sniffled and then wiped his nose on his sleeve, his blue eyes watery. He took a deep breath and pulled open the top snap of his tunic, then reached into the inner pocket. He pulled out a small data disk.

"I took this," he said with a faint air of defiance. "She started 'scouting,' as she called it, using the computer to spy all over the ship. She can do that, you know. And she taped this. The captains don't know she has it, and she's waiting to use it somehow. Like she used me against you. So I thought you should have it, sir." He put the flat square disk on the table and slid it over to Pov. Pov covered it with his palm, staring at Benek.

"What's on it?" he asked.

Benek shook his head. "Listen to it. It won't need explaining."

Benek stood up and swayed off balance, then righted himself and walked to the door. Pov started to call after him, but hesitated, wary of attracting the attention of the two Russkis eating nearby. Then Benek was gone, walking quickly out of the cafeteria and not looking back.

Pov looked down at the disk under his hand, then glanced again at the Russki techs. They ignored him, laughing at some joke one had told. Some spies, he thought wryly, pocketing the disk in his own tunic. Just slide it across the table with all the world watching. But the two techs stayed oblivious, chattering Russian to each other as they ate from their plates, chewing with gusto and swigging their beer. At least somebody on Omsk seemed happy. After a few minutes, Pov stood up and casually strolled out of the cafeteria, taking a different route back to *Siduri's Net*.

Pov passed another group of Forcer soldiers on his way back to *Net*, but no one challenged him. He checked in through *Net*'s docking lounge, chatting briefly with the chief on duty. Then, the flat shape of the disk palpable against his chest as he walked, he went up to his office on Sail Deck.

Tully had the watch and turned his chair around affably as Pov walked out of the elevator, then raised an eyebrow. Pov shrugged at him and smiled, then walked into his office off the Sail Deck lounge and library. He shut the door and sat down behind his desk to load the disk into his computer. He waited through some static, flickering shapes across the screen, a quick flashing of code numbers, then watched as the screen slowly built up a stylized lyre, *Dance*'s ship symbol. The tape had no visual, only audio.

"—if *Net* comes back," the computer suddenly blared.

Pov hastily adjusted the sound level, then bent forward to the speaker. He recognized the voice of *Dance*'s chaffer, Antek Molnar, nasal and deep.

"Oh, they'll come back." That was Sailmaster Ceverny, resonant and gruff. "Andreos will see to that. And they'll buy out and we'll get repaired, just as *Net* promised they'd do."

"That is an item I wish to discuss," Captain Rybak said, his voice rumbling harshly. "We cannot permit *Net* to buy out."

"And how are you going to stop it, Sandor?" Ceverny asked irritably.

"Ceverny, I am tired of your constant obstructionism."

"That is *too* bad, Sandor."

"*Captain,*" Rybak growled. "You will call me captain."

"Only when you call me sailmaster and mean it," Ceverny retorted.

Pov bent closer as the *Dance* meeting fell silent, trying to discern the faint noises in the background. A shushing sound of a ventilator, a rustling of papers, a long and pained silence as Rybak and Ceverny probably stared at each other, one openly defiant, the other determined to keep his absolute authority, even with a senior captain.

"Gentlemen," Molnar said placatingly, "this gets us nowhere. I suggest we ask Nikolay to join us, to hear what he wants to say."

"I object," Ceverny said. "The holdmaster and pilotmaster aren't here—you didn't invite them, did you? Since when does *Dance* have restricted captains' meetings?"

"Ask Mr. Bukharin to come in," Captain Rybak said, ignoring the question. "And you will keep your mouth shut, Mr. Ceverny. We need a united front here, for the sake of *Dance*."

"*Now* you talk about *Dance*'s sake." Ceverny's sarcasm was heavy. "This is new."

"Or else you can leave," Rybak said disdainfully. "Just take yourself away." Pov could practically hear the tension in the room shoot up as Ceverny's chair squeaked and he started to do just that. "Sit down, Miska!"

"I have trouble with dares, Sandor. Twenty years and you don't know that yet?"

Pov heard the sound of a door chime, then realized it was his own office door. He put the disk on hold and got up to answer it. Tully stood in the doorway when it opened, looking at him quizzically. "So when do you dash into your office," he asked humorously, "and don't even sit down by me for a while, just to show off you're boss?"

"So when does it take you this long to get the courage to ask?"

Tully snorted. "Sail watch just changed, you fuzz-brain. *I* show responsibility. I have moral charm. I wait until Roja shows up early and takes over the deck." He puffed out his chest, posing. "*Can* I come in?"

"Do so, charming one."

"Thank you so much." Tully stepped in and closed the door behind him, then glanced quickly around Pov's small office. "I could have sworn I heard Sailmaster Ceverny in here."

Pov grunted. "You did. Pull up a chair. I'm listening to a gift from Benek."

"Benek?" Tully's eyebrows climbed.

"He brought me a disk." Pov sat down and pressed a key.

"—Hello, Nikolay," Rybak said genially. "Please come in."

Tully's eyebrows climbed even more, his eyes widening in surprise. "Bukharin's aboard *Dance*?" he asked incredulously. "When?"

"The disk isn't dated, but recently." Pov turned up the audio a little to let him listen, too.

"Friends, friends," Nikolay Bukharin boomed in ship-Czech. Pov shifted uneasily as Bukharin's Russki accent reminded him of Avi. "So good to see you."

"Please sit down," Captain Rybak said, in a pleasant tone Pov had rarely heard except at meetings where Rybak wanted to please someone, rare as that was. Tully picked up the nuance, too, and leaned forward, cupping a hand behind his ear, then closed his eyes to concentrate.

Tully was better at picking up voice signals, heard things Pov sometimes missed.

"A pleasure to be invited aboard," Bukharin said, followed by a wheeze as the portly man sat down, then the idle creaking of a chair. "I've often wished to see more of *Dance* than the glittering exterior."

"We try to glitter," Rybak said fatuously.

Tully made a face. "Excuse me while I barf," he muttered.

"Quiet," Pov said. "I'm trying to hear."

"You wished to talk?" Bukharin said, getting down to business. "About which of my several suggestions?"

"This concerns *Net*."

"Ah, yes. When do you expect them back?"

"A week or so. If they succeed, they may bring back several holds of tritium, enough to pay for *Dance*'s repairs and our annual franchise fee to Omsk."

"And *Net*'s buyout," Bukharin said flatly. "You will remember when we signed our last annual contract, you agreed that your daughter ship would also serve Tania's Ring as long as *Dance* held contract here. It is your responsibility—"

"I remember the clause," Rybak said impatiently.

Pov and Tully looked at each other in perplexity. "I don't remember it," Tully said. "And I read the entire contract, theirs *and* ours. Rybak made a secret agreement?"

"Shh."

"Do you think Milo knew?" Tully asked, his eyebrows climbing again.

"I doubt it," Pov said, "or he would have waved it around when the ship voted for T Tauri. Shh."

"So what are you going to do, Captain Rybak?" Bukharin said over the speaker, his tone no longer as friendly.

"Yes, indeed," Tully growled. "Tell us, Captain Rybak."

"Will you shut *up*? Pov asked irritably. "I want to hear." Tully snorted, then sat back, scowling, and shut up.

"—open to ideas," Captain Rybak said. "We can expect, if *Net* is successful, two to three times our usual annual harvest of tritium, based on Sailmaster Ceverny's projections—and they may exceed that."

"That's a lot of tritium," Bukharin said noncommittally. "Could glut the market."

"Indeed?" Pov could practically hear Rybak's ears twitch to attention.

"Too much of anything," Bukharin said pompously, "always lowers the value."

"Tritium is tritium," Sailmaster Ceverny growled. "And there are other colonies than Tania's Ring and Earth herself. You can resell."

"Why should I resell?" Bukharin protested. "And ruin the tritium market?"

"*What* tritium market?" Ceverny asked impatiently. "The colonies can't get enough of it. Tritium can't lose its value, no matter how much *Net* brings back."

"Please, sailmaster," Molnar said soothingly.

"Still," Bukharin said blandly, rolling along, "we can't be too careful. A tritium glut could have severe consequences for our economy, and I must think of Tania's Ring. The value of a triple harvest would be quite uncertain."

"Exactly," Rybak said, pouncing on it. "I doubt we could value *Net*'s cargo at even half current market price."

"*We*?" Ceverny exploded. "What do you mean, 'we'?"

"That's enough, Mr. Ceverny," Rybak said coldly. "If you insist on being obstinate, perhaps you should busy yourself on Sail Deck. It's mainly your sails that are in shreds, thanks to *Net*."

"I don't believe Kozel. And I still want to know what 'we' means, captain. Why aren't Hold and Helm at this meeting?"

"That's enough! I can make that an order, if you wish."

"Don't bother," Ceverny said contemptuously, and his chair creaked loudly as he stood up. "I'll see myself out." Pov heard Ceverny's angry footsteps, then a short silence.

"You should replace him," Bukharin observed, his voice hard. "Divided command is always dangerous."

"That's *Dance*'s affair, Molnar retorted. "Not yours."

"I could make it my affair," Bukharin said menacingly,

"if *Dance* violates its contract with Tania's Ring. I agreed to not buy Aldebaran collector ships so that you could keep your monopoly here. *You* agreed I would have *two* cloudships producing tritium for my colony. I intend that agreement to be kept."

"It will be kept," Rybak said.

"I've heard otherwise, Captain Rybak. You allowed yourself to be outmaneuvered by *Net*'s captain when he protected that gypsy sailmaster of his. You allowed *Net* to leave system for T Tauri. Now I see consequences for *my* colony in *your* failure to restrain your junior cloudship. And so I am asking, on behalf of Tania's Ring, what are you going to do about it?"

"We are discussing that now," Rybak said coldly. "Uncertain tritium value, and your exclusive right to our tritium production, another part of our contract. *Net* cannot legally sell tritium elsewhere. Am I right, Antek?"

"Yes," Molnar said reluctantly, his voice almost too low to hear.

"That does not satisfy me," Bukharin said loftily. "I point out that *Dance* is not spaceworthy, and so cannot perform its contract. You owe me additional tritium this biannum."

"We aren't due for another cloud run for weeks."

"*If* I provide repair services, you'll be able to go." The threat lay on the air a long moment before Rybak began to sputter.

"You have a contract—" he said.

"So do you. I would, however, consider a modification, a small change to our arrangements. Right now I pay you market price for tritium. If I didn't have to pay market price, only the crew salary and amenities of your junior cloudship, I'd consider it a fair exchange for last year's guarantee." Pov and Tully exchanged a wide-eyed glance.

"You can't be serious," Rybak said slowly.

Bukharin's chair creaked. "Why not sell me *Net*? Ashkelon is looking for a new cloudship since *Alkat's Gold* and her daughter ship left for the Pleiades last year. *Dance* might prosper there."

"*Net* will not agree," Antek said, his tone ice-cold. "Of that I can assure you."

"So?" Bukharin said. "She's your junior ship, and you still own most of her. Make her agree."

"We don't operate as you do," Molnar said tightly. "*Net* has personnel guarantees—"

"We will consider your suggestion," Rybak interrupted. "Be quiet, Antek. Allow us a few days, Nikolay."

"Certainly, of course," Bukharin said, his voice affable again. "*Dance* is a beautiful ship, captains. You must be proud of her." The disk ran through the sounds of Bukharin's leaving, then abruptly ended in a hiss of static. Pov stopped the disk and put it on rewind, then looked at Tully.

"Well, that explains a lot of our recent mysteries," Tully said. "Rybak got scared by that Aldebaran vendor and signed his ship away—and us, too. The fool!" He got up and paced a few steps. "What a mess."

"Actually, it makes things rather clear—at least for *Dance*," Pov said, leaning back in his chair. "Selling us is a good way out for Rybak."

"You think he's done that? Agreed to sell us?"

"I saw more security troops on Omsk, their Forcer troops that patrol the planet cities—lots more than usual. I'm thinking about what Omsk could do to *Net*, parked here, if they wanted to. How many people does Omsk have on staff—a thousand, two thousand? And we've got three hundred on *Net*, nearly half of them children. It would be a very short war."

Tully stopped. "You think it would go that far?"

"God, I hope not. But when the gaje police get too active, gypsies prudently move on, and so should we—before Bukharin brings more troops up to Omsk. But what happens to *Dance* if we leave?"

"I surely don't *care*." Tully's face was flushed with anger. Tully had not expected this, that was clear: in some ways, for all his acerbic opinions about common humanity, his skeptical attitudes and his fierce loyalties that sometimes blinded him, Tully believed in certain truths. There would be others on *Net* who shared those beliefs, and who would not see beyond *Dance*'s betrayal. Pov looked down at his hands and slowly twisted his fingers.

Tully leaned on his desk. "Are you saying *you* care?" he demanded, still visibly upset.

"I do, Tully. And so will a lot of people on *Net.* Half my family lives on *Dance,* and the Slavs and Greeks have family on both ships, too. We leave them behind in Bukharin's clutches? We leave *Dance* behind for Bukharin to own?"

"And so we stay and join *Dance* in the slavery?" Tully stared at him.

Pov shook his head. "I'm not saying that." He stood up and walked around the desk, then gripped Tully's arm tightly. "Hey, coz," he said softly in Romany. "*Net*'s here. I'm here. Look to your own. The gypsies always say that. And you're half gypsy by now, I'll hazard, after all these years around me."

"I am most certainly *not*." Tully made a show of shaking off Pov's hand, then unthinkingly used a gypsy gesture to ward him off, catching himself in mid-gesture. He scowled ferociously. Pov laughed and finished the gesture for him.

"See?" he teased.

"Well, quarter gypsy, maybe," Tully said grudgingly. "I'll have to work on transmuting back to pure Greek."

"That's a deal. Let me know how you do that. Come on. Captain Andreos has to listen to this." Pov popped the disk out of the computer and motioned Tully toward the door.

Chapter 3

Captain Andreos was not surprised, but looked much older after he heard the disk confirm some of his fears for *Net*. He shook his head, saying that he had to think awhile, then talk to Milo, *Net*'s chaffer.

"Milo?" Tully asked, making a face. As *Net*'s principal lawyer, a rank given captain's status on the cloudships, Milo Cieslak had opposed *Net*'s trip to T Tauri and had tried to spread dissension ever since, opposing *Net*'s other four captains at every turn.

"He's still *Net*'s chaffer, whatever his oppositions," Andreos said tiredly. "He can tell me how legal this 'sale' might be. As Antek said, we have personnel guarantees in our ship contract that date back to *Fan* herself, promises we'd have to sign away expressly. If Tania's Ring tried to cancel them, we could appeal to Earth under the colony's own charter. Nikolay knows that. If he really thought it was legal, he wouldn't have troops on Omsk." Andreos scowled.

"Troops won't change our guarantees," Tully objected. "We could still appeal to Earth."

"Troops can do many things," Andreos said sourly, "including seizing our ship until we sign Bukharin's waiver of rights. Or maybe they'll put hull shots into *Net*'s holds to vent our tritium. No tritium, no problem, and Bukharin ends up with title to *both* cloudships. A very deft gamesman, our Nikolay. He's gambling we won't risk *Net*."

"Rybak will agree to sell us," Pov commented.

"Yes. He has to—or lose *Dance*. Bukharin has him neatly pinned, and both of them know it. Bukharin's target now is us, and he wants us pinned as nicely. As you said, Pov, this news explains a great deal. Go away now, you two. And keep this quiet, please." He shot a sharp look at Tully.

"Of course, sir," Tully said, sounding a little offended.

"Dismissed."

Pov returned alone to his apartment and stood for a time in front of his window, looking out over *Net*. Beyond the central core and the portside holds, the high walls of Omsk's docking bay rose half as high as *Net*'s tall prow, boxing her within metallic arms. The local sun, just now rising over Omsk, touched the prow and amidships structures with a shimmering gleam, casting long shadows. At this angle, the Pleiades rose just above *Net*'s starboard wing, a brilliant group of diamonds closely set. He traced the group with his eyes, naming them to himself, matching each brilliant blue star with the ionized gascloud that surrounded it. The Pleiades were a different medium for cloudships, a new challenge for *Net* if the ship took the chance, took her own justice for *Dance*'s betrayal.

As he and Andreos agreed, Rybak's promise to Bukharin explained much of *Dance*'s behavior this past year—the tension in several intership meetings, the careless risking of *Net*'s safety during recent comet runs, Rybak's overt search for a scapegoat in Pov when *Dance* had caught the dust instead. It explained many things, but Pov would rather have had other answers.

You wanted answers, he reminded himself sourly. Now you're complaining?

If *Net* took the chance, the choice would leave *Dance* behind, in peril. Nearly everyone on *Net* had family aboard *Dance*, with the majority Slavs having the strongest ties. No way to warn, not if *Net* hoped to break free. A single whisper to Captain Rybak on *Dance*, and *Net* would lose her one opportunity of surprise. He thought of his family on *Dance*, of Athena's parents and sister, the hundred ties that would be ripped apart. He doubted his *Dance* relatives would tell Rybak anything, not caring for gaje ties to any ship, but others could.

If we broke contract, took our tritium to the Pleiades, he thought. If. We could be called outlaws. *Ishtar's Jewel* still had a marginal existence in the Pleiades, they had heard, disdained by the other cloudships, plagued by one mishap after another. After she had broken contract with *Fan* at Perikles, *Jewel*'s great hopes had dashed themselves on the realities of a cloudship with older-design sails that never caught that run of good fortune, however brief, that could pay for the refit she needed.

We have the better sails, he reminded himself, pricked by worry. Would it be enough if we go? Will *Net* vote for the chance, if that is needed? And what about Bavol and Lasho? Should I warn them? And what if I somehow destroyed *Net*'s one chance if I did? He found himself caught again in the web of his conflicting loyalties, tugged in two directions as sailmaster and Rom did not mix, each demanding different answers.

He turned away from the window, flexing his shoulders to relieve the tension, then padded into his bedroom for his belated sleep, wanting it more now than ever. He was a stride through the connecting door when he caught himself short, startled by the sleeping figure on his bed. Pov backed up a step in alarm and moved his hand toward the light switch.

"Don't turn on the light," a woman's voice said softly from the computer alcove on his left. A shadowed figure stood up and moved forward, coming into the shaft of light from the living room. "He's sleeping. He's slept so little recently." As she moved closer to him, bringing her face into the light, he recognized Katrinya Ceverny.

"Mrs. Ceverny?" he blurted.

"Hush." Katrinya took his elbow and firmly escorted him back into the living room. "Let him sleep."

"Who?" Pov asked stupidly, astonished to see her, then realized who the sleeping figure had to be.

Katrinya smiled, her old eyes crinkling. She looked Pov up and down. "Have you grown again? You look taller." She reached out and pinched his arm, feeling the muscles. "Lifting weights? That's good." Katrinya Ceverny had always taken a motherly interest in her husband's sail techs, including Pov during his years on *Dance,* an interest he had always appreciated.

"No, ma'am, to neither. Sorry. What *are* you doing here?"

Katrinya smiled again, then abruptly looked forlorn. She glanced involuntarily toward the bedroom.

"Twenty years of captain's ranking," she said softly, "thirty years of absolute devotion to a cloudship—and all those profit shares adding up, speaking practically, the savings of a lifetime, now gone. Do you have room in your gypsy family for us, Pov?" She tipped her head. "I can cook fairly well," she joked. Katrinya Ceverny was *Dance*'s principal chemist, and had personally trained Karoly and *Net*'s other chemlab chiefs. Then he saw the glimmer of tears in her eyes, and a raw pride, an utter determination. Katrinya Ceverny came from the toughest of the First-Ship stock, had stood by her husband in every breach. Consistent, as always.

"Ma'am, you can adopt *me* anytime. Have you eaten?"

"I didn't want to presume. Your sweet young cousin, Tawnie, let us in here. She said it would be all right; I hope it is."

"Tawnie?"

"We asked." She reached out her hand tentatively, and Pov swept her into his arms for a quick embrace, then led her to one of the living-room chairs and insisted she sit down. She flushed slightly. "I'm sorry. We didn't know where to—"

"Tawnie was absolutely right. Does *Dance* know you've left ship?"

"Not yet," she said, looking up at him. "At least I don't think so. They'll search for us." The sad smile again. "Once my family fled from Poland to escape the Russians. Here we are, running again." She sighed softly. "I'm a little thirsty, since you're offering."

Pov went to the kitchen and opened the refrigerator, then held up a jug of Patia's marshberry juice that Tawnie must have left. "Something pink?" he asked.

"Please," Katrinya said.

He poured two glasses of the juice and brought them back to her, then sat down in the other chair.

"*Dance* has done something terrible, Pov," Katrinya said in distress, her hands fluttering. "I don't know what it is, but I see it in his eyes, and it involves *Net*. He would have stayed with *Dance,* I think, but past a certain point even loyalty must end, when argument has lost all purpose." She took the glass and sipped at it, then cradled it in her hands, stilling them, her head bowed. "So I insisted."

"Someday, if I am in a similar place, I hope my wife will insist, too."

She raised her head and looked at Pov bleakly. "It gives him me to blame."

"Nonsense. He won't do that. Miska Ceverny? Are we talking about the same husband?"

"Well, I only have the one," Katrinya said with some spirit, then smiled again, her face easing. "He always liked you, Pov." He saluted his thanks with his glass, and made her smile more broadly. Then, for a brief moment, she looked completely bereft again.

"*Net* will welcome you both," Pov said softly, taking her hand, "and with great honor. You must believe that. I already know most of what has troubled him, and in time you'll know, too, and know that your insisting was justified. He will never blame you."

"Blame her for what?" a voice growled behind them.

"Oh!" Mrs. Ceverny said, and almost dropped her glass. She turned around apprehensively to look at her husband.

"Want some juice, sir?" Pov said firmly. "You can have my chair."

He got up and waited as Ceverny walked forward, shuffling a little with fatigue. Ceverny collapsed into the chair with a groan, then rubbed his eyes and looked at his wife.

"Well, Mother, here we are," he said dryly.

"Yes." She lifted her chin, as if for a blow. Ceverny tsked at her chidingly.

"Pov is right, you know," he said. "I will never blame you. How can you think that?" Ceverny rubbed his hand over his face again, then yawned. "And he's right that you'll know it's justified."

"We know most of it already, sir," Pov said.

Ceverny eyed him. "The nonvalue value of your tritium?"

"Yes."

Ceverny blinked. "Exclusive production for Tania's Ring?"

"That, too."

"God, Tully has good spies! Or is it those pesky skyriders that flit back and forth? You know about selling *Net* to Tania's Ring?"

"That, too, at least the suggestion. So Rybak agreed?" Pov poured another glass of juice and carried it to Ceverny, then retrieved his own from the sideboard, leaning against the counter. "We would have known, anyway. It's not your doing."

"I didn't know how badly Rybak erred last year. He didn't tell us." Ceverny set his jaw and glared fiercely at his glass. "Molnar knew, but Rybak *ordered* him to keep it from the other captains. Poor Antek. He wanted to come, too, but *Dance* is going to need her lawyer a lot more than her sailmaster, believe me." He grunted to himself, then squinted at Pov. "Need a new sail tech? I heard Benek's slot is still available."

"I doubt that application was preapproved by Captain Rybak," Pov said wryly.

Ceverny shrugged. "Let him be surprised. Aside from the general treachery of *Dance*'s behavior, I have my other reasons. Katrinya will approve: she thinks I give too much of myself away, don't you, my dear?" Katrinya smiled tentatively, then sat back farther in her chair, relaxing a little. Ceverny shrugged at her, amused. "Stop flinching, Katinka."

"You old fool," she retorted. "I am *not* flinching." She tossed her head.

"That I am, and yes, you are. Aside from Sandor's treacherous behavior to a daughter ship, in which I do *not* choose to join, I want to go to the Pleiades. See, Katinka? There's hope for me yet. And, competent as you are, Pov, you don't have the experience to give *Net* her best chance. Nothing against you in that—it's just a matter of years on deck. Lack of experience got *Jewel* into trouble when she first got to the Pleiades, and she's still playing catch-up. So for *this* Slav ship I'm coming along to lend what *Dance* owes her daughter ship and chooses to withhold." He set his jaw. "If that's betraying *Dance*, then I'm a traitor."

"Sir," Pov objected, "you are *not* a traitor. I told you we knew most of it already—from a source other than yourself." He grimaced. "Though *Dance* will think it was you. I'm sorry about that."

"True," Ceverny said. He scowled down into his glass, looking troubled and old. "Do you have anything stronger than this bedamned fruit juice?" he growled.

"Vodka?"

"Excellent. You'll go far, Mr. Janusz. Just pour it in with the juice." He held out his glass.

"What about your sons, sir?" Pov asked as he brought over the vodka bottle. He glanced at Mrs. Ceverny, but she looked serene.

"Oh, they'll wait for the dust to settle," Ceverny said casually, "then maybe cash in their ship shares and catch a transport to GradyBol Station to rejoin *Net* there. Captain Rybak will confiscate Katrinya's and my ship shares as a penalty, of course, but we've faced that. My sons can make their own choice: the eldest will probably stay with *Dance*, but perhaps the younger will follow ..." He shrugged. "They're both grown and can choose for themselves. This crisis will cause many divisions, but division is often a process of change."

"A tough choice, sir."

"Not so hard," Ceverny said, adding an unconvincing shrug. "Chasing comets until I'm doddering while others are testing the seas elsewhere? I'm too much of a sailmaster to miss this chance: I suspect it'll be the last I'll have. By the way, speaking of last chances, I'm aware of a few other stowaways that would interest you. I alerted your Rom family on *Dance*, though they already suspected something was up. They announced a *slava*, I think it's called, and told ship security it was a gypsy thing it would be just awful to miss—all of them banished from the tribe or some what-all. The whole family trooped over a few hours before we did."

Pov felt a sharp relief, keen enough to be a pain. "That is a comfort, sir."

"*Is* there such a thing as a *slava*?" Ceverny asked curiously.

"Surely, sir. Except I thought it was next week. I guess I was wrong."

Ceverny snorted. "Well, I owed it to you. *Dance* was wrong to make you a target."

"Benek goofed the dust reading, sir," Pov said uncomfortably, looking down at the glass cradled in his hands. "He got distracted and misread the screen right before the dust hit our bow wave. I don't think it made any difference in *Dance*'s accident, but Dina Kozel erased the computer record. I didn't find out until just before the intership hearing." He looked up and saw Ceverny staring at him. "Sometimes you choose for your ship, have to. To speak—or not speak."

Ceverny sat back and regarded him a long moment. "You think I would expect you to tell that to me, when your ship might be hurt by it? When *you* might be disranked?"

Pov looked away uncomfortably. "I just thought I should tell you now, let you know."

"Dina's story was not believed, but how did you know we knew?"

"I have an audio disk you'd love to listen to. A little recent meeting with Nikolay."

Ceverny glowered, then made a disgusted gesture. "Pov, let's go to the Pleiades soon. Back to where life is normal. When you put too many Slavs in one place, life ties itself in knots." He drained his glass and put it down on the table, then looked casually around Pov's living room. "You won't mind if we bunk in here, I suppose, until *Net* leaves. Bring in a mattress or something, let me use your toothbrush in the mornings."

"Oh, I think we can find a bed somewhere else," Pov said dryly. "Does Captain Andreos know you're aboard?"

"Probably," Ceverny growled. "*Net* is riddled with spies." He looked at his wife, then leaned over to kiss her soundly. "But, thanks to my good wife, who is my moon and stars and all spaces between, I can welcome life even among spies. Spy away, sailmaster. I can handle it."

"If you say so, sir," Pov said, smiling.

He went into the bedroom and put in a call to Captain Andreos, asking *Net's* shipmaster to come to his apartment.

"Why?" Andreos said from the comm screen, looking irritable.

"Gypsy thing, sir," Pov said lightly. "Can't be missed."

"Do you have more detail on that, Mr. Janusz?" Andreos growled, lowering his eyebrows to menace him. Captain Andreos looked badly harried, more than Pov had ever seen Andreos show. That'll ease some now, Pov thought.

"Afraid not, sir," he said.

Andreos scowled and tapped his fingers, studying Pov's face for clues. Pov grinned at him, refusing to say anything more. Captain Andreos had great radar with people, better even than Tully, and had practiced at reading Pov like a data scan—a habit Pov sometimes managed to baffle. After another minute or so of scrutiny, Andreos grunted in defeat, then turned and looked at someone offscreen.

"We'll continue this later, Milo," he said. "Write me up a brief I can show to the captains."

"If you insist, captain," Milo's voice replied sulkily. "I still say—"

"And I've heard you," Andreos interrupted sharply, visibly trying to keep his temper. "That's all." Andreos's eyes shifted to follow Milo as the chaffer got up and walked out. Then he looked back at Pov, not at all pleased with his sailmaster, either. "Tell me now. I don't need both of you harassing me, not today."

"Just come down here. You'll like it."

"I'm busy, Pov."

"Not too busy for this. Wait a minute." Pov stepped out of the alcove into the bedroom and beckoned at Ceverny in the outer room. "He won't come unless he sees you, I think. Says he's too busy."

"Who are you talking to?" Andreos demanded.

Ceverny obligingly ambled into the bedroom and

moved into pickup range of Pov's monitor. As he saw Ceverny, Andreos's jaw dropped open in surprise.

"You!" Andreos exclaimed, stunned. Ceverny rocked on his heels and gave Andreos a wicked smile. Then, abruptly, Andreos's long face filled with open relief and delight, easing every line that had deepened with worry. "You!" he repeated. "But when—"

"I'm applying for sail tech on *Net*," Ceverny said loftily, his nose in the air as he posed. "Couldn't convince your sailmaster, so I insisted on going over his head. Still too busy, Leonidas?"

"I'll be right down," Andreos said, laughing, and clicked off.

Twenty minutes later, Pov found himself bundled out of his own apartment and left to shift for himself. Rather than stroll the Cevernys through *Net*'s corridors to other accommodations, bringing more people into the secret, Captain Andreos had grandly offered them Pov's apartment, at least for the interim. Pov got some clothes while Andreos talked to the Cevernys, then managed to get himself out of the apartment without too many apologies from Katrinya. He leaned against the wall outside, his arms filled with a change of clothes and a toothbrush, and considered his possibilities.

Sleep, he thought. It's wonderful.

He blinked tiredly, trying to get his mind to work, then looked at his wristband. Avi was almost off watch. He pushed himself away from the wall and headed off to throw himself on her mercy.

He had another restless night, sleeping fitfully through the early evening and on through the night, dreaming of data scans and T Tauri. He woke up in Avi's arms, still tired and yawning. Sex ended up a botch, disappointing Avi, though she said she didn't mind.

"I mind," he muttered to himself in the shower. "I mind a lot."

He managed to dress himself, then went up to Sail Deck and sat lumpily through his morning watch. After lunch, he finally found time to go see his family, knowing his mother would complain about his delay in welcoming the *Dance* Rom, finding fault in his discourtesy. She had left a message on the all-ship board when he hadn't responded to the one at his apartment, the tone brisk with her displeasure. It gets worse, Pov told himself, if you wait until tonight.

When he reached the Janusz apartment by the chemlabs, he walked into controlled bedlam. Though the Janusz family shared a triple-space modified into two large open rooms, the Rom visitors from *Dance* had crowded an already crowded accommodation. The children ran around shrieking in the sleeping area in the back of the room, tussling on the several mattresses, while the adults sat on the seating cushions in front, drinking drinks and eating small cakes as they talked. When Pov walked in, his mother paused in filling Uncle Damek's glass and gave Pov a raking glance, checking God knew what, then took her pitcher back into the kitchen, too busy in social duties to talk to her son. Typical, Pov thought, knowing his mother was unhappy with him and would do her best to air it.

Apparently the welcoming of *Dance*'s Rom still went on, though the group had arrived the night before. Uncle Damek genially conducted Pov to sit down with the group, his broad face crinkling with a rare smile, then sat himself down with a great gusting of breath. Damek, usually a humorless man, always enjoyed any feast for the chance to see all his family in one place: a gypsy man saw his heritage in his large family, and it made Damek a benevolent grandfather to all his sons' brood. Damek grunted as five-year-old Shuri slammed his head with a hefty backswing of her pillow, then waved a teasing finger at his little granddaughter. Shuri gestured back impudently, giggling, then squawked and ran as Damek pretended to get up to chase her. The children's noise was overwhelming in the room, but that, too, was part of the ceremony, the initial indulgence of the children's excitement. Later, when they had played themselves out and had been put to bed again, the adults would have their quieter talks. Pov drew up his legs into a comfortable arrangement on a cushion and smiled at Patia, Bavol's wife, who sat next to him.

"Pov," she said, leaning toward him to touch his arm, her earrings swinging with her dark long hair. "Good to see you."

"You, too, Patia."

In honor of the occasion, Patia had dressed in the flowing bright-colored skirts and kerchief of a proper *romni,* a costume that suited her complexion and pretty eyes. In other guises, she was one of the best biolab techs on *Dance,* Tawnie's model in choosing that cloudship trade, even if other parts of Patia's life gave her less joy. Bavol, Damek's middle son, had been a difficult boy, and had grown into a difficult husband, already losing one wife in divorce, though that hadn't been entirely Bavol's fault.

Pov accepted a glass of a cold fruit drink from Tawnie, smiling his thanks, then watched Tawnie bustle back into the other room. His mother walked across the kitchen doorway, a large kettle in her hands, and spotted him again with another unfriendly glance. Pov felt like a shrimp on a dish, about to get speared with a fork.

Patia smiled, her lean face openly pleased to see him. "Good to be here on *Net,*" she said in Romany.

"More than you know, Patia."

"Oh, that!" Patia asked airily. "Can any gaje hide such a thing from gypsy eyes? Though I admit your asking Sailmaster Ceverny to send word to Bavol was a good thing."

Pov opened his mouth, then wisely shut it, leaving Patia in her assumption that a certain sailmaster's loyalties always cut one way. Patia would not understand why he would even hesitate to send a warning to the *Dance* Rom, would not see the other loyalties.

Patia sighed feelingly, patting her dark hair. "I admit I regret leaving our ship shares behind—we can put in a claim later, but I doubt Captain Rybak will be moved to honor it." Her eyes followed Shuri, her oldest girl, as the little girl followed the toddler Nusi around in a game of tag, making the two-year-old squawk as Shuri pounced on her, tumbling her onto the mattresses in the back of the room. "I must think of a bride price eventually," Patia said, her young face looking unpleasantly old as she frowned. "Are there any Rom in the Pleiades?"

Pov stifled his surprise again. "Assuming we go there. That's not settled yet." Pov shifted uncomfortably. "I don't know. Might be a few on the larger mobile stations like GradyBol or AmTel. I haven't heard that any of the Matsvaya Rom joined *Arrow*'s group." The Machwaya gypsy nation had settled mostly in America and might have followed the American cloudships outward, as the Lowara Janusz had followed the Europeans.

Patia shook her head. "A mobile station wouldn't attract a gypsy. We need roads to wander, places to go, not a space station to circle endlessly." She wrinkled her nose. "I doubt if we could talk any Perikles tribe into paying for the girl's transport. They'd insist it be deducted from the bride price." She sighed.

"Shuri's only five, Patia. It's a little early, don't you think?"

"Not at all," Patia said, shaking her head briskly. "I married at fourteen, though I agree Bavol and I betrothed early because *Dance* was leaving system. And there's Lasho's Nusi and Lilike to think of, too." She frowned. "I wish we had more boys: it would have helped on the economics." She shook her head again.

"Lilike can marry your Kistur, Patia," Lasho's wife said, tuning in on her sister's bridal calculations. Judit, four years younger than her sister Patia and about Kate's age, shared her sister's prettiness, but had a gentler beauty, less cross, more contented. Judit caught up Lilike as the baby waddled by and cuddled her. "And Kem can marry Shuri," she said placidly. "What do we need Perikles for?"

"The children are too closely related, Judit," Patia said crossly. "Would you add a first-cousin marriage to our intermarriage problems since *Fan*?"

From Patia's frown, it was apparently a long-running argument, one that curiously paralleled his own recent discussions with his mother about inbreeding. Lilike had been born with a minor birth defect, easily corrected by surgery, true, but Kem was developmentally slow, and Patia had the genetics training to understand exactly why her stepson didn't thrive as he should. He looked at the two women as they continued their genial argument, ig-

nored by their husbands, who talked earnestly to Uncle
Damek, with Pov suddenly out of the loop on both sides.

In the older days, wives never sat down with their husbands: sexual barriers dominated most of the Rom's social affairs, a division repeated in the many niceties of the
purity rules that kept the Rom what they were. Even now,
a century past humanity's first star colonies, some division still remained in whom each chose as a conversation
partner. He liked Patia and Judit, but each time he saw
them, he found them obsessed with *romni* concerns of
marriages and children and family affairs, talking of little
else, even to the men. Patia's biolab duties at least gave
her some other concerns, but Bavol disapproved of her
job, liking better Judit's preoccupation with home and
children. Sometimes when they argued Bavol openly berated Patia for her unwifely preoccupations, then nicely
soured Patia's relations with Judit by holding up the
younger wife as a proper example to copy.

Does it have to be this way? he wondered, imagining
Avi's reaction to his cousins' behavior. Avi had thought
young Tawnie odd in her satisfactions with her baby and
husband: Patia and Judit had a few more years in the role,
married to two traditional sons of a traditional patriarch,
each son a decade or more older than his wife. Judit and
Lasho were happy, a genuine love match despite their age
difference, but they never talked together as he and Avi
talked. Judit had her children, Lasho had his job and his
artist's preoccupations, but still they seemed happy together. He puzzled about it. It was a pattern in his family
he had accepted and not minded: now he wondered more
about it—and wondered if he should wonder about the
wisdom of how his cousins managed their marriages.
Where does the line get crossed? Where does wondering
begin to change a Rom into something else?

I shouldn't have come, he told himself. He had wanted
to spend part of this time with his family, but now regretted he had. Not today when everything else was still suspended, when he wondered too much about everything.
He studied his hands, stuck with staying for a while until
the penalty of raised eyebrows and frowns lessened for
leaving early. Social compulsion, indeed.

Why does it bother me today? It never bothered me that much before, not among the family like this. Judit's happy: how can it be wrong if she's happy? Patia's not, but Patia could find some reasons to be happy if she tried, though she usually doesn't try.

Tawnie brought another cold glass to her young husband, Del, and knelt down next to him with a sigh, then put her arm comfortably around his waist. Del leaned over and whispered something in her ear, which made Tawnie giggle. Tawnie was happy with Del and her baby, despite the marriage arranged by her father, not by herself. Was that wrong? Pov wondered. If it was, why, if Tawnie was happy? He watched Tawnie as she got to her feet and went back into the kitchen.

You're thinking too much today, he told himself. Stop thinking.

Pov listened politely to the men talk for a while, not invited for his opinions nor offering any, then watched the children keep up their tireless game across the mattresses. Shuri tripped and fell, and Pov half rose as her face crumpled into a cry, but Shuri tossed it off and plunged back into the game with the boys, Judit's two little daughters following behind to and fro like puppies trailing the pack. As the noise level rose again to a painful level, Pov winced. Too many people: he wasn't used to all this chatter, hadn't lived among it for years. Later, if *Net* left for the Pleiades, Damek could ask for another apartment nearby for the Rom additions, but Damek did not look much distressed at keeping all the horde at hand. Knowing his uncle, Pov thought Damek might not ask. The older man liked having his family around him, reminded by their voices of the things important to him.

His eldest cousin, Karoly, looked at him quizzically, and Pov shrugged ambiguously back. I can't even explain it to myself, coz. He gestured a vague excuse and got to his feet, then carried his glass into the kitchen. Tawnie and his mother turned around as he walked in, then watched as he put his glass in the sink and ran some water into it.

"We could have done that, Pov," Aunt Narilla said, a little cross.

"Glad to help." He turned and faced his mother. "Hello, Mother."

His mother only tightened her lips, her dark eyes hard. Even in her fifties, Margareta was still beautiful. As a young woman, she had been magnificent, married at a high bride price to one of the handsomest boys available. Her early widowhood had hardened Margareta in ways Pov regretted—though how much was choice and how much misfortune? Margareta Janusz chose her own ways, whatever the ill luck of the roads, always had.

Tawnie started moving dishes into the sink, and Pov slipped his arm around her slender waist, letting his mother glare as much as she wished. Tawnie looked up at him and smiled.

"Looking good, Tawnie," he said. "How do you like having this mob around?"

"It's great," she said firmly. "I've missed them all so much."

Pov watched her small hands move deftly in the sink: the apartment had sonics and a food processor, but the Rom women still used soap and water most of the time, hand-washing the dishes as if it proved something. Maybe for Tawnie it did.

His mother tugged imperatively at Narilla's sleeve and began whispering in his aunt's ear, both of them glancing archly at Pov for some defect they saw now, whatever the hell it was. Games. Tawnie nudged him over a step with her hip, distracting him, and reached past him for a dish on the end of the counter.

"Have I ever told you," she said in a low voice, her hands moving busily in the sink again, "that I often wish you'd arranged our parents a little better?"

"What do you mean?" he asked indulgently.

"If you were second cousin instead of first, all matters would be smooth. I'd have glommed you as my husband years ago."

"Years ago you were just a kid."

"So? Don't underestimate me, coz."

"Aren't you happy with Del?" he asked worriedly, frowning at her.

"Of course I am." Tawnie shook water off her hands

and turned to press closer to Pov, her own arm slipping around his waist in a hug. Behind them his mother and Aunt Narilla stomped out, each bearing a pitcher like votaries with a sacred relic. Tawnie watched them go, then looked up at him, her small face a little sad. "I was teasing, Pov. Sometimes you look so desolate lately. What's the matter?"

"She glares that way and you wonder why I look desolate?"

"Your mother's glares have never bothered you before. You've been fighting with her as long as I remember, when you choose to fight, that is. Most of the time she's fussing and you won't play. What has changed? Can I do anything?"

He kissed her forehead, then smiled down at her. "Little mother of the world, that's what you are."

"Of course." Tawnie started to say something more, then rolled her eyes expressively as his mother and Aunt Narilla trooped back through the kitchen door, their faces intent.

"Pov!" his mother said. Whatever the topic of the whispered conference, action had obviously now begun. Pov dropped his arm from Tawnie's waist and turned around to face his mother.

"What now?" he asked sourly.

"You are ignoring your social duties," Margareta said pompously. "Go in and sit with the men."

"No thanks. I've got sail duty."

Pov kissed Tawnie's cheek again, traded glare for glare with his mother, and stalked through the other room to the door and on out. Let them talk.

Chapter 4

As the door hissed shut behind him, he heard his mother call out sharply, making everything obvious to everybody, another fight, another blot on the family named Pov Janusz. He kept going, taking a quick turn at the next corridor and a long way around back to the central companionway in case she decided to chase him down the hall. When he reached a good measure of safety, he slowed down and put his hands in his pockets, slouching along comfortably.

Not a great idea to go home today, he thought glumly. Not today. What's wrong with me?

He didn't have duty, and it'd be like his mother to check the rosters, but he didn't care that he'd lied or that she'd check. He didn't care, he told himself firmly.

On the main companionway that linked the prow with the rearward modules of the ship, he stopped in the middle of the companionway and turned toward the large windows that lined the long corridor, letting traffic find its way around him. He tracked his way around the stars and corrected several degrees to face the right direction. Over there, he thought, counting the Pleiades stars, then began naming them possessively. Maia, Electra, Asterope—

"Staring off into space again, I see," a voice said behind him.

Pov turned around, mildly embarrassed—for he had been doing exactly that—then smiled at Irisa Haralpos, Tully's dark-haired wife. Clutching the bottom edge of Irisa's tunic with her tiny hand was their youngest, Poppyea, dressed in bright red overalls. The three-year-old girl stared at Pov, blue eyes round, a chubby thumb stuck firmly into her mouth.

"Hello, Poppyea," he said and bent down to her. Poppyea took a cautious step backward, then edged prudently around her mother's leg. "Give us a kiss," Pov said.

Poppyea eyed Pov dubiously and retreated another step. Then she shook her head decisively.

"Why not?" Pov asked, pretending disappointment.

Poppyea took her thumb out of her mouth. "No!" she declared.

Irisa grimaced. "She's in that stage now," she said. "Everything's 'no,' don't care who you are. Right, Poppet?"

"No!"

"See what I mean?" Irisa rolled her eyes, then frowned reprovingly at her youngest daughter. "Poppyea, that's not nice."

"No!" Poppyea declared, then hid her face against her mother's leg and giggled.

"Sorry, Pov," Irisa said humorously.

"I can wait. When she's grown up and is as pretty as her mother," he said, giving Irisa a neat bow, "it'll be worth the wait."

"Hmph." Irisa dimpled. "I'm going to tell Tully you said that."

"Of course. That's why I said it. Make him jealous, so he'll appreciate you like he should."

"I'm also going to tell Avi," Irisa warned, shaking her head.

"Now *that* could be a little difficult."

Irisa smiled knowingly. "Have you seen Tully? He's wandering like you are, and I can't find him. I *hope* the boys are with him. They surely weren't in school. The entire ship's abuzz with rumors. You had a secret meeting of some kind on Omsk, according to *Net*'s lounge chief, who told all his friends, and then you came back looking ominous. How do you look 'ominous,' Pov? You must teach me. Then Tully was overheard shouting something after he closeted himself with you in your office. Then you two barge out and rush off to Andreos."

"We did not rush. We strolled, I'm sure."

Irisa made a rude sound, her eyes dancing. "Buzz, buzz. And now Andreos is scheduled to talk to the ship about something important." She grinned.

Pov grunted. "This ship is a sieve."

"Has *Dance* sold us out somehow?" she asked curiously, pumping him. "That's the general consensus, I think. All that rushing about, you know, hither and yon."

He shrugged, then turned and looked up at the Pleiades again. "I think *Net*'ll vote to go, don't you?"

Irisa sighed, then clucked her tongue with satisfaction. "I'm sure we will. Is there any real choice? My concern is for those who'll vote against it. Hard choice, losing *Net*." She shook her head. "Wander awhile with me, Pov. Maybe we'll find Tully—and if we don't, it's his loss. You can tell me more about how pretty I am, stock me up." She smiled and tipped her head.

"My time is yours, madam."

"You're a gracious dear, Pov Janusz. And Poppet, you be nice."

Poppyea opened her mouth, then hesitated as her mother raised an eyebrow. Poppyea stuck her thumb back in her mouth, smiling around it. Then she giggled again.

"Smart girl," Pov observed.

"Takes after her father," Irisa said dryly.

Irisa moved off, and Pov fell in step beside her. "Tully in that much trouble?" he asked lightly.

"Not really. But he has an infallible sense of when it's his time to baby-sit—something usually turns up, dire and desperate. It was *his* turn with Poppet an hour ago. When you and Avi have kids, Pov, put it in writing—with penalties."

"No!" Poppyea declared loudly.

"Yes, dear."

Pov ambled with Irisa into the starboard residential quarters and stopped to visit several times as somebody buttonholed them to chat. To Pov's surprise, a few were First-Ship Slavs, who usually kept it brief with *Net*'s sailmaster, whatever the need. Now each took the time to offer a vaguely apologetic socializing of some kind that Pov never did quite track. He watched the last walk off with her face slightly pink around the edges, then glanced at Irisa. Irisa looked openly amused.

"Nice of everybody," she remarked, "to care about your ranking."

"Is that what it's about? I'm not the cause of every problem?"

"Easy to blame," Irisa said briskly. "Harder to apologize later. I think you're getting a few apologies today, Pov. Are you also picking up how the vote's going?" Poppyea started to complain, and Irisa stooped to pick her up, settling her firmly on her hip.

"Yeah. I thought there'd be more argument."

"I think it'll be fairly close to unanimous. We became one ship at T Tauri, and most of us still feel it, Greeks and Slavs together. What counts is *Net*." She lifted her chin proudly, then smiled at him, a very pretty Greek in a ship suit. "Nice that you get some of the benefit—personally, I think it's about time."

"Thanks."

They turned down a side corridor. A few doors down, Irisa leaned her elbow on the doorplate. "Come on in. I'll put some music on or call some people for a party or something."

"Do I look that bad?"

"Hell, no. I'm just appointing you baby-sitter. The rest is a bribe." She put Poppyea down and waved him grandly into the apartment.

Pov bent down to Poppyea, who had her thumb in her mouth again.

"It's you and me, kid." Poppyea's eyes widened in alarm, and her lips worked harder on her thumb. Pov held out his hand to her and waited, letting her think about it. A moment later Poppyea's lips curved and she shyly put her little hand into his.

"I don't believe it," Irisa said, sounding amazed. "You must have some kind of magic charm."

"Gypsy stuff, I think."

"If you could sell it, you'd get rich," she observed.

"Probably. If I only knew what it was."

Irisa headed out, leaving him with Poppyea, and Pov had a pleasant time trying to woo Poppet's good opinion, not an entirely successful enterprise. Tully's little girl had her father's generous skepticism, and showed a wise understanding of the problems of trusting a gypsy horse dealer, however camouflaged as sailmaster he might be. He and Poppyea were building blocks into a pile of the little girl's design when Irisa returned with Tully.

"My, you do look domestic," Tully commented.

"Soar off," Pov advised. "I see Irisa found you. How's the sieve?"

"Voting for the Pleiades, I think," Tully said, and flopped down on the couch. Poppyea promptly left the blocks, abandoning Pov heartlessly, and climbed into her father's lap. She gave a little sigh, then curled up for a nap. "So much for you," Tully teased, winking at Pov. "You know, I think something really happened with *Net*'s people at T Tauri. I'm not hearing Slavs versus Greeks, we-owe-*Dance*—except from Milo, of course." Tully scowled, thoroughly irritated with Milo. "How *long* can that man talk?"

Pov sat back and hugged his knees. "Is he making any progress?"

"Not at all. *Net* trusts Andreos, always has. And, for your information, oh lofty one, there's a lot of talk about you."

"Me?"

Irisa came out of the kitchen with a tray of juices and offered one to Pov.

"Thanks, Irisa," he said, taking one of the frosty glasses.

"Yes, you—and Athena," Tully added. "It's called leadership, I think."

"Nuts." Pov lay back on one elbow and sipped at the fruit juice, then put it on the side table and lay back on the floor. Poppyea had a good idea. He closed his eyes, relaxing bonelessly on the carpet.

"Nuts to you back," Tully said. "It was you and Athena who pushed for the third run into the gas-jet when more prudent types argued against it. People know that, say they trust your 'greater vision.'"

"Nuts."

"Stop saying that. And don't you dare go to sleep on me: this is an important strategy session."

Pov opened an eye, grunted disparagingly, then yawned suddenly, surprising himself. "I haven't slept much lately," he explained. "I'm tired." He heard Irisa give a ghostly chuckle and walk out of the room. When Tully didn't nag again, he opened his eyes and saw Tully smiling at him, his blue eyes wise and canny and highly amused. "What?" Pov demanded.

"I can't believe you. Why aren't you pacing the floor?"

"I *have* been pacing, all over the ship, here, there, up, around. Now it's time for the gears to run down, I guess. Out of fuel." He yawned again and started to sit up, then collapsed backward again as Tully gestured at him indulgently.

"So snore away. The floor's free."

"Thanks." Pov closed his eyes and drifted awhile, listening vaguely to Tully and Irisa talk in quiet voices, to the rustle as Tully stood up and put Poppyea down for her nap, then the murmur of other voices he didn't bother to track. His thoughts wandered into weird dreams, snatches of rolling sail diagrams, *Net* sailing into a glowing gasjet, a series of faces, Kate, his sail crew, Captain Rybak, Benek's pinched misery. He roused when someone touched his shoulder and opened his eyes to see Avi kneeling beside him.

"Hello, love," he said, and yawned.

Avi sat down and shifted his head onto her thigh, then bent over and kissed him lightly. Tully's young boys marched by toward the bedrooms, shepherded by Irisa.

"Beds are more comfortable," Avi suggested.

"A floor gives good support for the back." He yawned again.

Avi gave a sharp tug on his ear. "Wake up. Captain Andreos is about to broadcast to the ship."

"I'm awake," he muttered, feeling so utterly relaxed it was easy to close his eyes again. He smiled as Avi caressed his hair, then dutifully responded as Avi tugged on his ear again, opening his eyes and trying to look alert.

Tully turned on the apartment wallscreen and accessed the all-ship channel, then sat down on the couch, his arm around Irisa. Another couple came in, neighbor friends of Tully's, then Athena and her tall Slav husband, Gregori, with their three girls. Gregori sat Athena down in a chair as if she were made of delicate crystal, then shooed the girls away when they tried to climb aboard, all at once. As Irisa played hostess again, fetching drinks from the kitchen, the only show on the wallscreen was the test pattern of *Net*'s ship symbol, Siduri's graceful hand casting a glittering net.

Then Captain Andreos appeared in the screen, larger than life size, his expression tired but pleased. The captain had dressed in full uniform, and had a smaller display screen behind him, his notes on his desk in front of him. He straightened his shoulders and looked squarely at the camera, then smiled slightly, perhaps amused by his own dignity. Andreos was a very human captain, easily surprised into the most disarming behavior: it was a gift he cultivated, blending deliberate tactic with a natural talent as shipmaster. Pov watched as Andreos signaled his aide, a woman far more nervous about an all-ship performance than Andreos. Then Andreos turned back to the camera.

"Some of you may know," he began as a preamble, "the general point of my presentation today—this ship is a sieve and nothing stays secret long. But my purpose is not to preserve a secret, but to give *Siduri's Net* her choosing of what we will next do." Andreos cleared his throat and glanced down at his papers.

"First, I wish to relay to you information we have received. As you know, *Dance* is undergoing repairs for the dust accident a month ago. *Dance* blames *Net* for that damage. To finesse the issue, your captains suggested our recent trip to T Tauri. We returned with enough tritium to pay for *Dance*'s damage, to finance another year of comet runs for both ships, and, if *Net* chose, to buy out and continue with *Dance* as equal partner or go elsewhere. This was the announced purpose, and our harvest at T Tauri made it possible."

He shrugged his shoulders. "I will be honest with you. All of us know of the recent strains between our ships, some of which have divided on bloodline and rank—

though not all. *Dance* does not want us to be independent: she fears we will leave Tania's Ring, as we most likely would. *Dance* wants her damage repaired, and we are the means—but still she does not want to let us go. It appears now that *Dance* erred in her last contract, a subclause we did not know about, and now Bukharin is in a position to insist *Dance* act against us. And so *Dance* will not recognize our full credits from T Tauri. Bukharin has even suggested outright sale of *Net* to Tania's Ring."

Pov heard a gasp of surprise from one of the neighbors. Athena crossed her arms and scowled, glancing at Pov to make a face.

"I won't detail the excuses," Andreos continued. "The chaffer's written report of the legal arguments are available on general computer scan. The upshot is that *Dance* intends to sequester most of our tritium credits and release those credits to *Net* when and in what amount *Dance*—or Bukharin—chooses. *Dance* is caught in a trap of her making, and much of what has confused us in her behavior stems from that."

Andreos cleared his throat. "We have all been part of *Siduri's Dance*," he said slowly, his voice heavy. "Many of you grew to adulthood on *Dance,* served your first years as part of her crew. *Net* is new, only three years old, but I have hoped that during our three years together, we have become a people of one ship, *Siduri's Net,* and can choose for that one ship when it becomes necessary. I suggest this may be one of the times."

He turned to the aide and nodded. The woman touched some controls on her computer substation, and the smaller video screen lit up, then relayed to the all-ship screen. Andreos's voice continued through the speakers as the prepared presentation began. Pov sighed as the familiar asterism of the Pleiades cluster appeared in midscreen, an open jewel box of brilliant blue stars.

"The captains propose," Andreos said, "that we go to the Pleiades."

"Beautiful," Pov whispered.

Avi suddenly leaned over and kissed him, her dark hair enveloping their faces in a warm tickling shadow. As her lips moved on his, he suddenly wanted her with the same intensity as he wanted the Pleiades, wanting to take her right then, drive into her to make her his, again and again and again, erasing all the doubts, all other needs, possessing her. His fingers tightened hard on her arms, and she broke off the kiss to look down into his eyes. *Love you,* she mouthed.

Want you, Pov said back.

When? Avi brought her face closer again, brushing his lips with hers.

Now, Pov replied, then chuckled as Tully pointedly cleared his throat from the couch.

Avi straightened and gave *Net*'s Second Sail a dirty look, but colored slightly as she caught one of the neighbors glancing at her. Pov sighed to distract her, just softly enough for only Avi to hear, and saw her eyes smile as she looked back at him.

Then he sighed again, moaning the press of fate and a sailmaster's propriety, and sat up to listen dutifully to *Net*'s shipmaster. Avi chuckled softly and wrapped her arms around him, holding him close.

Feeling her closeness, for the first time that day Pov felt normal, not at odds with everything and everybody. The music and the dance, family and a wife, Siduri had told Gilgamesh—all a man needed to be happy. And a road to wander, he added silently, when you're Rom. A good road, a place to explore and learn, never tied down, always free. He looked at the Pleiades hungrily, and Athena shared his look.

"*Diana's Arrow* has developed an advanced sail technology," Andreos was saying, "suited to the heavy dust and limited ionization of the Pleiades veils. The star cluster is relatively young, but is now dispersing, with the bulk of its interstellar gas already absorbed by the four hundred suns of the cluster. Of the remaining gascloud veils, three are most prominent—the northern cloud of Maia's Veil, the Merope Drift in the south, and Alcyone's Shield in the west. Each gascloud measures several light-years in its dimensions; each has a density exceeding a hundred thousand ions per subcubic."

The wallscreen shifted focus and displayed legend titles by several small stars near the major gasclouds. "The mobile processing stations are run by Earth commercial combines, and the cloudships currently in the Pleiades sell their product directly to the mobile stations. Contracts are not exclusive at any of the stations, and competition is fierce. *Diana's Arrow* and her daughters have prospered; other ships have not done as well. As we have heard on occasion from your relatives on *Ishtar's Jewel,* good fortune is not guaranteed. *Jewel* has struggled; so might we."

The presentation ended, and the screen returned to Andreos. The shipmaster folded his hands in front of him. "I suggest that half the tritium is *Net*'s share after proportioned allocation for *Dance*'s dust damage and our buyout fee. That calculation, too, is available on computer scan. The choice is whether we take our tritium and leave for the Pleiades, or accept *Dance*'s self-created problem and stay at Epsilon Tauri."

He spread his long fingers. "Admittedly, we could argue more with *Dance,* perhaps convene a formal intership hearing, maybe even sue in Bukharin's courts. And we might win a court battle—a few years from now, true, depending on several factors—or we might not. We might get boarded by colony Forcer troops, or we might not. We might persuade *Dance* to authorize another trip to T Tauri, though I think that highly unlikely. It would only create the same kind of crisis that has prompted *Dance* into its current intentions. But it could be an option available to use if we stay."

"He's right about the unlikely," Tully muttered.

"Quiet," Pov shushed him, then smiled when Tully scowled. They both knew how the vote would go, and so did Tully's neighbors and Irisa and Avi. So did everybody on *Net.*

"I'll admit I have doubted my proposal," Andreos said on the screen. "I admit that I am troubled—and furious and saddened and outraged. High emotion is not a good foundation for wise choice. But as your shipmaster, and with the majority consent of *Net*'s other captains, I am now presenting to you, the people of *Net,* this choice. Vote your conscience: apply your own wisdom. If emotion suits your choosing best, don't be ashamed to follow that plea of the heart. If close reasoning suits, apply your judgment."

Captain Andreos straightened his papers and looked squarely at the camera. "This vote," he said solemnly, "will be by strict majority, without weighting by preference shares. I invoke that clause of the ship contract, for this is of major significance for our ship's future. The majority will choose for us, and you others, who disagree, will choose, I hope, to accept that other choice—for *Net*'s sake. Good faring, *Net*. The choice is in your hands." He nodded to his aide, and the screen blanked.

Pov rolled to his feet in a sudden lithe movement, then threw a punch at the ceiling. "Yes!" he said. "I vote yes!"

"So should we all," Athena said from her chair, then saluted the neighbors grandly with her glass. "To the Pleiades, friends!"

"You're sure, Athena?" a woman asked, her eyes wide. "Should we?" She glanced uncertainly at her husband.

"Absolutely," Athena said fiercely.

Pov took Avi out into the corridors and they wandered *Net* for a while, listening to the various talk in the lounges, then ended up on Avi's flowered sheets for a long afternoon together.

"You don't have to prove anything to me," Avi said humorously when Pov started them into a second time. "I could see you were tired this morning." She sighed softly as his lips moved slowly down her neck, then caressed him. "And you're doing your damnedest to end up that way again, I can see. You should conserve some energy. Be prudent."

"The hell with energy," he murmured and kissed her shoulder, breathing in the scent of her long hair tangled on the pillow.

"Energy is useful," Avi suggested.

"For many things," he said and lifted himself on top of her. Avi wrapped her arms around him and smiled as he made love to her, taking his time to please her.

"I told you I wasn't fat," he said after a while. "Here, why don't you do some of the work?" He rolled onto his back, pulling her over with him. "Get some exercise, Avi. Be a fanatic."

"I didn't say you were fat," she protested. She braced her arms and smiled down at him, then moved sweetly on him, her dark hair brushing his shoulders, framing her face in its shadow.

"Oh, really?" he asked languidly. "I don't remember it that way." he caressed her back slowly, feeling the silky touch of her skin, the rippling of her shoulder muscles beneath his hands.

"I merely hinted. A hint is not a say."

"Oh ho. Sounds like an Avi rule to me." Avi leaned forward and kissed him lingeringly, stilling their bodies for a long moment. "Marry me, Avi," he whispered when she lifted her head and smiled at him.

"Yes, love. Yes, I will."

"It won't be easy," he admitted. "I don't know if my family will ever accept you. Kate will, but you know her troubles right now. I don't know how that will end."

"I haven't had a family for a long time, Pov. I won't miss it if it doesn't happen."

"I want more than that for you. I want everything for you."

Avi leaned her face close, making a dark tent of her hair around their faces. Her lips brushed his. "I know. That's why I said yes. But I don't need everything, Pov. All I need is you."

Pov smiled at her sadly. "I don't think so. I think you want a family to love you. You can't fool a gypsy, you know. We're too good at fooling gaje, had generations of practice." He twined a finger in her hair and watched her face as she thought about it, her expression a delicate frown. "Avi?"

"The answer's still yes, however you think you ought to argue me out of it. You think I'm crazy enough to say no? Now, shut up, sailmaster: we're busy." She leaned back and brought his hands up to her breasts, then moved so deliciously on him that he groaned. "Concentrate on energy," she told him, her dark eyes dancing. "While you've still got some left."

"Just enough, I think."

"That's good."

Afterward, Pov drowsed for another hour, his arms around Avi. He was nearly asleep when Avi's comm chimed insistently from the outer room. He opened his eyes and saw Avi open hers. As the chime persisted, Avi wrinkled her nose.

"We could ignore that," she said.

"How?" When the chime upped its volume into a screech, Pov groaned and rolled off the bed, then staggered a little as he found his feet on the carpet.

"You don't walk very straight," Avi observed drolly.

"Don't brag. I'm lucky I can walk at all, thanks to you." He leaned over and kissed her. "And I do thank you, ma'am, most sincerely."

"Anytime, I'm sure." The comm screeched again, and Avi pulled the sheet over her face. "Blasted thing," she said. "And they say technology is wonderful?"

Naked, Pov padded out into the living room and luckily remembered at the last instant to key off the video. "Yes?" he said to the blank screen.

"Sailmaster?" a voice said uncertainly. "This is Celka on Sail Deck. Captain Andreos is looking for you. The vote's in, and he's calling all the captains."

"How'd the vote go, Celka?"

"For the Pleiades, of course!" Celka exclaimed, almost indignantly. "Uh, sir, I mean. Anyway, Captain Andreos wants you to come to admin level, like *now,* sir. I've been hunting for you for twenty minutes. Do you know who's in your apartment right now?"

"Yeah, I do."

"A gracious surprise to me, I'll tell you, but he was very nice. So I tried a few other places when you didn't answer the chime at Avi's the first time." Celka hesitated. "I hope I haven't disturbed you," she added primly.

"That's all right, Celka. I'm on my way."

The captains' meeting was short, ending with Milo walking out in a fury. Pov and Janina looked at each uncomfortably, the Slav holdmaster turning delicately pink at Milo's behavior, as if somehow Janina as Slav were responsible for Milo's conduct. Athena watched Milo go, her wan face nearly as angry as Milo's. Then, abruptly, she sighed and leaned her head on her hand, looking exhausted.

"It never stops," she said tiredly. "Ever since *Dance*'s dust accident, he's been this way. And I haven't been provoking him, sir."

"I know," Andreos said tightly. "Milo chooses to act as he chooses. The vote was well over ninety percent. It is a captain's duty to accept the vote, however it falls. Milo is forgetting that."

"Will he tell *Dance*?" Janina said in alarm, her trust in Milo now wholly gone. As one of *Net*'s most senior Slavs, Janina's opinion alone could cost Milo his chaffer's rank, if she chose to move against him. As she might.

"He won't," Pov and Athena said at the same time, then looked at each other wryly.

"I don't have any specific arguments why not," Pov said, "but I'm sure he won't. How about you?" he asked Athena.

"Me neither," she said, shaking her head. "What are we going to do, captain? How do we reach Milo?"

Andreos gathered together the sheaf of papers in front of him. "Is it necessary we do?" he asked irritably, then got up to leave. Janina accompanied him out.

"Poor Milo," Athena said sadly. "In his narrow tight-fisted way, Milo loves *Net*, too. And he's going to lose her, if he keeps this up. Why won't he listen to reason?"

"I don't know." Pov got up and walked around the table, then offered her his hand to help her up. "You can't fight for everybody, Athena, especially right now. You have to take care of yourself. That's important, too."

"Oh, I'll rest up." She took his hand and got up, then allowed Pov to entwine her arm in his. "Keep nagging, Pov," she said dryly, making a face. "After a while, I might even like it."

"So you say," Pov said, then smiled as Athena made a rude noise.

"You and Gregori, nag, nag," she said, a slight edge to her voice. "Do something different for me: come to dinner tonight and bring Avi. Marisa's cooking, and feels so proud she can—though I can't promise what dinner will be. Last night we had honey-flavored goulash—Marisa loves honey, and figures it does just fine in anything else she likes, like any eight-year-old. Honeyed peas, honeyed sandwiches, honeyed salad. The whole family's going to lose their teeth."

"Sounds okay to me," Pov said. "I like honey, too."

Athena smiled. "That's exactly what Gregori said, bless his heart. And he eats it all, too. So if you could set aside your *marime* rules for—"

"Of course, Athena."

"It would be a favor," she persisted. "And if you could tell Marisa you like it—"

"Athena, of course," he said quietly and pressed her arm to his ribs. "We'll praise her to the skies."

"It's just that she's so little. . . ." Athena trailed off and looked bereft for a moment. "I worry for her," she added soberly. "You know, if I get worse and . . . well, that. The other two are younger, but Marisa's at that age when she's starting to copy me, following me around and wearing my clothes and ransacking my cosmetics. She knows something's wrong but doesn't really understand what, thank God. I think that's why I'm on her honey diet: it's her personal cure. Honey is so wonderful that it has to fix anything, right? Even whatever's wrong with Mother."

"Sounds logical to me. Marisa's a smart girl." He pressed his lips to Athena's forehead and held her for a long moment, feeling her shiver sickly against him, her knees trembling despite all her trying to stop them.

"Thank you, Pov," she murmured. Then she straightened and pushed him away. "Come at six. A final meal while *Net*'s still at Omsk, damn their black hearts, and then we're away."

"On the green, Helm." Athena's eyes flashed and she took a step away from him, her anger toward *Dance* building again in her pallid face, an anger that exhausted her too easily, that she couldn't afford.

"If I have to die," she said tightly, "it surely won't be here. Never that." She stalked out.

Chapter 5

Sneaking a cloudship away from Omsk Station won't be easy, Pov thought as *Net* began backing out of her docking bay, but *Net* had timed her departure carefully. By leaving far into Omsk's night shift, *Net* might gain useful time while tentative subordinates awakened grouchy chiefs. While the debates climbed up and down Omsk's authority ladders, Captain Andreos hoped to put some distance between *Net* and Omsk's laser defenses, then slip around Tania's Ring before either Omsk or *Dance* thought to ask *Net* for reasons. The captains of *Siduri's Net* sat at the interlink computers they had used at T Tauri, ready for anything, as *Net*'s crew held its collective breath.

The ship cleared the walls of the bay and fell slowly away from the station, descending toward the planetary atmosphere far below them. As the sails caught the upper wisps of stratospheric ozone, *Net* slowed still more and descended faster, falling around the curve of the planet toward nightside. Pov tracked *Net*'s sail pressure on a subsidiary interlink screen, watching the data steadily fed to him by Tully from Sail Deck's main computer. On the green, he thought.

"Tracking into planetary shadow," Athena said on screen from her own interlink room on Helm Deck. Behind her through an open door, Pov could see Helm Deck's huge screen track *Net*'s trajectory, slowly shifting its courseline as *Net* plunged into the planet's thin upper atmosphere, molecules screaming into her sails. "Beginning ascent out of orbit."

"Sit tight, people," Andreos said over the interlink, his long face tense. "They'll be asking why in a minute or so. Sailmaster?"

"We have the touring sails rigged, sir," Pov said, adding a sail display to the bank of monitor screens on his panel for the others to see. "You can have full acceleration whenever you want it. *Dance* will notice our sails, if they look fast enough, but Bukharin doesn't know enough about our configurations to recognize the outsystem set."

"Good," Andreos grunted. "Bukharin's the one with lasers and guard ships. Maybe he'll argue with *Dance* about our sailset instead of where we're going. Janina, is *Dance*'s share of the tritium ready for offload?"

Janina looked up from her Hold console and smiled. "Yes, sir. But not at this speed, please. I don't want the canister frame taking our engine assembly with it." She sniffed. "Would be embarrassing, suddenly parked short like that, if you get my meaning, Athena."

"Heard and obeyed, oh prudent one," Athena said. "What speed do you want for offload?"

"Slow down to a few klicks when we're a planet diameter out. That's in skyrider range for *Dance* to grab the canisters before the Russkis do."

"Can do."

Net fell more rapidly through the planet's shadow, accelerating into a hyperbolic curve that would carry her away from the planet's gravity pull. Behind them Omsk dwindled to a distant speck, then slipped out of view behind the darkening curve of Tania's Ring. They all relaxed slightly as *Net* put more of the planet between them and Omsk's lasers. Though intended for meteoroid defense, a laser capable of pulverizing a significant rock had enough power to cripple *Net* if Omsk shot them in the right places. Andreos blew out a breath, then raised an eyebrow at them all, getting weak grins back. *Net* increased speed still more, lifting away from atmosphere into open space, counting off the minutes to safety.

"Contact signal, captain," a voice said over the audio channel. "*Dance* to *Net*."

"*Dance?*" Andreos asked, sounding a little surprised. "Not from Omsk?"

"No, sir. It's Captain Rybak, via a circumpolar satellite."

Andreos drummed his fingers on his desk, thinking

about it a moment, then scowled worriedly. "Put him on the interlink," he said, "but send him the return signal only from my screen."

"Yes, sir." One of the upper interlink screens promptly lighted with the sour patrician face of Captain Rybak.

Half the time I've seen him the last year, Pov thought, he looks like that, furious and unreasonable. He sat back and tried to get more comfortable in his chair, half his attention on *Net*'s steady course away from Omsk Station, putting precious distance between his ship and a Russki colony that coveted the tritium fortune that *Net* now carried away in her holds. Andreos had hoped for Omsk to call first, and worried that it hadn't. Why?

"Captain Rybak," Andreos said courteously, then waited the few seconds for the radio beam to bounce around the circumpolar comsat back to Omsk. Already *Net* had moved far enough to create a slight delay in unassisted radio. The signal wavered as *Net* slipped through the solar wind eddies that trailed behind Tania's Ring, then steadied as the comm chief compensated for the particle interference.

"Why aren't you at Omsk Station?" Rybak demanded angrily. "I didn't get any request for *Net* to undock."

"We're leaving," Andreos said. "And you know why, Sandor. Take your 'nonvalue production clause' and 'uncertain market glut' and stuff it."

Rybak blinked in shock, then looked genuinely surprised, for once jarred out of his usual display of contemptuous pride. "Ceverny told you?" he asked incredulously. "Is that where he is? On *Net*?" He sputtered a moment, then glared at Andreos as he realized exactly what Ceverny might have told *Net*, that *Net* knew everything now. "You told me that he wasn't on . . . Bukharin's been combing half the planet trying to find him!"

"Helpful Nikolay," Andreos said unsympathetically.

Ceverny had appeared in the doorway of Pov's interlink room, leaning on the doorjamb to listen. He and Pov exchanged an ironic look.

"He's surprised," Pov commented.

"I can't imagine why," Ceverny said tartly. "I told him I was taking my vacation, the hell with him."

"You sort of left out *where,* sir," Pov reminded him. "The Pleiades are a bit far away from Omsk."

Ceverny shrugged elaborately, an unconcern that he didn't quite carry off. Whatever the good reasons for his decision, Sailmaster Ceverny still saw himself as a traitor to *Dance.* Many on *Dance* would agree with him, and that grief showed in the old sailmaster's shadowed eyes. Pov looked back uncomfortably at the interlink screen.

"I'll deal with Ceverny in due time," Rybak said ominously. "As shipmaster of *Dance,* I am ordering *Net* to return to Omsk Station."

"Sorry, *Dance,* I can't do that," Andreos said cheerfully. "*Net*'s crew has voted, and as shipmaster of *Net* I am obeying that vote. I think you can guess what the vote was." Then he grinned deliberately, provoking Rybak.

Rybak flushed darkly red, then visibly tried to control himself, not too successfully. "We have a legal duty to Tania's Ring," he began lecturing at Andreos, his tone as harsh and proud as ever, as if *Net*'s senior captain were a half-wit.

Pov curled his fingers in his palms and looked down, his stomach churning with an all too familiar response to that particular voice. How many times had he heard Rybak speak like this, whatever the other's rank, whatever the need, the stern parent to a disobedient child? He had never changed, never would—and now his inflexibility was costing him *Net* and risking *Dance* to Bukharin's greed, yet still he could not change, could not moderate that hectoring tone. Did *Fan* lose *Ishtar's Jewel* this way? Pov wondered. By a mere tone of voice, by a prideful unreasonability?

"Your duty, Captain Andreos," Rybak continued, his voice heavy with his displeasure, "is to negotiate any dispute you might have with us or with Tania's Ring. This precipitate action is—"

"He's stalling," Ceverny said and closed his eyes in pain, knowing what it meant that *Dance* would stall for Omsk's advantage. Pov looked up at him, not knowing what to say to *Dance*'s sailmaster, who still loved *Dance* more than life itself. "How's our distance?"

Pov glanced at the small screen showing Tania's Ring

and a schematic of Athena's helm map. "Out of range of the weapon sats now. Haven't seen a guard ship yet."

"Wait a bit," Ceverny said. "You didn't see the lust in Bukharin's eyes when Rybak agreed to sell *Net* to Tania's Ring." He shrugged tiredly. "I'm going elsewhere. I don't want to watch this."

"Of course, sir," Pov said. Ceverny straightened his lanky frame, shot a quick bitter look at Rybak's face in the monitor, and left.

"We're *not* going to sell you to Bukharin," Rybak was saying to Andreos, his hold on his temper growing ragged again. "That is not reasonable!"

"Bullshit," Andreos said, not smiling now.

The two shipmasters glared at each other for a long moment, and Rybak abruptly changed to open menace. "*Net*, you're risking breach of contract," he said coldly. "I could demand penalties for this." Stalling, Pov agreed. He quickly scanned the telescopic shots of Tania's Ring, looking for the first flicker of ship metal as Bukharin sent his ships after *Net*.

"Assess away, captain," Andreos said, waving his hand. "We'll pay them. For your information, *Net* plans to offload half our tritium cargo as we leave—if Bukharin allows us to. Tell him he'd better allow it, or you're dusted for sure, *Dance*. That tritium is intended to buy out our contract and pay for *Dance*'s repairs, *plus* your penalties if you want. I suggest you detach a skyrider to get the tritium before Bukharin steals it."

"You can't do this, Leonidas!" Rybak shouted, his fist hammering on his console. "I will not accept—"

"Oh, no? Watch me."

"Two guard ships just came out of planet shadow," Athena reported over the interlink. "They're accelerating toward us."

"Goodbye, Sandor," Andreos said, his face saddened. "We wish *Dance* good fortune, whether you believe it or not." He gestured to his offscreen aide, and Rybak's screen abruptly blanked in midword. "Increase speed, Helm," he ordered.

Janina blinked, startled. "But, sir," she protested, "we have to offship *Dance*'s—"

"Look again, Janina," Andreos said heavily. "Those aren't just guard ships with a few hot lasers to shear off our antennae. They're Bukharin's orbital *warcraft*, the ships Tania's Ring used to put down that grain revolt a few years ago. You may remember what they used on one of the villages."

"Fusion bombs?" Janina said, her eyes widening. "On us?"

"As long as they aim for the prow, the hold canisters should survive just fine for pickup. I accordingly suggest we continue accelerating and put them well behind us." Andreos looked at Janina with quiet sympathy, knowing how this decision would impact *Net*'s Slavs. First-Ship families had crewed the Slav cloudships for two generations, and such ties would linger even through a quarrel as bad as theirs with *Dance*. "Janina," Andreos said softly, "if we drop *Dance*'s tritium here, one of those ships will break off and confiscate it as 'abandoned salvage.' You can guess what luck *Dance* would have in Bukharin's court trying to get it back."

Janina's plain face showed her obvious distress. "Maybe we could orbit the tritium around an outer gas giant as we leave," she said. "Then tell *Dance* to hire a retrieval ship to go . . ." She stopped, thinking about it, then slowly shook her head as she found her own answer. "And what if *Dance* does pick it up and decides to lie, saying we still owe them the buyout? You've thought this out, haven't you?"

"I considered the possibilities," Andreos acknowledged. "Especially the chance Bukharin might use his warships. We need an impartial witness to the transfer, Janina, someone to document that we *did* pay—not Bukharin, and not *Dance*. We want to be free without question, without entanglements in courts up and down the chain for years. So we'll sell the tritium in the Pleiades and send back the credits to *Dance*." He spread his hands. "It's the only way."

"And what if Bukharin declares *Dance* bankrupt," Janina said, "and nationalizes her as Omsk property? Before we can sent our credits back?" They looked at each other bleakly.

"I didn't ask for this, Janina," Andreos said softly. "You know *Net* did not ask for this—all we wanted was our freedom."

"I know sir," she said heavily. "I know."

"Sir, the warships are gaining on us," Athena said in surprise, then leaned back in her chair to look out onto Helm Deck, rechecking her screen data against the visual track on the helm map. "They're angling to intercept, too," she added, sounding even more startled, "trying to cut us off. They must think they have speed to spare."

"*What?*" Andreos said. "*Net* can outrun any planet-bound craft."

Athena shook her head and straightened her chair with a thump of her feet. "I think our friend Nikolay is a lot smarter than we thought—and we weren't fools in guessing about him." She quickly tapped at her computer board to display data on one of the interlink screens. "See? My monitors say their engine emissions are star-drive frequency. Bukharin must have cannibalized one of the Tania's Ring freighters, then put the jump engines on the warships. They can indeed outrun us, sirs. We have more tonnage than they do and they aren't using sails for shielding, just slag armor on their prows." She glanced ruefully at Pov. "Our sails are slowing us down, Pov."

"We can't drop them, Athena," Pov said, alarmed. "Not running through insystem dust."

"I know, I know, I was trying to be amusing." She winced. "Sorry. Even if Janina dumps tritium at full stream into the engines, I'm not sure we can outrun them. *Net* has too much mass to compete with the kind of stripped-down speed they're getting."

"So let's use some different atoms," Janina suggested. "I've got lots of superheavy pets from T Tauri to play with."

"We haven't run spec analyses on that material," Andreos warned. "Most of it's already degraded into lighter isotopes."

"Not all, sir," Pov said, jumping onto Janina's suggestion. "I'd rather risk *Net* than let Bukharin enslave a cloudship, however much he thinks we deserve it." He waved at the monitor screen, where two lean fast ships hurtled after them. "Omsk hasn't tried to contact us: they obviously intend force, sending ships like that after us. We aren't going to turn back meekly with a shot across our bow—you know that and I know that. Even if they aren't planning the worst, it'll escalate to hull shots the moment we won't slow down."

"And once they close on us, sir," Athena said, "we won't get away again."

Andreos scowled, his eyes flicking from face to face. "Does anyone have a better idea?" he asked. "Please take time to consider, for *Net*'s sake."

They all thought furiously, watching the warships steadily advance on *Net*, visibly faster and on intercept course. One had already shifted slightly to strike across *Net*'s bow ahead of its companion, a pincer movement that would box *Net* neatly between them. Athena was right: *Net* was not a warship, and hadn't the weaponry or maneuverability to fight those twin combat craft at close range.

"What if we call Omsk?" Janina suggested. "Try to reason with Bukharin?"

"And say *what*?" Athena asked, waving her hand. "Leave us alone? We already did that. *Dance* talked to us through Bukharin's comsat relays, and I can't see Nikolay not tapping in to listen." She shook her head ruefully. "We didn't think about that engine overhaul, sirs, and now we're stuck. I say it's T Tauri all over again. Ride the wild wave or get fried. God, what a choice."

"I can't think of anything, either," Andreos said, then closed his eyes a long moment, took a deep breath. "We'll dump your atomic pets into the engines, Janina," he said then. "How long until they're in effective laser range, Helm?"

On her screen, Athena leaned back and conferred with Stefania through the door for a brief wait, then straightened back up and raised her hand, still looking over her shoulder into Helm Deck. "Helm Map is computing it now, sir. Six minutes, forty seconds ... mark." Her hand dropped sharply.

"We dump at two minus that tick," Andreos said. "Put the interlink on all-ship. Let *Net* see this."

"Yes, sir." Athena complied briskly. "Sir, we just had a ranging laser splash on our starboard wing. No damage, not at this distance." Athena set her jaw. "And I confirm launch of two torpedoes, aimed to intercept our forward track. Sir, they have *fired* on us."

"Burn out the torpedo sensors, Pov," Andreos said. "Use your skysail laser."

"Yes, sir." Pov took the function from Tully's main console and slowly rotated the skysail laser toward the pursuing ships while Tully laid Athena's course data into the sail computers, overriding the automatic programs that watched ahead for dust, not behind for pursuing torpedoes. The two torpedoes crawled steadily toward them, their own engines adding more speed to the momentum of the ships that had launched them.

"How long to impact?" he asked Athena.

"Our engines are now at full exhaust and we're overhauling some of the torpedo speed. It'll moderate their climb. Say eight minutes, maybe nine. Time enough, Pov."

Pov watched the sail-laser data change on his interlink screen, the columns of numbers shifting into new patterns as the skysail laser began to track on its different target. Tully boosted the laser's power and let it cycle upward.

"Tracking now," Tully called from the outer room. "Power climbing. . . . Ready!"

"Fire!"

A ruby-red beam lanced backward from *Net,* hitting squarely on the nose of the forward torpedo, blinding its sensors into a melted slag.

"Recycling. . . . Ready!" Tully called out again.

"Fire!"

A second bolt lanced out, splashing hard on the other fusion torpedo. An instant later, the torpedo exploded, shattering itself into a cloud of scintillating gas and sending a lethal rain of invisible particles in all directions. One of the pursuing ships hastily changed course, dodging before it plowed straight through the deadly remains of its torpedo. Pov heard a cheer go up on Sail Deck outside his interlink room, echoed on the audio channel from other decks.

"Radiation count!" Andreos shouted.

"Not much hard stuff, sir," Janina answered. "Within safety limits." She smiled tightly. "The Russkis got it worse than we did, I'd say. I hope Bukharin has good hospitals for those crews." She shot a meaningful glance at Athena, who smiled wanly.

"I'm glowing less in the dark now, thank you so much. And not enough to care that they're going to." She gestured contemptuously at the Russki warships.

"Veer course ten degrees," Andreos said. "Get the other torpedo out of our wake. I don't want it following us to jumppoint, blind or not."

"Yes, sir," Athena said.

One of the warships returned *Net*'s laser bolt, badly aimed and out of range. The attenuated bolt splashed through *Net*'s engine emissions, creating a cascade of sparkling ions in its wake, a ripple quickly gone. A second bolt, better aimed as *Net* finished shifting her course, hit *Net* amidships, damaging a minor sensor. *Net* had sensors to spare, but it was not damage they needed, not when the Russkis promised heavier shots as they closed the range. Andreos scowled, his fingers drumming a slow beat on his console.

"Prepare for dump, Janina," Andreos said.

"Now?" Janina looked at him wide-eyed.

"Now."

Janina turned her head and gave quick orders to her hold crew. Then she turned back to the interlink and smiled almost gaily. "Hold on to your seats, *Net*. We're about to ride the wave."

"Or maybe get fried," Athena said, shaking her curls, then glanced at one of her lower interlink screens. "No, I take that back. Sirs, they have just launched two more goddam torpedoes. Dump it fast, Janina."

"Dumping now."

Janina spilled a canister of the superheavy atoms from T Tauri into the roar of tritium falling into *Net*'s fusion engines. As the heavy fuel exploded in the plasma stream, *Net* surged forward suddenly, overriding *Net*'s internal gravity field and swatting hard at Pov's chair, tipping it over and backward. He fell in a crash on his back, and heard the squawks on the deck outside as Janina's "pets" upended others on Sail Deck. Cursing, Pov tried to untangle himself and get up, then lost his balance as *Net* surged again, then fell a third time as the last of the heavy atoms exploded in the engine exhaust. By the time he had dragged himself up on the console and looked at the interlink, Bukharin's warships had vanished from his screen and Tania's Ring was only a tiny white speck far behind them.

He whistled, awed. "And that was *one* canister? Pretty hot stuff."

Then he looked at *Net*'s acceleration curve and whistled again. In only minutes, the heavy fuel had boosted *Net* up to one-quarter of lightspeed, acceleration that usually took a whole day at full power. Hot stuff, indeed, he thought elatedly, realizing that *Net* had done it. *Net* was free.

"I think one canister was rather enough," Andreos growled, dusting himself off as he righted his chair and sat down again. "Next time we put belts on the chairs and bolt them down."

"Let's use some more pets, sir," Athena suggested enthusiastically. "Let's jump for the Pleiades *today*."

"No!" Andreos said. "No more pets! But lay your maps, Helm. Steer for Maia's Veil and we'll go fishing new seas in a week or so. How about that?" He grinned at her, looking a little giddy himself.

"That's *on,* sir," Athena exclaimed, and thumped her console in delight.

Net's chiefs checked the ship for damage, relieved but not wholly pleased with what they found. Several hull plates had buckled, breaching atmosphere from a minor hold compartment, and some of the equipment in one of the chemlabs had been badly damaged when a ceiling beam abruptly tore loose from its brackets and fell, narrowly missing two techs. A number of people, taken unawares by the sudden lurch in acceleration, had suffered minor injuries, including a broken ankle on Sail Deck.

Pov knelt by Celka Matousek, his youngest sail officer, and gently pressed her already swelling ankle. Celka winced and looked pale, and then yelped as he touched the bone the wrong way

"Sorry, sir," Celka said, gasping a little. She winced again. "It hurts."

"Permission to yell, Celka. We'll get Medical up here."

"But I want to *see*!" she exclaimed, aghast. "I want to see the Pleiades!"

Pov sat back on his heels and grinned at her. "And how will you be left behind, sail?" he asked.

"Well, true." Celka smiled, embarrassed. "You know what I mean, sir."

"Yes, I do. I'm afraid it's broken, Celka. You'll be in a walking cast for a few weeks, but who says you can't sit your sail watch up here and let us pamper you? Poor Celka, injured Celka, pat, pat."

"Don't you dare!" Celka tossed her blond head, glaring around the deck at the watching sail staff. "I'll *bite* anybody who tries."

"Oh, no," Pov said. "We're warned. Just sit there for now until the medtechs can bring a gurney." Pov stood up and looked around. "Was anybody else hurt?" He got a shaking of heads, though Tully sported a purpling bruise on his forehead. "Have you called Medical?" Pov asked the tech on comm duty.

"Sir, they say they're awfully busy. They said it would be a help if we got Celka down to Medical ourselves."

"That's bad news," Pov said solemnly. "I've heard she bites." He joined in the laughter as Celka blushed. Then she raised her arms peremptorily to Pov.

"So carry me, sir. Why should Avi get everything?"

"I'll think about that comment, thank you." Pov crouched down beside her, slipping his arms under her legs and shoulders. "Grab on."

"Grabbed." Celka put her arms around his neck and held on.

Pov grunted as he lifted her, then shook his head at Tully as Tully moved to help. "I've got her," he said. "Why don't you see if our computers are in one piece? I have a feeling the lurch didn't pull evenly at things, especially chairs and maybe equipment interiors." He looked down into Celka's face and smiled. "Right?"

"You're the sailmaster," Celka said. "It's always smart to agree with the heavy guys."

"Hmph. I'll think about *that,* too."

Celka waved gaily at the sail staff as Pov carried her to the elevator. "Whee!" she said as the doors closed.

"And you haven't even had the anesthetic yet," he observed.

"It only gets worse, sir. Next time I grab at the computer board, who cares what buttons I hit." She tightened her arms around his neck and grinned at him, smart and pretty and all of seventeen. "This is fun, sir. You have good hands."

"Calm down, Celka."

She snickered, her eyes dancing as he felt his face grow a little hot. "Why?" she asked innocently, then teased him mercilessly all the way to Medical.

Pov put Celka down on a couch in the Medical Section's waiting room and made sure she was comfortable. The outer lounge was filling up fast, with the doctors and medtechs moving people in and out as fast as they could. Pov sat with Celka for a while, keeping her company, then heard a general page for captains and chiefs on the all-ship.

"I've got to go," he said, getting up from the couch.

"Ah, too bad," Celka exclaimed. "I wanted so much to be an item. You know, 'Celka and the sailmaster were noticed sitting together,' buzz, buzz."

"For what? To keep your four boyfriends in line? I think that was the last count I noticed, all of them following you around with ardent sighs and pinings."

"Every bit helps," she said brightly. Celka took his hand briefly, smiling up at him. "Thank you, sir, for carrying me down—and being so gracious about getting teased. It's nice. Let me know if I'm ever out of line."

"Of course." He pressed her hand, and then left her talking to a subchief with an injured arm, waiting her turn to see the doctors.

* * *

Net's captains and senior chiefs crowded into the large conference room by Andreos's office. For good measure, Captain Andreos put the meeting on the all-ship channel, inviting everybody else aboard *Net* to listen in as the chiefs delivered their initial reports. Pov sat down between Andreos and Athena at the long arc of the front table, then watched the last of the chiefs straggle in and find chairs in the middle rows. Milo's empty chair on the other side of Captain Andreos was conspicuously empty, though Pov saw Milo's Second Chaffer, Danil Tomasik, and two other subchaffers among the people in the chairs.

After everyone was seated, they waited a few minutes, each tick of the clock lowering Andreos's eyebrows another millimeter. Finally Captain Andreos turned to his aide.

"Temya, please call Chaffer Cieslak again and tell him we're waiting."

"Yes, sir." Temya put in the call and waited, her head tipped close to the speaker when Milo answered. When Andreos heard her low voice get tense, he swiveled his chair back and looked at the security chief in the third row.

"Chief, will you bring Milo? Take a few men to carry him if he insists."

The security chief's eyes widened, but he stood up and nodded, then left the room. Andreos slowly tapped his fingers on the table, waiting.

The chief and two of his men appeared with Milo, who looked a little disheveled and utterly furious, Milo's usual expression ever since *Net*'s captains had outvoted him at T Tauri. Milo glared at Andreos, then half-turned as the security chief gave him a slight push on his back, propelling him forward. Milo whirled around again to Andreos, his fists clenching.

"You have no right!" he sputtered at Andreos.

"I have lots of rights," Andreos said coldly, "given to me by our ship's contract. And I'm about to sanction you, chaffer. A half-month's profit share, and the price goes up by the minute. Keep it up and I'll demote you and make Danil your boss."

"You can't—"

"On the contrary, I can. You wanted to make a public comment by your behavior: now you've had it. Sit down."

Milo didn't move.

"Chief?" Andreos said, glancing at the security chief. "Will you assist?" That got Milo moving. Reluctantly he circled the table, giving innocent Temya a ferocious glare, and sat down hard on the other side of Andreos.

Captain Andreos tapped the table, stilling the soft murmuring in the room. "This is a general ship's meeting," he said, "to let people know the initial news. We'll put the reports on the all-ship for review, as usual, as they get completed."

"I have an item," Milo said sullenly.

"In due time," Andreos said, glancing at him.

"*Now* is the time," Milo insisted, "*before* we commit ourselves to jump and this idiot venture. I speak for many of the ship's personnel—"

"Four percent is not 'many,' Milo," Andreos said calmly, "but I recognize the minority opinion and I respect it. I've promised the ship that *Net* would accommodate the minority, including returning them to Tania's Ring if that is their wish. But the actual *going* to the Pleiades is not on the agenda, if that's your point. The ship has voted, and we are committed. As I said, accommodation will be made."

Milo stood up and headed for the door. The security chief, still blocking the exit, glanced at Andreos's face, and then stepped aside, letting Milo storm out. Andreos sighed, then slowly rubbed a hand over his chin.

"Milo Cieslak has served this ship faithfully for three years," he said to the assembled chiefs. "But I would point out that refusing to reason, to discuss only with anger, is the fundamental root of our recent action against *Siduri's Dance*. Even so, I will give Milo some latitude. It has been a difficult time for all of us. Chief Razack, will you begin?"

The engineering chief stood up and cleared his throat nervously, unaccustomed to so many watching eyes. An older white-haired man and one of Janina's hold officers, Chief Razack was charged with keeping *Net* in one piece, sending his crews inship and outship to repair minor meteor damage, dust abrasion, broken antennas and faucets, sprung hold plates, and the thousand and one other irritating items outside the purview of the computer section and the labs. He cleared his throat again, then looked down crossly as he got nudged by the hold chief seated beside him.

"I'm fine, Jenz," he grumbled. "Keep your pokes to yourself." He reached into a pocket and pulled out a much-folded sheet of paper.

"Well, folks," he said, unfolding his paper with fastidious precision, "we're in one piece, though a few pied-eyed intellectuals in the physics lab can't imagine why. When Holdmaster Svoboda dumped the heavy atoms in the engines, we skipped through a series of microjumps, something that isn't supposed to happen. That's what blew out the gravity fields and knocked over chairs." He harumphed. "The pied-eyed sorts are getting more pied-eyed reading all their little numbers right now. Lucky for us the good Lord is still thinking up His own rules: we could have left half of *Net* behind with that kind of acceleration."

"Speaking as a pied-eyed sort," Sergei interjected, "I resent being called pied-eyed. At least until *after* the party celebrating the why, when I *will* be pied-eyed." He grinned.

"Did I hear a flutter over the ventilator?" the chief groused loftily. "Sounded like a rattle to me. Have to check that." He peered nearsightedly at his sheet of paper. "We're repairing the hull plates in that breached section and I have robots scanning *Net* outside section by section for other damage. If anybody notices something that doesn't work inship, alert my crews and we'll get around to it. Let's see. A few dust particles punched through the sails and vaporized on the upper prow, melting a radio assembly. Hmm, hmm." The chief pulled at his chin. "That's about it." He sat down and blinked rapidly.

"Thanks, chief," Andreos said. "Dr. Cherinsky?"

The chief of Medical didn't bother to stand up. "So far only minor injuries, sir, a few broken bones, lots of bruises. As the chief said, we were lucky." For some reason Pov couldn't scan, he looked straight at Pov and smiled.

Andreos turned toward Janina at the end of the front table. "What about your superheavy pets, Janina?"

"Not many left, sir," Janina said regretfully. "They degrade quickly once they're out of the high-energy environment that packed their substructure." She smiled, tipping her head. "Maybe we can find another gas-jet in the Pleiades and stock up, give the physics lab some more to play with. They've been asking."

"That's at the *bottom* of my list," Andreos said firmly. "I want some nice tame fishing for a while without pets, do you hear me, Mr. Janusz?"

Pov was still puzzling about the doctor's odd look and jerked straight in his chair. "Sir?" he blurted. He heard Athena snicker softly beside him, then felt her slyly poke his hip under the table. Take that, share the fun. Usually Athena got the ribbing, with her usual ways.

"Of course not, sir," Pov said virtuously, then turned his chair and looked straight at Athena. "Of course, there's still *her*. You can't help hot-jets."

Athena goggled dramatically. "Me?" she asked, aghast. "I haven't said a word about gas-jets. That was Janina."

"So you say," Pov said skeptically. "I'm sure you put Janina up to it."

"I most certainly did not. Why do I get blamed for everything?"

"Past experience," Andreos retorted, ending it. "Just focus on fishing, *both* of you." He looked at one of the physics chiefs. "I'd like a summary on those microjumps as soon as we have some preliminary analysis. People, we might have accidentally discovered the next advance in ship-drive technology. As Chief Razack said, what we just did isn't supposed to happen. We'll find out why."

He smiled at Razack, who was still busy refolding his paper and didn't look up.

"In the interim," Andreos continued, "the news of our rather startling escape will likely precede us to the Pleiades. Even if Bukharin squelches his ship crews from talking, the out-planet freighters from Earth and Aldebaran at Omsk were probably watching through Bukharin's comsats." Andreos made a wry face. "*I'd* watch, if I saw a colony send warships after a commercial ship and fire on her. If so, I am informing the ship officially that we may possess a technological secret of great value to *Siduri's Net,* one that we must guard until that secret can be turned to *Net's* best benefit."

Captain Andreos tapped his long fingers on the table, looking over the assembled crowd, then lifted his eyes to the all-ship monitor at the back of the room. "I can make that warning as formal as you like, though I'm sure everyone can see the importance. There will be no blabbing, and I will personally vaporize any skyrider who talks about it to the mobile stations or any other cloudship. Leave that timing to me. Skyrider gossip has helped us in the past, but this is not such an occasion."

"And after he fries you, flock," Athena added, shaking her curls, "it's *my* turn. Think about it."

Andreos smiled. "She's meaner than I am, so I hope our hot-jets are listening well. Thank you, pilotmaster. Anything else on initial reports?" Andreos looked around the room and got a shaking of heads. "Fine. Finish your inspections and log the reports. We'll jump in two days." He stood up.

Chapter 6

Pov went looking for Avi, who had been off watch during the recent excitement. He looked in several places but couldn't find her, getting more worried the more he looked, illogical as that was. She's all right, he told himself. Of course she is: nobody got badly hurt. Stop worrying. He looked in the skyside lounge, wondering ironically if Avi might be tracing his circuit, half a ship behind. Medical would know to page him if she was hurt. What's the point of a sieve knowing everything, even a captain's romances, if you can't have a page when she's hurt? And Avi would tell them to call him if they forgot. If she could, that is.

Stop this.

Finally he reached the middle of the midship companionway and turned around and hesitated, wondering if she had returned to her apartment, wherever she'd gone. The foot traffic parted around him as people passed to and fro, setting *Net* to rights, a few people nodding genially as they passed him. He nodded back absently, scanning the faces for Avi.

This is ridiculous, he thought. Where is she? He could put a call over the all-ship channel, but the steady parade of announcements blaring through the speaker suggested about a hundred people had already beat him to the message center, parents looking for missing kids, chiefs calling for extra repair crew, some meeting calls. He'd probably *find* Avi before his call got through the queue.

Maybe I'll stand right here, he decided, and wait for her to pass me. She has to eventually, if I wait long enough. He perched against the sill of the long windows and watched the crowd move back and forth, not really

expecting to see Avi, whatever his probability rituals.
And so, of course, there she was.

She saw him first and smiled, then walked up to him.

"I've been looking for you," he told her.

"I've been looking for you." She kissed him quickly,
then slipped her hand into his. "I'm all right. Are you all
right?"

"I'm fine. Celka broke her ankle."

"So I heard. *And* I heard you carried her to Medical."
Avi arched an eyebrow.

"Medical asked."

He studied her expression, wondering if Avi might be
jealous. Celka liked to flirt with him, a little too much,
and sometimes Avi frowned about it, making half-serious
threats at Celka. He liked the possessiveness, but knew
Avi linked it with feeling insecure, not really able to joke
about Celka's flirting, not yet.

He reached out and solemnly pulled at one of her hairpins, letting a long lock of dark hair fall loose, then sys-
tematically pulled out the others, tumbling her hair around
her shoulders. Avi tolerated it well, a smile tugging at her
mouth.

"Are you done rearranging?" she asked as he pulled
out the last pin.

"Are you done being jealous of Celka?"

"I suppose so." She bit her lip, flushing a little. "You
must think I'm ridiculous. Like I don't believe in you or
something." She looked away down the companionway,
obviously uncomfortable.

"Of course not. I think you're just better at keeping me
reassured. I need to do more for you, probably." Her dark
eyes flicked back to him, then suddenly filled with tears,
alarming him. "What did I say?" he asked. But she was
smiling at him, shaking her head.

"Don't worry, Pov," she said. "You do just fine." Then
she kissed him enthusiastically, twining her arms around
his neck. "Why don't we make a spectacle of ourselves,
right here on the companionway? I'd like that."

"Hard on traffic patterns, making obstacles that way.
There's probably a rule saying you can't."

"Ah, well." Avi sighed and laid her head on his shoulder. They stood together for long minutes with her arms around each other, watching the people go to and fro. Avi wiggled her fingers hello at a disapproving glance.

"What do you think she disapproves of?" Avi asked. "Hugging in public or the intimation of better times in private? Can't have better times: it's not decent."

Pov lifted their linked hands, where Avi's ivory-white Russki skin, paled by her shipboard life, contrasted against his darker brown. "Maybe it's that. The Rom are darker than most of the Slavs, except those with outship tans, of course, like the skyriders. We're noticeable."

"That is ridiculous," Avi said angrily. Pov restrained her as she impulsively started after the woman.

"Let it go, Avi. It doesn't change anything between us, what she thinks. And she's not most people on *Net*."

"You ought to stand up for yourself, make her *see* she's wrong."

He smiled down into her face. "Why? She's just a gaje. Who cares?"

"*I* care." She looked at him rebelliously.

"That's because you're not *romni* enough yet. Give it time."

"It's not right," she muttered, but leaned back against him again as he wrapped his arms around her, contentedly nestling her shoulders against his chest.

"I love you, Avi," he said softly, bending his head to her ear.

She sighed and was silent for a moment. Around the curve of her face, he could see her smiling. " 'And I looked for him,' " Avi said softly, " 'in the streets of the city, but I could not find the one I loved. And I asked the watchmen if they had seen him, and scarcely had I passed them when I found the one I loved.' " Her hands tightened on his where they were clasped at her waist. " 'And I held him, and I would not let him go.' "

"Sounds familiar," he said, vaguely recognizing the verses.

"Song of Solomon. My grandmother used to read Scripture to me when I was little, when Father wasn't around to object. It bothered her tremendously that I'd never been baptized. I think she thought if she read the

Bible to me a little every day, my soul would escape hell somehow, by her good Lord's mercy."

Avi raised her head and looked up at the stars visible through the long windows of the companionway. "She died when I was nine, and they ground her up into fertilizer, the Great Rodina in its early years 'conserving biowaste.' Sometimes later I'd go outside at night and look up at the stars and wonder if Grandmother was one of those beautiful stars, still watching over me. Somehow her God didn't seem the sort to dispose of her as fertilizer. I think He made her a star, His comment on the soulless Great Rodina. I miss her still." She raised her hand and sketched a gesture he didn't recognize. "She used to do that over my head, warding away the Devil, and it always made me feel blessed somehow, warm and happy. Is your Rom family like that when you're inside it?"

"Sometimes. Not always. Things are mixed up now, and it's not the best."

"Do you think they really won't accept me? You keep worrying about that."

"Kate likes you, Avi. That's a start."

"But *accept* me," Avi insisted, "as Grandmother did."

He heard the yearning in her voice and wished he could promise such things and make them true, for Avi's sake. When he didn't answer, Avi turned her head to look at him and saw his troubled expression. She smiled gently and touched his cheek, leaning close to him.

"How we wish for each other," she said, almost wonderingly, "such good fortune and peacefulness, such joy and comfort. With that wishing between us, love, who needs anything more?"

"You think so?" he asked dubiously. "You know what my mother is doing to Kate right now, and Kate is her own daughter. And a few others of my Rom aren't particularly kind, won't be kind to you." He scowled. "I don't want you hurt. I won't permit that."

"Do you think the Russki diminutive is 'Povushla'?" she asked lightly, changing the subject. "I need a pet name—we seem to be at about that point. You know, something I can call you in public to show off you're mine."

He winced. "Please, no. Not Povushla. It sounds like a Russki cereal."

She wound a lock of his hair around her finger. "Povinya?"

"You'd better not," he warned her.

"Poverksky?" She chuckled. "Povinko? Sailmaster Povinko Janusz. Now *that* has some potential."

"Want to find out what happens if you try? I don't advise it."

She smiled contentedly, unimpressed by his menaces. "Tough guy."

"That's me."

Avi chuckled and turned around in his arms, wrapping them around her waist again. "I've done a lot of thinking the last two weeks," she said, "while you've been dashing around doing sailmaster things and Rom things, tiring yourself out. I hadn't realized how much time I had for thinking, when I wanted to use it. And I've been thinking about how we can cheat ourselves out of living. I find you and then I convince myself that it won't work out, doing my damnedest to make the prediction into reality. Stupid. Now I'm making other predictions."

She gestured at the windows, where a thousand stars glittered. "*Net* is free, despite their boxes they wanted for us. We decided we should be free, one ship deciding, and found the ways. And when we get to the Pleiades, whatever's there, we will find the ways to stay free. I believe that." She tightened her fingers on his hands. "When I got up to Omsk Station, I always thought somehow Andreiy would get me back, even after I transferred onto *Net*. Somehow he'd do it. Somehow he'd put me back into his box, and keep me there forever. But if we wish it, if we decide strongly enough, there's always a window in the box, one to climb through." She smiled. "Grandmother told me that. I had forgotten."

"I've never felt imprisoned like that, not really," Pov said. "I suppose gypsies are raised differently, and I always had my family." He grimaced. "Now it's my family that makes me feel confined, the way we're behaving."

"Confined because of me?" she asked.

"Not because of you, *for* you, if you get my meaning.

It's all muddled up with *Net* and *Dance*. And part of it's Kate and part of it's the gypsy labels that got thrown at me at the intership hearing. I've just been seeing things differently, and I worry about it. I wonder if I'm losing the Rom."

She shook her head decisively. "You *are* the Rom, Pov. You can't be anything else. I know you're worried about my amazement about Rom this and Rom that, especially what happens to Rom women. I like how you worry about me, but you do it too much. All I have to do is look at you, and it all fits. I suppose that makes me sound totally mind-fuddled."

He smiled. "It's called love, they say."

"I've noticed you don't get too critical of me, either. I've heard it wears off in about six months, so I've decided I need a plan. How many kids do you want to have?"

"Excuse me?" he asked. Sometimes Avi managed to change orbits at right angles, leaving him adrift in her wake.

"Kids, as in children. Remember? Smaller versions of you. Kids? So I was thinking maybe I can go down to Medical and have my implant counteracted and then cajole you into lots of useful bedtime the next several weeks and get pregnant with our first. I was thinking about six."

"Six what?" Pov asked blankly.

"Kids. I've read that gypsies like large families. Why? Do you want more than six? We'd have to get awfully rich to support more."

Pov blinked. "Uh ... wait a minute. Let's back up a bit."

"To the lots of bedtime?" she asked humorously. "Or to my plan?"

"To the implant is far enough. Are you sure?"

"I am positive. Absolutely, beyond question, decided. Is now when I ask if you're getting cold feet about marrying me?" She turned around and smiled at him.

"No, of course not. But what if my family—"

"I told you that I cherish what I have," she said solemnly. "If there's more, I'll be glad. But I'm making the rules now, Pov. Remember what I told you about arranging matters? Well, I'm arranging. I want us so solid that no one else can take us apart, not even you, if you decide I'm better off without you. Isn't that where some of this worrying could lead? Well, I won't permit it." She tossed her head. "You're dished, Pov, and you're mine and I'm not letting you get away. You had your chance, but you're in my box now." She grinned. "And don't even look for the window." She pressed closer to him. "I'm the window, there in the box with you."

Pov caressed her face. "Actually, I was thinking about four."

"Well, kids come one at a time. We can discuss it as the count goes up. Though I've got twins in my family—we might have to think faster."

"Are you serious about this?" he asked, studying her face. "I'm not going to give you up, no matter what my family does. You don't have to worry about that. I just want the best for you, Avi."

"You are the best," she said.

"Nuts. Think rationally, please, though I admit we're both mind-fuddled and it's getting worse. We don't have to rush on the kids."

"I want to rush. I want children—your children—and I want to get started now." She wrinkled her nose thoughtfully. "Though I admit I'm rushing, and I'm not entirely sure of my motives. But I've wanted children for a long time, and now I've found the father I want for them. Isn't that a good reason?" She bit her lip, hesitating. "I'm about to give up on this topic, you know, with you looking so reluctant." She grimaced. "Now that's a manipulative comment, isn't it? I'm sorry, Pov. I just thought it was a good idea. . . ." She trailed off and bit her lip again, then looked away.

"You're a good idea for me," Pov said comfortably. He made a small ceremony of arranging her hairpins in a bundle and putting them in her tunic pocket, waiting until she was ready to look at him again. He and Avi got tangled up sometimes, trying to find the ways across the gap between Rom and gaje, but it got easier as they practiced. Avi looked back at him cautiously. "Sometimes I can't see the window in front of my face," he said. "Righteous Rom and all that." He lifted her hands to his lips and kissed it. "You want a baby? We'll make a baby. Be sure it's a girl, though, looks like you."

"Are you sure? Maybe I should have waited on suggesting it." Now Avi looked hesitant. Pov laughed at her expression.

"We'd be great at Milo's job, you and me. Never a clause settled, not one. Yes, I'm sure. It might take a few months for your implant to wear off, won't it? Why wait until later?"

Avi seemed to relax, as if she'd veered them toward a chasm, narrowly averted, just because she mentioned something she wanted, something the other might disapprove. Not allowed, someone had told her, wanting what we don't want. Something's wrong with you. And they looked at her with the cold glances, the sour mouths, the berating, the silences. That kind of indifference was worse than fights, he decided: it erased you as a person. At least his mother had a reason for her wars—not to erase, but to keep. And that was a good reason, even if she was pushing too hard.

He looked over Avi's head at the stars winking through the windows, wondering if that was the answer. Maybe caring alone could turn it around, find a window. A different window from that which Rybak had forced upon *Net,* driving her away to keep herself free. Margareta Janusz might drive her children away, too, but maybe not. He could hope for that.

"Pov?" Avi asked uncertainly.

He looked back at Avi and smiled. "Sorry. Just thinking. So you want a baby as a lucky charm? Just to make sure of everything? Sounds like a good reason to me. There are lots of Rom names that would fit. Gypsies believe in luck, name their children after it."

Avi opened her mouth, then closed it. "Pov, I didn't—" she started. "I mean—"

"Personally, I think it's smart to find your luck. And, personally, even if I *was* reluctant, which I'm not, I'd do it anyway—for you, Avi. Just because you want it. Sometimes that's all the reason you need. Right?"

Avi sighed. "It's easier to talk about being jealous about Celka."

"Suits."

She fisted his shoulder, then laughed. "I'm getting better at this."

"We both are. Listen, want to get yourself all nervous for a few days? I was thinking about taking you to the *slava* a few nights from now. Tawnie's invited you. That's a Rom feast, big family event, everybody there." Avi's eyes widened. "We'll dress you up as a *romni,* the whole display, skirts, jewelry, ruffled blouse—Kate will love helping. You can sit with the women and listen to Patia and Judit talk about bride prices and the utility of sons."

"Come again?" Avi swallowed as if her throat had gone dry, as it probably had.

"You'll find out." He took her hand. "Think of it as a window—or the start of a war. Sometimes it's both, I think. But they'll never *not* care about you, Avi: they'll never ignore you. They care about children and preserving what the Rom are, about keeping the roads open. Marriage is an important event for the Rom, one of the fundamentals. Children are another. It's our stability, however much we argue and carry on. They *can't* ignore you, not when that's involved. You'll see."

He pushed off the window ledge and pulled her along with him.

"Where are we going?"

"Starting the conspiracy. Come on."

Kate and Sergei were home, Sergei lounging in a chair reading reports, Kate's Tarot box on the couch table, with several of the cards spread out on the couch cushions where Kate had been sitting. Kate smiled as she answered the door and saw them, then gave Avi a smile all her own. "Avi!" she exclaimed. "How good to see you!"

"Hello, Kate," Avi said, a little shyly. Kate promptly took her by the arm and pulled her into the apartment.

"What kind of limp greeting is that?" Kate hugged her enthusiastically. "You'll notice, Pov, the attention you're deserving."

"I'm just the older brother, I know. I've been around

for years. Boring." Pov strolled by haughtily, gesturing a threat.

"Oh, ho," Kate said. "You and who else?"

"I missed that," Avi said, watching them. "Hi, Sergei." Sergei waved one of his reports and smiled.

"Gypsy gesture," Kate told Avi. "I'll teach you a few—but be careful how you use them. Some have a few nuances you'd better learn first." Kate pretended to shudder. "Awful what happens to you when you don't know."

Pov sat down in the chair by Sergei. The young Russki physicist, blond and stocky, shared his sister's intensity, but had a quite different temperament. Sergei was one of the brightest people Pov had ever met: he always seemed mildly abstracted, as if coping with life used only part of his brain and left the rest free to roam, most of it thinking math. Pov looked over at the Tarot cards on the couch. "Reading your cards again, Kate?" he asked.

"Just looking them over. Sit here, Avi, by me. Sergei's got his nose buried again, divining quark spells. See how patient I am?" Sergei pointedly raised his report higher in front of his face, reading ostentatiously. "He was such a drudge at the university, I'm sure, reading and reading. Eventually you read so much that your eyeballs fall out, so I'm reading my cards so mine can fall out, too."

"They do *not* fall out," Sergei rumbled from behind his report.

"You'll find out. I'm sure I'm right." Kate snickered as Sergei lowered his report to look at her, half irritated and half amused. "It's called management, Avi," Kate said. "How are you doing with Pov?"

"Fairly well, I think," Avi said lightly. "I'm still figuring out the rules, though."

Sergei rolled his eyes at Pov, then raised his report again. "I am reading," he said. "Important stuff."

"I'm sure," Kate said skeptically. "And Pov and Avi are here and you're behaving like a physicist. It is not polite to sit there and read when family's here." She waited a long moment until Sergei moved his report slightly and eyed her.

"I can talk to Pov about my reports," he said mildly. "He'll be interested."

"Weak, Sergei," Kate said, "really weak."

Sergei sighed and put his report down on the others in his lap, then shuffled them into a neat stack. "Sounds like social compulsion to me," he complained good-naturedly, adding another sigh. "And I thought I left that behind on Omsk." He winked at Avi.

"I've got news for you, Sergei," Kate said severely. Sergei smiled at her, all his heart in his look.

"Maybe it lasts longer than six months," Pov said to Avi.

"What?" Kate asked.

"Mind-fuddling. I've proposed. Avi said yes."

"Wonderful!" Kate exclaimed, openly delighted. "I knew you would." She looked down at the cards beside her and smiled, then picked one up and showed it to Avi. Avi took it from her hand and bit her lip as she studied the picture, then looked at Kate. The first time Kate had read the cards for Avi, Russki skepticism had collided with Rom prophecy, though Avi had found it wasn't exactly what she expected. "See?" Kate said. "Two of Swords. That's you."

"It is?"

"Of course. Pov's been moving around a bit in the cards. He used to show up as the Hermit, always chasing his whichness of the sails like some arcane Diogenes looking for an honest man. You've been a good distraction, Avi. With him, his legs'll fall off, all that chasing around." Pov crossed his arms on his chest and shared a look with Sergei.

"We're outnumbered," he said wryly.

"Looks like it," Sergei agreed. "I doubt that'll change much."

Kate picked up another card to show Avi. "That rather looks like him, doesn't it?" Avi took the card and glanced at Pov.

"It does!" Avi said, sounding startled, then looked at Pov again in open amazement.

"That's the Prince of Wands, Avi. Secretly, Pov's a skyrider in spirit, always has been, but he won't admit it."

"Don't have the reflexes," Pov objected. "I'd clip the strut every time."

Kate laid a third card in Avi's hand. "And that's the twins. Name the boy after the paternal grandfather: it's good luck for the first boy. Garridan was Dad's name, if Pov hasn't told you. And I think something pretty in Russki for the girl. Something Pov'll dote over." Avi was staring at Kate, her mouth open, then nearly dropped the card. "What's the matter, Avi?" Kate asked, teasing.

"Gypsy spells, Avi," Sergei said. "That's as good an explanation as any. The Rom don't pay attention to scientific rules. Who needs science? Magic is better."

"It's not magic, Sergei," Kate reproved. "I know better than that."

"So you say. What matters to me is that *you* believe in those cards, my love, whatever your dodging and add-ons and disclaimers. You're a *puri dai*'s daughter: how could you not believe? And I'm damned glad they stopped telling you all those disasters and bad luck. I was thinking of feeding them to Janina's engines, maybe seeing how those cards explode. All that packed magic is probably as good as quarks. How about that, Pov? Touring to Orion's Nebula on gypsy magic. Think Thaddeus Gray might be interested?"

"I'd put that idea on backup, myself," Pov said equably. "Maybe float a few other things at *Arrow* first."

Sergei smiled as Avi looked down at the card again and curled her fingers protectively around it. "Now watch," he said humorously. "When the genetic scan shows it *is* twins, boy and girl, Avi'll start believing, too. Goes with being a *romni*, Avi. It's a strength, thinking magic is real, that anything's possible, when you believe." He caught Kate's hand and pulled her over for a kiss. "Kate taught me that. Changed me from a grunge reading reports all day to half a grunge. She continues to improve me as time goes on. And she keeps hoping her mother will relent. Magic." He scowled, his mood shifting.

"And if she does," Kate said softly, "will you believe? You and your scientific mind, where everything has rules and limits. Where magic can't exist because it doesn't fit your rules?"

He pointed at her. "I just want you to have a healthy baby. On the rest, I want you to be happy, and I will do my damnedest to make up for whatever happens. That's enough for me." He glanced at the reports on the table beside him. "And maybe I want a new ship drive, one that can get us to the Orion Nebula, just to see what's there."

"You really think we've got one?" Pov asked, startled. "Can we control the power?"

"See, Kate? I told you he'd be interested in reports."

"Oh, you," Kate said, flipping her hand.

"I am definitely me," Sergei agreed. Kate collected her cards from Avi's lap and put them in their box, then took Avi into the kitchen. Pov watched them go, pleased that both Avi and Kate had a new friend in each other, that what had started well seemed to be getting better. Better than friends, actually: family. Even if he couldn't give Avi the others, he had given her Kate. And somehow it had been a gift to Kate, too.

He looked back at Sergei, and saw Sergei watching him, a half-smile on his face. "I'm doing what I can, Sergei. My mother's a stubborn woman."

"I agree the pregnancy wasn't wise," Sergei said with a sigh, "but at least we'll have a resolution of all this. Kate wants a Rom marriage, the entire panoply, and she wants the baby christened as a Rom, made a part of your family, no questions, no buts. The way it was going, your mother could have stalled us indefinitely."

"Well, she can't now."

"True." Sergei looked glum. "But I'm happy to see Avi has finally found somebody, and I'm glad it's you. You'll be good for her. The Rodina was not kind to our Avi, made her doubt things about herself that she shouldn't."

"You knew her on Omsk, didn't you? Before she joined *Net*."

"Yeah. I even met Andreiy, when he made his one token visit to demand she come back to the planet and be a proper wife. What a lacklife *he* was. He stands there, arms folded, expecting her to apologize—and, maybe, if she begged him hard enough, he might take her back. Thank God they never had children. That would have trapped her for sure. Avi would never leave her kids, no matter what the price she had to pay to keep them."

"Hmm." Pov looked at the kitchen door and frowned.

"A suggestion, Pov," Sergei said. "Don't want to meddle, of course, but I'd like to suggest."

"Of course," Pov said. "I think I can use the help. What?"

"Don't worry so much about the gaje and Rom differences. Let Avi find her own way into the Rom. She'll like what she finds there. I do, whatever our troubles lately, and even though I'm still on the outside, looking in. And go talk to Karoly. He helped me in the beginning, still strolls into my lab to talk regularly. Margareta might think she can pick her heir as *puri dai* and get it all locked up the way she wants it, but I think the leadership will go elsewhere when it changes over. To Karoly. He has the balance."

"Really?" Pov blinked.

"Speaking as the expert I am," Sergei said with a smile. "After I got dragged up to Omsk and stuck in that bedragged lab, who cares what I wanted, I got interested in power structures, the people kind, not just nuclear fusion. And I've spent three years studying your family, with lots of motivation to figure out the whys. It won't be you when the family votes: you'll be a shipmaster and have too many choices that'll conflict you, Rom and ship. So it'll be Karoly, I think. And that's *my* fortune-telling." He leaned forward and shut the lid on Kate's box. "I'd really rather not have my Rom marriage *after* your mother's funeral, not with her excellent health and years of living ahead. So if you and Karoly can put your heads together on outwitting her, maybe you can help us out, too."

"She's a stubborn woman, Sergei."

"But she loves Kate. That I've never doubted." Sergei sat back and sighed. "I get tired of fighting for my place in the family," he said softly. "It's been three years, after all. I wish it was over, but only the way Kate wants it to be. I wish Kate could just be happy, thinking of the baby and me and her skyriding. I wish for too many things, maybe." He shrugged.

"Like a ship drive," Pov said. "And a way to the Nebula."

"We *are* supposed to talking about that, aren't we? Kate's blighted my reading for a week about checking my eyeballs. What a comment." He laughed. "Where does she get these ideas? I never know what she'll say next."

"She's always been that way," Pov advised him. "*I'm* the expert on that."

"Just part of being outnumbered, coz." Sergei smiled.

"That's true."

"Give us a few days to finish the initial analysis. We should have something put together by after jump. Janina wants to drag in everybody who knows something about magnetics, then have a big theoretical confab. I don't *think* our pets are little sails, but I've been surprised before. Actually, there are some math links to maser technology, too, like little freighter beacons spinning around, zipping their quarks in a particle beam off the scale. Imagine that: a pulsar on an atomic level." He tapped the reports. "We may even have discovered a new state of matter. Earth's labs have been looking for two centuries for something below quarks, ever since we isolated the top quark and decided that must be it on subatomic structure. But it's all a matter of power, sheer power." He smiled at the sheaf of papers. "And that was just a protostar. I wonder what it's like in the galaxy's center, where that black hole eats a thousand stars a day."

"Not in our generation, Sergei."

"But maybe our children's, or their children's. I'm going to start early with the baby. Put up math formulae over her crib, get her started right."

"You *are* a grunge, coz. Kate'll make her a skyrider first."

"So maybe she'll be both." Sergei smiled. "And if I lose the war for our daughter's heart and mind, there's always the next one, maybe a boy. Or maybe your boy, if you'll cooperate. Don't give them all to Sail Deck; leave me one to train up right. How about that?"

"I'll think about it."

"And I'll bet you it *is* twins, too," Sergei said humorously. "A tenth of a profit share that Kate's right. But don't tell Kate which side of the bet I asked for. I'll never hear the end of it."

"No bet. *I'd* never hear the end of it."

Sergei grinned and handed Pov one of his reports. "Key up your math and read with me. See if you can find some sails in there. I think there might be one or two."

"It's a theory," Pov said wryly, then opened the cover on the report. Kate stuck her head through the kitchen door, about to say something, then made an act out of clutching her head, aghast, when she saw them both reading.

"I do *not* believe this," she announced loudly and plunged back into the kitchen.

"War," Sergei said as he turned a page. "It started in prehistory, when we men were still swinging through trees, having a wonderful time, and the women wanted to try walking on the ground. Nag, nag, nag."

"They won that battle, coz."

"True. But there's always hope. You just have to find better trees."

Chapter 7

The next day *Net* accelerated steadily, preparing for her convulsive leap across three hundred light-years to the edge of the Pleiades. Pov spent most of the afternoon watch with Athena on Helm Deck, trying to refine *Net*'s Pleiades maps. The hunt frustrated them both, especially when they found gaps in *Net*'s astronometrical database, missing data that should have been there and wasn't.

"God, for a decent map," Athena exclaimed and threw up her hands as the Helm Map program made another hash of the finer detail. She cleared the screen and took them back to the opening scan, the fifth time that afternoon. "Let's try the bigger view again. What the hell." Athena keyed the screen display to the larger wallscreen on her office wall.

The nine great blue stars of the Pleiades blazed against a starry backdrop of thousands of other stars, a standard field view of an observatory photo. Drifting clouds of gas, the blue-tinted veils still lingering in the Pleiades' star nursery, obscured large parts of the screen. It looked like a traffic jam in fog, with half the stars in near-collision. Athena enhanced the stars, then the gasclouds, both of which reduced the original to a blurry glare. Athena muttered a curse and leaned her forehead on her computer console. "What's the penalty for computer murder? I'm considering it."

Pov sat back and scowled at the wallscreen. Athena wanted a route inward from the cluster edge to GradyBol Station; Pov wanted a good patch of nebula for a cloud run on the way. Helm Map should easily convert a field map into three-dimensional local modeling to give them both. "It shouldn't do that," he said, perplexed. "What's wrong with your map program?"

"Nothing I can find. Watch." Athena unloaded the Pleiades starfield, and then keyed in a starfield map of the Outer Hyades, then mapped back to T Tauri. A few minutes later, T Tauri's local space displayed on the screen, three infant stars linked by a gas-jet. Helm Map laid four suggested courses into the system, highlighted its own choice, then waited for Athena's next command. "See? No problems." Athena took Helm Map back to the Pleiades starfield.

"Try a virus check, Athena," Pov suggested, a chill snaking down his spine as he thought of a bad possibility. "How long until we jump?"

Athena glanced at him, her eyes widening as she caught his hint. She leaned back and looked through her door onto Helm Deck at the tracking screen. "Not yet—another hour at least. I'll run the virus check."

She straightened and rapidly cleared the helm computer down to its basic programming, then began the systems check. If a computer virus had penetrated one helm program, it might have penetrated another, and a singularity jump across interstellar distances depended on an exquisitely precise control of engine power at the instant of jump. It was a split-second adjustment of thrust manageable only by computers, and computer error might deliver *Net* a hundred light-years short of her goal—or crash her right into the midst of the cluster, no matter what stars might be in the way.

The helm computer announced itself satisfied with its jump program, and Athena bit her lip. "Should we believe it?" she muttered. "Protostars and atomic pets I can handle, but not a sick computer with maybe a shaky hand on our drive pivots."

"We've got some time," Pov said. "Let's find the virus. Maybe it only infected one area."

"Still, I'm going to ask the computer chief to verify the safety check." Athena put in a quick call to Computer Deck and talked to the computer chief on watch, then reloaded the Pleiades map again. She windowed in the virus check and let the computer start hunting.

"There you are," she said malevolently several seconds later, and followed the virus coordinates down into the database, taking Helm Map's virus hunter with her. "There it is, in one of the data dumps we bought." She pointed at the virus with her stylus, and Helm Map attacked instantly, obliterating the alien program in a brief wink of light.

"Helm Map couldn't see it until you pointed," Pov remarked.

"Right. The virus was made inside the Helm Map program. Indigenous. And every time we've tried to make a map the last few hours, that virus has been eating more data." She blew out a breath and pushed back her hair tiredly. "That probably eliminates our friend Nikolay as the maker. Freighters map point to point, not in cubic as we do."

"A cloudship? But who? And how'd it get into our database?"

"Beats me. Let me give the chief the coordinates." She called Computer Deck again and spoke briefly with the chief, then flexed her fingers a moment over her computer board, giving Pov a wry look. "Let's see what damage we've got. Hold your breath, friend."

They both winced as Helm Map began its data listings. An entire section of astrometrical data had gone dark, with inky tendrils lacing from the hole through the entire Helm Map database. "What's the linking?" Pov said, leaning forward. "A key word?"

"As in 'Pleiades,' maybe?" Athena asked with disgust. "I don't see any fingers into the jump programming." She sent the screen data down to Computer Deck for analysis, then windowed into one of the tendrils, following it to its destination. A moment later, the screen lit with the text from a technical paper on freighter beacons, with a number of isolated words nicely scrambled. "I see 'Pleiades' missing there. That's definitely one of the virus keys."

"Try hunting outside of Helm Map and see if it's all gone."

Athena set up a global search and got a fast data listing with dozens of references. Pov sighed in relief. Athena opened up one of the data files and got a glowing corporate news release about GradyBol, part of EuroCom's annual media blitzes to recruit personnel for its mobile stations. Another file had a legislative summary of an Earth senator's speech about the future of humanity, in which the Pleiades featured prominently. A third was a smaller version of the map Andreos had used in his speech to the ship, its source another EuroCom report, not *Net*'s map files.

"I thought that map looked a little off," Athena commented drolly. "You know, GradyBol and TriPower in *big* letters, blink, blink, here we are, and everybody else labeled in eye-squint size."

"Ask for a map," Pov said wryly, "get a map. Temya asked for something with labels, I guess."

"Right." Athena scowled at the screen. "So how do we make a map?"

"Maybe Helm Map will work now."

"Most of the Pleiades database is gone, Pov, at least the mapping part. Corporate big talk elsewhere won't help."

"Try it on global, anyway. Make me happy."

She gave him an unreadable look and loaded the Pleiades starfield again, then told Helm Map to localize. Three-quarters of the wallscreen abruptly went blank, but several dozen stars stayed, dominated by the nine Pleiades blue giants.

"There's GradyBol," Pov said, pointing. In screen center, two yellow names blinked neon-bright, the bastions of EuroCom's corporate pride. Here I am. Blink.

"Thank you, EuroCom," Athena said dryly. "What else can we load?" she asked. "Helm Map's still looking by mapping keys, and the virus zapped most of those."

"Do we have general sky surveys? I'm thinking radio and infrared to spot the hydrogen."

Athena keyed out into the general database and found a very small arc of an Omsk Station dish survey. Helm Map added the ghostly outlines of gasclouds to its map, broad patches glowing in dim shades of dusky red and pink. "Here's an x-ray survey," Athena said, and the blue giants abruptly brightened. Near Pleione, the neutron star

in Lucifer's Deep was a brilliant white point, the marker
of the starry grave of another Pleiades blue giant, the first
of the short-lived blues to die. "Well, that didn't help,"
Athena muttered. "We already know where you guys
are." She took the data back out. "What else?"

"That showed Lucifer's Deep," Pov argued. "Leave the
x-ray in."

"We aren't going anywhere near a neutron star, Pov.
Don't even think about it." Lucifer's Deep had already
killed two research ships that had strayed too close to the
star's enormous gravity, and Pov conceded her point with
a shrug. "What else?" Athena prompted.

"Carbon monoxide and ionized calcium," Pov said after a moment. Athena raised an eyebrow, inquiring.
"Earth originally discovered interstellar gasclouds with
those two spectrum lines, so maybe we have some chemistry sky surveys in visible light and ultraviolet. Try the
chemlab database. Ionized hydrogen should show in ultraviolet, too."

"You've been reading up," she commented.

"I indeed have. We can't do it by star name or we'll hit
the data hole. Try it by stellar coordinates." Athena windowed out in the general database again, and their map
acquired new ghostly colors of violet and faint yellow.
The familiar outlines of Maia's Veil took on more defini-
tion. Pov got up from his chair and walked over to the
wallscreen. "Hmph. Not much detail here."

"It helps," Athena said. "At least we can see where the
veils are, more or less. When we slow down into decent
light readings again, we can map more detail from Sail
Deck's light sensors."

"True." He turned. "Which data dump was it?"

Athena windowed out again, then traced through the
Helm Map hole to its original data source. "That general
update library we bought from Earth two years ago," she
said. "*Net* took delivery directly from the freighter captain, as I remember, then shared with *Dance*. Remember
how Rybak complained about the cost and made *Net* pay
for it?" She frowned. "That does eliminate Bukharin, actually, even if he somehow got his hands on a Helm Map
program. He wouldn't dare meddle with Earth's regis-

tered mail, not if he wants to keep his freighter contracts. And we got the dump first, so it couldn't have been *Dance*. But why would Earth care if more cloudships go to the Pleiades? The more ships, the lower the product prices."

"I think the source is father out—and it doesn't mean EuroCom or even GradyBol knew. A virus can ride inside a lot of packages."

"*Arrow?*"

"I don't know. Captain Andreos said it's competitive out there."

"I'm thinking they couldn't be sure their virus wouldn't mutate and invade the jump programming, whatever their safeguards. Contamination like that can kill a ship during jump. Maybe they don't care about that." She looked grim.

"Maybe not." He turned back to the map.

Net jumped an hour later, and Pov forced the sail computer to take a lightning-quick look through the ship's speed distortion to confirm *Net* had jumped safely. Afterward, the sail computer did its equivalent of blinking dazedly and put itself on mandatory shutdown for a full system recheck, a process that would consume an hour.

"It says it has a headache," Pov said drolly to Athena over the interlink.

"I would, too, if I had to look at light that loud." Athena chuckled wanly, then propped her head on her hand. "How long until it's willing to peek again?"

"About an hour. Even then, I wouldn't recommend it if we're over eighty percent of light speed: it'll just get another headache and shut down again."

"Hmm." Athena turned and looked at the screens on Helm Deck. "I'm turning the ship now. We'll brake at full power."

"On the green, Helm."

Athena turned the ship on its axis, braking with *Net*'s engines, and *Net* began to decelerate rapidly. When the sail computer sat up again and announced itself still alive, Pov told it to activate the Sail Deck wallscreen at normal resolution, getting a painful gray glare that they usually kept turned off this close to jump. He filtered it to spare his sail staff's eyes, then put the riveting image of nothing onto the interlink. Gradually, as their speed dropped, nine brighter points took shape in the grayness, the first hint of the blue giant stars that dominated the cluster ahead.

"We have long-distance starfield photos," Athena reported to the captains as the others joined the interlink. "Plus some long-range radio and chemical surveys: at least we'll know generally where the hydrogen is. Plus lots of general gossip—tourists news about the aurorae at Maia and you gotta see the view someday, so-and-so's corp chief got promoted at some station, so-and-so got an award, other corporate in-talk, but not the science. Like how to get from here to there *inside* the Pleiades, or even where the stars are exactly. The chemlabs are finding a similar lack of data on Pleiades gascloud composition, though we have general data on gasclouds elsewhere."

"Data scouring?" Andreos asked mildly.

"Apparently." She shrugged. "Basically, sirs, Helm Map no longer has any practical map information about the Pleiades. It is simply not there, and the computer chief agrees with me that it's not. We have data in other places. For instance, the computer knows that GradyBol is circling 167 Tauri because of a corporate news release a few years ago, and—fortunately—our generally astronomy database includes star coordinates for 167 Tauri in its list of 'Fifty Important Pleiades Stars,' unquote, apparently because 167 is a double star with enough spectrographic irregularities to be interesting. If whoever'd made their virus a little smarter, we could have had a wipe of our other astronomy databases, too."

She unrolled a computer starfield scan and held it up so the others could see. Pov recognized the scale from Earth observatories: it was little more than an enlargement of the view from Earth, not much better than the guide map he and Athena had used earlier.

"It gives us proportions," he commented.

"I want the edge of Maia's ionization front," Athena said, a little irritably. "Where *your* sails can catch some *atoms,* not lose ninety percent of it because the hydrogen doesn't have an electric charge. And I don't want to blunder into smog and get our hull scoured by all that dust floating around. We need a decent map, and it looks like we'll have to make our own." She tapped the computer photograph. "This is a flat photograph of the starfield taken from Luna Observatory. It's a CCD print, so we can take it down to the photons and pick up every star in the field and a large part of the visible gas. Unfortunately for our computer, this is a flat projection of the entire visible starfield and we can't tell which stars are in the Pleiades and which aren't. A few we know are Pleiades—they're in the Fifty Most Important list. Yay. Some of the dimmer stars are undoubtedly much father out and not part of the cluster at all. Of the few thousand stars on that picture, four hundred belong to the Pleiades, but we're sure of only fifty, basically the big ones and the weird ones."

"Bukharin?" Andreos asked, frowning. "He's more far-sighted than I thought."

Athena shook her head. "I don't think so." She explained why not. "It looks like maps are trade secrets in the Pleiades, sir."

"Not surprising, since—" Andreos began, then stopped as Athena gave him a warning stare.

"You had better not, captain," she said.

"I can speculate, Helm. I am speculating: I am not claiming omniscience."

"Sometimes it's hard to tell, sir," Athena suggested meaningfully. She shook her head.

Andreos chuckled. "It *is* predictable. Maps show cloud concentrations, where the dust is, where the gas is, the good stretches of veil to harvest. That virus might have been a database guard that got loose elsewhere, and wasn't aimed at us at all."

"Maybe," Athena said darkly. "And maybe not."

Andreos shrugged humorously. "I agree with the maybe not, unfortunately."

"But even hide the star coordinates?" Janina asked. "What does that accomplish?"

"The only ships that need practical star locations in the Pleiades," Andreos said, "are us, the dread cloudship rivals. The combine freighters go by beaconed routes." He shrugged again. "So what do you suggest, Helm?"

Athena sighed. "Well, there's the long way, which we've started. We have light-ranging equipment on Sail Deck. We can make our own maps from light readings when we slow down into some meaningful frequencies. If we do it fast, we won't lost too much speed before we accelerate to jump again. So a quick peek and take off, sir. Then, after we arrive again, we can run parallaxes on the star positions and get a general estimate of star distances, add a few more stars to the fifty."

"In the old days," Pov said ironically, "it was called dumping a weight overboard to see how deep the water was. And you put a lookout in the crow's nest to watch for reefs and rocks and your stray ocean liner. If you were lucky, you didn't run aground or hit a submarine or a whale." Athena chuckled as Andreos started to react. "And if you were *really* lucky—"

"I get the picture, sailmaster," Andreos grunted.

"—you didn't get blown upside down," Pov continued blithely, "by hurricanes or waterspouts."

"I doubt," Andreos said dryly, "that the Pleiades has waterspouts."

"You never know." Pov waved his hand. "I can cite about ten scientific agreements, including Earth's guarantee of purchase on that library dump, that promise untampered data. And a few other agreements that make killer viruses illegal, for exactly this reason. Do you know how *long* it'll take us to map thirty cubic light-years?"

"We don't need all of it," Athena said. "Just a course to Maia along a shock front." She made a face.

"Put your senior people on watch, Pov," Andreos said.

"Yes, sir."

"Can you scan usefully above half light speed, Pov?" Athena asked. "I'd hate to lose more speed before we accelerate again."

"There'll be some distortion, but we can compensate, enough for a reasonable guess. Janina, I'll want to ask your chemists about other spectrographic frequencies as the data come in."

Janina nodded. "Improvisation, isn't it wonderful?"

"Yeah," Pov said sourly.

"So we'll buy maps from *Arrow*," Janina said. "What's the problem?"

"If they'll sell them to us," Pov said. "It was *their* virus, probably."

Pov stood up and walked out onto Sail Deck, then glanced around the deck, checking who was on watch. Lev had the comm duty at Avi's usual station; the other staff were several junior sail techs normally on Roja's night watch. "Is Celka still on sick leave?" he asked Lev.

"Walking cast, sir. Champing to come back."

"Fine. Call her and tell her we need her on Sail Deck. Tully and Avi, too." Pov scanned the duty stations, matching each to one face among his senior people, then made his decisions. "I want Celka on ultraviolet, Avi on radio lengths. Roja, you take visible light. Tully will take the deck when he gets here. Marya, you take x-ray and gamma." He stopped and blew out a breath, scanning the deck again. "You other folks can watch if you want," he said. "We're going to make a map from light-ranging, and you'll all have a part in the analysis after we launch again, but first Helm needs a course into the Veil as soon as we can see. We won't have much time to peek. What's our speed, Marya?"

"Sixty-eight percent of light speed, sir," she said.

"Let's try a look. Run a light resolution, Roja."

The view in the wallscreen flickered as the computer tried to compensate for the speed distortion, giving them a flicker of a window onto the Pleiades, a glitter of hundreds of stars, then a buzz of static when the resolution failed. The gray light returned, with its nine dim gray-white stars in screen center. "Hmm. Close, I think. Take your stations."

As he turned around, Celka and Avi came out of the elevator together, Celka hobbling awkwardly on crutches. "Special watch," he told them. "Put your boards onto the interlink. Did you get Tully, Lev?"

"Yes, sir. He's on his way."

"Fine."

He took Avi's hand briefly as she passed him, smiling at her, then made sure Celka navigated safely to her chair. Tully bounded onto deck a few minutes later.

"What's up?" he asked.

"Making a map. You've got the deck. I'll be on interlink."

Tully nodded and sat down in the central chair. Pov checked Sail Deck one more time, then walked back into the Sail Deck lounge. He sat down at the interlink board with its banks of data screens and logged back into the linkage. As his screens lighted, Janina popped into view in a lower-left screen and winked at him, then handed him two more hold screens from the chemlabs, where Katrinya Ceverny and one of *Net*'s chemlab chiefs sat talking to each other. He looked around as Sailmaster Ceverny walked into the sail lounge.

"Pull up a chair, sir," Pov invited. "We're making a map."

"So I've heard. I won't be, uh ... presuming?" Ceverny hesitated, still dancing his two-step of not treading on Pov's sailmaster toes and those of the other authorities on *Net*. It was not an accustomed discretion: Ceverny had too many years in command, and was awkward in assuming less.

"Nuts to that," Pov said forcefully. "Sit down."

Ceverny smiled and ambled forward, then sat down next to Pov and stretched out his long legs, looking with interest at the screens on the interlink board. Before *Net*'s journey to T Tauri, the two Slav cloudships had not used *Arrow*'s technique of interlink among its captains, with secondary staff taking actual command of the main decks. *Net* had found the interlink essential at T Tauri, and the convenience of the coordinated command was gradually changing *Net*'s basic ship operations, one after another. Andreos had also decided, as a new protocol, to put the interlink onto the all-ship comm channel so that all *Net* could watch, a vastly popular choice among *Net*'s off-duty crew.

Pov loaded his sail screens from the light boards, radio and infrared, visible light, ultraviolet, and the harder radiation. He deliberately made himself slow down to do it right, knowing they had time.

"Ready," he said.

"We are building a map, people," Athena said. "I want

a course that will skim Maia's ionization front for a short cloud run, anywhere along the border, yet head generally toward GradyBol. We are looking for hazards: dust, mostly, but also your stray star here or there." She smiled at Pov. "Consider them reefs and sandbars. What are our markers, Pov?"

"Radio at twenty-one centimeters for one, not that we want neutral hydrogen. The ultraviolet Balmer lines will show us the ionized gas. The dust is cold here, so infrared will help us a little, but not much." He frowned.

"I'd look for the aromatics," Katrinya suggested, "principally benzene and other carbon rings. The dust grains produce simple molecules fairly well, and some of the hydrocarbons can run several dozen atoms, with the ring structures the most stable." She frowned and glanced at the other chief.

"Lattice carbon?" the other suggested.

Katrinya nodded. "Maybe. The fullerenes are exposed to UV radiation here, but heavier dust will probably shield some of it from destruction, enough to show us where the dust is heaviest. We might be able to see the smoke." She smiled. "To find the ionization front, I'd hunt double-ionized oxygen, too. The blue giants put out enough heavy radiation to knock two electrons off oxygen, and that'll give us another line to hunt in visible-light frequencies. With the UV lines for hydrogen, it should pick out the front's shock wave fairly well."

"Why don't we try for the hydrogen first, Pov?" Athena said. "It'll pinpoint the stars and outline more of the veils."

"Celka, key up your board," Pov said. "Celka?" He leaned back and looked out the door into Sail Deck. "Tully—tell Celka to put herself on interlink audio."

"Yes, sir," Celka said a moment later on the interlink.

"We're UV ranging first for hydrogen, Celka. Tell Avi to scan for the neutral gas, too, then we'll put the data together. We're looking for stars and clouds, people."

"Yes, sir. Ready to scan."

"Let's try to look, Tully." Tully keyed the computer resolution, holding the clarified image for three seconds before it collapsed again. A moment later, a color map, partly red, partly deep violet, appeared in a lower screen,

combining the brief observations in two kinds of light.
Athena bent forward and studied the picture.

"That's a start," she said. "Let's do that about three
more times before we shift frequencies."

"Will do," Pov said. His sail team repeated the exercise, adding more and more detail to Athena's hydrogen
map. Each of the blue giants was dimly surrounded by a
ghostly sphere in yellow-green and violet, demarking the
gas ionized by the blue stars' hard-light radiation. Beyond
the ragged edges of the fronts, the Pleiades veils glowed
softly red, the thin drifting clouds of neutral hydrogen
and dust still lingering in the cluster. Ceverny leaned forward and peered at the screen with as much intensity as
Athena.

"We have the stars defined," Athena said, pursing her
lips. "At least we won't run into one while we're going.
I see a channel there on the western edge of Maia's Veil,
south somewhat. It looks like it's nicely on the way to
GradyBol." She pointed on the map, then remembered
and used her computer to point for her. "Neutral hydrogen on both sides, hydrogen radicals in the middle. Looks
like a shock-front eddy detached from the main front.
Hmm. No depth ranging on this. I wonder how long it is."
She fiddled with her Helm Map program, trying to range
on the nearby stars. "Well, the hell with you," she muttered as Helm Map balked again, wanting another point
for depth triangulation and getting stubborn about the geometry. "It looks like it's far enough from Maia to keep
us from the worst of the radiation, almost two light-years,
but it's definitely an edge of the ionization front."

"Try ranging in molecule frequencies," Katrinya suggested from the chemlabs. "It may outline more of the
heavier dust."

"Let's look again, Tully," Pov ordered.

The computer tackled the light readings again and took
several longer looks at the Pleiades, adding Katrinya's
other frequencies. The map acquired new shades of
darker purple, some of it overlaid onto the detached front.

"Dusty," Ceverny said, shaking his head in dismay.
"Thank God that's a gascloud instead of a comet. Interstellar dust is smaller, about a micron, as I remember.

Run a polarization scan in visible light, Pov. Let's see how regular it is." The map suddenly blurred out in a broad wash of blue, the cumulative effect of the dust's reflection of the blue starlight that gave the Pleiades their distinctive blue color. Ceverny harumphed. "Well, don't drive by polarized light at those frequencies, Athena. Just a suggestion."

"I'll say," Athena snorted, and switched it back. "What a fog. We'll be using UV to see, I think."

"Will the dust damage our hull?" Andreos asked Ceverny.

"It won't penetrate, of course, not at that size: it'll vaporize on impact. We'll get slow metal damage, probably, enough to be a problem over time, maybe a very long time, but still a problem. We'll have to refit with slag shielding, Leonidas, especially the stress points anchoring the sails. They'll catch the worse of it. And the forward sensor assemblies won't like it much. Razack's outship crews are going to get busier, I think." He shook his head.

"Are you recommending against the course, sir?" Athena asked.

"No, not at all," Ceverny said, a little hastily, then smiled. "Forgive me: I'm still adjusting away from comets. We'll get dust wherever we go here, and that shock front looks good."

"Then that'll do it, sirs," Athena said with satisfaction. "Let's go fishing, people. Laying the course into Helm Map."

Net turned to a new vector, adding her engine power to her speed, and began to accelerate again. Pov shut down the Sail Deck wallscreen and turned the watch back over to Roja, with the junior staff resuming their stations. When Pov came back to the sail lounge, Ceverny was still sitting in his interlink chair, slowly pulling at his ear. Pov leaned on the doorjamb and crossed his arms.

"Dust," Ceverny muttered. "Have you modeled sails for the different parameters?"

"Not yet. I thought we'd wait until we had some better data from a first run. Right now we'd just be guessing, especially with most of our practical stats somewhere in Athena's data hole."

Ceverny nodded. "Perhaps I could help you with the modeling."

"What do you mean, 'perhaps'?" Pov asked. "I'm counting on it, sir."

"I have lots of ideas," Ceverny said lightly, "about all sorts of things out here. I've been daydreaming about the Pleiades for years, what we could do if we had the chance, had the ships to do it. Ask Katrinya; she'll tell you. But Sandor would never listen, not once." He pulled at his ear again thoughtfully, then sighed. "Cloudships belong on the frontier, Pov. Gray knew that twenty years ago and took the chance and then made it work. I'm glad we took our chance, too, at last." He smiled. "Katinka's been working on me, telling me I was smart to come with *Net,* that it was the only right choice. She's making progress."

"Still want to be a sail tech?" Pov joked, pleased that Ceverny's tormented look had eased. All of *Net*'s people had done their best to welcome the Cevernys with open arms, knowing what it had cost Miska Ceverny to choose *Net.* "Benek's ranking is still available. We haven't promoted staff up to fill it yet."

"We'll work out my ranking later, not that I care, particularly. I *do* care about sail specs. We made some modifications to *Arrow*'s sail designs when we built *Net,* remember, to fit sailing comet plasma. We'll have to modify them back. More work for Razack."

"He's going to be a busy man," Pov observed.

Ceverny chuckled and tugged at his ear.

Chapter 8

Net jumped that night and decelerated quickly into a new sea. In the near distance, the blue star Maia blazed in its brilliant glory, its light painfully bright even through filters. Pov kept an eye on the x-ray radiation impacting on the hull's sensors, safe enough at this distance, then scowled as the scans suddenly shot off the scale when Maia flared. Unlike T Tauri, the Pleiades blues had not spun off companions as they formed to dissipate part of the starcloud's angular momentum, and the Pleiades giants rotated at tremendous speeds, each star several times Sol's mass and spinning a hundred times as fast. The blues trembled on the edge between gravity and centrifugal force, burning their hydrogen fuel at a prodigious rate, hot stars destined by their large mass to a short life. One of the original blues had already collapsed into a neutron star, creating Lucifer's Deep, and Pleione was now in the process of shedding gas shells as it, too, began to die. Maia would likely be next.

The radiation made any outship maneuvers by a skyrider chevron or Razack's crews out of the question, and so *Net* spread the sails she had. Athena's mapping had taken them directly into the drifting shockfront, a thin band of ionized gas and dust about a million kilometers wide and more millions long. The radiation shockwave had compressed the hydrogen into a gas density of several thousand atoms per subcubic, a good harvest for *Net*'s first trial of the Pleiades. In the distance Maia flared again, zipping particles through the gas ahead of *Net*, and Pov noted his sail efficiency went up as the UV radiation reionized some of the hydrogen. On the light frequencies *Net* was using to watch the gas drifting ahead, radio and

UV, Maia's light shimmered as a palpable wave propagating through the gas, a cosmic ripple in a nearly intangible pool.

"Busy star," Athena commented on the interlink.

"Well, it's helping the catching," Pov said judiciously. "Some of the dust is ionizing, too, which helps."

He looked at Sailmaster Ceverny, who was scowling ferociously at the other dust escaping the sails. Pov had accessed camera sensors on each wing to give them exterior views of *Net*'s forward hull. As the charge-neutral dust vaporized steadily on the forward hull, unimpeded by the magnetic pull of the sails, the hull metal glowed in infrared over its entire surface, warmed by the several degrees of heat generated by the dust impact.

"Damned dust!" Ceverny exclaimed. "Look at that infrared!" He threw up his hands.

"Calm down, Miska," Andreos advised. "You'll get your opportunity to fix."

"Don't humor me, Leonidas," Ceverny said with a snort. "It's *your* ship that's getting worn away, one molecule at a time."

"Your ship, too," Andreos said, laughing at him. "Our hull can take it. Calm down." Ceverny glowered and crossed his arms on his chest.

"Lots of molecules, too, sir," Pov said, adding his own cajolery. He tapped into Janina's hold readings and displayed the dozens of emission lines on the spectrograms, each marking a molecule or double ion that cloudships never saw except in clouds like these.

"Those molecule chains won't last long," Ceverny sniffed, "not with the UV bombardment." The glower did not change.

"Nor will the ion charge as they swirl in," Janina said. "Double ion oxygen eats atoms, given half a chance. I've got organics forming in the hydrogen stream, all those busy oxygen and hydrogen radicals eating busily. Chemlab will have fun trying to sort all that out."

"Any pets like T Tauri?" Athena asked with interest. Captain Andreos lowered his eyebrows but didn't comment. Athena waggled her fingers at him.

"No," Janina said, sounding disappointed. "Just standard chemistry. Good tritium count, upper percentages. Better than comets, worse than T Tauri. I've restocked a third of our canisters." She turned her head and looked at the wall displays on Hold Deck. "Do you want to save anything special besides tritium, captain?"

"What's chemlab's idea?" Andreos hedged.

"Oh, they want everything, naturally," she said, then smiled as she heard a muttered comment behind her on Hold Deck. "I thought basic solvents, some catalysts, a few of the odd molecules to study." She raised an eyebrow. "At least until we find out what the mobile stations want, what's rare and best worth catching."

"Sounds good. Let's not lose all our speed."

"Ten percent light speed now, sir," Athena reported. "I was thinking of falling to eight. That'll take another half hour. As we accelerate, I'll put us on trajectory for GradyBol." She raised an eyebrow.

"Fine." Andreos leaned back and ran his eyes over the banks of his interlink screens. "Fishing is nice, Helm. Nice and peaceful."

"Hmph." Athena snorted sourly, unconvinced. She looked desperately haggard in the interlink screen, too pale and thin after all the hours spent the last few days with Helm Map and worrying *Net* through her first hurdles. Pov saw her close her eyes and sway slightly, then determinedly sit up straighter.

"Are you all right, Athena?" he asked with some alarm.

"I'm fine," she said crossly. "Forget it."

"Stefania will plot the course to GradyBol," Andreos said quietly. "I want you off duty and down to Medical."

"Sir—"

"That's an order, Helm."

Athena looked at him resentfully for a long moment, then sighed. "Yes, sir."

She started to get up, then suddenly had to grab for support. "Got up too fast," she muttered, her legs visibly shaking as she leaned on her chair, breathing heavily. She smiled with embarrassment, then swayed off balance and slowly collapsed downward, fighting it all the way. "Help—"

"Stefania!" Andreos shouted, loud enough to carry onto Helm Deck, and footsteps rang outside Athena's interlink room, coming fast.

A moment later, Stefania burst through the doorway. She barely caught Athena as she fell, too late to stop Athena's head from bouncing hard on the chair arm. Athena's eyes rolled up and she went abruptly limp in Stefania's arms. Stefania eased her down onto the floor, then pivoted on her heel to face the deck outside.

"Get Medical! *Now!*" she yelled, then turned back to face the interlink screens, her face nearly as white as Athena's. "She's out cold, sirs. She's not breathing very well." Stefania gulped and looked down at Athena.

"Medical's coming, Stef," Andreos reassured her. "Hold on now."

Stefania nodded dumbly, then wrapped her arms tightly around Athena and began to rock her slowly, her blond head bent low over Athena's slack face.

"Athena . . ." she whispered, and began to cry.

Pov sat in his apartment chair in front of his window, nursing a glass of vodka, far into the late hours of the night. The first reports from Medical on Athena's condition were not good, but she was still alive. Her collapse had stunned the ship: as Pov had, the others had believed Athena's act as she drove herself beyond all reason, fueled by skyrider panache, Athena's personal brand of reckless courage.

He sat dully in the darkness, feet propped on the table, the vodka glass slowly warming in his hand, as he faced as a real possibility the first serious death for himself since his father had died years ago. Athena the bold, Athena the brave. You're just like Kate, he had told her angrily before the second T Tauri run. You go barging around and someday you're going to get yourself killed, all of it pilot panache. Let's lift a glass to Athena, but you're still dead and nothing will change that. And she had promised him not to get herself killed. She had promised him.

He looked down at his vodka, wanting to get drunk and knowing it wouldn't solve anything. He wanted to smash something, heave away at the immovable weight, push at Creation until his bones cracked, whatever would make Athena safe, and he couldn't do a thing. Nothing. He and Athena had an ambivalent relationship, more than friend or even sister, only marginally less intense than lover, and were brought closer than most by their twin duties of sail and helm. Athena was happily married to Gregori and had three daughters that looked exactly like her; he had Avi and Sail Deck and his Rom family. But there was a bonding between them for all that, something different from his big-brother love for Kate, his wary respect for his mother, his affection for his Rom cousins. If Athena died, she would take an irreplaceable part of his soul with her.

He silently voiced a prayer to his ancestors, those shadowy Rom spirits, half ghost, half deity, who watched over the wandering Rom wherever they traveled, and asked them to include Athena in their protections, if they would.

He got up and put the vodka on the kitchen counter, then solemnly went through the Rom rituals of purifying himself, washing his hands carefully, saying the necessary Romany prayers, and then asked again, this time aloud. Afterward, he stood for a long time in front of St. Serena's table, looking at the small statue that stood on the shrine. I'll make you a bargain, Siduri, he thought. Any bargain. Do the gods bargain for a life? What are the rules?

St. Serena looked back at him with unreadable eyes, saying nothing. He turned away and put more vodka in his glass, then sat down again in his chair, propping his feet, and watched the stars blur as *Net* accelerated again, heading for GradyBol and whatever awaited her there.

His door chimed again, and he ignored it, as before. Avi was with Kate, who needed her more tonight: the skyriders idolized Athena, Kate as much as the others, and Avi had gone to her when Kate asked. Pov preferred to be alone, praying to *Net,* as he supposed he was.

The door chimed again and Pov stirred irritably, but did not get up. A moment later the door opened when somebody with the necessary code overrode the lock. Pov heard the door shut and the soft tread of footsteps, then looked up at Captain Andreos. The captain lowered himself into the other chair and stretched out his long legs.

"Want some vodka?" Pov asked him solemnly.

"Yes. Thank you."

Pov got up and got another glass, then brought the bottle back. He walked steadily enough, probably reassuring Andreos on that point—though he guessed Captain Andreos would tolerate anything tonight. He gave the captain the extra glass and bottle and then sat down again.

"She's stable," Andreos said quietly. "Not out of danger, but stable."

Pov sighed and closed his eyes.

"She'll be on medical leave for weeks now," Andreos said, and poured vodka in his glass. "And I will personally tie her down to see that it sticks, too. You had no suspicions?"

"You know Athena. She doesn't want help, never asks. She *gives* help."

"Well, maybe she'll learn something new." Andreos tightened his lips. "Another fact I will see to." He sipped at the glass and leaned back farther in his chair, looking at the view out the window. "Athena gets her latitude this time, but if you ever do this to me, Pov, I'll kick you back to Perikles. And I mean that."

"Understood, sir."

"Oh? I don't like you sitting alone like this."

"I'm not alone." He gestured toward Siduri on her shrine. "I'm never alone. I've always got *Net,* and all my other Rom ghosts." He smiled affectionately at the statue. "Gypsy thing, sir."

"Hmph." Pov looked at Andreos and saw the captain's teeth flash with amusement. "Will you make me a promise?" Andreos asked. "An important promise—make it another gypsy thing, if you will."

"What, sir?"

"Come to me before you're even near the edge. Never risk yourself as Athena did and make *me* sit in the darkness like this. Will you promise?"

"Yes, sir. I promise."

"Good." Andreos put his vodka glass on the table and

stood up, then rested his hand on Pov's shoulder a moment. "Don't sit up too long, son."

"I won't, sir."

Pov watched the stars a little longer, then drained his glass and went to bed. He was nearly asleep when Avi came in, tired and heartsore, her feet dragging. When she saw he was awake, she turned on the small lamp on the bureau and began slowly pulling off her clothes, getting ready for bed. "Kate's asleep," she said dully.

"Athena's better."

"Yes, we heard." Avi opened his bureau drawer and rummaged for some kind of nightdress among his clothes, then blinked tiredly as the choice utterly defeated her.

"Come to bed, Avi."

Avi yawned and turned off the light, then plodded over to the bed in her underwear and climbed into bed with him. She curled on her side, turning away from him, and nestled backward against his body. He put his arms around her and held her.

"Don't ever die on me, Pov," she said, almost inaudibly. "Promise me we'll both live forever."

He kissed her shoulder. "Can't promise that," he said with regret. "Eventually you have to turn into an ancestor, watching over the Rom. Ghosts are important. All the Rom think so."

"That's all right." Avi yawned again and then turned in his arms, wrapping her arms around him. They lay together, their faces close, and Avi watched his eyes until they closed and he slept.

Athena improved slowly over the next few days, according to the regular bulletins on the all-ship, still weak but conscious and responding to Medical's therapy. The day before *Net* arrived at GradyBol, the doctors finally allowed visitors on a limited basis. Pov stopped by after his morning watch. When he looked in the door of her hospital room, she saw him and waved vaguely, her face pasty white and looking totally exhausted. Gregori sat in a chair in the corner and smiled as Pov stepped into the room.

" 'Lo, Pov," he said genially.

"Hi, Greg. How's she doing?"

"Doing nothing at all—and she'll keep doing nothing for quite a while." He gave Athena a fierce look, and she smiled weakly in response.

"I hear you," she said humorously. "I hear you every time."

"Good."

Pov bent down and kissed Athena lightly on the lips, then took her hand. "You look awful," he commented, looking her over more closely.

"I hear a lot about that, too. I thought people were supposed to cheer me up, pretend, you know." She sighed deeply. "I'm sorry, Pov," she said softly, so softly he could barely hear her. "I'm sorry I broke my promise."

"Almost broke it. Almost doesn't count."

"Oh, sure." He saw the tears start in her eyes. "And now I've let *Net* down, too. I've let everybody down."

"That is ridiculous," he said, a little angry with her. "Who do you think you are? Neutron Woman, who thrives on radioactive blood? So who says you can't get sick? Who says you have to be invulnerable?"

"I say."

"Athena . . ." he said helplessly.

"I say," she repeated, "but I'll admit I may be wrong. How about that? I think I'm going to have lots of time to think it over, revise some opinions." She glanced at Gregori and smiled wanly. "But I wanted to apologize to you while I'm still myself, you know, Neutron Woman." She wrinkled her nose. "What a label. You've totally ruined any chance of my enjoying my self-pity, calling me that."

"Good," Pov said, mimicking Gregori's earlier inflection, which made her smile again.

"Will you ask Berka to watch over Stefania?" she wheedled. "Gregori won't."

"Neither will I," Pov said firmly. Berka Kozak was Athena's Third Helm, an older skyrider from *Dance* whose steadiness suited him at Third, supporting Stefania's occasional nervous behavior on Helm Deck when Athena was busy elsewhere. "Berka can figure that out himself, as you know he will. And Stefania might sur-

prise you. That's another assumption about yourself you
might think about."

Athena closed her eyes and smiled. "Nag, nag, nag,"
she said faintly.

"You'd better believe it. Someday Stefania will have
Net's Helm Deck all to herself, after we build our daughter ship and you transfer to her as pilotmaster. She'll be
built for the Nebula, and there's no way you'd miss that.
Right? So it's about time Stefania started practicing."

"Nag." She chuckled. "I hear you."

The medtech stuck her head in the door and cleared her
throat briskly. "Time's up, sir. Doctor says to keep it very
short."

"I hear you," Pov said dryly and squeezed Athena's
hand, then smiled as she opened her eyes and looked at
him, amused.

"Come back tomorrow, will you?" she asked.

"You can count on it."

That evening Avi stopped in the corridor several paces
short of the Janusz apartment door, then sidled to the wall
and leaned, looking pale. Pov walked the few steps back
to her.

"I don't know if I can do this, Pov," Avi said, gulping.
Her hands tugged at the long red skirt, then flew to her
throat. She toyed a moment with her golden necklace,
then neatened the lace at her sleeves, totally, utterly nervous. Hair clips and earrings borrowed from Kate sparkled as Avi shook her head helplessly. "I'm not a gypsy,"
she said in a low voice and gulped again. "I don't know
the rules. What if I ruin everything?"

Pov leaned his hand on the wall over her shoulder and
brought his face close to hers, breathing in the sweet
scent of her hair and skin. "How will you 'ruin' everything?" he asked.

"Your mother probably hates me."

"My mother doesn't even know who you are, and she's
preoccupied with Kate. But, yes, she'll notice you."

"She'll hate me, I'm sure."

"Avi, my family has its weird behavior, but they aren't
like your Russki family. Karoly is open-minded and he's

seen you before, and his boys are nice normal kids. And Tawnie's heard more about you from Kate, and Kate likes you, and Tawnie always likes people, no matter who they are. Good people, Avi. I love them, whatever goes on. You will, too."

Avi took a long shuddering breath, her hands moving restlessly again as she straightened and tucked. Then she scowled, getting mad at herself. "You must think I'm a coward!"

"Not at all," he assured her. "You just think that if you blow it tonight, our romance is off, flat, no recourse, you're done. Right? And my mother's sitting in there just hoping to help it along."

"Well . . . not quite that baldly." She looked up at him and turned up the corners of her mouth. "I was thinking more of Avi Hash as the main dish at the feast, maybe served up with peppers. Is that possible?"

"Definitely."

Avi hit him hard in the ribs and glared. "Some sympathy, Povinko," she said, her eyes flashing. "What a thing to say!"

"So get mad at me. I don't mind." He leaned close to her again, their faces nearly touching. "Love you, Avi," he said softly. "I always will, forever. You want to cancel tonight, we can."

Avi took a deep breath, then grimaced. "No," she said regretfully. "It'd only be worse next time." She shook her head, making her earrings dance again. "Say 'suits' to me, Pov, so I'll feel better."

"Suits."

Avi smiled, then looked nervous again.

They walked to the apartment door and he pushed the door-chime button. The door opened and Karoly smiled at them both in greeting, then made a small ceremony of handing Avi a glittering metal coin, pierced in its center and tied up with bright ribbons of red and green, the Rom's lucky colors. Avi hesitated, then closed her fingers over it.

"For luck," Karoly said, his handsome face slightly mischievous. It was a Rom gesture for a favored guest, and much like Tawnie to think of it and for Karoly to agree.

"Thank you, Karoly," Avi said shyly, then tightened her fingers on Pov's arm as she looked past Karoly into the crowded room.

Tawnie, Kate and the two *Dance* wives, Judit and Patia, sat with Aunt Narilla on the front-room cushions, each dressed in a flowing colored skirt, bright jewelry, and a lacy blouse, their dark hair bound up with bright clips like Avi's. Pov didn't see his mother and wished, without much hope, that maybe she wasn't home. The children ran and shrieked around the women, playing an elaborate game of keep-away. To the right, through the open kitchen door, Pov could see Uncle Damek's broad back, cinched by the green ties of his apron as Damek toiled over dinner.

Karoly was wearing an apron, too, and handed Pov another. "Time for work," he said drolly. On St. Stephan's feast day, the Rom men cooked the meal while the women lolled around in the front room enjoying themselves, gossiping, commenting on their men and watching the children, and generally whooping it up, a neat turnaround on the usual patriarchal privileges. Pov sighed and tied his apron around his waist.

"Avi," Karoly said courteously, "why don't you go sit by Tawnie or Kate? Come on, Pov."

Kate looked over and beamed at Avi, then patted the cushion beside her. "Sit by me, Avi," she said loudly.

A dozen *romni* eyes swiveled and inspected Avi in a quick glance from head to toe, but Avi walked stiffly forward to Kate and sat down, pulling up her long legs, then arranging her skirt neatly on her knees. Kate bent and whispered something to her, making Avi smile.

Karoly grasped Pov's arm and dragged him toward the kitchen. "Duty," he declared. "You get to cut up the lamb, coz."

Pov looked back at Avi and saw her laugh with the others at something Tawnie had said, then gave in to his cousin's pull. "She's all right," Karoly said reassuringly. "Your mother's in the kitchen right now, giving Shuri a bath. That'll take a while, the way it's been going."

In the next room, Damek and his other two sons, assisted by Tawnie's slender husband, Del, were relentlessly making dinner. In the far corner, Pov's mother bent over a wide bathtub as Bavol's little girl, naked as a jaybird, splashed and shrieked happily in the water. Shuri spotted Pov and split her moppet's face in a broad grin, and would have climbed out to race for a hug if Margareta had not grabbed her.

"No, you don't, Shuri," she said.

"Coz!" Shuri cried out in a high-pitched squeak, splashing water into fountains. "Help me, help me. I'm being eaten by a monster! Ahhhh!"

"I'll monster you," his mother said, her voice tight with suppressed laughter, then grunted as Shuri's flailing arm hit her solidly in the rib cage. "Shuri, stop that," she said crossly.

Watching them, Pov remembered the last bath his mother had given to him, when he was nine and thought himself too much a man to be bathed by his mother. Margareta had bent over him then, much as she now bent over Shuri, while Pov glowered indignantly in the tub, his arms crossed, his arguments utterly futile. She had been ungainly that day in her pregnancy with Kate, but Pov remembered how she had smiled, cajoling him, until the women had come to the wagon and she had straightened and looked out as they called to her to come, had called about her husband, suddenly dead.

Would she be different if Dad hadn't died? he wondered. Would Dad have tempered her, made her happy?

Bavol turned away from the stove and gave his daughter a sour frown. "Shuri!" he said, his voice a crack of warning. "You behave!" Shuri grinned at him and giggled. Shuri loved baths, and nothing could dent the experience, not even her father's sour attitude toward the joys of living.

"Oh, Da!" Shuri wailed dramatically, windmilling her arms to splash even higher. "Can't you help me!" She shrieked again as Margareta forced her into the water to rinse her hair. "Help me, help me!"

Pov grinned and joined Bavol and Karoly at the long kitchen counter. Bavol handed Karoly some peppers and onions to scrape and chop. "Patia should be bathing Shuri," Bavol said irritably. "It's her duty as mother."

"Aunt Margareta offered," Karoly said smoothly. "How often does a grandmam get to have such fun with her granddaughter?"

"Fun?" Bavol asked sourly, then sent another frown at his cavorting daughter.

"Fun," Karoly said more sharply, but Bavol typically ignored the subtle signals.

"Patia forgets her duty," Bavol whined onward.

"With you as a husband," Damek rumbled, giving it to Bavol from both sides, "how could she ever forget?" Damek turned and smiled at Pov. "Welcome, Pov."

"Pov!" Shuri shrieked joyfully in her bath. "Pov, Pov, Pov!" She shrieked and splashed the water sky-high. "Boom!"

Damek looked at his granddaughter and crinkled the corners of his eyes. "Ah, to be young," he said, and nudged Pov affectionately, an infrequent gesture for Damek but made often enough. "You can start cutting up the lamb on the other counter, Pov."

"Yes, sir," Pov said, and headed for the lamb.

According to Rom tradition, St. Stephan was the guardian of male purity, the model and guide for a Rom husband and father. Centuries ago, women had been barred from the feast gathering, an old and isolated practice which most gypsy families had discarded as contrary to the importance of family gatherings. Pov could hear the murmur of the women's voices in the other room, rising and falling as they talked, the children's play a happy noise weaving in and out of the quiet murmur. It was a good feast for Avi's first.

Balance, Pov thought, with a smile to himself.

He eyed the joints of half-frozen lamb on the sideboard, then picked up a knife to start worrying them into pieces for the stewpot. With a half-dozen men in the kitchen, it was a tight fit. Lasho elbowed him accidentally as he poured milk into a jug, then turned his head and gave Pov a smile.

"Crowded in here," Lasho commented.

"That it is," Pov agreed.

In the family, Damek's youngest son was overshadowed by Karoly's rank as eldest and Bavol's assertive role as a guardian of tradition. Lasho, a slim short man with quick hands, bore it well, happy with his young wife and two babies. He had held a minor hold ranking on *Dance*, Pov remembered, and brought in extra income by working silver, some bangles for family gifts, others on commission for the gaje. Lasho had an artist's skill with the metal, a gift sadly more admired by his father for the credits it brought than for the skillful designs Lasho worked into the metal.

"This family needs more room," Pov said. "Are you and Bavol going to ask for another apartment?"

"We're negotiating with the neighbors, though the asking for knocking down another wall is ascending the authorities." Lasho grinned, showing his white teeth, and turned back to his work. Pov sawed at one of the lamb joints, reminding himself not to add a fingertip to the piled meat. As he sliced, he bumped Lasho again, and they turned toward each other, both pretending vast offense.

"Keep your elbows to yourself," Lasho advised him severely. Beside him, Del laughed, his knife chopping rhythmically.

"Same to you, coz," Pov said and brandished his knife. "Watch out. I'm armed."

"So am I." Lasho brandished his knife back. In the background, Shuri shrieked joyously, splashing water high. Lasho glanced over and grinned. "I wish I was Shuri right now," he said, making a show of wiping his forehead with his sleeve. "This is hot work."

Uncle Damek looked over and grumbled, and both Pov and Lasho turned back dutifully to their work. Pov heard a ghost of a chuckle from Lasho, then another snigger from Del, and felt happy that a few of the Janusz Rom seemed in good spirts today.

By the time Pov finished cutting up the lamb, his mother had finished Shuri's bath and dressed her in a pretty costume of long skirt and ruffled tunic. She began to comb the tangles from Shuri's wet hair, another circumstance of great fun for Shuri's dramatics. Finally,

Margareta gave up on perfection and shooed the little girl into the other room. Red-faced and damp all over from Shuri's splashing, Margareta straightened and rubbed her back, then gave Pov a mild glare.

"Good afternoon, Mother," he said gravely, trying not to show his amusement. Some things apparently exceeded even his mother's great powers: he judged the bath had been a draw.

"Hmph," his mother said noncommittally. Then her dark eyes flashed with her own amusement, and for a brief moment he and his mother shared something warmer than the conflicts of the past weeks. "Another year or two of her growing and I may lose completely."

"Another year or two and she'll start fussing more about her clothes than Patia does, true?"

"So we can hope." She walked over to inspect his pile of lamb, then backed up a step, startled, as Damek whirled around at her.

"Out!" Damek declared, pointing at the living room. "Only men here. St. Stephan's Day, Margareta. Be warned!"

"Pfui," his mother announced, but turned obediently and walked out of the kitchen. Her foot missed a step in the doorway as she saw Avi among the chattering women, but Pov saw her shoulders square and she walked onward out of his sight.

This was a mistake, he knew with sudden conviction. I should have known better. Not now, when Mother has too much to prove. He hesitated, caught between wanting to swoop out like an avenging hawk and carry Avi away before his mother pounced. But Tawnie had asked, the first gesture from his family other than Kate, and he risked offending Tawnie if he did. He craned his neck to see Avi around the doorjamb.

"Done with the lamb?" Damek said to Pov. "Good. Go shape the biscuits."

"I'd rather go out and sit by Avi, Uncle."

"Avi can take care of herself, nephew."

"Oh?" Pov asked pointedly.

Damek hesitated, giving him a cautious look. "*You* brought her to the *slava*, not me."

"Tawnie asked her." Pov practically danced in his anxiety as he heard the voices rise in the other room, then the sharp sound of his mother's voice.

"Who's Avi?" Bavol asked, confused.

"Our guest," Karoly said firmly, forestalling his father's own answer, whatever it might have been. "Go ahead, Pov, I can do the biscuits."

Pov nodded and tried to walk slowly out of the kitchen, his heart thumping. As he paused in the doorway, he saw the women sitting in a circle, his mother among them. Margareta leaned forward and said something directly to Avi, and Pov saw Tawnie's hands flutter in shock, heard Judit's gasp, then saw the wash of utter rage flush across Kate's face. Avi sat still as a white statue, she was so pale, as she looked blankly at Margareta.

His boots strode forcefully on the carpeting as he crossed the distance to the women. His mother looked up and smiled a crafty, malicious smile, and he knew suddenly why she had done it. It had nothing to do with Avi, only pressure on her son, pressure to take her side against Sergei. It erased Avi. His anger changed into a deep and bitter rage that his mother would hurt Avi, who had done nothing to her, nothing at all. Margareta's crafty smile wavered as he looked down at her with open contempt.

"She is my intended." he told her in Romany, using the word for Rom betrothed, and saw the flickers of surprise in the other women's faces, the quick appraising glances at Avi. "If you want the breach now, you can have it, Mother. Let's end it now. Kate doesn't even have to be involved."

"Today is a feast day," his mother responded tartly, looking up at him. "Do not say such words to your mother on a holy day."

"What mother?" he asked bitterly. "I don't see any mother." He stared at her squarely, letting the words hang on the air for a moment, and Margareta hesitated. In the back of his mind, a warning voice shouted at him, but he ignored it. He bent down to Avi and took her elbow. "Come on. We're leaving."

"Pov—" Avi said weakly, her face stark with alarm.

"This is St. Stephan's Day!" his mother protested incredulously. "You can't leave. It is tradition!"

"This is tradition?" he said, raising his voice. "One that twists and hurts, one that gives you power to be cruel?" He helped Avi to her feet.

"I only said—" his mother began.

"I don't care what you said," Pov interrupted. "Kate's face was enough to guess the gist."

"She is gaje." His mother's voice was loaded with contempt, the contempt of centuries of gypsy disdain for every outsider.

Pov met Avi's eyes, and felt abruptly filled with a great sadness. "I'm sorry, beloved. I'm sorry my people are the way they are."

Avi had tears in her eyes, but firmed her chin. "I'd rather not leave," she quavered. "I was having such a nice talk with Tawnie and Patia." Even so, she glanced uncertainly at Margareta beside him. He took her elbow firmly.

"It was a stupid idea," he said. "I was wrong to suggest it."

He saw the distress in Tawnie's sweet face, an odd calculation in Patia's eyes, then the startled faces of the children in the back of the room as they stopped their play, like young fawns caught still by the sound of sudden danger.

"I'm sorry, Tawnie," he muttered. "I'm sorry I ruined your feast." He and Avi left in complete silence.

Chapter 9

Avi said little on the way back to her apartment, her feet stumbling a few times. As he keyed the doorlock to the apartment, she disengaged his hand and walked through the doorway, then stopped and put her hands on her hips.

"What she said wasn't that bad," she declared to the open room. "Do you have to be so damn protective?"

"Nice act, love. But I know my mother too well." He walked on past her to the small kitchen along the wall and opened the refrigerator. "Want some wine?"

"*Are* we going to discuss this?"

"Not now, not unless it's really important to you. I'm too angry." He turned his head and gave her a tight smile. "The famous Rom male temper. Well, it was inevitable, I suppose." He rummaged in the refrigerator among the bottles and jars, then wrinkled his nose reflectively. Avi stayed where she was, watching him. Finally he turned back to her. "It's not you, Avi. You're just the excuse."

"I *am* a gaje."

"So? Maybe that's what the fight is really about. It started when I was ten and brought Tully home to dinner. My mother's afraid of what the gaje are doing to the younger Rom, afraid you're stealing our souls."

"I don't mean to," Avi said abjectly, then grimaced at herself. "Listen to me."

"It's called culture, I guess. Wine?"

"Sure."

Pov found the wine bottle, then got two glasses from the cupboard. They sat down in the chairs in front of the outside window, looking over *Net*, a different and narrower view from Avi's window. Pov popped the cork from the bottle and poured her a glass of the sweet red wine, then filled his own.

"To St. Stephan," he said, raising his glass, "and to Siduri, blessed be She." He propped up his feet on the table. "I've thought sometimes that maybe *you're* Siduri, Avi my love. I'm considering how to test that by experiment."

Avi twisted her glass around in her hands, watching the liquid slosh. "All she said, Pov, was some crack about gaje girls behind the barns. I didn't even know what it meant."

Pov took a sudden breath in shock, then closed his eyes. He had never struck his mother in anger and intended never to start: it had been right to leave when he did, he thought, before he heard what was actually said. "Forget what it means, Avi," he said. "It's not important."

"I insist on knowing," Avi said faintly.

Pov sipped at his glass, reluctant to hurt Avi any further, wanting anything but that. When Avi stirred impatiently at his silence, he looked at her in open anguish. Her dark eyes widened as she saw his face, but she sat very still, her long fingers curled around her glass.

"Please," she said quietly.

"It has to do with . . . the way that . . . well, basically it's how young Rom men find whores."

Avi's mouth dropped open and she sat up hard, nearly spilling her wine. "She doesn't even know me!" she sputtered.

"So why should that matter? Kate knew what she meant, and I saw it in Kate's face, not yours."

Avi slowly sat back in her chair, then raised one foot and crossed it over his ankle on the table. They sipped at their glasses, watching the lights twinkle outside Avi's small living-room window. The stars were blurred by *Net*'s speed as she accelerated.

After a while, Pov gave a short bitter laugh. "And I complained that my mother walked out."

The door chimed, and he hesitated before he got up to answer it. When it opened, Patia stepped through the door in her brisk way, followed by Tawnie and Judit. They marched over to Avi, scarcely sparing him a glance, took the wineglass from her hand, and lifted her from her chair. As they were step-marching her back toward the door, he blocked their path. "Wait a minute!" he said.

"You are ill-mannered, Pov Janusz," Patia declared, her chin high. "Avi is Tawnie's guest and not yours to whisk away from her *slava* feast."

"I won't have her humiliated by—"

"Avi is ours to protect," Tawnie declared, "not yours." She smiled and touched his arm. "This is women's work, coz. Out of the way."

Pov hesitated, then looked at Avi. She looked a little dazed.

"Avi?"

"I am a twig swept by a remorseless tide," Avi said, then giggled oddly. She looked at the two women holding her arms, then craned to see Judit behind them. She laughed again, deep in her throat, then looked back at him, her eyes shining. Pov scowled.

I don't understand women, he thought helplessly, *either* kind.

Patia lifted her hand and pushed him firmly to the side. "You can come back, too, if you want," she said, her tone snide. "It would be proper to show up at our family's *slava,* but do as you will."

They marched Avi out of the apartment, leaving Pov behind in their wake. As the door started to close, he hit the door control again and followed.

He caught up halfway down the corridor, wondering what kind of odd procession they all made to the people who passed them, then tried to overhear what Patia was whispering to Avi, without success. Avi laughed oddly again.

When everyone re-arrived at the feast, the women sat down and started chatting as if nothing whatsoever had happened, though Kate had left and his mother was in the kitchen again. Pov hesitated, glancing at the kitchen, where Uncle Damek still led the crew, then stubbornly sat down by Avi, making Patia move over. Patia's protectiveness was welcome, if mysterious. He suspected other motives at work, maybe Patia's challenge to his mother as a senior wife, maybe a challenge to Patia's unpleasant husband. He suddenly tired of all the maneuvering that constantly delighted his family, and decided sourly that none of this had anything to do with Avi, either. Avi was an object to them. Then he caught Tawnie's eye and saw her sweet smile, and could not believe it of Tawnie.

Sensitive to his mood, Avi leaned closer to him, then laid her head on his shoulder with a sigh. "Not what it seems?" she whispered.

"I'm not sure. I'm sorry, Avi."

"S'all right."

They sat uncomfortably in the circle, listening to Patia talk to Tawnie about some news from *Dance,* as if *Dance* were just over the horizon and this were only a family visit. His mother came back into the room and retreated to the mattresses in the back to watch the children play, keeping herself apart from the women. A few minutes later, the men trooped in from the kitchen, bringing the plates of hot food. Wine bottles were uncorked, glasses brought, and Damek led the opening salute to St. Stephan, as if nothing were different, all were unchanged. Pov entwined his fingers in Avi's and squeezed hers briefly, then let himself drift away to a remote place, building the walls. Across the circle, his mother stared at him, without expression.

I want to leave, he thought. I don't want to see the family die for me like this, not like this. He caught Tawnie's eyes watching him with open concern—leave it to Tawnie to see right through his pretending. Karoly glanced at him, too. He swallowed uneasily, knowing he was understanding more of what his sister had endured in the past three years since her first and only attempt to bring Sergei into her Rom family. He understood much more now of his sister's anger—and the desolation that fueled it. He saw a choice coming, walking malevolently toward him. He had thought he could pass that door in a fit of temper, easy, quickly over.

Patia smiled at him archly, then turned to chatter something to Judit as they dished vegetables onto their plates. What does Patia want? he wondered suddenly, seeing his cousin's wife in a new light. On Perikles, Patia's father had ruled one of the major Rom families, a rich and in-

fluential elder whose will often prevailed: marrying
Bavol had been thought by some a step beneath her. He
watched Patia covertly. With Margareta's daughter in disgrace, Patia was senior of the other wives after Narilla—
and Narilla had deferred to Margareta years ago. *Puri
dai?* he wondered, eyeing her—and suddenly knew he did
not want to be ruled by Patia. Patia would be colder, her
decisions fed by her own unhappiness that she could not
admit. His mother, at least, had known love with her husband, had once cherished her children.

His mother turned and called to one of Karoly's boys,
and he brought over Lasho's toddler, who had wandered
off. Margareta cuddled the girl, whispering in her ear to
make her giggle, then fed her a fragment of biscuit from
her plate—and Pov closed his eyes in pain, remembering.

We must have peace, he thought. I was wrong today,
however right I thought I was, but wrong in other ways.
By publicly defying her, I gave Patia her entry, her
chance. My earlier meddling made it worse for Kate, I
think; I erred even worse today, though thank God it
won't make things worse for Avi, only me. He studied his
plate, then began to eat slowly, the voices rising and falling around him as his family talked and joked with each
other.

At the end of the meal, when the final scraps were being picked off the plates, Uncle Damek raised his glass
and began the first of many songs of the evening. Tightening his fingers on Avi's hand, Pov joined in with the
men's bass line, listening to the women pick up the mel-
ody. Then his mother got up to turn off the room lights,
casting them into the dim light of a single lamp in the
kitchen. She handed out candles to each of her family,
pointedly bypassing Avi. As Patia reached for the box to
make her correction of Margareta's lapse, Pov gently in-
tercepted her hand, forestalling her.

He saw his mother's eyes flash in the dimness, then the
shadowed tightening of her lips as Pov entwined Avi's
fingers around his own candle, holding it together with
their two hands. His mother continued around the circle,
giving each a candle, child and adult alike, then circled

again, touching each head in a silent blessing. As she
reached Avi again, her hand went into the box and
brought out a candle, and held it out to Avi.

Avi took it wonderingly, looking up at Margareta's
shadowed face bent over her. His mother's hand brushed
Avi's dark hair, then rested on Pov's own head for a long
moment. Then she moved on, continuing the round of
blessing. Finally, Margareta seated herself and lit her candle with a long match, waiting until the flame caught,
then bent it gracefully to touch the wick of Damek's candle. Damek passed the flame and, solemnly, the lights lit
around the circle, lighting their faces.

Damek began another hymn, his bass voice rumbling
through the opening verse of the chant, and Pov warily
watched his mother's face across the circle, suspecting
her of anything and wishing it were not anything he
thought. After so much opposition, too many schemes
and pretenses, he no longer trusted her.

The *slava* lasted far into the evening, graced by a second smaller meal of cakes and fruits, more songs, and
finally, at the family's urging, Judit's dancing, accompanied by her husband's guitar. Though out of practice,
Judit still showed her proud flair as a dancer, and Lasho
played onward after Judit had stopped, joking that her old
age had caught her. As Lasho played, Avi tipped her head
to listen, obviously amazed by the furious movements of
Lasho's fingers over the strings, the fast arpeggios, the
strumming thumps on the guitar. Near the end, noticing
her smiles, Lasho gave Avi a smile just for her, pleased
by her open admiration.

Pov looked at Avi. She does charm, he thought. His
mother had ignored Avi the rest of the evening, choosing
to talk to *Dance*'s Rom, to play with the children, and
even joke with Damek, something she rarely did with her
gruff brother. Games, he thought wearily. Don't they ever
stop? His head ached with trying to guess his mother's
next feint, and he finally gave up the attempt. He and Avi
left at midnight.

The following morning, Pov decided to store his
mother in a holding file, not that she'd stay there long,

knowing her, and watched with satisfaction as *Net* made her approach to GradyBol Station. Avi sat at the infrared post, taking over Benek's former position in an informal promotion that would become legal in a few weeks, and Lev Marska had moved up to Sixth Sail at the comm station. The change put Avi next to Celka, and Pov watched them both out of the corner of his eye, relaxing a little as he saw Avi smile at something Celka said, then laugh.

Avi had surprised him, shrugging off his mother's insult as unimportant, and had already gone back to visit Patia and Tawnie—though prudently when his mother was elsewhere on Hold Deck duty. He watched Avi talk to Celka, mind-fuddling until she looked around and smiled at him. That made Celka turn around, too: she waggled her fingers hello. Pov ignored her with lofty dignity and turned his gaze back to the wallscreen, guessing he was outnumbered again, this time on his own Sail Deck. It seemed to get worse as time went on.

Suits, he thought, and smiled as Avi snickered something to Celka and Celka snickered back.

An Earth freighter passed *Net* as she decelerated into the edges of the star system at 167 Tauri. Earth maintained a regular freighter traffic, carrying product back and forth across the long gap to the Pleiades. The mobile stations, though possessing a near self-sustaining environment, were still dependent upon their Earth employers for certain catalysts used in their cloud processing and the luxuries that made crewing a mobile station less of a stark frontier. The freighter sent a brief acknowledgment to *Net* as she passed, but continued on her way, obviously less interested in new cloudships than racing a schedule. Stefania settled *Net* comfortably into the freighter's wake several thousand kilometers behind her.

As *Net* came within visual range of the station, Pov began trimming back *Net*'s sails, preparing her for docking. As *Net* came still closer, Sailmaster Ceverny diffidently walked onto Sail Deck, too much a sailmaster to feel truly comfortable anywhere else. Ceverny fidgeted around the walls for a while, then finally sat down in the chair next to Pov to watch.

"Well, we're here," Pov said. He waved his hand expansively at the wallscreen, as if he, Pov Janusz, had arranged it personally. "The Pleiades, sir."

"We've *been* in the Pleiades for a week, Mr. Janusz," Ceverny corrected, deciding to get technical. "And, yes, I can see it's GradyBol."

"You're in a fine mood," Pov said. "Where's your sense of adventure, sir?"

Ceverny just smiled, rocking his chair a little.

Together they watched *Net* make her leisurely approach to the station, letting the freighter increase her lead. In the distance, GradyBol Station looked like a silvery toy spinning against the backdrop of a swirling dust cloud as 167 Tauri condensed its protoplanets.

EuroCom had stationed its principal processing station on the fringes of an infant double-star system a few light-years from Maia, just beyond the edge of the Veil. To build its station, according to a corporate press release, EuroCom had harvested several meteoroids plummeting around the outer system, using the waste lead and heavy silicates to build a huge slag wall a kilometer long between itself and Maia's hellish glare. Behind the slag wall, the wide torus of GradyBol floated in open space, slowly turning on its axis. In the center of the open ring floated GradyBol's huge processing facility, connected by permanent transport tubes to the habitat ring like spokes of a wheel.

As *Net* came within a thousand kilometers of the station, GradyBol sent a terse greeting and directed *Net* to one of the floating ship bays drifting beyond GradyBol on the other side of the slag wall. As *Net* rounded the broad slag wall, heading for the ship dock, Pov sighed. There, floating in space a half kilometer from the ship-bay arc, were *Arrow*'s two daughter ships, *Diana's Moon* and *Diana's Hound*, glinting dimly in the starlight.

Thaddeus Gray had rebuilt them both for size, adding a third tier of labs and residential quarters and a second engine assembly, then widened and deepened the wings and prow to handle the larger sails. *Diana's Moon* was easily twice *Net*'s size, yet retained the graceful lines of a cloudship in her sweeping prow and sail assemblies. She gleamed in the bluish shadows, every line perfect, a buzz of skyriders arcing gracefully around her as chiefs made their inspections. Pov took a data-track recording of the viewscreen, saving the images for later study. Several of the sail modifications were unfamiliar to him, so much so that he hadn't a clue as to function.

"Save me a copy, too," Ceverny muttered. "Look at that extension on the skysail, the one amidships. Why would they need an axial support there? For what?"

"I've heard," Pov said, "that *Arrow*'s sails at full extension are five kilometers wide."

"I've heard that, too," Ceverny said skeptically. "I'll believe it when I see it. I had no idea he'd built his ships this large."

"They're beautiful," Pov said enthusiastically.

"And they're our chief rivals at this mobile station, Mr. Janusz, so much so that *Arrow* owns the game." Ceverny scowled and crossed his arms, then glanced at Avi and Celka talking together excitedly at their stations. Both ladies had excellent sailmaster radar and immediately dropped the chatter when Ceverny's gaze swept across them.

"Hmph," Ceverny said, watching as Celka got busy again at her duties. He cleared his throat again, making it louder.

"What happened to diffident sailmaster?" Pov teased. "You know, 'I don't belong at this table' and 'maybe I should sit in the side chair.' Now you're prodding my staff about proper duty?"

Ceverny gave him a perfect imitation of Captain Rybak's frosty stare, one Pov had seen countless times, complete even to the exact cant of the eyebrows. Then Ceverny made it better as he slowly pursed his lips outward, considering what hells and other mayhem he could inflict on one Pov Janusz, the upstart. It was a formidable stare, one of the best.

Pov laughed. Ceverny tried to hold the fearsome stare and lost it.

"You young pup," Ceverny growled. "Leave me alone."

"Once a sailmaster, always a—"

"*Arrow* hasn't given us her maps yet, and we hardly

need two of us," Ceverny warned. "But I do admit," he added, his lips curving upward as he looked back at *Arrow*'s daughters, "that they are magnificent ships. You have the right of that. We must be prudent in showing we think so, or we may find ourselves working in GradyBol's laundries."

"They have laundries?" Avi asked. "As in tubs of water and acres of linen to wash?" She wrinkled her nose.

"I was speaking metaphorically, Ms. Selenko," Ceverny said. "And you leave me alone, too. I will not be plagued."

"We don't *know* that *Arrow* is hostile," Pov argued. "The Arabs might have made the virus, or maybe a mobile station."

"We'll find out." Ceverny crossed his arms and studied *Moon* and *Hound* with concentrated attention.

Net drifted to one of the floating ship bays and made her connections. Pov left the watch to Roja and went up to the admin level to meet Andreos. He found the captain in his office, Janina in a side chair looking upset, and Danil Tomasik, Milo's second on the chaffer staff, standing uncomfortably by the door. Pov nodded pleasantly at Danil.

"Hello, Danil." He looked at the other two faces and raised an eyebrow. "Where's Milo? Or should I ask?" Danil shifted his feet and shot a glance at Captain Andreos.

"I tried to persuade him, sir," Danil said, "but you know what he's thinking." Danil set his lips, looking unhappy and apprehensive and stubborn at the same time. Pov sat down slowly and looked at Janina for an explanation. She looked very angry.

"Milo refuses to go over to GradyBol," Janina explained tightly. "The captain's asking Danil to step in. Danil's willing, but mighty uncomfortable, as you can see." She gave a tight smile to Danil, who shifted his feet again. Then, abruptly, Danil sighed and looked down.

"Milo *refuses*?" Pov asked incredulously.

Janina scowled. "Milo has finally made up his mind, Pov. It took a while, but he's decided. He thinks we're illegal and won't have anything to do with making it worse." She turned to Andreos. "I doubt if you can argue him out of it. He can't stand being wrong. I warned you at T Tauri that it might come to this."

"We *need* Milo," Andreos said. "Danil doesn't have any experience as lead chaffer."

"Neither does Milo," Janina pointed out, "except *Net* talking to *Dance*. Molnar always took the lead with Tania's Ring." She spread her hands. "I say that if Milo wants to be left behind, we should let him have what he wants. How effective will he be as chaffer if he's reluctant?"

"There are other considerations, Janina," Andreos said. "Milo's still a *Net* captain—"

"I know. If we don't take him, it's a door we close for Milo and can't reopen." Janina did not sound sympathetic. "This will get around the ship, and *Net* won't tolerate a chaffer who won't defend her. Milo's misread the Slav loyalties on *Net,* sir. Those loyalties changed at T Tauri, and he can't accept it. He thinks if he holds out, I'll hazard, eventually the Slavs will turn to him and ask to go back to Tania's Ring. And, crazy as it sounds, I think he's trying to blackmail *you* into proving you'll stand up for him as you stood up for Pov." She shook her head. "I don't think he's rational, and I'm tired of the fighting."

"This is not the time to ask for that kind of proof, I agree," Andreos grumbled. "Nor the context." He sighed and rubbed his nose slowly.

Janina shifted her eyes to Danil. "You're it, Danil."

Danil raised his head and smiled tightly. "Not the way I like my promotions, I'll admit." A severity settled into the clean planes of his Slav face. He gave Pov a neutral glance, the appraisal unmistakable, then raked Janina, too, with that cold blue-eyed glance. Pov had always thought chaffers too sly for their own good, but he didn't know Danil Tomasik well: the man had always kept carefully in Milo's shadow, as Milo had once shadowed Molnar with Tania's Ring. On the ship, Danil had his Slav friends and didn't socialize much outside a small select circle—an intense type who could probably recite contracts word by word as easily as Milo. What had Danil learned in Milo's shadow? He gave Danil the cool appraisal back, and saw amusement light deep behind Danil's blue eyes. Different from Milo, Pov decided.

"I see no reason to compete with a sailmaster," Danil said softly as Andreos and Janina started for the door.

"I want a chaffer I can trust," Pov said, just as softly.

"Hard to find. Doesn't come with the breed."

"I keep looking, Danil. Maybe uselessly, I admit."

"Prob'ly so, sail." They smiled at each other.

Danil nodded for Pov to precede him out of the room, and they both followed Andreos to the docking lounge and its access to GradyBol's ship bay. Sailmaster Ceverny joined them there, asked by captain Andreos.

"You're my senior computer chief, Miska," Andreos told him. "I want some camouflage for you while you watch. Explaining a second sailmaster is a nuance I'd rather not give away, so let's keep it simpler."

"You and your magic tricks," Ceverny said indulgently.

"That they are." Andreos winked at Pov. "I'm also changing your name. *Arrow*'s people might be leery of anyone named Ceverny, given your reputation. How about Moktov?" Ceverny rolled his eyes.

As the dock chief opened the hatch door, Pov copied Andreos's cool behavior as the tall and lanky shipmaster managed to hang himself loosely on the empty air, casual-like. He looked like he was about to whistle, and Pov felt delighted all over again at Andreos's play-acting. *Net* was obviously loaded for bear, a nice European-type brown bear, mostly the German and other MittelEuropa variety.

Andreos's practice at coolness came in handy. *Net* had a welcoming committee.

The hatch irised open, and the *Net* captains found five sets of cool eyes looking at them as their owners waited in a phalanx in the station's ship-bay lounge. Captain Andreos moved forward easily, nodding his thanks to *Net*'s lounge chief, then stepped onto the carpeted deck, glancing around in interest, all of it probably an act. Pov schooled his own expression into noncommittal iron competence, and followed Andreos, with the others bringing up the rear.

"Good evening," Andreos said to the GradyBol contingent. A stocky, ruddy-faced man stood in the center of the group, his small feet set apart combatively. He gave Andreos a harried frown.

"I am Gunter Weigand, stationmaster of GradyBol," he announced in English, still the lingua franca of Earth's outposts, but did not offer his hand.

As the one language commonly used in all Earth nations, especially for commerce, English was taught in all colony schools, and *Ishtar's Fan* had included it in its own curriculum. Pov had learned English as a boy, but hadn't had much reason to use it since, not when *Net*'s computer routinely translated everything into Czech when the ship bought data. He tried a few English phrases in his head, and wasn't pleased with the result. Understanding was one thing, composing a sentence another. God, it'd been years. What did you expect? he chided himself. German just because GradyBol's mostly German? You don't speak German at all.

"Captain Leonidas Andreos of *Siduri's Net*," Andreos replied, switching languages smoothly. "May I introduce my officers, sirs. Sailmaster Pov Janusz, Holdmaster Janina Svoboda, my senior computer chief, Miska Moktov, and *Net*'s legal representative, Danil Tomasik."

Weigand nodded stiffly to each of them as Andreos introduced them. Pov suddenly noticed a dark-haired young man behind Weigand: he wore a stylized hound on his sleeve, bound about with woven gold, though the cut of his ship's uniform was subtly different from *Net*'s and a light tan rather than dark gray. A woman stood beside him in similar uniform, a half-moon on her sleeve. Both looked back at him coolly, their eyes level and detached.

So *Arrow*'s daughters get themselves invited on GradyBol's official greetings? Pov wondered.

"My aides," Weigand said, introducing two other men standing with him, but not the cloudship officers. And invisible? Pov wondered. Why? *Arrow* had made a golden reputation for herself and her two daughters: somehow Pov wanted to stand straighter and have a warmer reception than that in those two pairs of eyes, one brown, one blue, with their cool detachment. Weigand extracted a sheet of paper from his tunic pocket and unfolded it. Pov heard Danil's breath sigh softly behind him.

"As stationmaster of GradyBol," Weigand intoned harshly, reading from the paper, "it is my duty to inform you of a protest lodged with my corporate offices, accusing *Siduri's Net* of contract breach, theft, and forcible emigration of unwilling cloudship staff. It is also my duty to—"

"Who lodged the protest?" Andreos asked pleasantly, as if that might be a total mystery. Pov looked down at his boots for a moment to keep his expression solid, then looked up for Weigand's reaction. Weigand blinked.

"Who do you think?" Weigand asked sourly. "Your dramatic exit even made Earth's global datanet channels. You were in the news, *Net.*" Weigand's tone made making the news sound immoral.

"Indeed," Andreos said coolly. "Why don't you listen to both sides before you decide, stationmaster? We've been busy jumping three hundred lights and haven't had time to write up our side." He shrugged. "I do resent the 'theft' part. We tried to give *Dance* her share of our T Tauri cargo, but the Russkis fired on us. If we hadn't dumped some free quarks into our engines and jumped right then, we might have been hulled." He smiled slightly as the officers from *Diana's Hound* and *Diana's Moon* reacted, then exchanged a glance. "We hope to make arrangements with you for transfer of the credits due to *Dance*. For moral reasons, mostly," Andreos added virtuously. "After all, we owe a great deal to *Dance.*"

Danil sighed again, just loudly enough for Andreos to hear, sending his signals.

"T Tauri cargo?" the *Hound* officer asked sharply.

"Quarks?" added *Moon*, her full lips curving upward in a smile.

Weigand snorted impatiently and gestured them both to silence. "Let me finish reading this, please. So I can tell EuroCom I followed their damn order." Andreos waved calmly for him to proceed. "It is my duty," Weigand rumbled on, reading from his paper, "to inform you that lawsuits are pending and you are hereby enjoined to return to Epsilon Tauri for formal hearing. You are hereby ordered by *Dance* and the government of Tania's Ring to proceed immediately."

"Thank you. Is that it?"

"That's it." Weigand folded his paper and put it back in his pocket. He looked them all over for a long moment. "Are you and your officers free for dinner? Before you leave for the Hyades, that is."

"We weren't planning on leaving right away," Andreos said dryly. "More than enough time to share a meal."

"I'm just the stationmaster here, captain," Weigand said irritably. "I buy product, make things with it, and then ship what I make back to Earth. You cloudships can do what you want—at least until Tania's Ring has a legal order saying I have to embargo you. Until then, come with me. The last thing I need is celebrities," he added with some disgust.

"Are we, indeed?" Andreos asked, his tone cool.

"You still have to prove it to me," Weigand said gruffly and turned on his heel, stalking toward the interior port.

Andreos moved forward easily, gesturing the others to follow. Danil caught up with Andreos and Ceverny in a few strides, Janina and Pov following behind. The *Diana* officers fell into step on either side of Pov and Janina, bracketing them neatly.

"Rachel Hinsdell, Second Sail of *Diana's Moon*," the woman said in a melodious voice. "This is Joshua Quarle, *Hound*'s Third Helm." They walked down a long carpeted hallway, passing the door to the next ship bay. "Quarks?" she prompted.

"A secret," Janina said slowly in English, hesitating over her vowels. "But open to trade."

"I'll let Captain Talbot know," Rachel said, switching smoothly to Czech. Janina looked her surprise, as Rachel obviously intended. "I was liaison to *Ishtar's Jewel* when she sailed at Maia several years ago," Rachel explained. "I look forward to a reason for acquiring Greek, too." She glanced forward at Andreos.

"*Net* is a Slav ship," Janina said, a little sharply. "Ship-language is Czech, by common vote."

"I will remember that," Rachel said coolly, taking the rebuff in stride.

They approached a long window on the right, looking outward into space. Pov abruptly hesitated in midstep as *Moon* came into a close-up view, hovering in space, her sails shimmering in full extension as her Sail Deck ran a sail drill. He stopped to watch. Quarle just walked on, though Pov saw him glance over his shoulder. Rachel walked back to Pov.

"I didn't catch your name, sir," she said, though likely she had.

"Pov Janusz, sailmaster." He tore his eyes away from *Moon* and looked at Rachel Hinsdell. *Moon*'s Second Sail was classically beautiful, with wavy brown hair framing a heart-shaped face and cool blue eyes. She was tall and athletic, like Avi, with the same long lean legs and high carriage of the head. As he looked at her, her full lips turned up. Pov suddenly resented her cool detachment and the subtle insult she had taken from Janina's reproof.

"Ah, the famous Pov Janusz." Her smile was dry, with an edge to her voice.

Pov looked away from her back to *Moon*, wondering what rumors exactly had preceded them. "Just Pov Janusz," he said in Czech, not trusting his English to keep him from being more a fool in her eyes than he seemed to be already. Suddenly he felt caught in another web of irrelevancies, where judgments were made and labels pasted. "On our ships, sail is a quality of mind. The skyriders understand it best, I think. With such ships as *Arrow* and her daughters, I thought you might, too." He turned and gave her a level look, then walked around her to catch up with the others. He heard her hurry her footsteps, then rejoin him with a neat stride.

"Quality of mind?" she asked, a touch of humor in her voice. Pov abruptly decided he did not like being patronized, even by *Arrow*'s daughter ship.

"I'm sorry to see *Arrow* has lost it," he said coolly. Ahead of them, he saw Danil glance back as the group ahead turned around the bend. Pov repressed a sigh, knowing he wasn't helping *Net*'s chaffer by provoking *Moon*. He looked back at *Diana's Moon* through the receding window, catching a last glimpse. I'm not a chaffer, he thought resentfully. I don't usually enjoy this kind of game, of feint and posturing and saying something that isn't so. Odd that a gypsy doesn't, but I don't. Rachel touched his sleeve, stopping him.

"Gunter's dinners run to badly roasted meat dishes and spicy sauces," she said, tipping her head. "*Net* already seems ably represented, I think." She tugged at his sleeve and pulled him toward a closed ship-bay door, the last before the turning. "*Moon* has better fare."

"You want me to go with you to *Diana's Moon*?" he asked.

Rachel stopped and smiled. "I'll trade. You tell me your mission as part of that group," she said, flicking her fingers toward the turn of the corridor, "and I'll tell you mine." Pov looked into her eyes, on a level with his own, and saw the humor there, not mocking as he had thought, but something a little warmer. Maybe an act, maybe not.

"I'm supposed to steal your sail designs," he said. "If it comes up casually at dinner or something."

"Ah. I'm supposed to kidnap you so Captain Talbot can meet you. Joshua had a similar mission for *Hound*, one I fear may be disappointed."

"Janina? Not her. Janina's going wherever Captain Andreos goes."

"Joshua does have a task for himself," Rachel agreed. "But Gunter is determined to get your Captain Andreos first, to see if he wants him for anything, of course. He may not. My skyrider's in there. Do you want to come?"

Pov hesitated. For whatever reason, *Moon* wanted to talk privately with *Net,* away from Weigand's listening ears. Why? He decided to find out. "Yes, I do."

Rachel walked to a wall panel and pushed a few buttons, then spoke rapidly into it in English, too fast for him to catch. "I sent a message through the intrastation link," she explained as he raised an eyebrow. "It should catch up with them over at GradyBol, so your Captain Andreos won't wonder where you are."

"Thank you," he said.

"Shall we go?" She gestured politely toward the skyrider bay.

Chapter 10

Pov buckled himself into the skyrider seat behind Rachel and watched her power up the skyrider controls, then roll them toward the irising exterior port. A few moments later, the skyrider lifted through the port into free fall, giving him that odd floating sensation that changed with acceleration surges, not a reliable gravity field that kept "down" steady. He folded his fingers in his lap and watched the view, then caught himself from grabbing at the chair arms when Rachel took them into a power dive beneath the floating ship dock. She glanced back, her look unreadable, then set a straight course for the two American cloudships a kilometer away.

Beneath them, the wide torus of GradyBol Station slowly spun in space, the habitats of the ring linked by slender tubeways to the huge processing plant and labs in the open center. A few small craft hovered above and beneath the center plant, manipulating tins and other equipment, shadowed by the massive mountain of slag that shielded GradyBol. Above them, another smaller ship left the ship dock and headed quickly toward GradyBol, bearing the dinner party to Weigand's feast.

"I have doubts about this," Pov commented.

"That seems inconsistent," she said, not looking around.

"Why?"

"Well, according to rumor, *Net*'s sailmaster deliberately damaged *Dance* in a comet run to get access to T Tauri, where his ship reaped a fortune, thereafter absconding with same when *Dance* presented its righteous bill for negligence."

"The chronology is a little mixed up," he said equably. "*Dance* presented its bill before T Tauri, not later."

"*And,* it's said," Rachel said, "the Slav crews still squabble endlessly about national origin, despite twenty years of mixed crews, and it's the fact this sailmaster is a gypsy that irks *Dance* most."

"Do you have any gypsies in your crews?" he asked, dodging the comment.

"Not yet. We're thinking about acquiring some, though." He heard a ghost of a chuckle.

"Do you believe all these rumors?"

"Oh, I presume you didn't damage *Dance* deliberately, though Captain Talbot will probably ask you to deny it specifically. Too hard to hide it when it's deliberate."

"It wasn't subtly deliberate, either," he said, feeling the sting of the implicit accusation. She's trying to nettle you by calling you names, he decided. He smiled slightly and looked past her out the skyrider window. Calling me gypsy won't work, Rachel: it's what I am.

"Good to hear," Rachel said coolly, glancing at him. "Mostly Captain Talbot wants a look at you."

"Why?" he asked.

"Slavs are always touchy," she commented.

"I'm not a Slav. And don't confuse *Net* with *Ishtar's Jewel,* whatever *Jewel* has been doing here."

"Oh, we don't. *Jewel* mostly sits and mourns her luck—it seems *Net* has a different character, a certain gypsy character, one might even say."

"Nuts." Whatever Rachel's motives in this baiting, he decided not to play anymore.

Rachel glanced at him over her shoulder. "Regretting this trip so soon?" she asked.

"Not at all. Nice view. I just don't like games."

"This from a gypsy?" she asked drolly.

He looked at her levelly. "On my ship, I get less comment about that in a month than I've gotten from you in ten minutes. I don't apologize to my people for what I am, and I'm certainly not going to apologize to you." He shifted his view to look out the wallscreen over Rachel's controls. Rachel turned around, and the rest of the ride was spent in silence.

The skyrider docked neatly with *Diana's Moon,* and Rachel led him off the skydeck to an elevator, which whisked them upward. They rode upward looking at each other without expression. Rachel led the way down a short corridor to a side lounge high in the prow. On one wall, a window opened onto space, showing the array of Pleiades stars and the bulk of *Diana's Hound* nearby. Sitting on a couch in the corner, his feet propped on a cushioned ottoman, a middle-aged bearded man with silvering dark hair sat reading a report. He looked up as they entered.

"Sailmaster Pov Janusz," Rachel announced stiffly. The man glanced sharply at Rachel, then dropped his feet from the cushion and stood up. Like Rachel, he was tall, but carried his height with more pounds, a sturdy strength. His uniform fit him well, smooth over narrow hips, outlining his chest muscles, and he obviously took great care with his short beard, neatly trimmed. When Talbot flicked his eyes over Pov, much as Patia had raked Avi the other night, Pov decided he might not like *Moon*'s shipmaster. Talbot smiled confidently as he came forward.

"Shipmaster Christopher Talbot," he said, introducing himself, then waved Pov to a nearby seat. "Welcome to *Diana's Moon,* sir."

"Thank you," Pov said.

"How is your English? I'm sorry I don't speak Czech."

Something in Talbot's tone implied he didn't speak anything else, either, and was glad of it. Indeed, Pov thought, and responded by deliberately mangling his English. "My English is ... many years in past," he stumbled pitifully. "No need ..." He stopped as if in frustration, then gave Rachel a helpless look.

Rachel arched an eyebrow and opened her mouth to comment, then shut it quickly as Captain Talbot's glance raked her, too.

"As you have undoubtedly learned from your own shipmaster," Captain Talbot said without preamble, "a ship's captain must be aware of nuances, and I know my Second Sail quite well. On behalf of *Moon,* I apologize for whatever insult she has delivered. Translate that, Rachel, if you please." He glowered at Rachel.

Pov caught the gist and felt surprised Talbot had so misread his play-acting, then realized Talbot had picked up an entirely different script. Had he told Rachel to insult him, so that Talbot could now nobly protect his guest? Pov relaxed, feeling himself on familiar ground: hell, Talbot is playing this like a Rom—but not a very good one. Talbot should have checked the guest first. He should also have told Rachel.

Moon's Second Sail stumbled badly through the translation, obviously taken by surprise, then flushed as she stammered. Talbot looked at her sternly until she was done, then sniffed audibly and turned to Pov. Rachel's color heightened even more at the pointed rebuff. "I have two other officers who speak Czech," Talbot said coldly. "Do you wish another translator? Translate *that,* too, Rachel." The order crackled through the room.

You bastard, Pov thought angrily when Rachel stammered again, still badly off balance. As Rachel finished, Pov threw up his hands in astonished protest. "Stop, please. Not her . . . fault. Please."

He turned to Rachel and spoke rapid Czech. "I don't know what's between you two, Rachel, but I'm suddenly looped into that and whatever agenda your captain has for this visit. But I do *not* wish your embarrassment." Rachel frowned uncertainly. "Tell him," Pov said, pointing at Captain Talbot, "that I am not offended. And tell him I do not object to your translating." Rachel hesitated. "Tell him, please."

Captain Talbot listened to the translation, then flicked his eyes once between Rachel and Pov, frowning. Then he turned and reseated himself on the couch and gestured to two other chairs nearby. "Please sit down," he said pleasantly.

Pov nodded and waited until Rachel sat down in one chair, then took his own seat in the other. He watched as Talbot put his report on a side table and propped his feet again.

"Why did I ask you over here?" Captain Talbot said lazily, though Pov had not asked him anything of the kind. "You're probably wondering." Rachel translated stiffly.

"And you're probably wondering why I came," Pov replied in Czech, then waited as Rachel translated again.

Captain Talbot smiled. "I agree it's unusual. Did you ask your shipmaster first?" His tone made it clear that such failures never happened on *Diana's Moon*, not with Captain Talbot in command.

"No. I was knocked to the floor and tied up before I noticed, practically." Rachel shot him a dirty look. "You can modify that any way you want," he told her genially. She translated, keeping the comment pretty much as he stated it. Captain Talbot's smile only widened.

"So you are Pov Janusz. The gypsy sailmaster."

Pov narrowed his eyes slightly. "The gypsy doesn't play that much of a role, except when I get into trouble for some reason. I prefer it that way." He saw Talbot puzzle over that a moment, then move on.

"Tell me about T Tauri," Talbot said.

"Show me your sails," Pov riposted. "I need some help with the higher dust ratios."

"Oh, not that much. You apparently did a cloud run in the Veil, and got through it without major hull damage. My congratulations." Pov looked his question when Rachel translated. "We pick up news from freighters and other places," she explained. "But not recently," she added and looked bland. "He's just guessing." Her lips turned up slightly.

"Freighter news? For a price?" he countered, as if he had guessed back. Rachel calmly translated it.

"Everything has a price. Like a tale of T Tauri data for modified field phasing to handle Pleiades dust."

"So what will you give us for what really happened at Tania's Ring?"

"Dinner?"

Pov shrugged, not impressed.

"Or we might buy some of your tritium. We noticed your extra hold containers, and, of course, some news of your success at T Tauri preceded you."

He waited for Rachel to translate, nodding his respectful compliments. "T Tauri wasn't that hard," Rachel said, amplifying again. Her eyes glinted.

"Most of the credits would go back to *Dance,*" Pov said carefully.

"To stay legal?" Captain Talbot looked amused.

"No. To save *Dance* from herself."

"Now that's an intriguing comment, one I'd like to follow up when you're ready. You should be aware that GradyBol may have difficulty buying your extra tritium. The corporate pressure has started: either Tania's Ring has more friends on Earth than expected or the Russkis are being very loud."

"Probably the latter," Rachel added in Czech. "EuroCom couldn't care less about the Hyades. And that's the end of your favors, sail." She smiled slightly.

Pov nodded, then wrinkled his eyebrows in puzzlement, playing it onward. "Then why did Stationmaster Weigand invite *Net* to dinner?" he asked.

"To buy time," Talbot said expansively, waving his hand. "Dinner is a small price for what time could give him. He has to figure a way around your notoriety and its effect on corporate blood-pressure levels so *he* can get your extra tritium."

"Tritium is still the main exchange, even here?"

"Tritium buys power, of several kinds."

"Why would *Arrow* want power, of any kind?"

Captain Talbot smiled, a wolfish look on his face. "Oh, we have reasons."

"You want to buy GradyBol, maybe," Pov guessed, trying to provoke him.

"I'm not giving you three guesses and the revelation, Mr. Janusz, whatever fairy tale you're wandering into. But why did I invite you? We couldn't get Captain Andreos personally—snatching him from Weigand would be noisy and too much trouble for the probable rewards. So I sent Rachel and Captain Ingram sent her officer to try to detach someone junior, anybody but the chaffer, who'd be even harder to detach. Someone like you, though I didn't expect to pick up *Net*'s sailmaster himself. Will *Hound* have any luck in snagging the other one?"

"Probably not."

"I see. Ah, well." Talbot got up and walked easily to a sideboard, opened a cabinet, and poured himself a drink from a wine carafe inside, then set two other glasses on the sideboard. "I have fruit juice, wine, hard liquor, water. Rachel, will you offer him a drink?"

"The juice is heavily drugged," Rachel told Pov in Czech. "So's the wine. We've got anthrax incubating in the Scotch and ptomaine in the water. Your choice."

"I'll take whatever you're having," he answered warily.

"Make it anthrax, sir," Rachel said in English. Captain Talbot gave her an odd look. "Scotch," Rachel amended.

"I wish I were recording this," Captain Talbot said distantly. "Then later, after I get the computer translation, we could have a talk ourselves, in private, you and I."

"He thinks you're recording it, anyway," Rachel said pertly, then translated both comments into Czech for Pov's benefit.

"Is he?" Pov asked.

"No," Rachel said levelly. "You use the other room for that, but he wanted to be comfortable on cushions."

Captain Talbot brought over the glasses and handed one to Pov and Rachel, then reseated himself comfortably. "To *Siduri's Net*," he saluted, raising his glass.

Pov rose to his feet and clicked his heels softly, then returned the salute. "To *Diana's Moon*." He reseated himself, then saw Rachel eyeing him.

"Are all Slavs so well-mannered?" she asked. "Formal bow and all?"

"Yes—and I'm not a Slav, thank you."

"You have a Slavic surname."

"Borrowed long ago, I assure you. Gypsies don't need last names to know who we are." He toasted her sardonically with his glass and saw her eyes dance with amusement. Captain Talbot looked at Rachel inquiringly, and Rachel hesitated a moment before translating.

"You have a problem with his being gypsy, Second Sail?" Talbot asked, back on the script he and Rachel had left behind some time ago. A faint line appeared between Talbot's brows as Rachel merely looked back at him, refusing to play. "My apologies again, shipmaster," Talbot intoned, then put on a genial look as he stabbed his sail officer again. "She's young." Rachel translated cooly.

Pov nodded back, and wondered how this man had ever made shipmaster.

Maybe Americans just behaved differently from normal people, he thought, eyeing them both. The Russkis had thought so for centuries, Sergei said, and never had figured out the rules, for all their trying.

Captain Talbot gave him an artificial smile, and Pov suddenly saw himself through his eyes, as young as Rachel, and foreign, eager, apparently a little stupid to fall so easily into Rachel's gambit. Pov's respectful bow had only confirmed what Talbot expected. That irked him, but the gypsies had made a living off such gaje condescension, and so could *Net*. Accustomed to *Arrow*'s preeminent position for two decades, Talbot had misgauged Pov's youth and had made a mistake in letting him see it. He had also misjudged Rachel.

As Captain Talbot chatted onward, talking carelessly about GradyBol and its stationmaster and the corporate politics that acted behind the scenes, Pov listened politely to Rachel's translations, catching more of the meaning from the captain himself as Talbot unwittingly brushed up more of Pov's English through the exposure. Talbot offered him another drink; he declined.

"So," Talbot said at last, putting his own glass on the table. "Will *Net* sell us some tritium?"

"That's not for me to negotiate, captain."

"But you'll let Captain Andreos know." Talbot smiled at him.

"Of course." Pov smiled back, copying the exact nuances of that knowing smile, and saw a flicker of uncertainty in Talbot's eyes. Then it was gone and Talbot rose to his feet.

"Good. Now I'm sure you'd like a tour of the ship. Rachel can guide you."

Pov put his own glass down and stood up, then opened his mouth, but Captain Talbot was already walking out of the room. He watched Talbot go, then looked at Rachel.

"Do you really want a tour?" she asked wryly.

"Do I get to look at your sail specs and copy what I like?"

She shook her head. "No, I don't think the captain had exactly that in mind. And I already paid back your favor, more than I should have, so don't cajole me." She looked uncomfortable, obviously regretting what she had done, minor as it was.

"Then I'll pass on the tour. Thanks."

Rachel made a face and headed for the door.

Pov caught up with her in the corridor and waited for some useful noise. As they passed a rattling air vent, he touched her sleeve. "Let me balance some of that extra favor," he said. "Come see *Net.*"

Startled, Rachel glanced at him, then looked up at the vent and laughed. "Picking up a gullible junior officer to pump for data?" She shook her head. "That talk wasn't recorded. Honest. I'm not in any trouble."

"You're sure? He doesn't seem the type to understand the nuances."

Rachel sighed. "Yes, I'm sure. I wouldn't mind absconding, but he'd know I wasn't fooled. As you weren't, sir. He told me to insult you, soften you up. I'm sorry."

"I know. And you got nicely even, with a little help from me." He smiled down at her. "Don't worry. I won't misuse it."

She shrugged tiredly, not wholly convinced. "Later, when the dust settles, let me come visit *Net.* I would like to repair some of *our* beginning, sir."

"I'd like that."

The ride back to the ship dock was easier, with Rachel making small talk, to which Pov responded in kind. At *Net*'s ship-dock doorway, she offered her hand. "I hope we meet again, sir."

"I'm sure we will. Goodbye."

"Goodbye."

He watched her walk back to the skyrider dock bay, the door hissing shut behind her. He turned around and watched GradyBol rotate for a while, then walked down to the next window and watched *Moon.* When the *Net* party still had not returned after an hour, Pov ambled back to *Net* and went up to Andreos's office.

He settled onto a couch in the small waiting room on the admin level, declining anxious offers from Temya for this and that, finally telling her that everything was fine, thank you, and she should please do her best to ignore him.

It was another hour before Captain Andreos returned, Danil in tow. Danil looked cautiously displeased, Pov decided, and wondered why. Andreos gave Pov an unreadable look and walked right on past without a word, then turned into his office. Pov crossed his leg over his knee and yawned at Danil, then watched Danil fight to hold his expression at the byplay.

Andreos had left his door open, probably to hear. Pov admired the niceties of Andreos's balancing—Pov disappearing from a ship delegation without asking, and Pov disappearing with *Moon*'s officer. Split the difference by walking by but leaving the door open. Pov split his own difference and stayed where he was. Danil sat down on the couch beside him and stretched out his legs.

"Nice conversation at the dinner?" Pov asked casually, lacing his fingers over his knee.

"About that—about *all* that was. Weigand's gruffness and bluster is probably real. I doubt he's really bothered by his order from headquarters—corporate heads tend to grandstand for politics' sake, and Weigand knows it. He spent most of the dinner needling Captain Andreos." He made a gesture at Andreos's door. "The captain dodged neatly every time," Danil added, speaking louder so it carried, doing his chaffer's work. "He's good at that."

Pov chuckled. Andreos did not come out of his office.

Danil frowned irritably at the open door. "I think this is called an impasse," he muttered.

"You'll get used to how Andreos and I interact. Don't worry about it. Right now I'm just doing what a good junior captain does—giving him someone to grump at when we've apparently just been snubbed by GradyBol, too. On *Diana's Moon,* I was a grungy junior officer that *Moon*'s captain wanted to pump for data."

Danil's eyebrows lifted. "Were you indeed?"

"That *Hound* officer was supposed to snatch Janina, another grungy junior officer for *Hound* to pump. Did it work?"

"Janina has more sense," Danil grumbled.

"Is that statement for real or for show?"

"What'd they want?" Danil asked.

"Our tritium. Can you think of any reason why they want *more* tritium?" Danil thought for a moment, then shook his head. "Also, *Arrow* doesn't think much of us." Pov frowned reflectively. "It wasn't personal to me—I wasn't really a 'person' to Captain Talbot, more a data carrier he expected to access. I offered to trade tritium for sail designs—he didn't like that, but didn't say no. I offered to trade what really happened at Tania's Ring, and he got cute. I don't think they care. It was ..." He hesitated, sorting it all again in his mind. "Careless, as if it really didn't matter. How do you read that?"

"Too used to success? Anti-Slav?" Danil suggested. "Maybe anti-gypsy?" he added uncomfortably. "Sorry."

Pov shook his head. "Gypsy didn't mean anything to them. They used the label only as a tactic. Talbot was more *amused* by me than anything else, without being particularly insulting about it. He didn't see much in me that matched the rumors, and that amused him even more. I've been sitting here trying to decide if I'm insulted." Pov smiled. "I think I'll be amused."

They heard a large thump in Andreos's office.

"His chair's been unstable ever since those microjumps," Danil offered, raising his voice again. He tsked. "Tough on furniture."

"It's a theory," Pov agreed.

Andreos appeared in his doorway a moment later, glaring at them both. "You worry too much," Danil said to him severely. "Pov is good for you."

"I won't comment on that," Andreos grunted and disappeared, splitting his difference again.

Pov smiled, and stayed where he was. "What are we going to do next?" he asked Danil.

"Go see TriPower. The hell with GradyBol." Danil got up, shrugged ambiguously, and wandered off toward the elevator. Pov waited another minute, and then strolled into Andreos's office and sat down.

Andreos studied him for a long moment. "Before, you didn't push at me this way."

"Before, I thought being a shipmaster was sort of easy, watching you in action. Now I'm not so sure." He smiled at Andreos. "*Moon* came after me: I thought it a good idea to cooperate. Was I wrong?"

"No, I suppose not."

Pov watched Andreos's face as it shifted from its pretended outrage to its very real disappointment. "*Arrow,*" Andreos grunted. Andreos had hoped for much from *Arrow,* more than he'd probably admit. A long nasty meal with GradyBol's stationmaster hadn't filled the gap. Pov smiled at him with sympathy.

"We can get along without them, sir," he said. "*Moon's* captain deliberately humiliated his sail officer in front of me, just to get on my good side."

"Indeed?" Andreos grunted, then scowled again. "Loyalty isn't the only criterion, Pov. We've discussed that issue before."

"He also missed every nuance possible. Whoever set him a task either overestimated him or underestimated us." He shrugged. "Maybe it was both. Interesting."

"You're as disappointed as I am," Andreos said accusingly. "Don't pretend you aren't."

"They don't need us, sir. It's probably as simple as that."

"Did they ask about T Tauri?"

"Hadn't heard much about it, didn't ask much. Rachel picked up on the quarks, but Talbot lumped it in with celebrity gypsy and missed it." Pov shrugged. "It was like talking sails to a chaffer—no connection. Though I admit Danil has surprised me," he added.

"You two mesh well," Andreos said absently. "If they're not really interested in us, why do you think you got invited to *Moon?*" He frowned. "I sure the hell don't know why I was invited to GradyBol."

"We're still an unknown, maybe. Curiosity. Nudging Weigand. Nudging *Arrow.* Maybe nudging you. It's a different mix from *Dance* and Bukharin. At Tania's Ring, we knew Bukharin was a wolf chasing the sleigh. He never had much reason to hide it, us being system-bound, anyway. Here it's just ..." He stopped, thinking more about it. "Like Athena badgering Milo? No, not that much of an edge to it."

"Like having a market cornered and not worried about it?" Andreos suggested.

"Like having it cornered for twenty years and worrying about something else, maybe."

"Worried about what?"

"Talbot wouldn't say."

"Hmph." Andreos scowled.

"Danil's right, sir," Pov said, spreading his hands. "Let's go to TriPower. Weigand won't buy our tritium until EuroCom decides what to do about Bukharin's complaint—or so he says. *Arrow*'s daughters would buy it, but with Weigand stalling, it's a buyer's market at a steep discount. They could both let us dangle here for a week, playing their games."

"So we just up and leave?" Andreos asked dubiously. He thought about that, juggling the nuances.

"It's a great gypsy tactic. 'The hell with you' always is. The family's fighting? So leave town for a while and let it calm down. The gaje are impossible? Go find some better gaje down the road. It's not exactly a friendly act to pounce on a junior captain and lead him off to be gulled."

"I don't like being patronized, either," Andreos grunted. They looked at each other ironically, then Pov saw Andreos start to smile. "Hell, I'm damn irritated. Who do they think they are? We sit here with the next ship drive in our treasure box and they sniff."

"I bet 'Chief Moktov' agrees with me. What did Ceverny say?"

"He said Bukharins seem to exist everywhere, in various levels of intelligence." Andreos grinned. "Weigand didn't even notice him. For him, computer chiefs just run the machinery, and he treated Janina like a *hausfrau*, which irked Janina, too. So I'm hearing the consensus, I suppose." He tapped his fingers on the table, looking it over again. "And if TriPower's the same, there's always the Japanese and AmTel. *Jewel* would know best, if we can find her."

Pov waved his hand expansively. "*Jewel* has maps, too. Who needs *Arrow* if *Jewel* will share? It's a whole new game here, sir. And we've got a great hand of cards that might give Thaddeus Gray his run at Orion's Nebula. He just doesn't know it yet." He smiled. "Maybe eventually we'll tell him. Talbot surely doesn't know—and he should have found out."

Andreos chuckled. "Oh, we'll tell them eventually—but not quite yet, I think. I think I'll stay irritated for a while. What about *Moon*'s sail officer? Same type?"

"No. She got even with Talbot, in a minor way. I helped."

"I'm sure you did. I know you."

Pov laced his fingers behind his head and rocked his chair, timing it, then smiled at Andreos lazily. "Then I invited her to visit *Net*. She was smart enough to say no."

Andreos tipped back his head and guffawed.

The next day *Net* blandly paid her docking fee to the dockmaster and left GradyBol, offering no explanations but many empty courtesies as she radioed goodbye, and not bothering to tell either GradyBol or *Arrow*'s daughters where she might be going. Ten minutes later, *Net* received a brisk contact signal from GradyBol, stationmaster calling *Net*, please respond. Andreos ignored it.

"Lay your course, Helm," he told Stefania.

For *Net*'s initial course away from GradyBol, Andreos had pointed *Net* directly at Lucifer's Deep, just to suggest certain people waste time on a nonsense fact. When *Net* was beyond GradyBol's scanning range, Stefania would shift course for TriPower.

"First course laid in, sir," Stefania said, a little nervously. "We are trimming the ship." She turned her head away from the interlink to watch the helm screens as the computer laid the course. "And launch, sirs."

Net's engines flared, accelerating her forward.

Chapter 11

Pov went to visit Athena in the hospital and brought her up on the news. Gregori had gone off to check on the girls, and Pov was sitting in Gregori's chair, one leg crossed casually across his knee as he told her the entire story, dinner and Talbot both. Athena watched him, amused, as he waved his arms, acting out the parts.

"Is this funny?" he asked when he had finished, pretending to be indignant. She looked much better today, less gaunt and with more color in her face.

"Come here," she demanded, holding out her arms.

He got up and walked over to the bed. She pulled him down and kissed him soundly. "Thank you," she said softly as he straightened and smiled at her awkwardly. "Thank you, Pov."

"For what?"

"For acting like a skyrider. Watch my jets." She chuckled. He looked down at her, mildly baffled and showing it. "No, I'm not losing my mind. I'm sure Talbot wasn't quite that stupid or Weigand quite that nasty. And I love you for telling me all about it."

"You didn't see either of them, Athena. Don't jump to conclusions."

"You shouldn't, either. Don't you realize what happened? We got second string because they expected a pushover: next time they'll be sure to use their first." She dimpled. "And leaving without a word was just perfect."

"I still fell off at the last turn, I think." He frowned at her.

"You and Andreos: it's all instinct, every time. You can give all your logical reasons, your careful analyses of personality, your measure of this and that, but you end up protecting *Net* every time. This is skyrider stuff, Pov: new kid in the corridor, swagger, strut, watch my exhaust. That's all it is."

"I thought it was commerce," he said lightly, pleased to see her smile.

"Oh, you! You know exactly what I'm talking about."

He grinned. "They thought I'd get offended when they called me a gypsy."

She made a rude noise. "Maybe they'll try to call me a Greek. It's about as reasonable."

"You're looking better. Good to see."

"Just keeping my promise." She smiled at him. "Will you do me a favor? I'm wheedling now, so get prepared."

"What?" he asked warily.

"Go talk to Milo. Will you? Don't let him go back to *Dance*. Please, Pov." She sighed. "I can't do it. I would, but I can't." She looked down at herself angrily, thin and pale. "Look at me, the idiot I am who put myself here."

"Neutron Woman," he agreed.

"That's me," she said, and he saw the shine of tears in her eyes. "Please."

"Of course," he said simply. "I don't know if he'll listen."

"Somebody should try. Janina won't: she's too angry at him for embarrassing the Slavs. Captain Andreos won't: Milo would misinterpret it and keep pushing the wrong way. That leaves you or me." She gave him a rueful smile. "And it's not me. Life does deal us some lessons, even ones we don't think we need. I'm learning I'm mortal and can use some help sometimes. Milo might need to know that, too."

"Please don't be too mortal," he said.

"Oh, Medical has good things to say, but I agree nobody's happy with my limping along. I'm supposed to get *cured*, after all: it's the way things work. Stars shine, planets orbit, hydrogen spins into sails—and when Medical applies its treatment, you get cured, damn it. Dr. Cherinsky isn't happy. But I'm learning something new. I'm only twenty-eight, Pov. I've been thinking about not seeing Marisa get much older."

"Athena—"

"My, what I've done in twenty-eight years," she said musingly, as if she hadn't heard him. "Pilotmaster of a cloudship, Gregori to love me as he does, three strong girls to carry on, good friends, a place I've made for myself. I ask myself, 'Well, can't that be enough?' If it has to be, of course—and I say no. No, it's not enough." She took his hand again, giving him a gentle squeeze. "Pov, if I have anything to say about it, and I have a lot to say, I am not going to die, not now." Their eyes met suddenly and locked.

"The chemistry still goes on, doesn't it?" she said softly. "Maybe yes, maybe no, I have Gregori, you have Avi."

Pov smiled. "It's that parallel reality that's bothering us, the one where it's only you and me, Athena. You know, the one where the gypsies didn't switch you with a gaje baby and the Janusz never went aboard *Fan.*" He waved his hand. "On that other Perikles you and I wander the roads together, town to town, with a pack of kids shrieking around the wagon."

"Is *that* what it is?" Athena dimpled.

"Absolutely."

She squeezed his hand hard, then released it. "Try not to worry about me too much, Pov."

"I'll try, Helm."

Pov exited the elevator on the portside residential level near Milo's apartment. He checked the wall register for the number and walked down the corridor, then turned left. Though apartment groupings weren't formally segregated, a few areas of the ship were entirely Slav, like this one. He nodded genially to several passersby, and stopped once to chat briefly with a skydeck subchief who greeted him, another First-Ship Slav wanting to socialize. He turned another corner and reached Milo's corridor, found his door.

He pushed the door button. When Milo opened the door, his eyes opened wide. Pov was probably the last person Milo thought to see, given Milo's open jealousy of Pov's status with Andreos. It was a wound never healed between them, badly complicated by Milo's devious personality. Milo blinked, then flushed with sudden anger.

"Come to gloat?" he snapped and reached for the door control. Pov walked forward, making him step back involuntarily.

"No," he said firmly. "Not at all."

On the couch in the living room, Milo's wife looked pale, her hands busy with some needlework in her lap. Fair-skinned, with flaxen hair, and pretty in a weak way, Pauli Cieslak was the daughter of a First-Ship Slav, an unquestioned part of *Dance*'s aristocracy. Milo had married well by marrying Pauli, though her relatives had sometimes whispered the marriage was beneath her, undermining the higher Slav status Milo had sought by courting her. As Pov took another step into the room, Pauli got up to leave.

"Please stay," Pov said. "This concerns both of you."

"I'd rather not," Pauli said stiffly and walked into the bedroom. Milo tightened his lips as he watched her go. Pov walked on past Milo, making him turn around.

"This is Athena's idea," Pov said, "but I agree with what she wants."

"And that is?" Milo asked sourly, poised for a fight.

"Stay with *Net*, Milo," Pov said. "Don't leave us."

Milo gave a bark of sardonic laughter. "You've *got* to be kidding. What kind of farce is this?"

"No farce," Pov said. "Come on, Milo. You know people well enough to know that Athena and I share a certain stupidity about people. Some would call it that. We get stubborn."

Milo hesitated, then decided to glare at Pov. "No thanks. Go be stupid about somebody else. I've got a free choice about leaving. I don't appreciate the pressure."

"I'm sure you don't," Pov said reasonably. "But what kind of life would you have on *Dance,* assuming *Dance* takes you back? Molnar won't retire for years, and you aren't guaranteed your old rank of Second Chaffer—Mihaly has that now. What will Pauli's First-Ship Slavs think of you, the chaffer who couldn't keep *Net* in line? What will Pauli's relatives do to you, with their sad faces about their daughter's bad choice, the careless ostracism, the forgetting you're there, the not-invites to family councils? And that assumes *Dance* keeps her independence: she might not. It'll be worse if *Dance* has to sell herself to Tania's Ring."

"Stop it," Milo said harshly. "Don't you think I know all that? Don't you—" He broke off and turned away, clenching his fists.

"Milo," Pov said, "stay with us. I am asking. Athena is asking."

"He promoted Danil over me," Milo whispered.

"What was he supposed to do? You defied him in public. You've opposed him ever since the ship voted for T Tauri. He put up with it for weeks, gave you every opportunity to relent. And after all that, when the ship *needed* you at GradyBol, you refused to go. You denied *Net*. Even if he wanted to, he couldn't keep you as chaffer. Not after that."

"Shut up."

"Facts, Milo. He has to think about the ship. But *we*, Athena and I, don't have to think about all the ship, as he does: we think just about ourselves and you. This was Athena's idea to ask. I assumed it'd be no use. Prove me wrong."

Milo turned around and stared at him. "Deft, sailmaster. Very deft. Ever thought of trying another trade?"

Pov smiled thinly, refusing to rise to the bait, and wondered if Milo hated him, truly hated him. Probably. "Milo, don't you see? Here we are in the Pleiades, where everything's open, not set by *Dance* and Bukharin. Here we are, scooting off to TriPower because we don't like the cut of Weigand's suit. *Arrow*'s daughters wanted to buy our tritium, but won't say why. *Jewel*'s over at Alcyone. Maybe we'll go visit her and set up a two-ship alliance to confound them all. God, what fun for a chaffer, all these devious plots and strategies."

"*Arrow* wanted to buy our tritium?" Milo asked, surprised. "Why?"

"Intrigued? Good."

Milo stared at him, then bit his lip uncertainly, his eyes

darting at the bedroom. "Pauli?" he called. "Will you come out here?"

Pauli appeared in the doorway, looking distant, the baby balanced on her hip. "Why?" she asked.

"What do you want to do? Go back or stay?"

"I will follow whatever you choose, Milo," Pauli said, her lip trembling. She absently juggled the baby as it squirmed. "It's not mine to say."

"Why not?" Milo asked impatiently. "I'm asking *you,* Pauli."

"You just want to give in to them, and this way you can blame me for it later," Pauli said, lifting her chin. "I put up with a lot of things living with you, Milo Cieslak, but living with you for three years has taught me a little about *strategies.*" She gave Pov a dirty look.

Milo turned fully to face her, with a desperation on his face he didn't bother to hide. "I promise I won't, Pauli. I promise. But what do *you* want to do, Pauli?" he pleaded. "You wouldn't tell me, when I asked all the times before. Please?"

Pov shifted uncomfortably, suddenly understanding a great deal about Milo when a sweet malice flickered in Pauli's eyes. She said nothing for a moment, staring at Milo, then shifted the baby again. "It is not mine to say," she answered, her voice laced with bitterness.

Pov abruptly made a disgusted sound. "What you *should* do, Milo," he declared, "is divorce this woman, ship her back to *Dance,* and marry yourself a good Greek girl, one who'll appreciate you as you deserve." He advanced on Pauli, who retreated into the bedroom in open alarm. "Pauli, I swear to God, if you do not stand behind your husband on this, you'll pay for it the rest of your lives. What kind of answer was *that*?"

"Get away from me," Pauli cried, clutching the baby to her.

Pov stopped short and took a deep breath. He didn't mean to frighten her, however angry he felt. "You two need marital counseling," he told her, his tone milder, "but I don't have the training. Can't you see that if you won't say, he wonders if it's what you want, and can't back down?"

"Pov," Milo said crossly, "leave her alone."

Pov ignored him. "Pauli," he said softly, "it won't be the same if you go back. You'll be married to a loser, with all those female relatives pitying you."

"He's not a loser!" Pauli said angrily.

"And all those uppity relatives won't care what you think about it, either." Pov spread his hands. "*Net*'s your home now, Pauli. *We* are your family, not *Dance*'s First-Ship aristocracy. Please stay." Pov let his hands drop and waited, looking at Pauli.

Pauli's eyes shifted beyond him to Milo. "Could you stay?" she asked. "Could you stay and be happy?"

Milo looked down at the floor for a long moment, considering it.

"No," he said sadly, almost wonderingly. "I'm not an adventurer like you, Pov. I never have been. I can't risk everything as you do, as *Net* does. It's just that simple. Even if I apologized and kept my rank somehow, it'd happen again." He sighed.

"Then think of something else," Pov suggested. "Anything but *Dance*."

"Another cloudship? Oh, sure. All that's out here are ships and mobile stations."

"So? What about a mobile station?"

Milo lifted his eyes and stared at him.

"The mobile stations need good lawyers," Pov said. "Patents, freighter contracts, personnel, intercompany negotiations. As long as you didn't deal directly against *Net*'s affairs, I think Andreos wouldn't invoke the anticompetition clause. And if we can build a deal with TriPower or another station, you could be liaison, valuable to both sides because you know *Net*. A whole new brand of law, Milo."

Milo frowned, but his dark eyes were interested. "Would Andreos recommend me?"

"Of course he would, you idiot." Pov threw up his hands. "How can you even doubt that?"

"He's right, you know," Pauli said softly, "how it would be back on *Dance*." For Pauli, Pov supposed sadly, that was the major item, status. Not that her husband was happy, not really. Not wanting a life with a goal. Only what certain Slav people thought of her personally, with herself as only a reflection of her husband and her important Slav relatives. Suddenly he pitied them both, especially Pauli.

Milo scowled again, then put his hands in his pockets and rocked slowly on his heels, his clever mind turning again. He thought about it, then looked at Pauli. "We'll talk about it. Thanks."

"Anytime, Milo."

Milo smiled bitterly and stepped to one side, obviously inviting Pov out. "Goodbye, sailmaster," he said softly, his dark eyes glittering.

Pov nodded, knowing it was the end between them, whatever Milo did with himself. "Goodbye, Milo."

He left and heard the door sigh shut behind him.

Pov walked up to Sail Deck and chatted with Tully for a while, then took his mother out of the holding file and went to see Karoly in the chemlabs. He found his oldest cousin in a small side lab down a corridor, bent over one of several flasks as he watched something angrily crimson bubble down a pipette. Pov pulled up a lab stool and sat down, then propped a foot on the stool's cross strut to copy Karoly's comfortable slouch.

A handsome dark-haired man in his forties, Karoly had steadily risen in the chemlab ranks during his nearly twenty years abroad the cloudships, first on *Fan,* then to a middle ranking on *Dance,* and now to senior chemist on *Net,* specializing in carbon distillation. The Pleiades gasclouds had given him an entirely new arena, and the chemists were working as much overtime as the physics labs right now, analyzing the catch of *Net*'s Maia run. Karoly had a founder's share in several patents *Net* had sold to Tania's Ring, a nest egg against the future that Margareta Janusz counted as part of the tribe's available wealth. Likely Karoly intended the patents more as an inheritance for his two sons, but he found it easier to wait until arguments had a point. It was Karoly's style in the family, quite different from Pov's prickly relationship with his mother. Karoly spent a lot of time watching odd substances bubble in flasks or swirl in vacuum chambers:

maybe it gave him a stolid patience about outwaiting that Pov had never learned.

Karoly had always taken the role of older brother to his cousins, including Pov, especially after his young wife had died from complications during their second son's birth. Maternity deaths were rare on the cloudships, but Terike's blood poisoning had moved too fast, complicated by her failure to respond to the available antibiotics. Cam had survived, growing into a vigorous small boy and an even more active teenager, but Karoly had never remarried, even when a Perikles family had offered. Pov had always wondered why, if Karoly even knew, but Karoly had gotten used to his widower life as the years passed, and seemed content.

Pov watched his cousin's face as Karoly's dark eyes flicked steadily between the pipette and the computer screen mounted beside the lab hardware, intent on his work. After several tedious minutes, Karoly punched some readings into the computer, then glanced at him in acknowledgment. "Afternoon, Pov."

"Hello yourself. Carbon radicals?" Pov asked, motioning politely at the pressurized flask.

Karoly shook his head. "More than a radical. It's a complex molecule, over a hundred atoms, with structure enough to be a partial protein. I'm trying to encourage it along to see what'll add to itself." He smiled. "Maybe I can build a germ."

"Oh, sure," Pov said skeptically. They watched the flask bubble some more.

"Nice to see you," Karoly said, prompting him.

"Kate won't give him up, Karoly. They need help."

Karoly straightened his shoulders, then looked at Pov and sighed. "You're sure she won't?"

"Absolutely."

"I feared so. Sergei says as much." Karoly contracted his eyebrows in a mild scowl, as if he were just thinking, not disapproving. "Why? Why would Kate risk so much? She must know this kind of opposition is dangerous." Karoly looked genuinely perplexed.

"She loves him. That's all the reason she needs. And I don't think she's doing the risking—Mother is." Pov set his jaw, his anger at Kate's dilemma rising again, then saw the laugh lines tightening around Karoly's dark eyes. Was Karoly laughing at him? He straightened and gave his cousin a glare all his own.

"Your father had that same kind of temper," Karoly said mildly, "and fought with Aunt Margareta just as much. I doubt you remember it all, but I do."

Pov shrugged again. "Sometimes I'd prefer your mellower frame of mind, I admit."

"I'm not the son of the *puri dai;* I don't have the same kind of stresses. And I was allowed to keep the love I chose and live with her for many years, gaining two sons. It allows a mellower mind."

"Unfortunately," Pov said, "you're not old enough to overrule her authority if my mother convokes a *kris* to expel Kate from the tribe. And Mother wouldn't act so boldly if she weren't sure of her support from your parents."

"I'm ashamed of that," Karoly said candidly, his dark eyes openly regretful. "I'm ashamed that the Janusz would use a tradition for power instead of bonding together. The Lowara Rom have always used the *kris* for family unity—settling squabbles, setting a bride price, announcing elder status, that kind of problem. The *kris* trials are for outright crimes, and even then the accused is allowed to make his penalty and return to the tribe eventually. The other Rom nations can do what they like with expulsions, but the Lowara Janusz haven't permanently expelled one of the family for, God, I don't remember how long. Generations, way back to Old Europe, if ever." He shook his head. "Unfortunately, my parents agree with your mother about Sergei, and those three constititute the *kris.* I worry for Kate—and you, Pov."

"Kate's pregnant."

Karoly's boot dropped to the floor, and he groaned. "God, no. *Why?*"

"She loves him." Pov crossed his arms and hugged his elbows. "She's told me, and she's told Tawnie, I think. I'm not sure about that, but Kate won't be able to hide the pregnancy much longer."

"Tawnie would keep it to herself until Kate wanted it

known," Karoly said, then shook his head worriedly. "It's not a good time right now. Bavol has been talking about cashing out for Perikles, the whole family, and your mother isn't discouraging the talk, just watching what the family thinks."

"And?"

"You know Bavol. The *Dance* Rom weren't particularly happy on *Dance,* and they never made much of an effort, either. They don't even miss *Dance,* and none of them has applied formally for a transfer to new posts on *Net,* not even Lasho." He frowned. "Maybe I could talk to Dad."

"He won't listen any more than Mother does. You know who pulls the strings between those two. And my mother thinks there's too much at stake."

"And what do *you* think's at stake, Pov?"

"Not what they're assuming." He stared at Karoly, hoping his cousin could help somehow, but not expecting he could. "I don't think you have to shut out the gaje to keep what we are. I don't think you have to give up all other loves. The Rom don't have to be that jealous. If you can't trust a way of life to keep your loyalty over others, can't risk even temptation, that doesn't say much for the way of life." He raised his hand. "Now don't start worrying that I've assimilated and forgotten what we are. You know me. I love the Rom. I like our traditions, what we are, the binding together, the certainty of family, the one certain place in an uncertain universe. Only it doesn't seem as certain as it did, especially now."

Karoly smiled wanly. "Maybe we should go join those Rom tribes who still keep the women in their place. It would surely make life easier."

"Is that the solution? Kate was talking about how Rom girls get raised. Do you really want to go back to all the rules about female contamination? Keeping women apart each month, throwing away anything their skirts touch? Making them wash downstream from the men and horses? Treating them like owned things?"

"Of course not." Karoly looked slightly offended, though he'd been the one to suggest it.

"Kate feels owned."

"Kate's a skyrider. They get too used to certain freedoms."

"Kate's a Janusz. The Janusz have never liked being owned—and also expect certain freedoms." Pov waved at the bubbling flasks. "Could you give that up? Go back to an older trade, an older life, leave the knowledge behind and never use it again, forget the purpose for the science? Could you leave *Net*, Karoly?"

Karoly looked at the lab equipment, then thought about it, giving him the courtesy of considering it carefully.

"Yes," he said reluctantly, though he grimaced as he said it. "If my boys went with me, wherever we go. But I grew up on Perikles in that other life on the road; I have memories to go back to. But it wouldn't be the same without Terike, of course."

"Cam would go with you, even Lenci, if you asked."

"To live as what?" Karoly asked, choosing contrarily to argue with himself. "Eventually all the Hyades colonies will end up like Earth, crowded and hostile to anything Rom, imposing their anti-nomad laws, their anti-gypsy laws, tossing us in prison because we won't conform to their gaje rules. Right now we're a novelty again, with lots of room to wander a new planet, lots of slack to tolerate some variations. But it won't last. Eventually the colonies will be just as 'civilized' as Earth and Mars. Eventually the roads will end, as surely as they did on Earth. I don't want a new version of the Spanish gypsies, living in caves on the edge of town at society's sufferance. I don't want to ever settle down." His lips quirked. "I'm thoroughly Rom in that."

"So am I. I want to stay in the Pleiades."

"The choice of road doesn't matter, Pov," Karoly reproved. "But you're right that the answer isn't stripping you of the love. But on the other, to go forward or back, *you* aren't understanding, not completely. This crisis could split the Janusz, elder against younger, with both sides convinced they're right. I'm in the middle generation, half Perikles, half *Net*: I was a grown man when we came aboard *Fan* and I remember the way it was with the other tribes. It helps me see both sides."

"That's what Sergei says. He thinks you'll be the next *puret dai.*"

"Does he?" Karoly raised an eyebrow, as if the idea had never occurred to him. It probably hadn't.

"You've helped him a lot, coz. Is Patia making more trouble? She sees herself as future leader, even if you don't. You saw what she did at the *slava*, using Avi." He tightened his lips.

"Patia isn't happy, Pov. You know that."

"Patia could be happier if she tried, but she doesn't try. I don't appreciate her using Avi as a weapon against my mother."

"Patia's not waiting for your mother to die, I agree." Karoly chewed on his lip and watched the flask bubble awhile. "From a Rom point of view, you know," he said softly, "your mother's right. She's absolutely right. We should go back to Perikles before we lose more of what we are. It's becoming all yes-no, nothing in between."

"I'm not going. Neither is Kate."

"I know that. I'm not suggesting we do, Pov, not even for myself. I might try, but I'd miss this desperately." He waved his hand at the chemistry equipment. "I'd miss this road for what it's become for me, what it could mean for my boys. Go back to stoop labor, tinker work? Know that the other tribes, as they all do, think everything we've sought on *Net* is irrelevant to living?" He shook his head. "It's too late. We've been aboard the cloudships too long."

"I don't think we have to give up being Rom to stay. I *don't* believe that."

Karoly looked at him dubiously, his dark eyes profoundly troubled.

"I don't believe it, coz." Pov leaned forward and grasped Karoly's arm. "Help Kate, Karoly," he said. "Find a way to help Kate. Keep us here."

"I'm not *puret dai.*" Karoly shook his head.

"Karoly, I can't do it. My mother won't listen to me. It has to be you. It has to be."

"I don't even know what *I* should do," Karoly said, his voice anguished. "I don't know what's right. I see one side and I see the other, and I don't see how they could be the same side. We aren't gaje, Pov. We just aren't. We're Rom—and that's something that can't be contaminated if you want to keep it. You give a little here, give away a little there, and eventually you don't have anything that's Rom left. Can't you understand that? Don't you see why we build the walls we do, why they *have* to be built?"

Pov sighed and pressed Karoly's arm, then dropped his hand. "No, I can't. I can't see it."

"I have to think," Karoly muttered. "You can come to me, but who do *I* ask?"

Pov stood up and embraced him for a long moment, then felt a warm breath against his cheek as the older man sighed deeply.

Karoly tightened his arms on Pov, then lifted his head and kissed him. "Fortune, Pov, and a good road," he said in Romany, smiling into Pov's eyes. It was a Rom blessing, two things the Rom had always thought important, wherever they wandered.

"Fortune, coz."

Karoly nodded. "I hope so," he said quietly.

Chapter 12

Maia had shifted sixty degrees across the sky when they emerged from jump, with Alcyone markedly closer, another massive star radiating blue streamers into the surrounding thin gas and dust, and an x-ray strength high enough to require filters on the exterior screens and a warning to *Net*'s crew not to watch Alcyone without protection. That caution would probably follow them around the Pleiades, inhibiting their use of skyrider chevrons unless they armored the pilot ships heavily. Pov watched from Helm Deck's wide windows, letting Tully take Sail Deck this time: Helm Deck had a better view.

Stefania Bartos eyed him irritably from the central chair. Pov stood with his hands clasped behind him, his back to Stefania, and watched Stefania's face in the reflection of a helm monitor screen nearby. She frowned at his back, patted her hair, drummed her fingers restlessly on the arm of her chair, a constant nervous behavior that always wore on Pov's patience. But Stefania was steady enough at helm, he reminded himself, brave when it counted.

Stefania chewed at her cuticle, then jiggled her foot, and Pov's flesh seemed to twitch in response. He closed his eyes to block out her jiggling, knowing he'd have to leave soon if she kept this up. Maybe Stefania just operates on a different energy principle, he thought, with fidgets as a data display. It's a theory. He opened his eyes and she was still fidgeting, her eyes roaming over her staff at their helm stations, the forward windows, the huge wallscreens of Helm Map, as she patted and jiggled and twitched. Pov sighed, and knew that he'd never feel comfortable with Stefania when she behaved this way, however hard he tried.

He and Stefania had always cooperated well enough when their duty intersected, were sometimes almost friends, though they'd never quite made the connection to a real friendship. It baffled him when he thought of it, and he'd made an effort the last few days as he and Stefania updated Helm Map with the new starscans from GradyBol. Stefania had been stiff and unresponsive, deliberately vague, offended by advice, making it perfectly clear she thought she could update Helm Map without his help. At the captains' meetings, to which Andreos had invited her during Athena's absence from Helm Deck, she watched Pov with hostile eyes. He could not, for the life of him, decide how he had offended her, and she had dodged his one attempt to ask bluntly.

Like Pauli with Milo, he thought, watching the tiny shape of TriPower turn slowly in the distance. *I will not say.* Could it be as simple as Slav bias? Stefania was Rumanian, one of the several East European peoples on *Net.* Centuries ago, Rumanian boyars had enslaved any gypsy who unwisely wandered into their territories, and later some Rumanians had helped enthusiastically in rounding up gypsies with the Jews for the concentration camps. Centuries ago: why did it have any relevance to a Rumanian now? It just wasn't like Stefania, in particular. It didn't make sense.

Whatever the reason, without Athena's intercession, which had kept matters smooth between them, his relationship with Stefania had soured immediately, and he didn't know why. He was thinking of talking to Athena about it, knowing he risked more offense to Stefania if he did.

As if I need more problems, he thought wryly.

"Are you going to stand there the entire approach?" Stefania asked him acidly. He turned around.

"You object?" he asked in surprise. Athena had never minded his visits to Helm Deck, had even welcomed them. And ship rules didn't bar visits to another deck, so long as visiting staff didn't overly distract the people on duty.

"I don't need you watching over me, Sail." She tightened her mouth.

"I'm not watching over you, Stefania," he protested, surprised again that she would think so. "I want to see the view from here, and let Tully take the approach watch. That's all."

"Oh, sure." She tossed her blond head, and several of the helm staff turned their heads, glancing around at Pov.

"I'm not watching you, Stefania," he repeated.

She only tightened her lips still more, glaring at him resentfully. "I'm not lying to you, either," he said tightly. "Either you believe me or you don't. If you don't, we'd better have this out right now. I don't like being called a liar."

More heads turned, a few expressions slightly shocked. But she had called him a liar, and in public.

"If Athena doesn't believe in me, she should tell me herself," Stefania declared loudly, her hands tightening on the chair arms. "She doesn't have to send you to watch me. I *can* do this."

Pov's mouth dropped open in surprise. "Is *that* what you think?"

Stefania hesitated, then abruptly looked uncertain. "Yes, I do," she said in a small voice. "You mean she didn't ask you . . ." Pov shook his head. Stefania's fair skin flushed deep crimson, the color flooding upward into her face. Then she glanced with horror at the helm staff, who had heard her every word.

"Athena told me," Pov said mildly, but loud enough to carry to everyone on deck, "and I agreed, that you're obviously suited to be *Net*'s next pilotmaster if Athena elects to helm our daughter ship, which she probably will. In fact, I told our mother hen, who worries about you and every other person on *Net* beyond all reason, to leave you alone up here so you can get some practice. Athena niggled a little about that, being Athena, but she gave in. Wasn't much of a fight." He shrugged. "You've got better windows, and Tully wanted his turn at an approach. Honestly, Stefania. That's all it is."

"Oh, Pov," she said, aghast.

"It's easier, Stef," he said meaningfully, "to tell me why you're mad when I ask, not let it go on and on."

"I'm sorry," she said faintly, still aghast. Her hands fluttered.

"Suits. Do you fidget on purpose to make me leave?"

That unblocked her. She blinked at him, then abruptly smiled. "No. You just make me nervous, Pov. You always have."

"I've noticed," he said wryly. "We have to get a solution to this, Stef. It can't go on."

"I *am* sorry," she said, blushing a little. "I just thought—well, you've heard what I thought."

Pov shrugged it away, smiling at her. "*Can* I watch?" he asked.

"Please do," she said shyly.

Pov walked over to her chair and bent down to her, taking helm staff out of the loop. "She really did agree, Stefania," he said softly. "You proved yourself to Athena at T Tauri. You proved yourself to all of *Net*. Nobody doubts you, especially me."

"I'm not used to captain's status," she muttered help-lessly, looking down at her hands. "I don't know what the rules are."

"You'll get used to it. Just takes practice." She looked up and smiled, then impulsively offered her hand to him. He took it and pressed her fingers. "Harder to be Helm after Athena, and harder for you, Stefania. I understand that. When I offer help, I'm not saying you can't do it by yourself. Maybe it comes across as that, but I don't mean it that way. And it would be easier if you'd tell me when you're angry. I get confused."

"I'll try," she said, biting her lip, then glanced at a helm officer watching them.

"They always watch," he said. "You'll get used to that, too. Comes with command."

"Does it?" She squinted at him.

"Always."

"I am sorry," she whispered. "God, Pov."

"No problem—and don't think you have to be perfect in front of staff. So you embarrassed yourself right now: big deal. Sometime I'll tell you some stories about what

I've done to myself on Sail Deck: a few are a *lot* worse. Staff will talk and watch, but if you try to be perfect, you end up losing the connections because you aren't human anymore. Be yourself, Stef."

Stefania instantly looked dubious. "But I'm not Athena," she said.

"Of course you're not. But you have a good personality, and you love Athena as they do. You're a skyrider as they are. They know you have to step in while she's sick. And you are good at helm: believe it. You know it's true, when you're honest with yourself. You don't have to be Athena: be Stefania."

Stefania thought about it, still dubious, then looked at the helm staff.

"Should I apologize publicly again?" she asked hesitantly.

"Hell, no. We're shrugging it off. Wasn't important, just a misunderstanding. Hard now when Athena's ill. No problem, Helm."

She looked back at him, her expression suddenly intense. "And what about us?"

"No problem, Helm." He watched a smile slowly spread across her face as she believed him. "I like you, Stefania," he said. "I do. You just drive me crazy, how nervous you get." He straightened and pressed her fingers again, then released her hand.

"I can tell you a few stories about *you*, too, Pov Janusz," she told him, tossing her blond head.

"I'm sure you can." They smiled at each other. Stefania waved grandly at the helm windows.

"So watch, sailmaster. The watching's free."

"Thanks."

Pov went back to the window and watched their approach on a long curving trajectory to TriPower, then noticed in the monitor screen, with some amazement, that Stefania had stopped jiggling.

Well, not quite, he amended, as Stefania patted her hair busily.

Pov solved the problem by shifting a few feet to a new view without the monitor screen and went back to watching the sky. TriPower grew steadily in size, turning slowly in space behind its protective slag wall. Apparently, he noticed, TriPower was experimenting with space station technology, building a second half-completed ring outside the standard torus, installing an extensive farm complex, and erecting larger machine shops to tend the station's workings. Though the feasibility of a truly independent space station had its critics, especially a station isolated by hundreds of light-years from a habitable planet, TriPower's Scandinavian stationmaster was obviously far enough from EuroCom's nags to try some newer ideas.

Our cloudship isn't that much different, he thought musingly, watching a toy-size freighter hover over the central processing plant, taking on product for Earth. A lot of our resupply is for convenience, not need. If we had to, we could make our food from gasclouds, especially hydrocarbon dust clouds like these. Process the air, fabricate cloth and metal, sustain ourselves indefinitely. Did TriPower have similar dreams? He smiled

When *Net* swung into her final approach to TriPower, Pov turned, nodded his thanks to Stefania, and went uplevel to Admin to meet Andreos.

Net docked at TriPower's curving ship dock and waited, but a greeting party did not appear in the ship bay. Andreos waited for twenty minutes in *Net*'s docking lounge, damned if he'd ask TriPower's ship-bay chief, then took Pov, Danil, and Ceverny back uplevel. Stefania looked around in surprise as Andreos marched onto Helm Deck.

"Undock," Andreos ordered.

"But—" Stefania blinked. "Yes, sir."

Stefania called the docking chief, and a few minutes later *Net* began backing out of the dock.

"Query from TriPower, sir," the officer at helm comm said. Andreos crossed his arms on his chest.

Stefania turned around to look at Andreos. "Should we reply, sir?"

"No," Andreos growled.

Stefania blinked. "What course, sir?" she asked hesitantly, obviously badly adrift. Stefania was still new to the inner view on Andreos's maneuvers, but she was obviously about to get some good exposure. Almost as one, Pov and Danil sat down in two side chairs and stretched out their legs. Ceverny stayed where he was, his arms crossed on his chest.

"Let's drift a little, Helm," Andreos said. "Keep it slow." Andreos looked at Ceverny. "Assuming we come back, how about shipmaster instead of computer chief, Miska? I'm not inclined today."

"Maybe they were just late," Ceverny grunted. "Can I keep my real name? Nobody'd believe I was a Greek."

"That they wouldn't."

Stefania looked around again, her eyes a little wide, then glanced wildly at Pov. He shrugged elaborately.

"Backing out, sir," Stefania said. "Drifting nicely." Andreos shot her a sharp look.

Net drifted away from dock, putting distance between herself and the space station, but not too quickly. TriPower sent another query, a little more urgently, as *Net* moved off another few kilometers.

"Sir?" Stefania asked, glancing around at Andreos.

"They'll query a third time," Ceverny judged, "if we don't answer again. Should we be nice?"

"Maybe a little mercy," Andreos agreed. He looked at the helm comm officer. "Comm, ask what they want, then put them on hold while I'm asked if I want to reply." The comm officer complied.

"This could take some time," Danil said to Pov, a slight smile on his face.

"Athena says it's all skyrider strut," Pov replied.

"With those two," he said, waving at Andreos and Ceverny, "I agree."

TriPower was on hold, and Andreos let the hold sit for another minute. "You answer, Stefania," he said finally. "Say you're Third Helm and maybe we had the wrong shipbay."

"Sir?" Stefania looked up at him, her face totally bewildered. She blinked. "But we didn't have the wrong—"

"Never mind, Stef," Andreos said kindly. "I'll do it."

"Sorry, sir." Stefania scowled, then laced her fingers on her lap and sighed. "I need a Captain Map," she muttered to herself. "Is there one?" Ceverny chuckled and gave her a wink.

Andreos walked over to a helm console and borrowed the comm officer's earpiece, then connected himself to comm. "Ms. Thorsen? Third Helm here. Yes. We thought perhaps we had entered the wrong shipbay. You did say A-42?" The audio squawked a bit, just below audibility to those listening on Helm Deck. "Ah, I see," Andreos said. "I'll ask our helm captain to realign and dock as before. Will you light a beacon to guide us? Just so we get the right shipbay. Thank you." Another pause as TriPower squawked busily. "I don't know, ma'am. I think he's taking a nap."

Danil sighed and covered his eyes with his hand. "I don't believe this," he muttered. Pov laughed.

"Disturb his nap?" Andreos was saying, aghast. "Ma'am, we *never* do that." Squawk. "I don't know, ma'am. I suppose someone will meet you. I don't know anything about that."

Squawk, squawk.

"Well, I can check, of course. I suppose somebody knows. Yes, we look forward very much to visiting your station. Goodbye."

Andreos straightened and turned around to Stefania. "Redock," he said dryly. "Same ship bay." He looked back at Ceverny. "I'm taking a nap, Miska, as you heard. You meet them with Pov and Danil."

"With pleasure, captain."

When *Net* redocked, a hastily assembled party of Scandinavians waited in the docking lounge, led by a small woman in a trim coverall, her white-blond hair neatly braided and pale under the lounge lights. Older, about Janina's age, the woman carried herself with conscious pride, looking at them with calm gray eyes. Ceverny eyed the Scandis like a wolf looking over a toothsome flock.

"Sirs, welcome to TriPower," the blond woman said in Czech, speaking slowly. Pov saw the tiny translator in her ear, and knew someone was giving her the Czech words over a radio link, a courtesy GradyBol had ignored and TriPower did not have to offer.

Ceverny bowed gracefully. "Thank you," he said in English.

"I am Sigrid Thorsen," the woman continued in Czech. "I am stationmaster of TriPower. I apologize for our delay in greeting you, as was proper." Her lips curved. "You are welcome here at TriPower, *Siduri's Net*, and we all look forward to meeting your people."

It was a gracious speech. Ceverny put his hands in his pockets and smiled at her, then turned to the lounge chief. "Tell Captain Andreos I'm bringing"—he ran his eyes over the TriPower group again—"five to lunch. Will you join us, stationmaster?" he asked courteously.

"Certainly," she replied in Czech, her eyes glinting with amusement. "We would be delighted," she added firmly.

Andreos set the tone for TriPower's meal with *Net*'s captains by speaking in English, sparing the others in TriPower's party the burden of missing most of the conversation. After a few more courteous attempts at Czech, Sigrid Thorsen smiled with relief and took the translator out of her ear. "Thank you. I have this horror of saying something unfortunate if I mangle a word. You have a beautiful ship, Captain Andreos. I hope you enjoyed your nap," she added.

"We think so, and, yes, I usually do." He smiled.

"I'm sorry for the delay," Sigrid said candidly, shaking her blond head. "It was not intentional at all. I was waiting for Bjorn, my plant chief, who had an emergency he should have delegated." She glanced at the dark-haired Swede seated beside her, who shrugged humorously.

"I'm in trouble," Bjorn said. "I've been there before."

"That's not an excuse, Bjorn, and we will discuss it later." She turned back to Andreos. "I'd like to meet your Third Helm," she said pertly. "He seemed a most interesting person."

Andreos's smile got lazier. "He is. We like him a lot."

"I think I do, too." Sigrid raised her wineglass and saluted him, then took a sip. "I had overlooked Gunter's effect on people, despite our past experiences whenever his guests stop here next. You have a most distinctive voice, Captain, very cultivated."

"I like to think so."

Sigrid laughed at him. "Shall I go first?" she asked.

"Please do," Andreos said, waving his hand.

"We are a subsidiary station to GradyBol," she said. "Second in everything—station size, staffing access, production quotas, corporate attention. Gunter makes sure of that." She wrinkled her nose. "From what I have heard on the freighter rumor net, Captain Andreos, that gives us something in common as junior."

"What have you heard?" Andreos asked genially.

"Only preliminaries, but enough to interest me." She glanced at Pov, then made the look a candid appraisal. "Your sailmaster dominates the rumors."

"I can't imagine why," Pov said grumpily, responding to her look. "I'd like to see those news disks and find out who I am now."

Sigrid smiled. "We'll give you a copy. When I was appointed stationmaster, I had rumors, too," she said. "I had been a chemist out here for a dozen years, running the gas distillation plant. Usually stationmasters have to cultivate corporate types on Earth for a year or two to get the ranking. It was assumed," she said, her smile broadening, "that I had some kind of dirt on the CEO. I've proved myself since—and find GradyBol as annoying as I always did." She looked back at Andreos. "Another sentiment perhaps we share."

"You see an opportunity," Andreos said humorously.

"And I'm hoping you do as well, Captain. Sometimes I get a contract with one of *Arrow*'s daughters for a season, if Gunter permits it. Usually I get GradyBol's product overflow, hauled over here by freighter and the cost added to *my* overhead. So I've been lusting for a cloudship all my own, one that looks to TriPower first instead of GradyBol. But I must be subtle in my lusting, given my corporate structures. I thought of sending a message down by freighter to the Arabs or *Rohini's Horn* at Merope, but the freighters go through GradyBol first, and I'm not certain of the captains' loyalty in keeping my secret. Occasionally *Ishtar's Jewel* comes close enough to be wheedled, but so far Janofsi won't listen to me, whatever his reasons. So I am unrequited."

"We'd like to sell you some tritium," Andreos said casually, "then ship the credits back to *Siduri's Dance,* with TriPower as formal witness."

"That could be arranged," Sigrid said, her fingers curling tightly on the stem of her glass. Her eyes fixed on Andreos's face. The four other TriPower officers did their best to copy her studied calm, but Pov sensed the tension that suddenly shot up. TriPower wanted *Net* very much, and chose to allow *Net* to see it, another unexpected courtesy. Pov saw Janina glance at him, her eyes amused and pleased.

"And a few of our people want transport back to the Hyades," Andreos added. *"Net* will pay the associated costs."

Sigrid nodded. "A freighter with passenger space is due to arrive next week. I am sure we can make all the necessary arrangements."

"Do you know where *Jewel* is right now?" Andreos asked.

"In the Shield, I believe. The last I heard, that is. We haven't had much news of her lately."

"We may go into the Shield then," Andreos said. "Some of my people have relatives on *Jewel,* and it's been many years since we last saw *Jewel*'s people. In the interim, I suggest a limited sharing of personnel, while *Net* and TriPower get acquainted."

Sigrid closed her eyes a moment, then relaxed back in her chair. "We would like that, very much."

"I could propose one of our chiefs as liaison to TriPower for the interim. Would you lend us an equivalent officer on our next cloud run?"

"Yes," Sigrid said, then smiled. "I may exercise one of my prerogatives as stationmaster and come myself."

"We would be honored, madam," Andreos said.

They smiled at each other. "Just so long as you don't take any naps," Sigrid added pointedly.

"I have to nap occasionally," he protested.

"I've noticed," she said. Andreos laughed.

"By the way, I have another rumor that might interest *Net.*" Sigrid reached into her pocket and pulled out a folded paper, then casually handed it to Andreos.

"*Moon*'s shipmaster sent me a private message by jump capsule, asking me to be on the lookout for you, then deigned to instruct me how to handle you. Apparently you surprised them, leaving GradyBol like that without so much as a fanfare. They expected you, I think, to drift around in the shadows, waiting for Talbot and Gunter to settle your future."

"Not hardly," Ceverny said tartly.

Sigrid chuckled. "Talbot's a self-important fool who somehow convinces Captain Gray that he's more competent than he really is. *Hound*'s Ingram is better, but Gray uses her for other things. I suppose Gray has his uses for Talbot, too, whatever they are. He bobbled something at GradyBol, I think, which intrigues my interest about what. Knowing the personalities, sirs, Talbot wouldn't have sent this unless Captain Gray told him to do so." She raised an inquiring eyebrow.

"Talbot stole my sailmaster to pump him," Andreos explained dryly. "Effect led from cause." Sigrid's eyes shifted to Pov, then crinkled in amusement.

"I see," she said in satisfaction.

"What do you see?" Pov asked.

Sigrid waved her hand at him. "Talbot asked me to let *Moon* know if *Net* docks here, then wheedle you to stay awhile until *Arrow* herself can come over. Gray wants a look, I think."

"We're going fishing in the Shield," Andreos said. "Sorry not to oblige."

Sigrid laughed. "*Arrow* has had her dominance here for twenty years, Captain," she said. "You could excuse a certain lack of courtesy, especially to newcomers who still have to prove themselves. I think Thaddeus Gray would have handled it differently at GradyBol if he had been on-site."

"Does Gray make a habit of meeting new cloudships?" Andreos asked.

Sigrid narrowed her eyes thoughtfully. "I've been watching *Arrow* for several years, sirs, enough for certain patterns to be obvious, and one of those patterns is Captain Talbot. *Moon* goes only where Gray tells Talbot to go." Sigrid shook her blond head. "*Moon* was sent to meet you, and Talbot botched it. Gray isn't taken unawares like that very often, and that's to your benefit. You'll like Gray: he's everything his reputation says he is."

Andreos sat back and fingered his wineglass. "So now Gray will come looking for us at TriPower?"

"If you're here."

"*Should* we be here?" he asked pointedly.

"If I ever got such an advantage, I wouldn't, at least not right away. That's my advice, as your new associate in the Pleiades." She raised her glass. "To our new association, sirs, and our mutual good fortune."

"To fortune," Andreos responded, echoed by the other officers of *Net* as everyone returned TriPower's salute.

Sigrid sighed, then glanced at Bjorn. "You're reprieved, Bjorn," she said wryly, as she watched Bjorn lolling in his chair, a lazy smile on his face. "Thank your stars. I was intending to feed you to your processors if we lost this chance at *Net*." Bjorn waggled his eyebrows at her, unrepentant, and made himself relax even more bonelessly, his smile unchanged. "And I'll fix those eyebrows eventually, too," she said with some disgust. "Don't you think I won't, sir."

Then she pushed back her chair and stood, raising her glass again. "To *Siduri's Net*," she said solemnly. "Welcome, *Net*, truly welcome. Not that I promise to be this genial in *all* our affairs," she added playfully. "I have profit margins to watch, too."

"I'll remember that," Andreos said, wary again and displeased with her wit and the implied comment that he'd ever forget.

Sigrid did her best, as lunch went on, to charm *Net*'s captains with pleasant compliments and her deft observations about business in the Pleiades. Unfortunately, she and Andreos had the same clever guile, and Sigrid could not resist poking at Andreos, a poke he returned each time. It wasn't as nasty as Weigand's meal, but nor was it entirely comfortable for either side. Pov could see that Andreos was not pleased. Pov began to wonder himself if TriPower might be another disappointment as Sigrid continued to annoy Andreos, missing a few signals—or perhaps misinterpreting them. Different script, Pov decided, eyeing them both.

After lunch, Captain Andreos took Sigrid and her party on a tour of *Siduri's Net,* and they ended up on Sail Deck. Sigrid showed intense interest as she looked around the deck at the several monitor stations. Andreos noticed her interest and glanced at Pov, sending signals Pov hoped he understood. "Why don't you run a sail drill, Pov?" he suggested. "Show her how it works."

"My pleasure, sir," Pov said.

Roja got up and moved to a side chair after getting his own signal, and Pov politely gestured Sigrid to the other chair at the central console. "Stationmaster?"

"Thank you." Sigrid sat down in the chair.

"In the meantime," Andreos said blandly, "may I continue the tour for your other officers?"

Sigrid looked around at him, then glanced at Pov in amusement. "I think they would enjoy that," she said. She watched Andreos shepherd everyone into the elevator, then looked at Pov. "In some quarters," she observed pertly, "this is called hold sorting."

"The magnetics are similar," Pov agreed, hesitating a moment as he hunted the technical word in English. "I haven't much of an idea why he just delivered you to me, stationmaster, though I got some signals I hope I understood. Would you like to watch one of our sail drills?"

"Definitely. Will it look like the real thing?"

"Yes, very much so. We use our drills to train our sail officers, and we try to make that training as useful as possible. In a few days, perhaps we can show you an actual demonstration in the Shield. Roja, will you start a sail drill?" he said in Czech, not sure if his Third Sail had kept up his English. Roja's blank half-smile ever since Andreos walked on deck suggested he hadn't. "Use the parameters from the Veil, skysails dominant."

"Yes, sir."

Sigrid leaned forward as the main wallscreen lighted, showing a starfield with drifting blue gas. The computer added the field lines of the sails reaching forward from the ship, then began *Net*'s simulated run into the gascloud, the hydrogen streaming into the sails. Sigrid watched, openly fascinated, as the Sail Deck crew gave quiet reports to Roja about gas flow, sail integrity, and light readings. Roja simulated a request to Helm Deck for a ten-degree turn to port, and the screen changed, stars shifting, as *Net* chased a thicker eddy. The gas fluoresced as Maia flared in the distance, the UV light rippling through the gas. Sigrid raised her hands, marveling.

"Beautiful!" she exclaimed, openly amazed. "I had no idea it looked like that!" The fluorescing atoms spun into the sails, sparkling as they descended the field lines. "Oh, my!" They caught a patch of ionized dust down one side of the sails and *Net*'s starboard spinnaker blurred to a warm deep red, then flared again as it caught more ionized hydrogen. "Oh, my!" Sigrid threw up her hands again.

Two of the sail officers looked around at her, a little incredulous at her open exclamations, and Pov instantly squelched them both with a frown. Sigrid caught it and laughed.

"I can't help it," she said, then laughed again, throwing up her hands. "I've never seen it before! Oh, look!"

The sails flickered as *Net* caught more dust and carbon radicals spun dizzyingly down the sails in brilliant crimson and blue, followed by a rainbow of colors as other molecules manufactured by the dust spun into the sails. Grinning, Roja ordered another turn to port, and *Net* plunged into a patch of heavy dust. The metal gridlines of the sails glowed dusky red as dust impacted hard across *Net*'s forward hull and reflected its infrared back into the sails.

"*Mr.* Korak," Pov said disgustedly. "What the hell do you think you're doing?"

"What?" Sigrid asked curiously, not understanding the Czech but catching his tone.

"We just lost about a millimeter of hull surface from dust impact," Pov explained. "It's not supposed to be deliberate." He gave Roja another scowl. "You can pay for the hull damage, I think," he told Roja in Czech. Roja chuckled, undented, but ran the rest of the drill without interpolations.

"Sail drill completed, sir," Roja reported as the wallscreen went blank. "Shall I run another one?"

"Another?" Pov asked Sigrid.

"Yes," Sigrid said promptly. "Please do." Roja nodded and turned back to his computer console. *Net* again plunged into a simulation of Maia's Veil. Sigrid watched, entranced, as *Net* spread her sparkling sails. She sighed deeply. "I envy you, sailmaster, more than you know."

"You can watch anytime, stationmaster," Pov said, "and be welcome."

She smiled at him. "Call me Sigrid. May I call you Pov?"

"If you like," he said with some caution, remembering she was TriPower's stationmaster and Andreos had sent signals. Her smile broadened.

"I'll make you a deal," she said impishly. "I won't tell him what you say to me, and you won't tell him what I say to you."

"I don't think he'd agree to that, exactly," Pov hedged, as Sigrid obviously remembered a certain fact about the same time he did. Pov found himself liking this tiny Scandinavian stationmaster with her braided sun-bright hair and clever wit: she was no one's fool. Yet for the several minutes that she had watched his sails, she had genuinely forgotten her rank and deft comments, and that had touched him. The new sail drill was a bad distraction as Sigrid tried to get back to business.

She turned and touched Pov's sleeve. "I meant that, what I said earlier. My lust is deep. What did you think of Captain Talbot?"

"He has good scripts," Pov said dryly.

Sigrid chortled, then exclaimed aloud again as the sails put on another dazzling display. "Oh, my," she said weakly. "What did he do exactly, for his script?"

"Embarrassed his sail officer in front of me. Got cute. Missed clues. Thought I was stupid. Didn't feed me dinner."

"I'll remember to extend that invitation, be assured," she said coyly. It was another false move, one like several that had annoyed Andreos during lunch, and was maybe based on whatever expectations she had learned about cloudship captains, maybe from Gunter's dealings with *Arrow* herself. But *Net* was not *Arrow,* and Sigrid didn't yet know *Net* well enough to play a sure hand.

"There's always AmTel and the Japanese," he said, copying one of Talbot's voice tones to provoke Sigrid hard. Her gray eyes immediately narrowed.

"TriPower is nicer than AmTel, believe me," she said, tossing her head, then poked back. "You have a new ship drive. I apparently watch the Earth news scans more closely than GradyBol. The Earth commentator dismissed that Aldebaran captain's story about your escape from Tania's Ring, but I'm entertaining a theory maybe it wasn't exaggerated. What do you think of my theory?" She watched him intently for any reaction. Pov smiled at her lazily, baring his teeth.

"You're good, Sigrid," he said admiringly. "I'm going to enjoy watching you and Andreos in action."

"*Do* you have a new ship drive?" she persisted. He shrugged elaborately, saying nothing. She sighed gustily. "Forgive me. My lust again."

"That's all right. I can understand lust."

Her eyes sparkled with amusement. "Captain Talbot hasn't lusted for years. His loss, I'm afraid.

"It looks like it," he said carefully, sending a hint he thought she needed. He could see Sigrid hadn't really believed the news scan, not really, and had used its bit of drift gas mostly to poke back at Pov. When she heard the confirmation in his voice, Sigrid's head swiveled around at him, her eyes widening in honest shock. Pov lifted an eyebrow and waited, then grinned as Sigrid quickly got hold of herself again. It didn't take long: he had a feeling nothing shook this very capable Scandi stationmaster for very long.

"Remind me, Pov," Sigrid said as she eyed him with new respect, "never to play cards with you for real money."

"I think that just went on the list of what we don't tell Andreos," he said lightly. "We don't have a working drive principle yet, much less engine designs, but put it under your hat, Sigrid. Captain Andreos likes you, but he thinks games ought to have a purpose—and only to a certain point. I just gave you some incentive to play by his rules."

She nodded. "I'll remember that." She studied his face

for a long moment. "Orion's Nebula? Could you jump that far?"

"We don't know yet. Maybe."

She pursed her lips, her gray eyes thoughtful. "Andreos will need some guidance on this, when we talk to Gray. I know the personalities and a few more facts he needs to know." She paused again, her eyes narrowing as she juggled the nuances, just as he'd seen Andreos do a thousand times. Pov relaxed: he'd been right to warn her before the inevitable byplay between two smart operators, already skewed by an awkward start, had gotten more out of hand. He only hoped Andreos didn't vaporize *Net*'s sailmaster when he found out what Pov had just told Tripower.

"You really should skewer that Bjorn of yours," he suggested. "We nearly left and went elsewhere."

"With this in your holds and after GradyBol's behavior? I wouldn't have blamed you a bit. I must remember to thank my lust," she added fervently, "for keeping me half civil. My, oh my," she said in awe.

"Another sail drill?" he offered, liking Sigrid very much.

"Oh, yes. Definitely."

Sigrid leaned back in her chair with a sigh, wiggling her small shoulders against the chair back for the best comfortable spot, then smiled with great satisfaction at the wallscreen.

"Do it again, sailmaster," she said. "I can take it."

Chapter 13

"You told her *what*?" Andreos hissed. His face flushed darkly red with his sudden anger.

"It was necessary," Pov blurted, startled by Andreos's reaction. "Not so loud, sir." He gestured slightly at Sigrid chatting with Janina across the Admin lounge. Pov hadn't found an opportunity to pull Andreos aside into a private conversation out of Sigrid's view, but Andreos had to know before he and Sigrid left for their tour of TriPower.

"Do you realize what you may have done?" Andreos said in a low but furious voice. "I told everyone I wanted no disclosure, and that included you, Mr. Janusz."

"Sir—" Pov said desperately.

"One voice for the ship, not two or four or a dozen," Andreos said tightly. "This is *Net*'s fortune in the Pleiades, and you had no right to disobey me. Do you realize what you've done?"

"Sir—"

Andreos seized Pov's arm and his fingers dug into the flesh painfully. "Do you *realize*?" he persisted.

"You want to disrank me, say so," Pov said angrily, then stopped himself short as Sigrid began moving toward them. "Sir, we are noticed." Pov shook off Andreos's grip and stepped away.

Sigrid's eyes flicked between their faces as she walked up. "Our list of secrets, Pov?" she guessed.

Pov looked down at his boots and clenched his teeth.

"List?" Andreos said, his voice dangerous with sudden suspicion.

Pov abruptly turned and walked out of the room, then broke into a run in the corridor, racing for the elevator. He hit the elevator button and saw Temya put her head out of her office, her mouth rounded with surprise. Pov looked wildly around. *Net* did not have stairs by this elevator, only a utility tunnel, a hundred-meter drop into nothingness if he lost his grip. Right now he recklessly wished for that drop, and took a step toward the access door.

"*Pov!*" Andreos shouted after him, coming out of the lounge.

Pov plunged through the utility door onto the narrow platform inside and grabbed a ladder rung at chest level, then looked down into the dizzying drop beneath the platform edge. What am I doing? he wondered and closed his eyes, feeling suddenly nauseous. What in the hell am I doing? He swayed and nearly lost his grip on the rung, genuinely risking a fall. He clutched at the rung hard, his breath suddenly coming in great gasps, then managed to back away from the ladder and sit down by the side wall.

He heard the footsteps coming and looked up as Captain Andreos appeared in the open doorway, backlit by the corridor lights.

"I'm near the edge, sir," Pov said in a strangled voice. "You said to tell you. Didn't mean it to be literal, though." He waved at the empty drop a meter from his feet, and heard his own ghastly laugh. The sound echoed down the well eerily, dividing itself into hollow reflections below and above.

Andreos turned his head to the side, looking down the corridor. "Stationmaster, if you'll withdraw," he said, "I would appreciate it."

"He didn't make a mistake, Leonidas," Sigrid's voice said quietly, muffled by the half-open door. "Let us dispense with all our master's games, every one, shall we? I offer you TriPower and all its resources. I offer you everything I know about the Pleiades." Her voice rose, ringing clearly. "I offer you alliance, mutual profit, and TriPower's friendship. We did not start well, you and I, and he knew it. He took a risk, because he decided to believe in me. I value that deeply, and I will not betray it. On my honor as stationmaster of TriPower and as a Scandi." Her voice dropped. "Please, sir."

Andreos stood motionless, looking at Sigrid for a long

minute. Pov saw him nod slowly. "We'll be with you in a few minutes, Sigrid," he said then, his tone entirely normal. "Could you take the others back to the lounge?"

"Certainly. Sirs, if you will?"

Andreos stepped into the utility shaft and slowly eased himself down beside Pov, then leaned cautiously forward to look down the well. "Long fall," he commented.

"That's what I thought when I looked down." Pov put his forehead on his knees, still dizzy, his heart pounding. He heard Andreos sigh and lean back. "I was telling Stefania today," Pov said, his breath hard to catch, "that captains can make asses of themselves. It's a good thing, I said. People won't mind at all, makes us human." He swallowed hard. "I think I'm going to throw up, sir."

"Just sit there a minute, son," Andreos said quietly, and Pov felt his arms come around him. "Put your head down between your knees. That's right. Everything's fine, Pov."

Andreos's voice was a gentle croon, and Pov felt the captain's hand on his hair, then the slow caress as Pov struggled against his nausea. It eased after several minutes, and Pov slowly sat up.

"I'm sorry, sir," he mumbled.

"It seems you vaporized yourself, son, all in about thirty seconds. Forgive me. I was taken by surprise, too involved in my clever schemes and what looked like another disappointment. It was my mistake." Pov looked at him and Andreos twisted his mouth. "It makes me human, I suppose."

Pov started to chuckle, then held his head as it began to spin again. "I *feel* vaporized," he muttered.

"Just sit. We have plenty of time." Andreos let his breath go in a long sigh. "I feel rather vaporized myself." He leaned his head back against the wall, one arm around Pov's shoulders.

"I wasn't going to jump," Pov said after a while.

"Don't worry about that. The elevator was too slow and you were coming after me, that's all."

"It gets complicated when it's father and son."

"That it does," Pov agreed. "I think Sigrid means it, what she said."

"Yes, I think so." Andreos sighed feelingly. "This is

not the way I wish to test a stationmaster's truth, Pov. Find some other way next time."

"I had to tell you before you went over to TriPower." Andreos squeezed his shoulder. "Pov, store that."

"Yes, sir."

The slow cool current from the well flowed into their faces, and Pov felt his dizziness finally recede as they sat together in silence for several more minutes. He tried to look more alert.

"What else is going on with you, Pov?" Andreos asked quietly. Pov glanced at him. Andreos sat with his head back, his eyes closed as the cool air flowed upward.

"What do you mean, sir?" he asked.

"Why was losing me suddenly the last prop taken away, the last stair tread into nothingness?" Andreos opened his eyes and turned his head to look at him.

Pov sighed and leaned back, thumping his head against the wall. "Family."

"Avi?" Andreos asked with concern.

"No, not Avi." Pov hesitated, then felt the encouraging press of Andreos's hand on his shoulder. He sighed again and laced his fingers in his lap. "You know about the Rom and their exclusions," he said slowly. "We keep the walls for a reason, and my mother thinks *Net* has broken the walls. Kate wants to marry Sergei Rublev, but Rom law doesn't permit it, and Kate won't back down and my mother won't back down and I'm in the middle. Now Kate's pregnant, and it's goading my mother into taking the Rom away from *Net,* back to Perikles." He spread his hands helplessly. "I tell her I won't leave *Net,* and she doesn't believe me. A Rom would never choose gaje over the family: it just isn't so, ever. So I wonder if maybe I'm not Rom anymore. But I see it all happening, coming straight at me, and I can't get out of the way. I can't give up *Net.* I love my family. I don't know how to stop what's happening. Nothing I've tried works." He grimaced, then looked wryly at Andreos. "I guess that's an edge, too, isn't it?"

"I'd say that's definitely an edge," Andreos agreed, just as wryly. He frowned. "She hasn't gone to the chaffers."

"The family's still talking it over. You know the *Dance* Rom came over to *Net* before we left Epsilon?"

"Yes, I know."

"They've never had the connections to the ship that we do—Kate, me, Karoly, Tawnie and Del. They never really tried. Patia's unhappy with Bavol, and Judit only wants her home life, and even Lasho wasn't that interested in a ship profession. They never fit in over there with all the Slavs, anyway. Most of the Greeks came over to *Net* when we built her, and you know what *Dance*'s First-Ship Slavs are like. So it was easy to keep the walls. Why bother with the gaje? They're just gaje." Pov shrugged tiredly. "They don't even miss *Dance,* and genuinely couldn't care less what happens to her. So half the family now is already on my mother's side, and she thinks she can force the rest of us." Pov spread his hands helplessly again, let them drop. "Kate won't. I won't. But I think the others will, if she makes it a *puri dai* ultimatum. It's part of being Rom, and they're all more Rom than I am, I guess."

"You *are* Rom, Pov. You can't lose what you are."

"That's what I tell Kate."

Andreos chuckled softly, then slowly ran his fingers through his hair as he stared unseeing at the utility ladder and the blank wall behind it, his long face backlit by the light from the corridor. "God above, Pov."

"That's the edge, sir." Pov looked down at his hands again. "But it's family business: it's not Rom to tell gaje about family. It's not done. It's—" He stopped as Andreos's hand pressed his shoulder.

"I understand," Andreos said. "I can't see an answer, either. I'll think about it, though."

"Don't tell anybody else, sir," Pov said uncomfortably, then grimaced at himself. "Please. Though I admit it's odd to ask after what—"

"Store that, sailmaster. That's an order. You weren't wrong: I was."

Pov sighed. "Yes, sir. If you say so." He looked down at his hands again.

"Someday maybe I'll convince you," Andreos said, a trace of laughter in his voice. "Well, I suppose we should go talk to Sigrid. Are you feeling all right now? No more dizziness?"

"No, sir."

"That's good." Andreos got to his feet and held out his hand to help Pov up. They walked back together to the Admin lounge, Andreos's steady hand on Pov's elbow, to where TriPower and *Net* were waiting for them.

Sigrid sent her staff back to TriPower and stayed another hour with *Net*'s captains in the lounge. Pov could see she was shocked, and she and Andreos quickly repaired the frayed relationship between TriPower and *Net* that had nearly gone awry. By the end, Andreos was smiling and Sigrid was smiling, too. Danil looked vastly relieved. Janina kept glancing at Pov, her concern quite frank at whatever she saw in his face. The entire time, every instant, Pov wished he were somewhere else with Avi.

At the end, he was caught unawares as everyone suddenly stood up. He struggled to his feet off the couch, and Janina stepped over and put her arm through his, holding him up.

"I'm okay, Janina," he muttered.

"Just wait until they leave," she said quietly, patting his arm. Janina watched Sigrid and Andreos walk through the door, followed by Stefania and Ceverny. Janina waved Danil out of the room, too, as the chaffer hesitated, looking back at them.

"Where's Avi's apartment, Pov?" Janina asked.

"Starboard," he said dully. "D Section."

"Fine." She pulled him forward gently and walked him out of the lounge and down the hall. The others had already left by the elevator. As they passed Temya's office, Janina put her head into the doorway. "Temya, will you please find Avi Selenko and tell her she's needed at her apartment, if she's not there already? Quietly, please."

"Yes, ma'am."

Janina steered Pov toward the elevator. He tried to straighten and walk more efficiently, and Janina pressed his arm.

"Forget that stuff," she said pertly. "Drag if you have to. Who needs an act?"

"Everything's piled up, Janina," he muttered.

"I know." Janina pushed the elevator button, and he tried to collect himself again. "Save your straightening for the companionway, if you insist on it."

She clucked her tongue, then took him to Avi's apartment, chatting normally as they walked arm in arm through the ship corridors and into the residential block. Janina pushed the door chime by Avi's door, and Avi opened it an instant later, her dark eyes wide with alarm.

"He's all right, Avi," Janina reassured her. "Here, Pov. It's Avi."

"Avi?" Pov said dully.

"Great stars above!" Avi exclaimed. "What's happened?" Janina pushed him gently, and a moment later the door had closed behind him. Avi led Pov to one of the living-room chairs, then rushed back to the outside door, but Janina had already left. Pov leaned forward and covered his face with his hands, then groaned.

"Pov?" Avi said, her voice tight with fear. He dropped his hands, hearing her fright, and turned toward her automatically. She knelt beside his chair and took his hands, her face contorted as she looked up at him. "Pov?"

"Don't be afraid," he said gently, finding a smile for her. "It's a kind of body shock. But everything's all right." He disengaged one of his hands and caressed her cheek, giving it all his attention for a long moment. "Everything's all right, Avi."

He pulled her up and into his lap, then wrapped his arms around her. She kissed his forehead, then began to tremble violently. "It's all right," he said, caressing her.

"You keep saying that, while you're looking like this? What happened, Pov? Who hurt you?" she demanded fiercely. "Tell me and I'll go kill him, right away." She sounded as though she meant it: maybe she did.

Pov chuckled softly, then took a deep breath and raised his head to look at her. "I told TriPower about the new drive when I probably shouldn't have, and Andreos—" Avi started to get up, about to charge out of the apartment to commit mayhem on *Net*'s shipmaster, and he held on to her tightly, pulling her back into his lap. "Wait. It's all right. I found out what it meant to me to lose *Net,* and I wasn't expecting it when it happened. That's all."

"How could you lose *Net*?" Avi asked, confused. "You're still sailmaster, aren't you? How could you *not* be? What *happened*?"

"Please don't be frightened, Avi. Just sit here and I'll tell you, and everything's all right."

Avi made an effort to collect herself, not successfully. He felt her hand trembling on his shoulder, but she tried. It helped him. "I told the stationmaster because she and Andreos were on the wrong tack," he said haltingly. "They're alike, but things got mixed up. It caught Andreos off-guard. . . ." Pov closed his eyes, then opened them quickly as she drew in a sharp breath. "But everything's all right, Avi. I had a pit open below my feet and I almost fell in. God." He pressed his face against her shoulder and shuddered deeply.

"But everything's all right," she quavered, and he felt her tentative caress.

"Yes. Everything's all right. I promise."

She kissed his hair and slowly rocked him. He felt his shuddering ease away as she held him and finally, at last, could look up and give her something of a normal smile.

"Sorry to frighten you, love," he whispered. "I'm sorry."

She touched his face. "Should I call somebody? Tully? Maybe Kate?"

"You're all I need, Avi. You and *Net.*" He sighed and closed his eyes, holding her tightly.

The next morning, Pov was in his office on Sail Deck, loading Helm Map into a data carrier to take over to TriPower, when he looked up to see his cousin Tawnie in his doorway. She was dressed in her biolab coverall, her long hair swept up and fastened with plain clips, making her look older, more a woman than the girl she usually was. Tawnie was struggling for control, visibly upset but trying her best to hide it in front of his gaje sail staff. Pov got up and shut the door, then seated her in one of his chairs. "What's wrong, Tawnie?"

"Aunt Margareta is taking us back to Perikles!" Tawnie exclaimed. "She's cashing in our shares and buying passage for everyone back to Perikles!"

Pov closed his eyes. She'd done it: she'd actually done it.

"She *said* it was an elders' decision," Tawnie said with a sob, "and that the elders had voted. Da and Mother always go along with whatever she wants, you know that. Oh, Pov, it's all my fault! I wasn't supposed to tell about Kate but I slipped and Patia heard it and she said something nasty to Aunt Margareta and suddenly Aunt Margareta's charging out of the apartment, saying she'll invoke a *kris* on anybody who disagrees!" Tawnie wiped away her tears angrily. "Pov, you have to *do* something! Karoly won't. He's just letting it happen. Do something, Pov."

"I don't know what to do, Tawnie," Pov said helplessly. "I've tried everything."

"*Please* go talk to her. Somebody has to try! I don't want to go to Perikles! I want to stay with *Net,* and I don't want *Net* thinking I ever didn't!"

"Tawnie—"

"Please!" Tawnie begged him. She took his hands desperately. "Please, Pov."

He sighed and squeezed her hands, then stood up. "You come with me, Tawnie. Maybe you can help."

"Me?" Tawnie looked amazed.

"Yes, you."

She sat another moment, staring at him, then leaped to her feet. Her small warm hand slipped into his and they left Sail Deck together in a rush.

At the sub-admin level where the *Net* chaffers had their offices, they stepped off into an air of studied calm, a few people waiting patiently in the long corridor in soft chairs, a murmur of voices beyond them in the several private meeting rooms that ringed the entry deck. Pov took a quick look around.

"I don't see her," Tawnie whispered.

"It looks like a short line. She must be in with a chaffer already. Most everybody voted to stay, after all."

"How do we get her out of the chaffer's office?" Tawnie asked.

"I don't know," he said.

Suddenly Tawnie threw her hands to her head and shrieked, and Pov practically jumped out of his skin at the earsplitting sound. He grabbed for her as she staggered away from him, letting out another shriek. She eluded him easily and ran full-tilt into the nearby wall, crying and moaning and tearing frantically at her head.

"Tawnie!" he cried out in shock. "What's wrong?"

He grabbed for her again, but she darted out of reach and then fell to the floor, still shrieking, jerking and twitching in some kind of fit. Pov threw himself down beside her and tried to control her flailing limbs, getting a solid punch on his nose as thanks. Two of the people in the chairs were already half to their feet, their eyes round with surprise and shock, and every head had turned.

At the far end of the room, a half-dozen doors were thrown open, and his mother came charging out of one of them. She ran to Tawnie and roughly shoved aside the two people who had reached them to help, then gathered the writhing girl into her arms.

"What happened?" she cried, looking up at Pov.

"I don't know, Mother," Pov said. "Tawnie just screamed and fell."

"Medical," Margareta said curtly, and tried to lift Tawnie. Pov quickly slipped his own hands under Tawnie's knees and shoulders, helping lift Tawnie upward. They carried her to the elevator, with Tawnie still jerking and moaning in their arms.

As the door closed and the elevator started downward, Tawnie raised her arms and gave Margareta a sweet hug. "Hi, Aunt Margareta," she said brightly. "Don't worry. I'm all right."

His mother nearly dropped her in surprise. When Pov laughed, she abruptly let go of Tawnie and glared at him.

"Oops," Tawnie said, trying to catch herself as she stumbled. She hung on Pov a moment and found her feet, then straightened up, a little flushed from her exertions.

"What is the meaning of this?" Margareta asked Pov coldly.

"Tawnie has brain cancer," Pov retorted. "She gets these fits now and then."

"Don't say such things, Pov," Tawnie muttered, crossing herself hurriedly. "It's bad luck."

"I will not be—" his mother started.

"Aunt Margareta!" Tawnie cried and caught at his mother's arm. "You *can't* do this!"

It shifted his mother's attention. "Child, you don't understand—"

"I *do* understand. Why are you so sure Patia would win? I love you, Aunt. I don't want anybody else as *puri dai*. But I also want to stay here on *Net*. You never asked me."

"You're too young, Tawnie, to know—"

"I am a married woman," Tawnie said with dignity, lifting her chin. "I am an adult in our tribe. I have a right to be heard. I won't go back to *Dance* or Perikles! I want to stay here!"

"You will do what the tribe decides," Margareta said, her eyes glinting. "It is your duty as *romni*."

"And *your* duty," Tawnie threw back, her chin lifting still more, "as *puri dai* is to be a wise leader for all your tribe. This isn't like you, Aunt. First you fight with Kate, and then you fight with Pov, not just squabbles, but *arguments* with too much at stake, yes you will, no you won't or else. Or else? Is that how a *puri dai* speaks with her children? Are you going to fight with me now? Who else? Del doesn't want to go, either. Will you fight with him? Do what I want or I'll cut you off, send you away forever?" Tawnie's chin trembled, her eyes filling with tears, and his mother made a soft sound of distress despite herself.

I wish I were invisible, Pov thought, so that this works. But the first time she looks at me again . . .

Then Margareta's eyes shifted to Pov and turned hard, as he expected. As she opened her mouth, he raised his hand.

"Don't say it, whatever it is," he said. "I don't want to argue anymore."

"They will go with me, if I say they must," his mother said proudly.

"Yes, probably they will. I won't, and Kate won't. But they probably will, even Tawnie." He smiled at his young cousin sadly, then brushed one of the tears off her cheek. "Even Tawnie, because she is an adult in the tribe." He bent and kissed Tawnie's cheek, tasting the salt of her tears. "And a married woman, who will be a wonderful Rom mother to her many children. But Kate and I will not leave *Net.*"

He saw his mother stare at him, her mouth dropping open, as she finally, at last, believed him.

The elevator door opened at the companionway, and Pov stepped off. "Goodbye, Mother," he said. He began to walk away.

"Pov!" his mother called.

He hunched his shoulders and kept walking, then heard their footsteps hurrying after him. His mother caught up with him and marched along beside him for a few steps. Tawnie walked on his other side, her dark eyes wide and hopeful as she watched both their faces.

"You really will," Margareta said incredulously after they had marched several more meters. "Allow me to leave you both behind."

"I've *told* you that, I don't know how many times. You just didn't believe me."

He refused to look at her, keeping his eyes on the carpet stretching far ahead, past the wide windows and the star spaces beyond. Then he heard his mother sigh softly and he glanced at her quickly, not believing his ears. She was scowling.

"Brain cancer," she said disgustedly, looking past him at Tawnie. Tawnie faded prudently behind Pov, putting him safely between her and her aunt. Pov gave his mother a look of disbelief. Their Rom world was falling apart, and all she cared about was Tawnie's gaje audience. Margareta saw the look, and her expression went unreadable. "You are *that* certain, my son?"

"Yes, Mother," he said tiredly. "I am certain. I don't think *Net* is a gaje place that ties us down and makes us lose what we are. I think *Net* is a road, one that never has to end." He gestured at the companionway windows. "Look out there, Mother: all those stars to find, all those places to wander forever. We are still Rom, no matter how we change our customs or borrow gaje ways, so long as we wander. We keep the road. And *Net* is a road. If you want to force a choice, go ahead, but I am telling you I will not leave *Net,* even if it means losing you and the rest of the family."

He stopped and she turned to face him, her head lifted proudly, slim and beautiful in her hold uniform. Her eyes shifted beyond him to the stars beyond the windows, then returned to his face. She said nothing, but her lips tightened stubbornly, an expression he had seen a hundred times the last three years. It exasperated him.

"It's *your* choice now, Mother, not mine," he said angrily. "I've made mine. So now you can either adapt to *Net* and cope with its gaje temptations, or you can go back to Perikles without your children. That's the choice. If you go back, you win your big point: Kate and I will know that how you define the Rom is more important to you than we are. But I can live with that: I can understand the reasons you would make that kind of choice, whether you believe that or not. I can also accept you'll never understand why I need only Avi and *Net,* if I had to choose yes or no, this but not that."

"But—" she started.

"And maybe in ten years, maybe twenty," he interrupted brutally, "you can afford a trip out here to see your grandchildren. I'll allow you to see my kids, I suppose, but I don't know about Kate. You probably ought to ask her, before you go, just to get things lined up. It'd be a shame to waste all those credits and get only half the benefit." He turned on his heel and started to walk off again.

His mother caught up with him in a stride and clamped her hand on his arm. He shook her off with a violent motion, then whirled around at her. "You can't!" she exclaimed. "You can't do this!"

"Watch me. Call Avi a whore, will you? Let's get to that issue."

Tawnie fluttered her hands and made an inarticulate cry. "Stop this, stop this!" she cried out, covering her ears. "What kind of family *is* this? Is *this* what Rom is? Then I don't want it, either."

"Tawnie!" Margareta exclaimed in shock.

"I'm not going to Perikles," Tawnie declared, her voice tight with rage. "And Del will pick me over you, and I won't let you see *my* children, either!"

She started to flounce off, but Pov caught her and wrapped his arms around her, stopping her before she ran away, as he had tried to run when his world had suddenly collapsed. She sobbed against his chest, and Pov saw every passerby in the companionway turn and look at them. More gaje audience, but this time his mother had eyes only for Tawnie and himself, more profoundly shocked by Tawnie's outburst than by his own ultimatum. She had expected Pov's defiance; she had not expected Tawnie's.

Pov kissed Tawnie's hair, holding her close, and looked at his mother over her dark head. "It's started, Mother, all the unraveling. Do you really think you can put the family back together again?" He sighed. "I'm sorry for you." And he did genuinely pity her.

His mother looked again at the windows and the stars glittering beyond them, then looked back at Pov and Tawnie. A man and a woman walked past them, arm in arm, and both nodded genially to Pov, two subchiefs from Computer Deck. Pov nodded back, and the woman smiled.

"Hello, sir," the woman called, waving her hand at him, then looked curiously at Tawnie, who was crying only quietly now. They walked on.

Margareta watched the subchiefs as they walked out of earshot. "They all know you," she said, almost wonderingly. "All the ship knows you."

"*Net*'s a road, Mother. All Rom know each other, when they share the road." She looked him up and down, as if he had sprung fresh-grown from the soil. "You choose, Mother," he added softly.

Margareta hesitated, then stepped forward and gently disengaged Tawnie from Pov's arms. "Go home, Tawnie," she said. "I'll be along later."

"But—"

"Go home. I won't be going back up to the chaffer deck, child. We'll discuss all this in the evening, and you, as an adult in the tribe, may have your say." Though dry, his mother's tone was not unpleasant. Tawnie gulped and looked at Pov, her face still wet with tears. Pov kissed her and gave her a little push toward the end of the companionway.

"Go home, Tawnie," he said gently. "Maybe we'll both be along later."

Tawnie pulled her sleeve across her face, then turned and walked off, her boots jarring on the carpeting. She disappeared around the turning at the end of the companionway.

"Well?" Pov asked his mother warily.

Margareta spread her hands. "Take me to Kate. Perhaps this Sergei person isn't as bad as I believed. Anything is possible, after all."

Pov looked at her skeptically. "Would you be offended if I said I don't exactly buy all of this? After three years of fights?"

"Yes, I would be offended, so keep your comments to yourself. And it's smart of you to practice a little skepticism, my son. It suits you better than all that nobility you toss about far too much."

Pov made a disgusted noise and turned to walk off, but she suddenly closed the gap between them and laid her palm against his cheek. "How much like your father you are, Pov," she said softly. "Ah, I miss him keenly, even after all these years."

"And you'll destroy his family if you force this," he told her distantly, not responding to her caress. "Is that what a *puri dai* does to her tribe?"

She broke the half-embrace and stalked off after Tawnie, marching along with long strides. Pov ambled along behind, not bothering to hurry, and made her wait for him at the turning.

"Brain cancer," she muttered as he caught up, back on that issue. "Falling fits and shrieking for a gaje audience."

Pov fell into step with her. "You were the audience that counted. I thought it was rather spectacular, myself."

"Oh, it was, that it was. Smart of her. You could have burst in on me with the chaffer and remonstrated loudly with logic and emotion."

"Or delivered my ultimatum in front of gaje. But why embarrass you in front of the chaffer when you'd have to back down later?" He gave her a tight smile as her head jerked around. Then he bared his teeth, provoking her before she got to Kate and worked whatever mayhem she might be planning now, if she was.

His mother opened her mouth, then changed her mind about whatever retort she was about to make, surprising him. Maybe this was half real. He stifled the first flicker of hope for Kate. He stifled it all. "Patia wants to be *puri dai*," his mother said instead.

"We know," Pov said casually. "That doesn't mean she'll get the votes."

"She's looped your Avi into her plots," his mother accused. "I saw them sitting together."

"No. Avi's just trying to learn how to be a good Rom wife. She'd like to help you."

"I cannot credit that," his mother snorted.

"It's true, anyway, whatever you believe. She wants the family to stay together, so that I don't lose the Rom. So she's trying to learn what the Rom are. She's even going to ask Kate to teach her the cards."

"A Russki atheist?"

"Yes. She says the cards are 'the spirit of the Rom.' "

"Hmph. Well, she's certainly an improvement on that Bulgar woman."

"I'm glad you approve of her, Mother."

"I didn't say *that*. Don't get ahead of events."

Pov chuckled, then laughed outright as his mother reacted. "Oh, Mother," he said, shaking his head. "You never give up, do you?" He saw her smile to herself, though she quickly turned her face away to look at a rivet seam on the wall.

"Take me to Kate," Margareta demanded.

Chapter 14

When Kate opened the door, her mouth dropped open at the sight of who stood on her threshold. She noticed Pov belatedly, started to greet him, then went back to staring at her mother. Margareta stepped forward, making Kate move back. Behind Kate, Sergei looked up from the couch, more computer reports in his lap, and his expression turned wary as he saw who had just marched in.

His mother took her time looking around the small apartment, which she had hardly visited, then turned back to Kate to inspect her, too. "How many weeks are you along?" she asked.

Kate's lips tightened. "Almost three months." she said. "And I'm not getting an abortion."

"Abortion?" Margareta said briskly. "Of course not. *My* grandchild? What would ever put such an idea in your head?"

Kate started to boil. "Don't you come here and play games with me, Mother! I know how you feel, and I don't need your taunts about it, either. You can just take them and stuff them!"

"Have you had the gene scans?" Margareta asked mildly. "Girl or boy?"

Kate hesitated, disconcerted by their mother's tone. She glanced at Pov.

"Tell her, Kate," Pov said with a shrug. "It's worth a try." He walked over to Sergei and sat down in a nearby chair, then put his feet one by one on the couch table.

"A girl," Kate said reluctantly. "A little blond girl."

"Blond?" Margareta pretended shock, drawing herself up. Games again, Pov thought, disgusted with his mother's playacting: it never stopped, no matter the crisis, no matter the need. He tightened his lips, staying out of it.

"A *blond* gypsy?" his mother amplified, aghast.

Kate glared at her. "Sorry, Mother. She's blond."

Margareta glanced at Pov as he missed his cue. When Sergei opened his mouth, Pov signed at him quickly. *Not now,* he mouthed. Sergei shut up with an effort, though he muttered in Russki and nearly purpled with the effort. His mother saw that, too. Pov put his arms across his chest, staying out of it.

"Well," Margareta announced airily, waving her hand at Kate, "I suppose we can always dye her hair black."

"The hell you will," Kate declared.

"I will trade you, daughter. Black hair dye for a Rom marriage *before* the baby comes—none of *my* grandchildren will be illegitimate, I can assure you."

"No trade. We can get a civil marriage anytime we want."

"Why haven't you?" Margareta asked curiously.

Kate set her lips. "Because I've been *waiting* for you to ... for you to ..." She shook her head fiercely. "Because I want a Rom marriage inside the family, where Sergei can belong and our children will belong and ..." She broke off and turned away, crossing her arms stubbornly.

"And you thought a baby would force me to accept him?"

"Until I found out it was a girl and another heir for *puri dai,*" Kate muttered, not looking at her. "Then it was a disaster. But I'm keeping the baby, Mother. That is not negotiable."

"We've already agreed on that." Their mother blew a breath out her lips, considering. "Well, I won't insist on the hair dye. When shall we have the wedding?"

Kate turned her head and looked at her mother icily. "If this is a scheme, another feint, some dodge of yours to retract later, Mother, I will never forgive you. I will take Sergei and our child and leave the Rom. You will not be allowed in my house. I will not speak your name within our family. My child will never know you."

"Don't speak such obscenities," Margareta said irritably. "Am I not allowed any dignity? Must my capitulation be a groveling?"

"Yes," Kate snapped. "After what you've put us through for three years? After the way you've treated Pov about me? After all the *fights* you've started?"

Margareta's face suddenly softened, making her look younger, less formidable. She glanced at Pov with a small bitter smile. Pov tightened his lips. "Then, my own," Margareta said with a sigh, "I submit." She clasped her hands at her belt and bent forward, offering humility to Kate. "Forgive me," she murmured.

Kate blinked, then looked at Pov.

"She means it," he told her, as startled as Kate was.

"You really think so?"

"Yes, I do. She might take a little of it back, but she's going to let you marry Sergei, Kate. A Rom wedding, Mother. You did say that."

Margareta straightened up and grimaced. "I said that. I agree."

"And the baby will be christened as Rom, taken into the tribe," Pov added.

"Not specifically said, but also agreed." Margareta sighed feelingly. "Your victory is complete."

"Nuts to that. I know you, Mother. But Kate means what she said: if you renege, she will leave the Rom and cut you off. And so will I. I won't accept this as a *puri dai* game."

Margareta pursed her lips, her dark eyes unreadable, then shifted her glance to Sergei for a long look. She sighed again, not pleased with what she saw. "I won't promise to like him," she said disdainfully, lifting her chin. "I won't promise to always be polite. I will probably even be rude." Sergei tightened his lips, nearly strangling with the effort not to retort back to that.

"You can talk now, Sergei," Pov told him helpfully.

"When do you ask *me* about this?" he exploded. He jumped to his feet, his reports scattering all over the floor and the table and Pov. Pov swatted hastily at the sifting pages that fluttered at his face. "What kind of game is—"

"*I* ask," Kate cried. She ran to him and threw her arms around his neck. "*Marry* me, Sergei. Please do!"

Startled, Sergei looked down into Kate's face. "You're sure?"

"About you? Oh, yes!"

"I mean about *her*," Sergei said, pointing at Margareta.

"She'd *better* keep her promise," Kate declared. "But will you marry me, Sergei?" Sergei looked back down at Kate and then swept her up into a passionate kiss.

Margareta looked pained.

"Get used to it, Mother," Pov advised her. "They do that a lot. If you'd been around more, you'd have seen."

"Gloating does not become you, my son." She sniffed.

"The hell with that. I'll gloat if I want to."

Kate laughed and kissed Sergei a second time. "When shall we have the wedding? Next week!"

"We need more time than that," Margareta protested. "The arrangements will—"

Kate's expression clouded, and she tightened her hold on Sergei. "Why not next week?" she asked stubbornly.

"Kate, I'm *not* going to withdraw my permission," Margareta said. "You needn't be distrustful."

"I want to marry him *now*!"

"What happened to 'next week'?" Margareta asked sourly. "You want a Rom wedding: that means posting the bans, consulting with the family, bringing him to meals, and all the rest for at least six weeks." Kate's face clouded even more. "Ekaterina," his mother said patiently, "we need time to bake the cakes and make the wedding gifts. And you need a wedding dress, and I won't have you wearing those indecent costumes in the ship's stores with their high hems and low bodices. St. Serena's feast is next month. At least wait for the luck of a good saint's day and a proper *slava*. Saints above, child, just sewing your dress will take three weeks in itself with all the women helping."

It was at that moment that Kate truly believed their mother meant it, and Pov saw the joy flare in her face. "Oh, I'll sew my dress, Mother. It'll be beautiful."

Pov saw his mother's dark eyes suddenly moisten as Kate so obviously trusted—foolishly trusted, perhaps, as was Kate's way. Margareta gave Pov a wry look, then walked forward and placed her hands on Kate's head.

"I bless this marriage," she said, her voice trembling. "May your road be always clear, your joy unchanging, your children a blessing to your old age. I consent to this marriage, and call all to witness." His mother removed her hands and gave a little snort of dismay. "We'll have to repeat that later, of course, when the rest of the family is present." As Kate straightened, Margareta added, "You will, of course, move home and live with the other Rom."

Kate stiffened. "Don't you even start, Mother!" she warned.

"Why not move?" Margareta looked honestly befuddled. She gestured at Sergei. "Doesn't that show how much I accept him? Don't you want to be with the family?"

Kate hesitated, then grimaced. "There's hardly room, with Lasho and Bavol there now."

"We can get the adjoining apartment to give us a bit more room. I think the Kerenskys will move, or maybe we can shift to a new apartment altogether—though purifying a new home will be a task, indeed." She frowned. "I'll have to think about it, but I do want you to move home, Kate. Come back to the family." She couldn't help sending a hopeful glance at Pov.

"No," he said firmly.

"Somehow," Margareta said acidly, "I think I have opened an ancestor's coffin, and now those ghostly fingers emerge to grasp my throat, one finger at a time."

"One issue does lead to another, doesn't it?" Pov said without sympathy. "But you haven't asked Sergei if *he* wants to move in."

Margareta shrugged. "I told you I'd be rude. Kate can ask him. I won't." She gave Sergei a disdainful glare, and Sergei glared back.

"I'll think about it," he said rudely.

Margareta dismissed him with a gesture and kissed Kate's cheek, an embrace Kate permitted stiffly. "Come along, Pov. So they can *think* about it." She headed for the door. Kate seized Pov's hands, her face ecstatic.

"Go plan your wedding dress, *chavali,*" he said. He grunted as Kate hugged him like a compactor crushing metal. Then Kate danced him around in a circle, which

Pov managed to move in the general direction of the door. He finally dislodged her and pointed her back at Sergei, then got himself and Margareta out of the apartment.

As the door closed behind them, Pov smiled at his mother, then put his hands at his waist and solemnly bowed to her, repeating the respectful bow she had given Kate. He could give her that, games and all, for Kate's sake.

"Honor, Mother," he murmured in Romany. "Thank you."

He heard her indrawn breath, then felt the feathery touch of her hand on his hair, then her fingers more firmly as she caressed him. As she withdrew her hand, he straightened up again.

"Once I had worried," he said softly, "that Kate and I had left you behind when the wagons moved on. I wondered how we could come back for you, Mother."

His mother sighed. "Sometimes, my son, the grandmam merely picks up her feet and manages to catch up herself. It is my disgrace, I suppose: I'm not Rom enough to give you and Kate up. And Tawnie ..." She grimaced. "I should, but I can't." She squinted up at him. "You knew that all along, didn't you?" she accused.

"No," he said, shaking his head. "I didn't. I thought you'd go back to Perikles."

He would never know—for his mother would never tell him—if she would have relented for his and Kate's sake alone. Perhaps Tawnie had been needed, with Tawnie's threat of the other *Net* Rom who might refuse. Go home to Perikles with only half her family? Face the other tribes with such visible proof of her failure as *puri dai*? Not Margareta Janusz. Never her. She'd rather put up with the gaje that afflicted them, for all that trouble.

He would never know. Somehow the pain stretched only a certain distance—and stopped, protecting him.

"You thought that?" she said. "Well, at least I *appear* a Rom. At least I have that." She moved off down the corridor, and he walked beside her. "We will still battle, you understand that. I will not give up our traditions willy-nilly."

"I understand," he said sourly. "I don't expect miracles."

"Why should I change when I don't have to? But you told me that our law must bend itself sometimes. I obviously must bend for Kate. I don't like it. I don't think this marriage is wise, but I will bend. And if you will not leave *Net,* I must bend on that, too. On other points I will not, so choose your ultimatums carefully."

"I will."

"Good." His mother sighed, then tossed her head impatiently. "Does your Avi have any ideas about how I'm supposed to deal with Patia?"

"Not yet. Why don't you ask her?"

"Spread this out, please," she said irritably. "For the sake of my old bones—and my dignity. I'll notice Avi later—maybe, if this so-called engagement of yours lasts."

"It will."

"How can it be a true betrothal when you haven't asked the elders for permission?"

"Meaning asking *you,* you mean. We'll see, Mother. After Kate is truly married to Sergei, then I'll think about talking to elders."

Margareta smiled and slipped her hand through the crook of his arm. Together they walked across the companionway to the other side of *Net,* where the Rom lived together, to tell the family that next month's *slava,* Siduri's own feast, would celebrate Kate's wedding, for the luck of the Rom.

"Patia will turn green," Pov noted as they turned into the Janusz corridor.

"And other colors," his mother said with great satisfaction. "I have always treated her well, better than Narilla does. I promised myself, after your grandmother treated me as she did, that I would be different to our younger women." In some Rom families, the older women of the tribe badly dominated the younger wives, proving their power by making other lives miserable. To be fair, excepting how she had treated Kate about Sergei, his mother had indeed forborne the worst of what she could do. He didn't rise to her bait, letting her win the jab.

"Patia won't win, Mother," he said. "She lacks the subtlety."

"Thank you," his mother said, as if he had complimented her instead of disparaging Patia. Maybe his mother saw some kind of logical connection, though the logic escaped him.

"Would you give the same forbearance," he asked cautiously, "to a daughter-in-law, even if she's a *gaji romni*?"

"I will *think* about that—when I am *asked* about a betrothal."

"*When* you don't want to play games," he told her calmly, "then I'll think about asking—but not until then."

"I will be waiting all that time," Margareta said complacently. "Let us hope something eventful happens in our lifetimes."

His mother patted his arm and smiled, then walked into the Janusz apartment. She held the door open and looked back at him. "My son?"

One thing at a time, he thought and stepped forward. He would go in, not to gloat at his mother when she told the others. He would go in to be with his family.

Pov was late in meeting Stefania on skydeck for their data mission to TriPower, and Stefania's fingers were tapping irritably on the control console of the skyrider when he arrived. As he buckled himself into the passenger seat behind her, Stefania dangled an arm over the back of her chair and opened her mouth.

"It's a captain's rule," Pov told her solemnly, "that one captain never comments when another captain is late. It's rude." He leaned over and snapped his data carrier into a floor bracket.

"Is it?" she said skeptically. "Are these rules published somewhere? I'd like to look that one up."

"Not that I've heard," he said blandly and straightened in his chair. "You sort of pick the rules up as you go along. Trust me on this, Stef."

"Right, Pov." Stefania wrinkled her nose.

She laughed and turned around, then started punching at the buttons on her console. The skyrider rolled smoothly toward the exterior port. After a short trip,

Stefania docked at a small-ship access on TriPower's inner torus ring. They cycled through the airlock, stepping out into a decor of cool white and restful pastels, with the windows oddly set into the floor instead of a wall. Pov walked over to the nearest window and looked down.

In the distance, TriPower's floating ship dock, with *Net*'s upper prow just visible above her bay, was moving sideways, the entire starfield moving with it. Unlike Omsk and *Net* herself, TriPower used centrifugal force for a working gravity, a far cheaper method than fielding artificial gravity for a station of TriPower's size. Pov's feet were now pinned to the outside wall of the torus, moving Pov sideways, too, though a different sideways from *Net,* of course. He blinked, untangling his mind from that fractured idea. Stefania joined him and looked down, too.

"I've decided," he said, "that it's not that the windows are in the floor. It's that people on TriPower walk on the walls."

"Now *that's* an illuminating comment," she said.

"I thought so."

They looked up as a tall and pleasant-looking young Swede came toward them, his bright blond hair swept back from his face. Sigrid's son, Lang, worked in the TriPower observatory, and Sigrid had arranged data access for *Net* to TriPower's astronomy databanks. The young man smiled broadly and stretched out his hand.

"Sailmaster Janusz?" he said. "Lang Thorsen. My mother said you'd be coming over." Pov returned Lang's strong handshake, then introduced him to Stefania. "Did you bring your Helm Map program?" Lang asked.

Pov tapped the data carrier in his hand. "And some other things you might like."

"I've heard about your cloudship's Helm Map program for years," Lang said enthusiastically, "and I've itched to look at it." His smile lit up his gray eyes, so much like his mother's, and Pov saw the other resemblances to Sigrid, not only in his features, but in his personality. Lang actually rubbed his hands in anticipation. "Come this way. We'll go up to the observatory and use the computer there."

Lang led them down the hallway to a cross corridor and past an atrium, something pretty with fountains and greenery and a ceiling twenty meters high. People passed to and fro, most of them blond, dressed in jumpsuits of several colors, all walking with a smart stride. Pov could feel the coolness of the water mist in the air and sniffed at the scents of the plants as they walked through the atrium toward an elevator. Avi liked fountains in a garden, Pov remembered, looking around with appreciation, something she missed from planetside: he should bring her here.

He felt odd, not quite reconnected to reality. His mother's warfare had so dominated his life the last three years that he found himself slightly unmoored without it. Sideways, indeed. He sniffed again, turning his head to look back at the garden, liking the sounds and smells. Avi will love it, he thought, and smiled. He caught Stefania eyeing him quizzically and smiled at her, too.

"Comm to skyrider," Stefania murmured pointedly, "*are* you there?"

"Mostly. Nice plants."

"Yeah. They're even green."

At the elevator, Lang waved them both into the cage, and they stepped out four levels above onto a suspended balcony far above the atrium. Walking briskly, Lang led them into a nearby suite of brightly lit rooms with large computer banks and a wallscreen. Above their heads, a wide curving dome gave a view of the processing plant overhead. Lang sat down at a chair before a large compute console and accessed the mainframe computer, and Pov sat down beside him.

Stefania put her hands in her pockets and looked casually around the room, then looked up and watched the activity at the huge processing plant. "TriPower also works upside down on ceilings," she observed, just loudly enough for Pov to catch, then smiled as he chuckled.

"Okay, I'm in," Lang said. "What do you need?"

Pov stretched his legs out comfortably. "We need a route into the Shield and a way to find *Ishtar's Jewel.* We've lost most of our Pleiades database, and that was mostly Earth data, anyway. So, to start, mainly astronomy, and more than a single vantage point, if you've got it."

Lang frowned thoughtfully, then keyed up some data lists. "Well, we do have some astrometrical research, mostly studies of the blue giants and some cloud processes. But that's all at long distance and all of it single-point from TriPower."

Pov sighed. "Long-distance scans will help, but not enough. A light-year to you to a few photo frames, but it's several thousand times the length of a cloud run. We need data up close." He scowled. "We need maps, especially cubic maps."

Lang chewed his lip thoughtfully, then brightened. "I have some observations off the freighter beacons for a second point. TriPower maintains the beacons on our segment of the route, and we've sometimes sent out a scanner package for basic research. Let me see what I've got." Lang ran through his datafiles again.

Pov leaned forward. "Do you have light surveys, all frequencies?"

Stefania stepped up to stand behind Pov, looking over his shoulder. "We're mostly interested in radio and UV," she added.

Lang nodded. "Uh, Helm Map?" he said diffidently.

Pov smiled and snapped the carrier into the access port. "Load it into a separate area with a virus fence," he warned Lang. "We had a virus buried in some data. As far as we can tell, the program's clean, but I'd hate to contaminate your computers."

Lang nodded and complied, then became quickly absorbed in his computer screen as Helm Map displayed its programming access. Pov nudged his chair over. "Here, let me show you how it works. Where's that data you identified? Okay, loading into Helm Map. Let's pick a local star in the Shield, maybe the area around 191 Tauri."

Stefania turned toward the wallscreen, then sighed with satisfaction. "First-rate!" she declared. Pov turned and looked. The screen showed a localized segment of the Shield, modeled in three dimensions, with a small orange star embedded in the drifting gas. Part of the screen was obscured, showing little detail, and other parts were not colored properly—but it was a map.

"Still long-range," Pov judged. "We aren't getting much depth ranging."

"Better than we had, Pov," Stefania said firmly. "I'll take it."

Pov looked back at Lang, and saw the astronomer's mouth still agape as he stared at the wallscreen. "It's called cubic, Lang," Pov said, amused.

"My God!" Lang exclaimed. "I had no idea." He got up from his chair and paced the length of the wallscreen, peering at the images. "My God!" he repeated again. Pov grinned. They'd have to take Lang on a cloud run, too. Lang turned around, delighted. "I had no idea it looked like this. You could map anywhere!"

"Want a copy?" Pov asked, smiling at him. "Modeling on Helm Map takes practice, but it'd give you a better idea of what we're looking for in sky surveys."

"*Would* you?" Lang turned around again and backed up to get some perspective. "I'd love that. It's wonderful!"

"When we have the data, it's even better," Stefania said, still looking at the map. "And we need two-point data to map, three to do it properly. Also, Lang, our version of Helm Map is programmed for ordinary solar systems and comets: it doesn't expect the heavy dust, especially in the smaller size you have here. When your Pleiades dust absorbs some frequencies and not others, we get a skewed plot. The *last* thing I want to do is rescrub Helm Map down to its light-wave assumptions."

"I could study that problem," Lang said eagerly. "We have molecular scans of local space, and once I understand the program fundamentals, I could—" He broke off suddenly and laughed. "This works, doesn't it? Sharing data. What a difference it'll make!"

"I'll say," Stefania said, turning to smile at him. "Don't the cloudships ever share data with you?"

Lang shook his head. "Not here at TriPower. A little at GradyBol, but Gunter had to pay a fee for it, then couldn't share it with us." Stefania raised an eyebrow. "The promise was a condition of the sale."

Stefania shook her head, then turned back to the map

screen. "It's better, Pov. I could plot from these data to that star."

"It's still got holes," Pov argued. "This particular star happens to be near a freighter beacon that TriPower happened to pick for a survey instrument package." Pov checked the datafile list. "I see only two other places in the Shield with that much data. Let's try someplace where it's less." Pov plotted into another part of the Shield and got mostly a blue glare, a ghostly star winking in the middle.

"Bad holes, I agree." Stefania rocked on her heels, scowling at the screen. "Where we come from, Lang, dust was red. Here it seems to be blue, like everywhere. But it's still better, Pov. We had basically nothing before, especially over here in the Shield."

"I suppose," Pov said reluctantly.

"TriPower could send out a scanner to pick up what you need for a second observation point," Lang offered. "We service the freighter beacons in our area, and two are due for a service check. That would cover most of the northern quadrant of the Shield."

"That would help," Pov admitted. Lang sat down again beside him and stretched out his long legs, still looking at Helm Map with a kind of wonder.

"Helm Map would be useful to an observatory," Pov commented. "Better than flat field, especially when you're studying local space."

"I agree, but we've never had access. *Arrow* won't sell it to us. It's a secret, they say. Everything's a secret, it seems. I've never even been aboard a cloudship. None of us on Tripower have, until you invited Mother onto *Net.* Mother just loved your sail drills, by the way." He looked at Pov, suddenly hoping.

"Come over this afternoon, Lang," Pov said indulgently.

"Aren't I supposed to be cautious?" Lang said, teasing as his mother teased. "You know, play the games, remember commercial advantage, and so forth? Mother keeps trying to teach me, but I like watching stars."

"Don't worry about that," Pov said. "I'm giving you Helm Map to play with, and I brought over some sail modeling, too. This exchange goes both ways, wide open. Captain Andreos and Sigrid are determined." Pov smiled. "Both sides want confidentiality with third parties, of course, but both sides have the other's data for retaliation if the agreement doesn't stay stuck, with the lawyers writing in penalties that bite."

"Somehow I don't think we'll need the penalties, sir," Lang said. "I think we're changing the rules about cloudships and stations."

"Looks like it," Pov agreed, smiling at Stefania. "What do you have on *Jewel*?"

"It depends on where she's been in the Shield recently." Lang turned back to his computer console and typed busily. "When she's on our side of the Shield, we can sometimes detect her engine exhaust close to jump. The frequencies range higher then, you know, and it can be enough to detect as a point source against the background radiation."

"Can you track her course when she jumps?" Stefania asked.

"Not in three dimensions," Lang said, then looked at Helm Map. "At least not yet," he added, then smiled.

"Do you have historical records about *Jewel*'s movements?" Pov asked. "Based on the times you've sighted her in the Shield?"

"I can assemble what I have. Why?"

"Maps again, and maybe where *Jewel* might be found. *Jewel* will hunt the ionization fronts, and might return to a particular segment of a front once she has it mapped." He shrugged. "I would. It's easier to jump back to where you've already been. Maybe *Jewel* has a route around the Shield, too. If she's been sailing the Shield for several years, she's had the light ranging to map most of it by now."

"I'll load everything I have, but I wouldn't know how to analyze that kind of pattern."

"We do. Maybe by the next time we come back to TriPower, so will you." He smiled at the young Swede. "One last thing. Do you have any pictures of cloudships? Especially *Arrow*'s group."

"Pictures?"

"Optical scans."

"Well, I can look. The telescope points in all directions over a twenty-hour schedule, so we ought to have some. *Hound*'s been here a few times, and *Jewel,* of course. Why?"

"I want to look at their sails."

"Why?" Lang looked confused.

"Commercial espionage, Lang. How to make my sails more efficient. How to get ahead of all the other guys."

Lang grinned. "Hm. Sounds corporate to me."

"That it is."

Stefania chuckled. "It's *all* corporate, I think," she said, turning back to the wallscreen. "I'm happy with Helm Map and its pretty pictures." She sighed. "Let's go here first, to this star. I like this detail. Part of that gas is ionized, too. Look at the color."

"If it's accurate. You'll note that part of that star's surface isn't ionized. Helm Map is sorting the dust wrong."

"So we'll scrub it and see. Think positive, Sail—unless you've got a better idea about somewhere else, better than mine."

"You're the pilotmaster, Stef." Stefania turned around and smiled.

Pov and Stefania took Lang back to *Net* and left him with Tully to watch sail drills, then spent an hour in genial argument about the new data for Helm Map. Pov thought there were too many holes, but he wasn't Helm. Stefania liked what she saw, but admitted some of his arguments had a point. Finally, after ascending the authority ladders to both Captain Andreos and Dr. Cherinsky, they invaded Medical and stole Athena.

They also stole her bed, rolling it out of Medical and down the hall toward the companionway, with medtech attached and already scowling ferociously. "My golden barge," Athena joked, pretending to paddle.

"The *Argo,*" Pov suggested. "And we're hunting the golden fleece. Paddle hard, Athena," he added as they neared the elevator. "Here come the Clashing Rocks."

The elevator was a tight fit, and the medtech pulled rank on Stefania, tossing her out to ride up by herself in the other cage. When Pov and the medtech rolled Athena onto Helm Deck, everyone on deck looked around and broke into surprised laughter, then applauded Athena happily as they came to crowd around her bed, excited and pleased. The medtech shooed them off briskly.

"Dr. Cherinsky says *no* excitement," she declared, putting her hands on her hips. "And there *will* be no excitement, or I'll take her right back to Medical. You hear me?" She included Athena and Pov in her awful glare.

"We hear you," Athena said meekly, and motioned the staff back to their stations. "Pay attention, flock. She means it. I'm on parole, and everybody's got rules now. Roll me up to the middle of the deck, Pov. Let's use the big screen." Pov pushed her bed forward and stopped it beside the central command chair.

Stefania joined them and sat down by Athena. "You can all help," she said, looking around at the helm staff. "We're making maps again, and Athena's here for a front-row view. Right?" She smiled at Athena.

"Right," Athena said with satisfaction. "What have we got?"

Athena frowned about the holes, but agreed with Stefania. "We can jump with it," she decided, then shook her head regretfully. "I was hoping for more from TriPower's database. But it's better than what we had, even with the dust distortion. And we've got all the star coordinates now, based on what we loaded at Maia and now this."

"The data's younger, too," Pov admitted. "Our Luna map was based on light four hundred years old, after all. The clouds and shock fronts don't drift far in a few centuries, but far enough if we're chasing something small. With this new data, the time lapse for the Shield is only a year or two, minimal. You can plot around that."

"True," Athena said. "I'd like to talk to Lang, Pov. Maybe he can do a targeted scan for us before we launch."

"No talk," the medtech declared. "Dr. Cherinsky won't approve."

"So I'll write a report," Athena muttered. "Five-minute

work units, two-hour rests. It'll only take all day and to-morrow." She squinted up at the medtech.

"If Doctor approves," she said with a sniff, "which I doubt."

Athena rolled her eyes. "So I'll dictate prone."

"If Doctor approves, maybe."

Athena crossed her arms and laughed. "So I'll think good thoughts." The medtech smiled, knowing her power.

Chapter 15

Later that evening at his apartment, Avi had gone to bed, but Pov sat in front of his window, watching *Net* and the starfields beyond her. Stefania had backed *Net* out of her ship bay to turn Sail Deck's sensors on the Shield, supplementing the scans Lang's night crew would run from TriPower's observatory. It gave Pov a new view for a few hours, one he had decided not to miss. Beyond *Net*'s glittering lights, TriPower's double torus dominated the sky, backlit by long thin veils of fluorescent clouds, the clustered stars, and the red hub of TriPower's processing plant. Like Pluto's forge, he thought.

The outer door opened and Tully walked in and plopped down in the nearby chair, then put up his feet on the table. Pov looked him over. "So how long have you had my override code, Tully?" he demanded. "I'm sure I locked the door."

"I've had it for years," Tully informed him casually. "Nice view."

"Yes, it is. If you keep strolling in this late at night, anytime you like, you could end up inconvenient."

Tully was unrepentant. "So I steal in, go 'oops,' and steal back out, and you and Avi never know. Just go right on with what you're doing," he said grandly, waving his hand. "I won't mind."

Pov chuckled. "Want a drink?"

"Absolutely."

Pov got up and brought glasses and a bottle, then poured vodka in both. "How's the sieve?" he asked, handing Tully his glass.

"Which one? *Net* or TriPower?"

"My, you move fast. Spies on TriPower already?"

"Of course. Sigrid told them to tell us all: it's a priceless opportunity. Of course, I have to tell *them* all, too, so now I'm one of TriPower's spies, too. Only in the Pleiades, I guess." He cradled his glass on his stomach comfortably. "They like Sigrid. She's got a lot of loyalty."

"She deserves it."

Tully turned his head. "Is everything okay between you and Andreos?"

"Yes," Pov said. "It was a misunderstanding. We're fine." He paused. "Is that on the sieve, too?" he asked uncomfortably.

"Not really. No real details, but enough to feel a vague concern. They worry about Athena, and now they're worrying about you. The *big* item is the fight with your mother on the companionway."

Pov grimaced. "Well, I suppose it was in public."

"She started it, not you," Tully said aggressively, "and I'm glad she lost. So don't sit there and flinch about gaje knowing about family: you know better than that, Pov. This is something the ship should know, if it happens. It's important when a captain is willing to choose *Net* over everything else. That's the sieve's consensus, and that's my opinion." He sipped at his glass, looking at TriPower.

"She had her reasons, Tully."

"Rom reasons, and I don't agree with them," Tully said stubbornly. "I'm a Greek. I don't have to get all tangled up in the rightness of gypsy tradition and the wrongness of everything gaje else. Hell, I'm damned angry at her." He scowled and looked down into his glass. "Don't invite me to visit your family for a while, Pov," he muttered. "I'd be rude."

Pov smiled. "Thanks, Tully."

"Anytime, coz." Tully looked at him closely. "So you're all right?"

"I'm fine. Avi and I are getting married."

"So I've heard." Tully said teasingly.

Pov hissed in exasperation, and Tully laughed, then saluted him with his glass. "Congratulations, Pov. She's the right one."

"I think so, too."

"I just hope your mother agrees," Tully added meaningfully.

"Oh, she won't, but I've been trying to warn Avi. So long as we don't get into Avi's old pattern with her own family, I think she'll be all right. It's hard enough to be a Rom when you're not born to it."

"Now *that's* a fatuous statement."

Pov looked at him quizzically. "Is it?" he asked, amused by Tully's expression.

" 'Born to it.' What an attitude." Tully snorted vastly and waved his glass.

"If you were a gypsy, you'd agree," Pov said mildly. "All the Rom know it's true."

"Just keep it up Pov, and I'll leave. *I've* got an attitude right now, too." Tully scowled at him, obviously inclined to argue about anything Rom tonight.

"I've noticed." Pov gestured peace and smiled, then watched Tully lose his ferocious scowl in a smile that lit up his blue eyes. Tully always lost the scowl, every time: *rai,* he thought with affection, the Rom word for a gaje brother, rarely found, a man to be treasured. Like Tully. Pov raised his glass to his friend. *"Sastimos,* coz."

"Stin'ya stass, adelphos. Down the hatch." They matched word to deed, and Pov refilled their glasses, then leaned back and slid farther down in his chair, getting his feet just right on the table. Tully yawned.

"What else is on the sieve?" Pov asked casually.

Tully shrugged. "Oh, pieces here and there. The news is out about the Orion Nebula, though how we get there is a mystery, of course. So's the why. Most of TriPower thinks we're crazy to even think about it, however Sigrid likes the idea."

"Gray's wanted the Nebula for twenty years," Pov observed. He balanced his glass on his stomach and saw TriPower's reddish light shimmer across the liquid surface of the vodka. It glowed, like the Nebula glowed, shimmering between the darkness of his hands.

"A man gets his compulsions, I agree," Tully said, unimpressed. "Yours are usually Rom, though I'm glad to see Russki enter the mix lately." Tully yawned again. "I seem to remember a conversation like this before, you smiling happily about a protostar that might eat us alive and me trying to impose reason."

"I'm *not* smiling happily, at least not about that. If I get posted shipmaster to our daughter ship, you'll be my sailmaster. If she goes to the Nebula, so do you."

"Yeah, I know." Tully was silent for a long moment. "It isn't about me, particularly. Sail Deck doesn't scare me, even with the challenges the Nebula would throw at us. I'm just wondering if all this dashing around, being heroes on the frontier and all, is overlooking some basic sense. We wanted the Pleiades and got it and now, after a month, we want something else. Basic greed is good for a man, I admit, but sometimes it can edge into megalomania."

"This is more than greed, Tully. The Nebula is—"

"I know. A treasure trove. A high-plasma cloud powered by a cluster of O-class stars, with a hundred light years of dark molecular cloud behind it. Access to the Nebula's dark clouds would change cloud chemistry as much as our new drive is going to change basic spaceflight. I know the reasons for the dream, not that they're particularly yours." He pointed at Pov with his glass. "For *you*, it's your gypsy road. I think a lot about that road, since I seem to be riding along with you. I keep pointing at all the nice scenery we're passing by, nagging we ought to stop and camp. Rom forever, you shout back, then wave your hat and cluck at the horses."

Pov snorted with amusement. "So? What about your Greek Fates that handed us the new drive? Without the drive, we might have tried something at the Nebula in ten years—what I don't know, but maybe something. With the drive, it got sooner, maybe five years to get the capital investment we'd need, plowing around the Pleiades picking up cash. Now with Sigrid's alliance, it's feasible in a year or two, and *Arrow*'s buying in will cinch it for next year. We're the first, Tully, the first who have the chance to go. How can we say no?"

"Oh, really? No choice, you say?" Tully waggled his eyebrows, affecting amazement. "You make your fate Greek and you might find it rolling right at you—and right over your wagon, squashing it flat. The Nebula has lots of ways to do it: supersonic gas streams, water masers, dust curtains, protostar jets—"

"Okay, okay," Pov complained. "I hear you. Marathon and dead Greeks, right. How serious is all this gloom, anyway?"

"It's Gray's dream, Pov: it doesn't have to be ours." Tully stared down into his glass. "I think Gray is going to railroad Andreos into trying it. I think we'll commit everything to the Nebula, all the good years we could have here, all the future for our children we would build *here* in the Pleiades. And I think we could indeed get fried." He grimaced. "Does that make me a coward?"

"Of course not. How serious, Tully?" Pov repeated quietly, watching his friend's face.

Tully blinked at him owlishly. "Hell, I don't know. You're drunk and I'm catching up fast—and I seem to lose these arguments whenever I start one, anyway. The Fates, I guess. Have you considered that our Slav ships and *Arrow*'s three aren't enough? We'd be idiots to send everything we have on the first try, and we'll need a phalanx to survive the Nebula's core. So maybe five or six ships to give us the sail coverage we'll need. That means asking the Arabs or Hindus, maybe both."

"Other ships, more besides Gray," Pov said slowly, considering the complications. "I hadn't thought that far ahead."

"Exactly. So I've noticed." Tully had his scowl back again, sharing it equally with Pov, TriPower, and his shot glass. "Our only protection is wider sails, stronger sails built into a shield by multiple ships in close maneuver—and so we need a consortium that works. If we get somebody with better ideas at the wrong time—" He sighed and stirred uncomfortably. "So we need the Arabs, probably, and what I hear of them is problems cubed. Allah's gift to the Pleiades, they think themselves, slick and smart and damned aggressive. The Hindus on *Rohini's Horn* won't even talk to them any more, TriPower says, and that after only a year of their sharing the Merope Drift."

"Andreos is good at juggling personalities," Pov said comfortably. "I'd rather worry about the Nebula."

"That's nice of you. I feel wonderfully reassured. Wake up, Pov. Andreos can't go. Sigrid has to be cultivated, *Arrow* managed, GradyBol insulted nicely, plus *Net* has to make some money to cover what we'll be wasting at the Nebula. *You're* the one who gets to juggle."

Pov sat up straighter. *"Me?"*

Tully chuckled wickedly. "I worry about you, I really do, going around in a fog like that."

"Nuts," Pov declared. "You're out of your mind."

Tully grinned. *"Net* is senior partner in this adventure; we own the new drive. No way would we let Gray lead it, and Ceverny would never take our daughter ship away from you. So it's you. You'll have help, of course—me, Ceverny, others—but you get to hold it together."

"You're crazy." Pov dropped a foot from the table and stared at Tully, aghast. "I don't have the seniority."

Tully grinned more broadly, obviously enjoying Pov's horror. "I beg to differ, coz. Andreos is openly grooming you now, including you in all the contacts with outsiders, deferring to you in conferences, showing open favor. It's obvious, you dope—and the sieve approves, by the way. I approve, too, of course—not complaining. You've got the potential and deserve it. But I'm selfish, too: I don't want you hurt—or dead, Pov, chasing after Gray's dream and letting the Arabs act off, getting stupid. The stars would dim, I think they say." He chuckled. "Listen to me, getting embarrassed about feelings. I love you, Pov. You're a brother I don't want to lose."

"We're the best, you and me," Pov agreed, then slowly re-propped his foot on the table. "I hadn't considered. . . ." He trailed off, his mind working frantically.

"Obviously," Tully said wryly. "As I've noted. Hell, two months ago Rybak was trying to make you the main course at dinner, and it was a short orbit that he didn't. But there's still hope. Do you know that you narrow your eyes just like Andreos does when he's thinking smart?"

"Do I?" Pov blinked at him.

"Yes, you do. I've enjoyed watching the changes. I've been sitting on our wagon watching my friend turn into a shipmaster, one that I'll be proud to follow. And I'm thinking this friend might be one of the great shipmasters, maybe the next Thaddeus Gray." He leaned forward and put his glass on the table by Pov's feet. "One to die for, if that's necessary." Tully shrugged. "So don't worry about me. After a certain point, you believe because he believes. That's Andreos, and that'll be you, Pov."

"So be my spy, Tully. Work the sieve and give me some warnings."

"Of *course* I'll do that. But I want you to listen about Marathon and dead Greeks, a little more than last time. Don't let your adulation for Thaddeus Gray warp your judgment. The glamor isn't worth it."

"Heard and observed, sail."

"Good. Not that it'll stick," Tully said with mock disgust. "I know you too well."

Pov laughed. "I'm not *that* bad. Hell."

"Oh, really? I haven't seen you as shipmaster yet, whatever my hopes. I'm not sure what kind you'll be. Some shipmasters can get crazy, risking their ship out of damnable pride like Rybak did. And it was stupid of the Arabs to alienate *Horn* so quickly. And Talbot was stupid, too, losing the chance at you. It's easy to be stupid. At the Nebula, stupid can kill you."

"That's why I have you, Tully," Pov said placatingly, "to keep me smart. Right?"

"You're so right," Tully retorted. "Like I said, fatuous. I'm needed—desperately. I can see it in your face. Glamor, power, authority—you'll change, right before my eyes, and I won't know you at all."

Pov laughed. "I most certainly will *not.*"

"Oh, sure, toss it off," Tully growled. "Be blithe. But when it happens, remember it was *me* who predicted it." Tully thumped his chest with his finger. "I want the credit."

"Nothing's happened yet, you Greek, but I'll remember. I'll listen: I promise." Tully kept his scowl. "Want to be best man at the wedding? It's about time you returned the favor I did you for yours."

The scowl vanished abruptly into a wide smile, lighting the eyes again. "Sure," Tully said. "I hate obligations that go on and on. When did you have in mind?"

"Let's get Kate married first." Pov sighed contentedly.

"They're getting engaged tomorrow. Everything's all right—for now, at least. The future might be something else. See, I'm listening to you, Tully. I always listen."

"Oh, *sure* you do." Tully got up. "I'm going home," he said dramatically. "You're hopeless."

"So maybe I don't want the next problem right away," Pov said reasonably, squinting up at him. "I just got over the one I had and now I'm nicely sloshed and Avi loves me and this is a good view. But thanks for coming by, coz. Take it easy, will you?"

"Oh, you . . . you. . . ."

"Go ahead, say it. As Sigrid says, I can take it."

Tully laughed. "Anytime, you crazy gypsy."

"Goes well with crazy Greek. Very well indeed." Pov raised his glass, saluting him. "Fortune, Tully," he said in Romany. "Sleep well."

Tully made an act of shaking his head, and then slouched out of the apartment, going home. After he'd left, Pov positioned his glass on his stomach and shifted his feet slightly on the table, then smiled at Sigrid's forge beyond his window, a fiery beacon against the brilliant darkness.

"The frontier," he said softly, saluting the forge. He looked at the dim shadow on the shrine table in the corner. "Your road, Siduri. Give us fortune, when we go, for the luck of the Rom, and the music and the dance, and for the stars between. Help me listen to Tully." He saluted her solemnly with his glass, then added, rather drunkenly, "Down the hatch." Siduri approved, smiling at him through the darkness.

The next afternoon Pov pushed the chime button at the Janusz apartment door, with Sergei standing nervously at his side. "Relax, Sergei," he said.

"I keep thinking she's going to pull the plug somehow."

"By Rom law, the engagement itself makes you married, though we do the rest, too." He lifted the bottle of wine and necklace of glittering coins that he held in his hand. "And you're about to get engaged. Relax."

Sergei made an effort, then smiled. "Thanks for everything, Pov."

"Surely, coz. Welcome to the family."

Tawnie opened the door. Behind her, the entire Janusz family sat on the guest cushions, watching, with Avi among them. "Yes?" Tawnie asked. "What do you want, old man?"

"I'm a sad father looking for a bride," Pov intoned mournfully. He gestured to Sergei, measuring him up and down with his hand. "Look at my son. Grown and without a wife." Pov tsked.

"We have no brides here," Tawnie said pertly. "Go somewhere else." She keyed the door shut, and Pov waited a few seconds and pushed the chime again.

"Yes?" Tawnie said, then took a step back in feigned dismay. *"You* again?"

"I'm a poor father looking for a bride for his son," Pov said pitifully.

"We have no brides here," Tawnie declared, and put her hands on her hips. "Away with you, old man," she added, then almost giggled, turning red as she tried to keep her composure. "No brides here!" she shouted.

Pov pushed her aside with a grand sweep of his arm and marched into the apartment. "Sergei!" she heard Tawnie whisper as Sergei missed his cue and Tawnie had to help him into the apartment. Pov took his stance, feet planted firmly, and glared at the waiting Rom.

"I'm looking for a bride!" he shouted.

"No brides here!" they shouted back.

"Hmph," Pov said dismissingly. "I don't believe you. You lie, I am thinking." Carrying his bottle of wine and necklace, Pov stomped into the kitchen and opened a cupboard about a foot square and looked in, which made the children laugh and whoop. He sighed and scratched his head, then marched back into the living room and crossed to a tall closet, then stepped right in, rattling and bumping around the contents. He heard the laughter outside as he made more busy noise, clanging and thumping, then stepped out of the closet.

"I'm looking for a bride for my son!" he declared, glowering at them all.

"No brides here!" they shouted back derisively, then laughed and catcalled.

"Leave, old man!" Tawnie declared, pointing at the door.

"Not until I find a bride for my son," Pov told her malevolently. He looked around the room, high and low, then looked a long moment at each of the people on the cushions, one by one, coming at last to Kate. "See!" he declared triumphantly and pointed at Kate. "You did lie! I see a bride, right *there!*"

Pov walked over to Kate and offered her his hand, then steadied her as she stood up. Then, with great ceremony, he unwrapped the long strand of pierced coins from his bottle of wine and settled it around her head and shoulders.

"I see a bride," he said softly, smiling at her. Kate threw her hands around his neck and kissed him. When Sergei missed his cue again, Pov turned around and saw him standing there like a lump, smiling shyly at Kate.

"Sergei," he hissed and gestured impatiently.

"Oh!" Sergei said and lurched forward, getting a little pink as everyone laughed, even Kate.

When Sergei managed to walk over without falling down, Pov handed him the bottle of wine. *"Sastimos,* coz. Don't drop it," he added, as if Sergei might.

Sergei glanced at him disdainfully. "Not a chance."

Margareta got slowly to her feet and waved for silence. "I consent to this marriage," she said. "My blessings, my children." She came forward and kissed both Kate and Sergei on the cheek, graciously enough, then joined their hands together under hers. "The marriage shall be on St. Serena's feast. *Sastimos!"*

"Sastimos!" the others echoed loudly, wishing the couple health and blessings.

Pov sat down by Avi, then watched as Patia and Judit brought out the engagement gifts, brightly wrapped in foil, one for Kate, one for Sergei. Kate held her gift for a while, not opening it, looking around at her family and so radiantly happy that Pov felt his own eyes fill with tears. Finally, at the family's loud urging, the couple

opened their gifts, a pretty lace kerchief for Kate, a fine
silver bracelet for Sergei.

"More later," Karoly promised. *"Sastimos!"*

Karoly opened Pov's bottle of wine while Tawnie
brought in two other bottles from the kitchen, and everyone had a glass, even a sip for the children. The relief in
the family was almost palpable, adding color to the many
faces, extra liveliness to the toasts given to Sergei and
Kate. Tawnie hung on Del's arm, smiling with her delight. Then Shuri, Bavol's five-year-old, began running
around the room in excitement, quickly joined by the
younger children, and the Janusz gathering again descended into its usual noise. Pov slipped his hand into
Avi's and smiled at her.

"Getting used to this?"

"She's so happy," Avi murmured, her eyes on Kate.

Pov looked at his mother, who was acting gracious, accepting the compliments of the family as if she hadn't
lost a battle at all. Patia was practically simpering as she
bent to press Margareta's hand. Well, win a battle, there's
always the future, Pov thought, and held out his glass for
Tawnie to fill, happy that Kate had won hers, the only
battle Kate really cared about.

Over the next two days, *Net* sold half its tritium to
TriPower and converted the payment into credits, then arranged transport for the two dozen of *Net*'s three hundred
crewpeople who had asked to return to Tania's Ring, one
family buying passage back to Earth itself. Then, after a
leavetaking with TriPower's senior staff even more cor-
dial than its welcome, *Net* undocked and headed for the
nearby Shield.

They jumped to the small orange star and found another detached shock front, weaker than the drifting arc
of gas at Maia but sailable, and farther from the local
blue star, which allowed *Net* to use a skyrider chevron.
Alcyone's Shield was a vast pool of dust and gas illumi-
nated by the blue giant Alcyone, located midway between
Maia and the twin blues of Pleione and Atlas. The Shield
was smaller than Maia's Veil and the even larger Merope
Drift, but rich in carbon radicals and the heavier isotopes

of hydrogen and lithium. *Net* spread her sails, reaping in another harvest.

It was a rich harvest, heavy in the silicate dusts that spun into *Net*'s sails with the ionized hydrogen. Janina stored extra tins of dust for analysis, then sorted the heavier atoms from the deuterium and tritium isotopes of hydrogen that formed *Net*'s main catch. Sigrid had shared data about other atoms worthy of sale in the Pleiades, and the captains and chiefs conferred often about the best products. The alliance worked well, and Pov saw the satisfaction in the faces of both Captain Andreos and Sigrid.

Sigrid had spent most of her time gossiping with *Net*'s staff, freely answering any question they asked, and genially insisting on a fair return as she marveled at *Net*'s sails and Hold Deck and all the points between, openly exulting to be aboard *Net*. She huddled with Janina, talking molecules and big plans, then sat a whole watch on Sail Deck with Pov, asking one question after another. She rode with the skyrider chevron, dined with Ceverny and Andreos and Danil, taught them all some bawdy Swedish songs, and generally made a pest of herself all over the ship, having fun all the way.

When *Net* had filled her holds, she jumped farther into the Shield to find *Ishtar's Jewel*. After several days of searching, *Net* jumped again and found *Jewel* near a small golden star on the far edge of the Shield, cruising slowly through the drifting dust. Even at a distance, *Jewel* showed her antiquated design in the smallness of her sails and the canted angle of her collecting holds.

"It looks like she still has her original sails," Ceverny commented from his interlink chair next to Pov. "In this dust?" Then he frowned as *Jewel* shifted course ahead of them and the local star's light fragmented into shimmering rainbows across her hull. Years of dust had scoured *Jewel*'s prow and collecting wings, etching complicated whorls into the metal on every exposed surface, refracting the light. "Look how she shines!" Ceverny exclaimed. "Why hasn't she replaced her hull plates?"

"That must be why she's moving so slowly," Andreos said. Sigrid sat beside him, the translator link in her ear so she could follow the Czech ship-speech. "She hasn't responded to our greeting yet, either. Odd." He thought a moment. "Have comm try an older frequency, something on long radio band. They might not have modified their comm equipment, either. Use *Fan*'s recognition signals."

"Strange that GradyBol didn't discuss *Jewel* much," Janina said thoughtfully. "I'd say they even avoided the subject."

"*Jewel*'s a Jonah ship here, Janina," Sigrid said. "She got off to a bad start, and it never got better. Gunter deals only with the *important* ships. What you got from him was mild compared to *Jewel*'s last reception there, gosh, it must eight or nine years ago. *Jewel* never went back, and I didn't blame Janofsi." She shrugged. "*Jewel* sells to me or the Japanese down at Merope when she has a full hold. It doesn't happen very often, from what I hear."

Andreos frowned thoughtfully.

"*Jewel* is responding, sirs," the Helm comm reported on the audio channel. He sounded perplexed. "They're telling us to go away."

Ceverny gave a snort and looked disgusted. "Goddammit, Karol," he exclaimed. "You stiff-necked bastard. This won't be easy, Leonidas, knowing Janofsi as I do."

"Difficult?" Andreos asked.

"Impossible," Ceverny replied. "Typical Pole," he added in a mutter.

"Watch out, Miska," Janina Svoboda said equably, "or I might get offended, cry and carry on and beat you up. What would Katrinya say, hearing you talk that way about Poles?"

"Offend away, Janina. Katrinya agrees with me every millimeter about Karol." Ceverny sat back and crossed his arms, then grimaced at Pov. "And he's still impossible. Gets up in his high orbit and never comes down. *Fan* was half-happy to see him go, all the trouble he made." He grunted. "*Jewel*'s crew adores him, though, the way he fights for *Jewel*."

"She's changed course again," Stefania said. "Moving away from us."

"Follow her, at her speed," Andreos decided. "Maintain the distance between us, but stay with her."

"Yes, sir," Stefania said. "Berka, change course, pacing *Jewel.*"

"Acknowledged."

"Comm, send the signal again," Andreos said.

They all waited, watching *Jewel* struggle away from *Net.* As *Net* followed behind, *Net*'s sails caught part of *Jewel*'s draft and swept in the ionized particles of the Shield, adding to the supply in her holds. "No reply, sir," the comm said.

"Hmph," Andreos said. "Well, keep trying."

Net slowly cruised behind *Jewel* for ten minutes, repeating her hail at intervals and getting no answer. Andreos slowly tapped his fingers on his console, his eyebrows lowered. "I can be as stubborn as you are, Janofsi," he muttered. "Comments?"

Pov shrugged. "Why is she still sailing with *Fan*'s sail designs? Their efficiency must be a third of ours, and *Arrow*'s designs exceed ours by as much. How can she make a profit?"

Janina shook her head. "If they'd made profits, they would have refitted. Something is very wrong here. Why is she avoiding us?"

"Because we're a Slav ship?" Pov suggested.

"Because we're half Greek, more probably," Andreos told him. He glanced at Sigrid. "They apparently avoid most everybody."

"True," she said. "I really don't know why, sirs."

"*Jewel* is signaling, sir," helm comm announced. "They are repeating their request that we withdraw."

Andreos blew out a breath. "Well, we can't storm and board her. Stefania, take us out in front of *Jewel.* We'll let her draft in our wake to help those sails of hers. I need some calculations from Sail Deck, Pov, about how much her sails can handle."

"We're on it," Pov said.

Net accelerated into a high looping trajectory, quickly overtaking *Jewel* and then slowly descending in front of her.

"This makes me nervous, sirs," Tully remarked over the audio. Such a slip course had damaged *Dance* badly at Epsilon Tauri. "Her sails don't look very stable."

"Here they're expecting dust," Sailmaster Ceverny said, unconcerned. "Even so, Pov, I suggest we sort the dust wider, reduce the proportions flowing into the bow wave."

Pov nodded, thinking about it, then modeled a few ideas on his computer. Ceverny added another suggestion from his own computer board, then let Pov look it over.

"I like your model better, sir," Pov decided, then looked at Andreos. "If we spread the skysails wider, it'll set up an attraction field to pull at the iron in that dust. Basically, we can put more of the dust in *our* faces instead of theirs."

"Sounds good to me," Andreos said, and smiled as Tully muttered something under his breath. "Anything from *Jewel,* comm?"

"No, sir."

Andreos leaned back in his chair and relaxed. "Well, let's cruise awhile then."

"What do you think is going on, sirs?" Pov asked curiously, then looked at Ceverny.

Sailmaster Ceverny grimaced, then ran a hand through his white hair. "I think *Jewel* is very tired and bereft. And I do know Slav pride, considering how I act myself, after all. What would you do when a Slav ship shows up, bright-new and spanking, and you're the back-luck Jonah of the Pleiades?"

"*Jewel* is calling, sir," the comm said. "Replying on the long radio band. They are asking our intentions."

"Reply 'slip-course, *Jewel*'s favor,' " Andreos said.

"I think they can *see* that already, sir," Stefania commented.

"Send it anyway."

"Sending."

Jewel spent some time thinking about it, though she did not move out of *Net*'s draft. Pov spread the skysails a little more, scrubbing out more of the dust, then decided to spill some of the hydrogen in *Net*'s mainsail under the spinnakers, diverting some of *Net*'s own catch into the wave that trailed back to *Jewel*.

"I assume," Andreos said wryly, "that you're not letting that charity be too obvious."

"Maybe it should be obvious," Pov said with a shrug. "Actually, I could dump the whole mainsail and it'd still be inside their sail capacity." He raised an eyebrow.

Andreos tapped his fingers on his console and rocked his chair a little. "Anything from *Jewel*, Helm?"

"No, sir," Stefania said. "They're just cruising back there."

"How much of the catch is tritium right now, Janina?"

"Standard percentages, sir, in good concentration," Janina said. "If *Jewel* can still sort isotopes, she could fill a few containers in about five minutes."

"Dump the mainsail for five minutes, Pov. Let's give her some tritium." Sigrid raised an eyebrow, but didn't comment.

"Dumping, sir," Pov tipped the mainsail and diverted all of *Net*'s catch to starboard for sixty seconds, then began dumping to port, filling the bow wave with the rest of the enriched hydrogen caught in *Net*'s mainsail. "Extending spinnakers, Janina. Get ready for some dust. Stefania, I could use some help from the skyriders."

"Skyriders, spread out and power your sails forty percent. Let's scrub some dust out of that hydrogen, Josef."

"Yes, Helm," the skyrider leader replied. "Let's do it, people."

The skyriders moved apart into two slant lines from the forward edge of *Net*'s sails, enhancing the horizontal pull of the mainsail. Pov fed more power into the thin gridlines of the mainsail, intensifying the magnetics to catch the dust grains ionized by the skyrider sails. As he dumped more hydrogen through the bottomsail, he spun the mainsail into a tighter cone to channel the dust into *Net*'s holds, then reversed polarity as he dumped through the topsail, filling the bow wave in all four quadrants. With the skyriders' help, *Net*'s sails had become a rougher version of the finer magnetic channels in Janina's catchers, processing dust and hydrogen by their atomic weight and charge.

"Pretty nifty," Pov decided as his interlink screens started reporting the results from Janina's hold counters and the aft sensors that trailed into the bow wave. "Hey, Tully, it works."

"Still sifting some dust into the bow wave," Ceverny judged, then sniffed. "Not bad, though."

"I wonder what we could do," Pov said, "if each of those skyriders were a cloudship. We could put out a field four kilometers wide, scrub it all."

"With a dreadnought cloudship behind, catching it all," Ceverny added thoughtfully, his eyes alight. "With the other cloudships out ahead, we could start the catchers ahead of the ship, not in her holds, and sort it all the way in."

"Or use a mobile station with enough speed to keep up," Pov said, "one big catcher as long as we want. Think TriPower might be interested, Sigrid?" he asked.

Sigrid opened her mouth, but Andreos waved her away. "You two are ahead of me on big ideas," he grunted, "but store them away for thinking later. You didn't hear that, Sigrid."

"I didn't?" she asked with a big smile.

"No. Keep a one-track mind, please. Right now I'm just trying to get *Jewel* to talk to us."

"*Jewel* to *Net*," Stefania reported. "Captain Janofsi calling. He is asking our intentions again. Getting a single video beam this time, sir."

Andreos sat back in his chair and grimaced. "God, this is like courting a First-Ship virgin. Uh, sorry, Janina."

"S'all right, sir," Janina said and chuckled.

"Put him on, Stefania."

Sigrid got up and moved out of the monitor's pickup range, deciding not to complicate *Net*'s problem. Stefania fed the picture to the upper-right screen on the interlink panel, which lighted to show a bearded saturnine face with suspicious black eyes.

"Hi, Karol," Janina said casually, keying her screen into the video link. "Haven't seen you for years."

"Svoboda?" Janofsi said, surprised. "God, you've put on weight."

Janina looked slightly offended, but let it pass. "It *is* so nice of you to talk to us," she said. "Why the coy behavior?"

"What do you want?" Janofsi said irritably. "We haven't asked your help."

"So give us back the tritium we just sent you," Janina retorted. "I'd say you *ought* to ask, with those sails. I doubt you're catching a third of the atoms that are passing you by." She sniffed. "So strain a little and be polite. . . . Captain Leonidas Andreos of *Siduri's Net*, this is Karol Janofsi, who I presume is still shipmaster of *Ishtar's Jewel*." She shifted the screen over to Andreos.

"Want some help?" Andreos said wryly to the scowling face in the monitor.

"No!"

"All right," Andreos said with a shrug. "We'll leave."

"Fine with me, *Net*." The screen abruptly blanked.

"Hmph," Andreos said in surprise, then pulled at his chin.

"I told you he's that way," Ceverny growled. "Imagine negotiating your intership contract with *him* every year, picky point by point. Captain Janda wanted him strangled, would have paid a whole season's profit to do it, too."

Janina smiled. "Karol was a tough old bird before he got out of boy-pants, captain, and the years have obviously made it worse. I remember him, too. I apprenticed under *Jewel's* holdmaster, and I know how he acts with his crew. He can be wheedled. Call him again, I think. Let him score his point."

"Call him again, comm," Andreos ordered.

"Sending, sir."

Janofsi promptly reappeared in the video screen. *"What?"* he barked.

"God save me from stiff-necked Slavs," Andreos said irritably. "According to my screens, captain, your skysail is twenty percent short of failure and you've a warp in your port spinnaker. And that's with scrubbed plasma. Do you always sail on that kind of dangerous edge?"

Janofsi opened his mouth, then thought better of another retort. He shrugged, visibly tempering his rude behavior. "We sail with what we have, *Net*."

"That's not much," Andreos said sympathetically. "Hard years?"

"Don't patronize me, Andreos."

"I'm not. I'm being sympathetic. Please observe the

difference. And are you going to let your pride stop us from helping you? A captain should think better than that."

Janofsi set his jaw and glared from the screen. "I don't need you to tell—" he started, then glanced distractedly to the side. "Uh, just a minute," he muttered, then muffled the pickup mike with his hand to talk briefly to someone offscreen. "No!" Pov saw him say, but then Janofsi hesitated as the other talked at him some more. He scowled and took his hand off the mike. "Uh, do you have some B-complex foodstuffs?" he asked reluctantly.

"Say again?" Andreos asked blankly.

"My medical chief's asking for anything with B-12 vitamins. We have a few children down with rickets. We'll pay for it," he added.

"Rickets?" Andreos asked incredulously. "Did you say *rickets*?"

Janofsi hesitated, his eyes suddenly looking trapped. Janina promptly put herself on the video channel. "Karol, are you saying you have vitamin-deficiency *starvation* on your ship? How could that happen?"

Janofsi flushed. "Janina . . ." he said desperately.

"That's enough," Janina said briskly. "I'm coming over there. Have your holdmaster ready to take me through your stores and we'll make a list. Stefania, can you spare a skyrider from the chevron?"

"Can do."

Janina stood up and disappeared from her interlink screen.

"Captain Janofsi," Andreos said softly. "Please tell us what you need for your people."

"We can't pay for much," Janofsi said rebelliously. "And I won't sell part of *Jewel* to you. We had enough of that in the Hyades."

"So did we, captain. And who said anything about payment?" Andreos stared him down until Janofsi dropped his gaze. "I suggest, captain, that we slow our ships to a safer level for your ship, and that you and your captains come to *Net* for discussions. Our offer is sincere, Captain. For the sake of your ship, please agree."

Janofsi sighed and closed his eyes. "Yes."

Chapter 16

The skyrider brought Captain Janofsi and his party back from *Jewel* after delivering Janina. *Net*'s captains and Sailmaster Ceverny waited on the skyrider deck as the *Net* pilot looped in under *Net*'s starboard wing and steadied on a flat course for skydeck midway up the prow. Sigrid stayed safely stashed in admin level, as both she and Andreos agreed. The airlock lights began rippling as the outer doors irised open.

"Maybe I shouldn't be at the meeting either," Ceverny muttered. "Janofsi and I never got along, and half the time he roars around like a duck imprinted by visual cues."

"I didn't know ducks roared, myself," Danil said, his hands in his pockets. He raised an eyebrow at Pov, his eyes crinkling with amusement.

"You know what I mean, Danil," Ceverny growled. "Stop splitting hairs on me, you chaffer."

"Your hair doesn't look split to me, sir," he said, unable to resist. As Ceverny turned on him, Danil backed away a step, raising his hands. "*Verbal* cues, sir?" he asked pointedly.

Ceverny scowled at him, then relented. "I'll yell at him. I can't help that."

"He'll survive it. And, yes, you should be here. He knows you. Janofsi has to ask us for help now. It won't be easy for him, not with the wars he's waged for twenty years. True?"

"I suppose," Ceverny said reluctantly.

The skydeck lights changed from amber to green, and the inner doors began to open, the skyrider visible in the outer airlock. The skyrider rolled through the portal to-

ward them, then stopped several meters away. Captain
Andreos moved forward, followed by the other captains.
Janofsi was the first to exit the skyrider, followed by two
others, a gray-haired woman and a younger man. Andreos
walked forward unhurriedly and shook Janofsi's hand,
then nodded to *Jewel*'s sailmaster and chaffer as Janofsi
made the introductions.

"My holdmaster is busy with Janina," Janofsi said uncomfortably. "And Helm prefers to stay on deck while
we're in your draft. But I brought Natalya and Ludek."
He gestured at his companions. "Sailmaster Natalya
Tesar, Chaffer Ludek Ziolka."

Natalya, gaunt-faced and thin, extended her hand to
Andreos. "Sir," she said firmly.

"Sailmaster," Andreos replied, taking her hand in his.
"Welcome to *Siduri's Net.*"

Natalya smiled. "A beautiful ship, sir. *Dance* built
well." Ludek cleared his throat, then shuffled his feet.
"Stop signaling at me, Ludek," she said irritably, then
raised her voice to even greater firmness. "I hope we see
much of *Net*, Captain Andreos, in the months ahead."

"That hasn't been decided," Janofsi growled. "Don't
get ahead of things, Natalya."

"Why not?" Natalya asked, turning toward him. "I told
you I was going to be difficult. I've been wanting new
sails for twenty years, and I'm going to get them, over
your limp body, Karol, if you insist. And I want food for
the children and air scrubbers that work properly and
more room for too many people." She pressed Andreos's
hand hard enough to turn her knuckles white as she
looked back at him. "I want many things, sir," she said
quietly.

"You will get them," Andreos replied, staring down
into her intense blue eyes. "What do we need chaffers
for?" he added lightly.

Natalya blinked, then flushed slightly and released her
hard grip on Andreos's hand. "Forgive me," she said, her
color deepening.

"Not at all." Andreos looked at Janofsi's conflicted
scowl, then laughed and spread his hands, inviting. "Wel-

come, *Jewel.* We have looked for you. Please come this way, sirs."

Andreos led them into a large conference room off skydeck. After everyone was seated, Andreos studied Captain Janofsi, then glanced at Natalya and Ludek. "I suppose there's no easy way to do this. We had heard you'd had problems, but not like this. How long has *Jewel* been desperate?"

"Desperate?" Janofsi started to bristle, then stopped as Natalya stirred in her chair and gave him a pleading look. He rubbed his hand slowly over his face, looking at her, then glanced beyond her at the other *Net* captains. "Oh, hello, Miska," he said in mild surprise, spotting Ceverny.

"Karol," Ceverny said, nodding.

"I thought you were *Dance*'s sailmaster. Change ships? Why?"

"I was *Dance*'s sailmaster," Ceverny growled. "Not anymore. Haven't you heard why we left the Hyades?"

"No," Janofsi said. "Why?"

"Captain Janofsi," Andreos prompted. "Tell us."

"I'd rather yell and carry on," Janofsi said gruffly, then quickly curled his hand over Natalya's, looking at her in a blend of irritation and perplexity, softened by the open affection between them. "After twenty years, she knows me so well. It's easier to yell, but she'll plead and forget all her dignity and melt my old heart." He sighed. "She does that, when she looks this firm. How long? It's mostly a matter of degree. We didn't bring much capital with us, but thought we could refill our holds easily. We hadn't counted on the dust."

"Has *Jewel* never had a profitable year?" Andreos asked.

"Profits?" Janofsi said bitterly. "What are those? I have people *starving* on my ship, and I don't have the credits to ship them home to Earth. Each time we go out into the Shield, we hope we'll get enough tritium to turn it around. Sometimes we do, but not enough to keep it going. *Jewel* is falling apart, and the ship is overcrowded— thank God we stopped having children five years ago, by ship vote. You can imagine how that went over with the minority, or the whole ship when I ordered several abortions when some women disagreed." He grimaced painfully and looked old. "That was a mistake," he said. "I shouldn't have ordered that. But what could I do? Our air scrubbers are antiquated and I've got carbon dioxide alerts twice a month. We tried planting more gardens, but then the scrubbers took too much CO and killed half the greenery." He scowled in frustration, the lines deepening in his face. "Blasted machines."

Ceverny shook his head. "Why don't you ask the other cloudships for help?"

"*Arrow?* Are you kidding? The elite of the Pleiades doesn't deign to deal with us, not when they found out we didn't have credits to pay for an upgrade. They just weren't interested. And GradyBol hiked their prices on supplies and a refit when we winced at the first quote. The hell with them all." Janofsi clenched his jaw. "We've gotten by. TriPower takes a catch, and sometimes the Japanese will buy." Then he caught himself and grimaced again. He looked down at his hands, then sighed as Natalya entwined her fingers in his. "I hate this," he muttered rebelliously grinding his teeth.

"By our luck," Andreos said quietly, "*Net* won a bonanza at T Tauri and we're holding even in our runs here." He spread his hands. "We have enough to spare."

"I don't need your charity, *Net,*" Janofsi snapped irritably.

"What charity?" Andreos said. "Call it a long-term loan with no interest. Pay us back sometime—but don't deny your people our offer."

"We agree," Natalya said, raising her head. "Don't we, captain?" She turned to Janofsi and gripped his forearm hard. "This is a *Fan* ship and they're offering, Karol. Don't be a fool. The people are so hungry. Please."

Janofsi crumpled again, his old face showing intense strain. "Of course, Natalya," he said, nodding dumbly. He raised his hand to her face and touched it. "Of course I agree. It's a kinder humiliation, after all."

"Humiliation?" Ceverny interjected sharply. "That's not what this is, Karol. It grieves us to see you in these straits. Of course we'll help."

Janofsi glanced around the faces, seeking escape, then noticed Pov.

"You don't look Slav, especially with that dark skin." Pov sensed the other *Net* captains tense at Janofsi's tone, and Pov braced himself, knowing what was coming. "Gypsy?" Pov heard the automatic distaste and tried not to react. Slav traditions, indeed—one that had persisted unalloyed on *Jewel,* if her captain was typical.

Pov smiled slightly, meeting Janofsi's eyes. *"Net,"* he said.

"And her sailmaster," Danil added smoothly. "And future shipmaster of our first daughter ship, when we build her." Pov glanced at him, startled. "Future elder of the Siduri Rom," Danil rolled on, obviously enjoying himself, "husband of the Russki beauty Avi Selenko, father of seventeen, grandfather of forty-two."

"God, Danil," Pov protested weakly.

"What?" Danil asked innocently. "The daughter ship or the progeny?"

Janofsi had flushed angrily, and Danil gave him a level stare. "In all my life, I have never heard such an ungracious captain for his ship. I don't know you, and I understand you're trying, at Natalya's pleading, but we are not humiliating you, captain. But you can't see it that way, can you? We ask friendly contact, and you tell us to go away. We offer help, and you prate about your Slav pride, then come aboard and insult our sailmaster." Janofsi started to get up, and Natalya dragged on his arm, pulling him downward.

"You don't know what it's been like," Janofsi shouted at Danil.

"You were welcome to tell us—we wanted to hear," Danil said coldly. "But that has now changed." Janofsi froze in place, and Natalya gave a small cry and stared at Danil in horror. Danil glanced at Andreos for permission and got a nod. *"Jewel, Net* offers a refit of your sails, supplies to restock your necessities, other system repairs as needed." Natalya relaxed as Danil spoke, and Janofsi slowly sat down. "In return, *Net* asks mutual slip-course for two joint runs in the Shield, to occur after your repairs are completed. We also ask for access to your maps for this area of space. Repairs for data, captain. Does that help?"

Janofsi squinted at Danil, then glanced at his own chaffer uncertainly. "You could get the data from somebody else."

"Not necessarily," Pov interjected. "You obviously haven't tried to buy maps here. In any event, we choose to buy our maps from you. At our valuation—and we think your data equals the value of repairs and supplies to refit your ship."

Janofsi glanced at Natalya, then swallowed painfully. "My apologies to those I have offended," he said gruffly, not looking at Pov.

"No offense taken," Pov said, copying Danil's smooth tone. "Have you ever seen *Arrow* on a cloud run?" he asked Natalya.

"A few times when her group sailed the Shield, some years ago," Natalya said. "You want pictures of her sails, don't you?" She smiled.

Pov nodded. "Trade you my sail designs for your pictures. How about that?"

"That's a deal, Sail."

Danil gave Pov a dirty look. "What *do* we need chaffers for?" he growled.

"I've often wondered." Pov grinned at him mischievously. "Just wait. Later when Natalya and I set up the ship consortium to pool the profits and rebuild *both* ships, you can work out the picky details, Danil. Give you and Ludek something to do while *Net* and *Jewel* go give *Arrow* a real run for her money. Sailmaster Ceverny has some ship maneuvers you'd love to see, Natalya, four or five cloudships at a time. Did you ever talk to *Rohini's Horn* down at Merope? Or the Arabs?"

"Wait a minute," Janofsi protested. "What consortium?"

"Captain Hanuman might be interested," Natalya said slowly as she caught on. "I'm not sure about the Arabs. I've heard they're pretty slick. AmTel's furious about how they bargained their first tritium harvest, but AmTel paid for it anyway."

"Maybe we should go ask," Pov said lightly.

Janofsi and Andreos looked at each other. "I think," Andreos said dryly, "that we just got run over by a gypsy horse dealer, wagon and all. *What* ship consortium?" he demanded.

"The one with TriPower's super-catcher," Ceverny broke in, winking at Pov. "The one that'll get us enough tritium and sail run practice to build a ship that can handle our T Tauri power pets and jump us all the way to the Orion Nebula." He made a sniffing noise. "And if *Arrow* asks real nice, maybe we'll let her come along."

"Pets?" Janofsi asked wildly. "Nebula?"

"I'm still trying to climb back aboard myself," Andreos told him wryly.

"And I said I'd yell," Ceverny said. He spread his arms wide. "Who needs chaffers? Hell, yes! Let's do it, Karol!"

"Do what?"

"Sail a sea you've never imagined. The Nebula itself! Oh, *Arrow* will buy in. Gray's wanted to go to the Nebula all his life. He won't miss this." Ceverny rubbed his hands in glee. "We'll rob him blind for the ship drive privilege, too, with franchise fees, consultant fees, major profit share, royalties every cubic. Snoot, snoot. That'll teach him to pump *Net*'s sailmaster." Ceverny got up and did a little dance. "Yes!"

Natalya looked overwhelmed as she watched Ceverny prance around. Pov leaned over the table and took her hand, then gallantly raised it to his lips. "Sailing," he said softly, "such as no one has every seen. Welcome, *Jewel.*"

Her eyes shifted to him and then a glorious smile filled her thin face. "That's a deal, sail," she said.

Pov saw the hope flare in her eyes, hope *Net* had put there—and now had an obligation to protect. What if *Net* assumed too easily that success was assured, as Janofsi had assumed and nearly ruined his ship, as Rybak had assumed at Tania's Ring? What if *Net* led *Jewel* into new disaster at the Nebula? *Net* had a duty to *Jewel*, like the Rom duty to protect and guard one's family. My duty, he realized, if I am shipmaster when we go.

Tully's right, he thought soberly as Natalya pressed his hands and turned to smile at Ludek. It would be too easy to assume, too easy to be stupid. He understood more of the burden that Captain Andreos carried as shipmaster, a burden that might be his too, and soon.

But his would involve the Nebula, he thought with a chill, understanding now why Tully had tried to warn him. Get out of your daze, Pov Janusz, he told himself. Get real.

Natalya laughed when Ceverny pranced over and swept her into a little dance around the table. Pov smiled as he watched them, then laughed outright at Janofsi's befuddled expression. Janofsi probably wondered if they'd all gone mad, as they likely had.

But the Nebula is a sea of light to sail, Pov thought yearningly, a wealth of rare atoms for a cloudship's catching, a place no human has ever been. We'd be the first, the first to see those O-stars up close, the first to sail the dark molecular clouds behind them, the first ever to see newborn stars still enshrouded in their natal starclouds. We're the first to have the chance. How can we *not* try?

But Janofsi did not like it, not one bit, when he discovered Sigrid Thorsen was aboard *Net,* and went right back to shouting. Andreos and Pov exchanged a look as they got a good example of what *Fan* had endured with *Jewel*'s cantankerous shipmaster. Ceverny stalked out, waving his arms in disgust, as Janofsi and Sigrid squared off in *Net*'s admin lounge, with Janofsi doing most of the glaring. Sigrid waggled her fingers at him.

"Why am I here? I'm studying to be a sail tech," she told him gaily, then winked at Pov. "Think I'll change careers. You just watch."

"Oh, sure you will," Pov said skeptically. She wrinkled her nose at him.

"EuroCom on a *cloudship*?" Captain Janofsi bellowed at Andreos. "Are you out of your mind, *Net*?"

"Not at all," Sigrid said forcefully. "I've given *Net* full access to TriPower's databanks—everything. I tipped the bag. An *alliance,* Karol, one that means something." She jabbed his chest with her finger. "If that alliance had existed before, your cloudship would never have suffered what it has all these years. You know how GradyBol

treated you, jacking up the price when they saw your
need. And what did *Arrow* do about it? Nothing. Shrug—
it's competition. Shrug—it's business. Shrug—we're *Arrow* and who are you? *Arrow* has always set the rules
here, hiding secrets, manipulating stations against
cloudships, running everything by *Arrow*'s design."

"But—" Janofsi started, his face purpling.

"Well, now *we're* designing something different!"
Sigrid shouted at him. "And you're invited in, whether
you like that or not, *Jewel*. I've offered help to you I
don't know *how* many times, you stiff-necked idiot! God
above!"

Janofsi sputtered, then turned and stalked out of the
lounge in a fury. Natalya sighed, watching him go. "He'll
come back. He has to." She smiled at Sigrid. "He does
carry on," she told Sigrid with some embarrassment. "But
his crew would die for him, because he bellows like that."

"They almost did die," Sigrid said, still angry and not
budging an inch, "because he bellows like that."

"We would have sold *Jewel* eventually," Ludek said
soberly, stepping in. "We would have had to, and soon.
He knows that, and hates it: you're seeing the result." He
looked at Natalya and smiled thinly. "But I can invoke
ship contract and force it to a vote by the captains. He
won't like it, but we'll outvote him. I've done it a few
times before to get a deal made. Then, if he pushes it to
ship vote, he might lose the vote, when it means life
again for *Jewel*. Mothers think of their children, husbands
think of their wives. So I am asking, sirs, for your patience. If the ship ever voted against him, however mad
he made the choice, it would kill him." He looked at
Andreos and Sigrid levelly.

"We understand," Andreos said.

"I hope you do. I've heard your offers, TriPower, and
I admit I was tempted, especially in the last few years—
but even my chaffer's judgment yields to my loyalty to
Janofsi. He brought us here, he has kept us here. Don't be
so sure that *Jewel* wouldn't sell herself, even accepting
that kind of death, to protect him." He looked at Sigrid
fiercely.

"Even beyond all reason?" she asked softly.

Ludek snorted. "We've been beyond reason for years."

"Now that has changed," Danil said. The two chaffers looked at each other, measuring whatever chaffers measured in each other.

"Perhaps," Ludek said.

Danil smiled thinly. "We will see."

Twenty minutes later, Janina came back from *Jewel,* shaking her head in mute dismay, then loaded skyrider after skyrider with supplies and sent them off to the other ship to restock *Jewel*'s near-empty essentials. Both ships slowed and retracted their sails, allowing *Net* to drift backward to shield *Jewel* from Alcyone's distant glare in *Net*'s shadow. Then, after some more expostulation by Janofsi, Pov asked Chief Razack to send his crews over to *Jewel*'s sail assembly. He and Natalya studied *Jewel*'s sail structures from Pov's Sail Deck, deciding on the immediate repairs. When Janofsi stormed onto Sail Deck, rampaging again, Natalya rose to her feet and raised her hand.

"No more!" she declared. "No more. That is *enough.*"

"I say—"

"Shut up!" she bellowed back at him. She had the lungs for it, and Celka looked around, startled, then rolled her eyes at Pov incredulously. "Gracious God above, Karol," Natalya exclaimed. "Do I have to tie you up?" She put her hands on her hips and glared at him, then pointed at the chair she had just left. "Sit!"

Janofsi eyed her. "Why?" he asked suspiciously, glancing at Pov and the other *Net* crew on Sail Deck.

"Sit, or I'll throw you out an airlock. Don't you think I won't, Karol. I'm right about that point."

Janofsi opened his mouth.

"Sit!" Natalya shouted, pointing at the chair. Janofsi sat down rebelliously, then crossed his arms on his chest. Natalya leaned forward over his shoulder. "Now you watch," she said into Janofsi's ear, "while Pov shows me the wonderful things his chief is going to do to my sails. And then," she continued inexorably, "you will thank him. I don't expect you to mean it, but you can say the words." Janofsi rolled his eyes as thoroughly as Celka had, then grunted. "You hear me, Karol?"

"I hear you."

"Good."

"I don't like this," he grumbled.

"Why the hell *not*?" she asked impatiently. Janofsi opened his mouth, then shut it. "They already think you're an ass. Giving in won't make you that much more of one, I'm thinking."

"I'm not an ass."

"You're an ass, Karol," she informed him. She leaned past him and picked up where she and Pov had been on the screen. "You say move this generator? Won't it weaken the spinnaker field?"

"Not if it's supported by this guideline on the mainsail." Pov glanced at Janofsi, who sat with his arms crossed, scowling at the wallscreen. "It's an *Arrow* design. *Dance* bought a module for building *Net*."

Natalya straightened. "Then that's the difference. I kept modeling on *Fan*'s sail settings when I saw your sail set." She pursed her lips. "Obviously more efficient."

"And *Arrow*'s improved her sails further."

"*Jewel* didn't get much of a view those few times," Natalya said, "but with *Net*'s sails as a foundation, we might get some better ideas about *Arrow*'s other designs. Did TriPower have any pictures?"

"Only you and *Hound*, and those just showed the touring sails during approach."

"Hmm. Enjoying this, Karol?"

"You'll keep this up, won't you?" Janofsi muttered. "Harassing me in front of strangers."

"Absolutely. So will Ludek, though you might get him to waver a little, if you shout loudly enough." Natalya shook her head. "But *Net* doesn't understand the shouting, Karol. Look how Pov's sail staff are watching you with wide eyes. Look at Pov's face, however much he's trying to hide it. Andreos trained him, and Sigrid's like Andreos. So I think this isn't a time when shouting protects *Jewel*." She rested her hand on his shoulder. "That's my advice. Do what you like, sir."

Janofsi turned his head and squinted at Pov. "Most of our maps are limited to the Shield," he said, not fussing at all.

"That's fine, sir. The Shield's a big place. Lots of good fishing."

"If you've got the sails," Janofsi grunted.

"We'll both have them now. How do you deal with dust, Natalya? *Moon*'s captain mentioned something called modified field phasing."

"You met *Moon*'s captain?" Captain Janofsi asked with surprise. "What did you think of him?"

"Don't ask."

Janofsi laughed. "We share an opinion, lad."

"He played games and embarrassed his Second Sail in front of me." Pov smiled. "I prefer shouting."

"I'll be glad to oblige you, I'm sure; you just wait. So he embarrassed his Second Sail? I'm surprised he'd take that kind of chance. Talbot likes his rank too much to risk it easily." Janofsi shrugged. "Of course, he could always tell Thaddeus Gray it was strategy. Probably did."

"I don't understand," Pov said, confused.

"The last I heard," Janofsi said, taking in his surprise, "was that Gray's daughter was Second Sail on *Moon*. Has been for a couple of years. You heard differently, Natalya?" he asked, turning around to look at her. Natalya shook her head.

"She said her name was Rachel Hinsdell," Pov said slowly.

"Hinsdell? Rachel *Gray,* you young ass. He's only got the one daughter." He looked curiously at Pov as Pov began to laugh, hard enough he had to hold his sides.

"What?" Janofsi demanded.

Chapter 17

They took a day to repair *Jewel*'s sails before the chief's crews vanished inside with new parts for *Jewel*'s environmental systems. Some of *Jewel*'s crew transferred temporarily to *Net* to ease *Jewel*'s overcrowding: *Net* had the quarters to spare, and several of *Net*'s Slavs contacted relatives on *Jewel* and insisted on a long visit back on *Net*. It helped, for many of *Jewel*'s people shared their shipmaster's wariness, even of a sister ship from *Fan*. As another day passed, *Net* transferred a full hold of tritium to replenish *Jewel*'s engine fuel, and the joy on *Ishtar's Jewel* became nearly palpable as *Jewel* became more spaceworthy than she'd been for a dozen years. Even so, Danil and Ludek published the first tentative ship's agreement as soon as they finished a draft, easing any lingering worries. It was to be a full consortium, as sister ships, not mother and daughter, with their common Slav heritage to bind them together.

Pov saw the change in Captain Janofsi as he watched his people rejoice. *Jewel*'s shipmaster watched them all with wondering eyes, as if he had to shake himself to believe *Jewel* had found an end to all the hard wandering, the trials to which he had led them. They embraced him, cheered him, even danced with him against his humorous protests, as if he were responsible for it all. He demurred—they laughed at him, wagging their fingers. He shouted, even at them—and they laughed and danced him around still more. And so they cajoled him, until even Karol Janofsi stopped his shouting.

"I think I see part of why *Jewel*'s followed him," Pov told Natalya as they worked through *Jewel*'s new sail configurations again on Sail Deck.

"I'm glad. Sometimes it's not easy for outsiders to see why." She shrugged her thin shoulders. "Sometimes all they see is how he carries on, ranting as he does, but he's kept *Jewel* free all these years. To us, that's all that counts." She smiled ruefully and shook her head. "We could have stayed with *Fan,* a daughter ship bound to *Fan's* bad luck, always indebted, always owned. Somehow that doesn't fit a cloudship, being owned, so he led us away to a different choice. Then, when we had our troubles here, we could have sold *Jewel* to GradyBol and gone back to Earth, given up the cloudships forever." She shook her head. "I couldn't do that. I'd rather starve than give up this life. Odd to say such an extreme thing, but that's how I feel."

"So do I, Natalya," he said quietly.

"Perhaps you *do* understand part of it." She looked at him intently. "Captain Janofsi does carry on—he won't change that, and he's not always wise with it. But of his devotion to *Jewel,* there is no question. It's a different mix than you and your Captain Andreos."

"I'll say."

"What if *Net* had failed at T Tauri, Pov?" Natalya insisted. "Would *Net* have followed Andreos then?"

"Yes. Devotion can be earned in a lot of ways, Natalya."

"True," she conceded, looking only half-convinced.

"But you're right about the other." Pov said. "It is a different mix. If you were a shipmaster," he asked curiously, "which type would you be?"

She smiled. "I won't be a shipmaster. I'm happy with Sail Deck."

"But if you were."

Natalya's smile widened. "I'd be myself, if that's the point of your asking. You'll get *Net's* daughter ship, won't you?"

"That hasn't been decided."

"Oh, I doubt that. Those matters are decided long before a ship keel is laid." She put her hand on his forearm and squeezed. "But if I had a choice of captain's personality? I don't know. Which is better: a ship's loyalty that will follow you into any danger, or the cleverness that finds the best choices? I don't think you can combine the two. One takes a certain madness that is not clever at all, and the other is too cautious to take the wild chances. Odd that Andreos would take you to T Tauri, with that kind of risk."

"Not so odd. We were facing getting sold to Tania's Ring." Pov shrugged. "What happens when the only choice is crazy? What kind of captain do you have then?" Natalya laughed. "What kind of captain is Thaddeus Gray?" he asked curiously.

"A different kind. Himself, like all captains are. You'll find out."

Net and *Jewel* jumped together to a second shock front in the Shield, then politely exchanged slip-courses as the two ships winnowed through the ionized gas, though *Net*'s sails were noticeably more efficient than *Jewel*'s older designs, a difference that had plagued *Net*'s relationship with *Dance*. Accustomed to cloudships far superior in sails, *Jewel* shrugged away the difference and openly admired *Net*. As Danil and Ludek got farther into their bargaining, they discussed a complete refit for *Jewel*, then snagged as the arrangement fell into the shape of a construction loan, with buyout payments and the lot. Andreos called the captains of both ships to *Net*'s admin lounge.

"No!" Janofsi shouted.

"Quieter, Karol," Andreos said. "No loans, I agree. Would you consider minority partner?" Janofsi looked stubborn, and Andreos shrugged. "Hell, neither would I. It's still being owned. So we're back to the value of your maps. I can jigger the figures on our expected profit flow without those maps, make it come out right." As Janofsi opened his mouth, Andreos pointed at him. "They're *my* profit projections, after all. And my sailmaster will back me up, if he knows what's good for him."

"Maps," Pov said fervently, then grinned as Andreos shot him a look.

"And later," Andreos continued, "after *Jewel* has the profits to spare and quite on her own initiative and in whatever amount she likes, *Jewel* may decide to pay a bonus to *Net,* for friendship, admiration, and general goodwill." Janofsi thought about it.

Danil winced, pained by heresies to a chaffer's ears. Ludek looked pained, too, then got nudged hard by Natalya. "A good idea, sir," he blurted, then rubbed his hip and looked at her irritably. "Ouch."

"I'll give you reason to look pained," she said. Even Janofsi laughed.

"Oh, hell," Janofsi declared, spreading his arms expansively. "This can work, the whole consortium. Let's keep it."

"We're determined," Andreos told him.

"That I can see. All right. *Jewel* needs a refit, that's obvious, and with two ships in slip-course and decent dealing with TriPower, it shouldn't take too long to pay your 'bonus,' *Net.*"

"Good. Janina is also suggesting some modifications to your holds, in line with Sigrid's production needs at TriPower. Ours, too. Sigrid's willing to buy into the cost of the hold modifications for a partial exclusive contract, term limited to one year, though likely we'll sell all the product to her anyway. She'll also lend us her facilities for the repairs. She wants into our consortium, Karol."

"Ships and a mobile station?" Janofsi squinted dubiously.

"Why not?"

"But you're dealing with EuroCom. That'll involve GradyBol."

"Not necessarily," Danil said. "We just make it a contract term that limits our deal to TriPower, with the necessary ban on data-sharing with GradyBol or we'll pack up and leave, with penalties we can collect for breach of contract."

"Sigrid thinks EuroCom will accept it," Andreos added, "and she can watch the corporate side to make it stick. If it doesn't, we take off and go talk to the Japanese. Right, Karol? Also, it's a long way to Earth, if Sigrid wants to remember her practical astronomy and show just how mobile a mobile station could be if it chooses."

"She'd *move* TriPower?" Janofsi asked incredulously. "That's a lot of credits to steal."

"How much is a new ship drive worth, Karol?" Andreos asked lazily, smiling at him.

"True." Janofsi began to smile. "This is like opening a box and always finding another box inside, all of them full of treasure."

"We think so," Andreos said with satisfaction.

"Who cares what the rules are?" Janofsi commented dryly, though he wasn't objecting now. "Let's make up new ones, any way we want."

"Why not?" Andreos asked lightly.

Janofsi snorted. "Be sure to let me watch, Leonidas, when you start in on the natural laws. Turn space inside out, run time backward, make a star and color it pink. That I've got to see."

Net and *Jewel* sailed the shock front for another day, then trimmed ship for TriPower, their holds full. When *Net*'s helm detected a ship decelerating toward them from jump, Andreos smiled.

"She's on a vector directly from TriPower," Stefania said on the interlink.

"Arrow?" Pov asked.

Andreos shrugged, still smiling. "I would, if I were Gray."

Stefania frowned, perplexed. "But how'd she find us so quickly? It took us two weeks to find *Jewel,* and we knew a few places to look. Now we're on the other side of the Shield with all that dust between us." Andreos glanced at Sigrid beside him.

"Beats me." She shook her head.

"Should we stay another day and see what they want?" Andreos asked her drolly.

"Oh, leaving a third time would be wicked, Leonidas. You have a dangerous mind." She looked approving, then chuckled.

"Net?" Janofsi bellowed, clicking into the interlink. "Do you see her?"

"Indeed I do. Let's hope it's not *Diana's Moon,* or I *will* leave." Then he chuckled. "This might be fun. Let's be careful not to show too much of how fun it is." He grinned uninhibitedly. Everything had gone so very well, so very well indeed.

"Skyrider strut, that's all it is, Athena says," Pov reminded him.

"That it is."

It was indeed *Diana's Arrow*. As Gray's cloudship decelerated into the shock front ahead of them, she spread her sails briefly, giving *Net* and *Jewel* a look, then trimmed back to touring sails and calmly cruised toward the two Slav ships, sleek and big and beautiful. *Jewel* spread her own sails, then fell back into *Net*'s draft, catching more hydrogen that she quickly spilled in a profligate show of defiance.

"Don't lose all of that," Janina told *Jewel*, a little irritably. "Tritium count is nicely up."

"Nuts," *Jewel*'s holdmaster replied. "I'm full to my brackets. Besides, we'll be back. I'll catch those ions next time." He laughed.

"*Arrow* to *Net*," the comm said over the interlink audio. "Shipmaster Gray, sir."

"Put him on," Andreos said. "My screen only."

Sigrid scooted her chair to the side, out of view, to keep a certain secret in *Net*'s larder. An interlink screen lit with a bearded face, square and rugged and space-tanned below a shock of graying brown hair, dominated by the eyes, dark and watchful. His lips, full like Rachel's, curved up.

"Greetings, *Siduri's Net*," Thaddeus Gray said in a baritone voice, as much control in its nuances as Andreos had learned to cultivate in his. The tone was welcoming but restrained, dominant but interested, Pov decided, admiring the magnetism in that face. He sighed involuntarily. Thaddeus Gray. Finally, at last.

"*Diana's Arrow*," Andreos replied as smoothly. "Our greetings."

"I can speak Czech, if that is more comfortable for you." The lips curved a little more, a little sly, knowing all about Rachel and her Czech.

"English will do fine," Andreos replied, comfortable

with anything Gray suggested, and knowing things Gray didn't know at all.

"I'm sorry *Arrow* missed you at GradyBol," Gray said, his regret tempered by having had more important affairs elsewhere.

"We enjoyed our dinner with Weigand and *Hound*'s officer," Andreos replied, having had important affairs elsewhere, too, part of what Gray didn't know about.

"Indeed?" Gray asked, amused.

"Most assuredly," Andreos said, just as amused. "I'm afraid my sailmaster missed that dinner."

"So I've heard, captain."

"Have you?" Andreos inquired, lifting an eyebrow.

"*Ishtar's Jewel* seems to have refitted her sails," Gray commented, changing orbits.

"Has she?" Andreos asked dryly, changing orbits just as smoothly. He pursed his lips thoughtfully. "I hadn't really noticed."

Gray smiled slyly. "And TriPower's stationmaster has left her station. Or so her staff said when we stopped by. They wouldn't say where she'd gone."

"I wouldn't know anything about that." Andreos smiled back, knowing everything.

"Wouldn't you?" Gray asked.

"That depends."

Gray shifted orbits a second time. "Gunter said he read you that directive from Tania's Ring. Are you going back to the Hyades soon?"

"No. We bought out. We think we'll stay."

"Do you have a new ship drive?" Gray asked bluntly.

"Maybe."

"I have maps," Gray dangled.

"So does *Jewel*." Andreos sniffed.

"I have other things," Gray added, leaning back in his chair.

"So do I." Andreos leaned back in his.

"Dinner, captain?" Gray said, smiling suavely.

"I'll see if Karol and Sigrid are free," Andreos said. "I'd like to bring them along, if I come myself."

"If you wish," Gray said indifferently, not entirely pleased. "*Arrow* out." The screen blanked.

Sigrid rolled back into view, her gray eyes narrowed. "Well, that was rather coy," she remarked.

"That's *Arrow* for you," Janofsi said irritably from his interlink screen. "I'm better than you, he thinks. I know more than you. I'm Thaddeus Gray, the Wonder of the Pleiades. I'll shout at him, I'm sure. You go by yourself, Leonidas. It's *Net* he wants to talk to, anyway."

Andreos shook his head. "Wrong signal, Karol. We're in consortium now." He glanced at Sigrid. "My scans detect another inimitable Pleiades dinner coming up. How about yours?"

"Gray's type," she agreed, "or Gunter's type. I don't know who started it way back then, but you're right. He'll sniff at Karol to make him shout and drop in Gunter's comments about me to keep me defined, then spend the rest of the time fencing with you." She made a face.

"A course for TriPower?" Andreos suggested, looking at them both. Sigrid and Janofsi nodded. "Lay in for TriPower, Stefania."

"Yes, sir."

"Skyriders never stop the strut, I'm thinking," Ceverny muttered beside Pov, obviously disappointed.

"Maybe *Arrow* will get the point eventually," Pov said dryly, "chasing us around the Pleiades like this." He crossed his arms and sighed. Ceverny chuckled.

A few minutes later *Net* and *Jewel* changed course together, turning away from *Arrow*'s steady approach toward them. Gray signaled as soon as the two Slav ships had clearly aligned for TriPower's distant star.

"Captain Gray calling again, sir," *Net*'s comm said.

This time Rachel Gray stood behind her father's chair, *Moon*'s insignia still on her sleeve. "I told my father, sir," she said to Andreos, her lips curving up, "that he reminded me just now of Captain Talbot, and that *Net* has already expressed her opinion of *Moon*'s shipmaster. Was I accurate?"

"Talbot serves my purposes," Captain Gray said indulgently, lounging in his chair. He smiled lazily. "One of which relates to you, Rachel, as I've explained to you."

She sniffed, not impressed. "I also told him that I'd

been invited to visit *Siduri's Net,* and that I wanted that visit now."

"So she insisted I call again," Gray said. "I forgot to mention that before," he added.

"Did you?" Andreos asked dryly.

Gray laughed. "Come have dinner with me, *Net,* damn it. Bring your friends. I want to talk to you. Just don't go gallivanting off again, please, and make me chase you somewhere else. You've made your point. So have I." He smiled. "Our dinner might be the first of many talks, if *Net* and her partners are willing."

"Thank you, captain," Andreos said. "I think it might."

Pov waited for Rachel on *Net*'s skydeck and watched as her skyrider rolled through the irising door. She stepped out and strolled toward him, then stopped a few paces away and put her hands in her pockets, her smile wide. He started to chuckle, then saw her laugh.

"Welcome, sail," he said.

"Welcome yourself. Were you surprised?"

"I won't admit anything of the kind," he retorted. "It's just not done." She stepped forward and her hand grasped his firmly. "Want a tour?" he asked, smiling at her.

"I'd love that. Thank you."

Epilogue

Siduri's Net celebrated Kate's wedding on St. Serena's Day as *Net* and her two cloudship companions decelerated toward TriPower's golden sun. The Pleiades stars gleamed through the wide windows of *Net's* companionway, a counterpoint to the wedding lanterns that hung from the window casements and lined the long aisle between the chairs. Red and green banners hung from the tall ceiling and framed the altar, where Kate and Sergei stood before Father Ilya, their hands joined.

Kate had invited everyone on *Net* and *Jewel,* and nearly everyone had come to give their best wishes. In a front row, Athena sat next to Gregori and her three young girls; nearby, Janina sat with Danil and his wife. Natalya had brought Captain Janofsi and other *Jewel* people, and across the aisle, Captain Andreos sat with Thaddeus and Rachel Gray, also guests. Pov sat with Avi in a middle row next to his family, his arm around Avi's shoulders, watching Kate.

His sister's wedding gown sparkled with a thousand silver beads every time she moved, and a long veil obscured her face with a cloud of white gauze. As they began the traditional Rom vows, Kate lifted her head proudly to her beloved.

"All night long," she said, her voice clear and strong, "I looked for him but did not find him. I will get up now and go about the city, through its streets and squares; I will search for the one my heart loves." Avi leaned her head on Pov's shoulder and sighed, her fingers moving in his. "I asked the watchmen," Kate declared, "I asked, 'Have you seen the one my heart loves?' And scarcely had I passed them when I found him. And I held him and

I would not let him go, until I had brought him to my mother's house, to the room of the one who bore me."

"Come with me from Lebanon, beloved," Sergei replied softly. "Come with me from Lebanon. You have stolen my heart, my beloved, my bride; you have stolen my heart with one glance of your eyes, with one jewel of your necklace."

"Awake, north wind," Kate cried, her voice lifting to resonate through the room. "Come, south wind! Blow on my garden, that its fragrance may spread abroad. My love is mine and I am his."

"Come, beloved," Sergei said passionately, his eyes locked with Kate's behind her veil. "Let us go to the countryside. Let us go early to the vineyards to see if the vines have blossomed, and if the pomegranates are in bloom." Sergei lifted Kate's hand and placed it firmly on his chest, then covered it with his own. "Place me like a seal over your heart," he said, "like a seal on your arm; for love is as strong as death, its jealousy unyielding as the grave. It burns like blazing fire, like a mighty flame. The raging waters cannot quench love; rivers cannot wash it away."

Kate leaned toward him intensely. "I, Ekaterina Marya Janusz, take you, Sergei, for my husband, to have and to hold, for better, for worse, for richer, for poorer, in sickness and in health, until death do us part."

"And I, Sergei Alexandrovitch Rublev, take you, Ekaterina, for my wife, to have and to hold, for better, for worse, for richer, for poorer, in sickness and in health, until death do us part."

Father Ilya raised his hands, blessing them. "May your union be fruitful, my children. May you have joy in each other in this life and the life beyond."

Kate and Sergei turned toward him and knelt on the riser, their hands joined, and Father Ilya extended his hands over their heads.

*"When one finds a worthy wife,
    her value is far beyond pearls,"*

he said, his deep voice rolling through the companion-way.

> *"Her husband, entrusting his heart to her,*
> *has an unfailing prize.*
> *She brings him good, and not evil,*
> *all the days of her life."*

Kate bowed her head, her features concealed in the gauze of her veil.

> *"She is clothed with strength and dignity,*
> *and she laughs at the days to come.*
> *She opens her mouth in wisdom,*
> *and on her tongue is kindly counsel.*
> *She watches the conduct of her household,*
> *and eats not her food in idleness.*
> *Her children rise up and praise her;*
> *her husband, too, extols her:*
> *Many are the women of proven worth,*
> *but you have excelled them all."*

Father Ilya lowered his hands and addressed Kate and Sergei: "The Lord delights in you, my children," he said, smiling at them both. "You are the joy of His heart." He traced the cross over their heads. "In the name of the Father, and the Son, and the Holy Spirit. On this holy day of St. Serena, Ekaterina and Sergei, you have been joined forever in a union of love."

"Thanks be to God," the crowd murmured. "Amen."

Sergei gently lifted Kate's veil and kissed her, then took her hand. As they stood and turned toward the audience, the crowd erupted in applause. Several of the skyriders stood up and yelled loudly, pounding their hands together enthusiastically as Kate and Sergei started down the aisle between the rows of chairs. Kate bent over and kissed Margareta, then smiled at Pov and Avi behind her. Then she raised her bouquet and waved it like a banner flag at the skyriders.

"I am married!" she shouted triumphantly.

"Thanks be to God!" a skyrider shouted back irreverently. Father Ilya scowled at him reprovingly.

"That's enough of that," he growled. "Have some respect." The crowd laughed.

Kate bent toward Captain Andreos and gave him her hand, then embraced him happily when he stood up and swept her into his arms. Captain Gray stood up, too, and bowed to Kate, then kissed her hand.

"A beautiful bride," he said, smiling. "My congratulations."

"Thank you, sir," Kate said shyly.

As the couple made their way down the long aisle, Kate hung on Sergei's arm, smiling and chatting with everyone, her face radiant. Avi squeezed Pov's fingers.

"Will I be as beautiful, do you think?" she asked, her eyes on Kate.

"Of course," he said, and leaned to kiss her. "As beautiful as Siduri herself." She turned her face to him and smiled, all her love in her dark eyes.

And Avi's smile told Pov that she, too, believed that the veil of toil and anger had finally lifted, revealing the stars, and their gypsy road that wound among them.

Would that road take them to Orion's Nebula? He looked beyond Avi at the glittering sky and tightened his grip on her fingers, intensely conscious of the risk, of maybe losing everything precious, wife, children, the road itself.

Give us fortune, Siduri, he thought. Give us the luck of the Rom when we go. Keep us safe, even in the maelstrom. Keep us smart.

Turn the page
for a preview
of <u>Orion's Dagger,</u>
the stunning conclusion to
<u>The Cloudships of Orion</u>
trilogy, on sale in the spring
of 1996 from Roc Books.

As the five cloudships started their sixth hour of light-ranging from the Nebula edge, Pov Janusz leaned back in his chair and sighed quietly, a little bored by perfectionist photon counting. Outside the open doorway of *Isle*'s interlink room, he could hear the murmur of voices on Admin level, a soft musical sound punctuated by the quiet hum of the computer at his elbow. Across the room, Miska Ceverny had given up watching the light-scans some time ago and now tapped idly at his computer board, playing with sail models.

Pov rotated his chair toward the wallscreen between their two consoles, where the Orion Nebula glowed as a sea of colored light. Currents of gas and dust, tinted pink and green and deep violet, swirled outward from the blazing Core, where the giant Trapezium stars burned white-hot among hundreds of smaller companions. The Trapezium's power house of newborn stars ionized a full twenty cubic light-years and now ate steadily into the dark molecular cloud behind it, triggering the formation of still newer stars, hundreds more, in the dust-hidden depths of the inner Core. Creation. Force. Beauty. The words didn't catch it, what lay there before them.

I want to go *there,* Pov thought, looking hungrily at the light-filtered blaze of the Trapezium. And I want to go *now.* He grimaced and glanced at his wristband, wishing alpha watch was over. Let Tully watch lines wiggle. Let anybody else watch.

Where's the drama? he thought crossly, then laughed inwardly at his own impatience. Be smart, you dope. They'd just arrived from the Pleiades, after a wish-and-prayer leap across the gulf that had worked right by the numbers. Be smart.

The cloudships' two days of light-ranging would scan a hundred square degrees of the Nebula, in several dozen frequencies done multiple times, with the computer delaying any upload of data until it finished the first complete scan across the spectrum. Thaddeus Gray had insisted on the detailed ranging before they dove into a dangerous unknown, and Pov had agreed, each cautious for different reasons—or maybe the same one. Before the cloudships plunged ahead, they both wanted to see what might be there to bite them.

And what if the biter is invisible? Pov thought wryly. *That's a wonderful thought.* A few of the suspected phenomena deep within the Core, chiefly the cloud-wide gravitational and magnetic effects, were indeed invisible, even to a cloudship's sophisticated sensors. But they would see what they could see from the Nebula edge.

Could see, could see, he thought, drumming his fingers on his outship console. Only he, dutiful Dope Shipmaster Janusz, sat and watched lines wiggle. He supposed it proved some point, though the point escaped him right now.

He rocked his chair and slouched, then took his time stretching out his legs in front of his chair. He laced his fingers over his stomach and admired the embroidery on his sleeves. He looked at his boots, studying the creases, and thought of a half dozen other things he could be doing instead of this, one notable item involving bed with Avi. He sighed.

"So model some sails," Ceverny said without turning around.

"Nuts," Pov said aggressively.

Ceverny snickered at his tone. "I can't believe you're bored. Already?"

"Bored? Me?" Pov declared. "Duty's never boring. You taught me that years ago." He waved at the blank outlink screens, where four other cloudship captains had found better things to do elsewhere. "See the fantastic interest? It's riveting."

"At least you outlasted them, even Gray," Ceverny

said. "That's good for morale." He turned his chair around and squinted at Pov. "*You* agreed we wouldn't do any course modeling until everybody had a chance to look at the first full scan. *You* agreed to the data hold until we got comparison data from the survey cutters. You agreed to all that."

"Thanks for reminding me. Why don't we sneak a look? I'm sure the Arabs are peeking, just to show off their advanced thought later."

"I'll bet you Thaddeus Gray is peeking, too, same reason." Ceverny drew a long face and looked down his nose, then sniffed virtuously. "But it wouldn't be moral, Pov."

"Nuts to moral."

Ceverny chuckled. "The first data capsule from *Traveler* should arrive soon," he said placatingly. "Katinka's had enough time to complete jump and start her readings. Be patient."

"Nuts to patient. I don't want to wait for the cutters."

Isle's cutter had jumped a light-year west, mirrored by a similar jump by Gray's cutter to the east, allowing two other scanning points that stretched their baseline two light-years long. The cutters' outranging was the reason *Siduri's Isle* and *Diana's Mirror* had built the larger skyriders, the reason both cutters had jump capacity. They were also part of the reason Pov had been watching lines wiggle, hour after hour.

"I want to peek," Pov insisted.

Ceverny pulled thoughtfully at his chin. "I could stare at the ceiling," he suggested. "I could even whistle a little, so you know when I'm not looking. I won't see a thing. Why are you asking me? You're the shipmaster."

"You're the witness. I need you subverted, so you're as guilty as I am and can't talk about it later. It's called conspiracy."

Ceverny grinned. "Subvert away, sir." He leaned back in his chair and gazed at the ceiling, then began whistling softly.

Pov laughed and turned around to his board. All right, he thought, deciding how to do it.

He took a fast surreptitious copy of the last hour of

scanning, then loaded it into a side program and pasted it with several security codes. Next he built a fence to keep it from drifting anywhere else in *Isle*'s computer banks. The computer chief had put in several new integrity safeguards after the Arabs tried their data theft at TriPower, but Pov chose to add a prudent extra fence, then made the entire data unit invisible to random search—should the Arabs come prowling again. He expected they would, knowing Captain Sharif.

"The data name is Adv.Tht," he said to Ceverny over his shoulder, "in case you want to look, too. I've got the top five security codes on it, so don't ring any bells."

"Got that." Ceverny thumped his chair upright and started typing at his own board. "Sneak a copy of Helm Map from Athena, won't you, so we can do some mapping."

"Can do." They both tapped busily, starting an analysis of *Isle*'s early light catching. It was conspiracy. It was breach of agreement. It was wrong. Pov smiled happily, glad to repay a few of Sharif's recent unwanted favors with this bit of mild treachery—not that Pov would ever admit it to the Arab ship's wily shipmaster. Never that.

"Loading Helm Map," he said two minutes later. "You better close the door."

Ceverny got up and closed the door of the interlink room, then ostentatiously locked it. "I believe only you and I have the codes to get past this lock."

"Tully's got those codes," Pov said absently, hunting for the radio lengths to load some hydrogen lines. "Sorry."

"Bad planning, Shipmaster," Ceverny reproved as he sat down again.

"No planning involved. Tully gets any secret he wants, no matter what I do. You know him."

"So turn him loose on Sharif."

"I did, right after Sharif rode that carrier beam into our database. Tully says he's making progress."

Ceverny laughed. "Some consortium," he said. "Politics! I hope we creak along somehow."

"So do I. Here comes the ultraviolet." He turned his head and looked at the wallscreen. "Beautiful!"

The screen glowed in a dozen shades of purple, superbly detailed. Pov got up and paced the length of the wallscreen, looking closely at the swirls of molecules and brilliant dust.

"Look," he said, pointing at a blurred disk in the western Nebula. "There's that active protostar at LP Orionis that you liked so much."

"It'd be a good alternative to the Core," Ceverny observed.

"I haven't given up on the Core yet. Don't think so fast."

"We can try the Core next time," Ceverny persisted.

Pov gave him a genial glare. "Think slower, will you? I want to go into the Core *this* time."

Ceverny leaned back and crossed his arms, smiling at him. "Gray will agree with me."

"No, he won't. Want to lay a bet on that?"

"No thanks. I'm afraid you're right." Ceverny looked at the wallscreen and scowled. "I don't see why Katrinya had to go out in the cutter," he complained. *"Diana's Mirror* didn't send *their* holdmaster."

Pov shrugged. *"Mirror* operates by different rules, as I'm sure you've noticed by now. So far Captain Gray hasn't let Rachel take the lead once. When *Mirror* talks to the Arabs, it's Thaddeus Gray doing the talking. Ditto us and *Jewel* and Captain Hanuman. Rachel gets to follow him around and wear shipmaster slashes on her sleeve, but everybody knows who's the real shipmaster over there. And now he's taken charge of the light-ranging, too, something he could delegate to her, even as a junior captain." Pov stopped pacing and put his hands on his hips, bothered by it. "Hell, he *should* have delegated it. I got duty like that from you when I was still Third Sail on *Dance,* and later I handed similar duty to Roja, as Tully's now giving to Celka. I don't understand it." He frowned.

"A princess doesn't need expertise," Ceverny said. "All she needs is a marriageable hand, and I understand Rachel's suitors are legion, considering the assets she'll inherit."

"It's not fair to Rachel," Pov muttered.

Ceverny shrugged, not that concerned for Rachel and

her inship problems with her formidable father. "On our side, it's called being a First-Ship Slav—or Rom. Some of us have to try harder because of it."

"True," Pov agreed reluctantly. "Even so, what's the point of making shipmaster rank too young if you don't get the show-off perqs, get the seniors to defer to you?" He gave Ceverny a mock bow. "Speaking from my recent experience, of course. If *you* had had as much sense as Captain Gray, you'd have claimed rank as *Isle*'s shipmaster and *you'd* be sitting in my chair, not me, running the show to suit yourself."

"Even if I *were* sitting in that chair," Ceverny corrected mildly, "Katrinya would still be off in *Traveler*. Don't confuse shipmaster with spouse: the authority lines just aren't the same. Avi'll teach you. You just wait."

"With my relatives helping her along, I'm sure she will. The *romni* set up all those rules centuries ago, then probably taught them to all you gaje. Blame the Rom, Miska. It's as easy as any other reason."

Ceverny chuckled, then glanced at his inship board as it chimed for attention. Second Hold Denny Lambos appeared in one of the small screens, looking harried—and oddly frightened. "Mister Ceverny?"

"What is it?"

"The jump capsule just arrived from *Traveler*, sir. It's too early but I downloaded the data into the computer, only it didn't have much to download, at least not as much as it should. So I looked at the holdmaster's realtime recording to see why." He hesitated.

"And?" Ceverny prompted, sitting up straighter.

"I think it's best you see for yourself, sir," Lambos said. The man seemed to wince at Ceverny's irritation, and Pov walked over to stand by Ceverny's shoulder. "Loading message," Lambos said, then sent a look of anguish at Pov.

A nearby screen lit with a view of the cutter cabin, as before, only now a reddish shimmer from the Nebula's glowing hydrogen filled the transparent wallwindow, silhouetted by Josef's lanky body at the pilot controls. In the foreground Katrinya Ceverny smiled into the monitor, her white hair coiffed neatly around her lined face, looking just as she had looked hours before when *Traveler* launched.

"Here we are," she said pleasantly. She pushed a button on her console. "Starting data recording now. We've got a dust wall north of us with a density you won't believe, and Josef is cruising us alongside it. Thin plasma to east and west, slow eddies, mostly hydrogen and some drift molecules from the dust wall. I'm counting silicates and carbons as the dust base, about the percentages we expected. Sending you the initial light scans." Her hands moved over her computer board again.

"Also sending you some microwave readings," she continued, her tone easy and unhurried. "It looks to be our first close look at a water maser. Apparently there's a protostar a half light-year beyond this dust wall, still quite enshrouded in its dust shell, but it's putting out enough energy to mase a water cloud between us. The maser winks on and off with the infall flares, no predictable pattern. Here's the outside view in short radiolengths."

The small screen filled with reddish shadows, a drifting curtain of dark gas flickering with infrared molecular frequencies. In the center, a dim sphere brightened and faded erratically, a near point-source in darker microwave. It flickered eerily, like a demon's eye winking through a smoke-hazed darkness. Pov felt a shiver of vague dread snake up his spine and glanced at Lambos.

"The microwave coherency is blurred," Katrinya said on the voiceover. "There could be a lot of dust mixed in the water cloud, refracting some of the light. Or maybe it's a function of the protostar flares. If the protostar is still dispersing its dust shell, not much radiation is getting out to mase the cloud. It's not a big star, anyway, maybe G-class when it settles down in a few million years."

The screen shifted back to Katrinya's lined face. "The maser readings are different from Earth's long-range scans of the inner Core, markedly so. Even watching for a few minutes, I can see the light curve is more diffuse, far more erratic. I can't tell if it's the dust over there at the protostar or over here in the wall." She shrugged.

"Sergei can figure it out, I suppose. Tell him to let me know when he does."

She turned her head to look at the large wallwindow above Josef's console. "Dust is getting thinner. That's odd." She frowned, then chewed her lip. "Josef, why don't you ... oh, never mind. Who says gravity waves have to be regular?" She tossed a quick smile back at the monitor. "If there are such things as rolling gravity waves, of course. Personally, I think Lobanov is an idiot, retooling Einstein as he does. Why do Russkis always think they—?"

She stopped, frowning again as she glanced up at a light-scan screen above her monitor. "Now, that *is* odd. Josef, will you polarize the window into infrared? Thank you." She turned her chair toward the wallwindow, obviously perplexed. "I would have thought—"

The next instant a brilliant red glare swept across her face, flashing through the pilot's window into the cabin. Josef gave a sharp cry and threw his arm across his eyes, then tumbled sideways out of the pilot chair.

"Get down!" he shouted.

Katrinya gasped and half stood, then turned and hit her hand hard on her panel, launching the jump capsule. Ceverny's sidescreen went abruptly blank.

Ceverny stared at its emptiness, frozen into immobility.

"We think the maser flared hard, sir," Lambos said into the silence, "just as the dust wall was thinning. The cutter's hull should protect them, of course, and the wallwindow should have polarized to opaque within another second, but the cutter's sensors have to be gone."

Lambos swallowed uneasily, his face very pale. They had all seen the infrared flash into Katrinya's cabin, and likely masered radiation had flashed with it. How much masered light depended upon how well TriPower's engineers had built the cutter's wallwindow—and how much power the protostar had flared into the maser cloud at a certain instant six months ago. Given enough power at the right frequency, a water maser could flash to X-ray intensity, penetrating space like a razor.

Not out here, Pov thought in dismay. Not by the Nebula edge. The hot masers are in the Core, not out here. It's safe out here. Isn't it?

"Losing the sensors means they can't jump back, sirs," Lambos continued. "The ship computer wouldn't permit it, not without working sensors. It's one of the jump program's imperatives."

Ceverny stood up convulsively. "Then we'll go get her right now."

Pov put his hand on Ceverny's shoulder, stopping him from charging off to Athena's Helm Deck to give the necessary orders, as Ceverny evidently intended to do, totally forgetting he could call her on the interlink. "Not with *Isle*, Miska," Pov said with regret. "She's one of the anchors for the light-ranging. It would gut the scan program."

Ceverny shook off his hand brusquely. "So we'll start over when we get back," he snapped.

"No, we'll send *Jewel*," Pov said more firmly. "The other cloudships can overlap to cover *Jewel*'s scanning share. *Jewel* can get there and back just as fast as *Isle*." Ceverny hesitated, blinking at him. "Let me call Janofsi." Pov took a step toward his own console.

"Then I'm going with *Jewel*," Ceverny declared.

Pov turned back to him. "I need you here on the inship board," he said, hating himself for having to insist. If it was Avi, he'd charge off too, in an instant, wherever it took him.

Ceverny set his jaw stubbornly, his eyes flashing. "I'm going with *Jewel*," he repeated, his shock shifting into anger at Pov's unexpected resistance. "What kind of order is that? Of course I'm going!"

"I need you here," Pov responded, just as stubbornly. "I need your expertise, your seniority, your presence beside me. I need you *here*, Miska, when we tell the other cloudships."

Ceverny's face clouded even more, not thinking clearly in his anxiety for his beloved Katrinya. He practically danced in place, furious at the obstacle, any obstacle, that prevented him from rushing away to *Jewel*.

"Goddammit, Pov!" he shouted. "What *kind* of order is that? You can't expect—"

"I need you," Pov said softly. "If you'd think a moment, you'd know why I can't let you go, not now. *Rohini's Horn* is on the brink of turning back and we just got here. The Arabs would love to pounce on this and blame me for it, with Gray just itching to take over everything. I'm on thin ice. I've been on thin ice with this group since the beginning, and you know it. You leave with *Jewel* and it turns into a comment on me, Sailmaster Miska Ceverny charging off to correct *my* mistake. You know that's how it would look to them—and you know what they could do with it. The consortium's too fragile, Miska. That might break it."

Anguish washed across Ceverny's face, and he looked at the wallscreen where the Nebula swirled in its many colors. Somewhere out there Katrinya needed him. But Ceverny also knew Pov was right, though Pov dearly wished otherwise. He wished he could let Miska go, how he wished it.

"They can't blame you for a maser—" Ceverny began, trying vainly to argue against it.

"They'll blame me for not expecting it, for not training Katrinya to see it coming. Me train Katrinya, oh, sure, but you've heard the way it goes once it gets started. Rachel's not the only captain with authority problems." He took a step and pressed Ceverny's arm. "It's only a few extra hours, Miska," he said softly, "a few extra hours until you'd know she's all right, just the time for *Jewel* to get there and send a message back. Can you give me that? I am asking."

Ceverny blinked and stared at him a long moment, then took a shuddering breath. He nodded, a slow agony. "Yes," he whispered, then closed his eyes in pain.

Denny Lambos still watched mutely from the inship panel, his anguish nearly matching Ceverny's. A Perikles Greek who had joined *Ishtar's Fan* a month after her arrival insystem, Lambos had revered Katrinya Ceverny from his first watches on Hold Deck, later following the Cevernys to *Dance,* then looking to Katrinya after his transfer to *Net* for the help she had freely offered any of Janina's staff. "Sir?" he asked Pov, lifting his chin. "Any orders?"

"Call the hold staff, Denny," Pov said. "Make the announcement right away before the sieve gets hold of it. I don't want this exaggerated." Ceverny made a strangled sound, but said nothing.

"Yes, sir." Lambos gave Ceverny a troubled look, opened his mouth, then shut it and cut the link.

Pov turned and called *Jewel,* asking for immediate contact with Captain Janofsi.

"She's my moon and stars, Pov," Ceverny said behind him, his voice faint and old. "My moon and stars."

"We'll find her, Miska," Pov said. "We'll find her and bring her back."

If you and/or a friend would like to receive the *ROC Advance*, a bimonthly newsletter featuring all the newest and hottest ROC books and authors, on a complimentary basis, please fill out this form and return it to:

ROC Books/Penguin USA
375 Hudson Street
New York, NY 10014

Your Address

Name _____

Street _____ Apt. # _____

City _____ State _____ Zip _____

Friend's Address

Name _____

Street _____ Apt. # _____

City _____ State _____ Zip _____